SECRETS OF NEVERAK

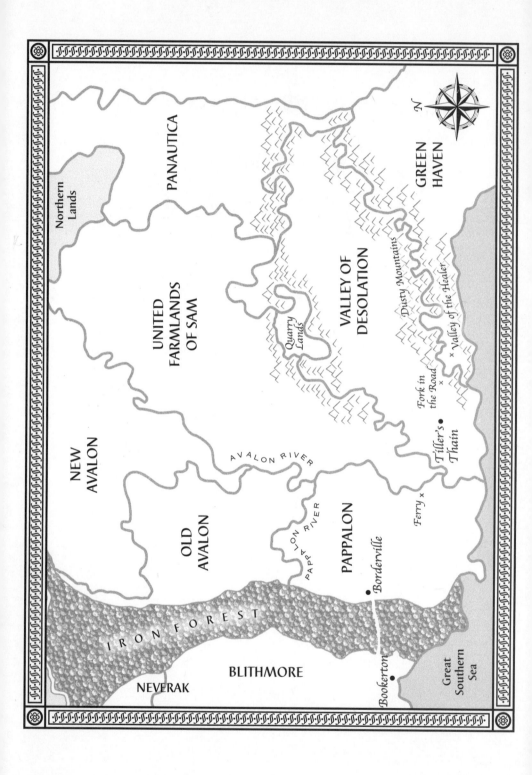

A TALE OF
LIGHT
AND
SHADOW

SECRETS OF NEVERAK

JACOB GOWANS

SHADOW
MOUNTAIN

Visit us at ShadowMountain.com

Library of Congress Cataloging-in-Publication Data

Gowans, Jacob, author.
    Secrets of Neverak / Jacob Gowans.
        pages cm — (A tale of light and shadow ; book 2)
    Summary: Henry Vestin, along with his sister and his friends, continues the quest to save Isabelle, the woman he loves, from the clutches of the Emperor of Neverak, whose plans for war draw ever closer.
    ISBN 978-1-60907-978-9 (hardbound : alk. paper)
    1. Kings and rulers—Fiction. 2. Fantasy fiction. I. Title. II. Series: Gowans, Jacob. Tale of light and shadow ; bk. 2.
    PS3607.O8963S43 2015
    813'.6—dc23   2014040882

Printed in the United States of America
Publishers Printing

10 9 8 7 6 5 4 3 2 1

For Jake, my little hero

Contents

CONTENTS

CONTENTS

The Old Woman

With my room situated directly above the tavern hall of the Silver Nugget, it often seemed that there was no floor at all between myself and the other guests. I heard each belted laugh, each slammed mug, and each roll of the dice with perfect clarity. I rested my head on my pillow for nearly an hour before giving up on sleep. Rather than waste time, I got up and lit the dry logs under the hearth. By the light of the fireplace and a few candles, I reviewed my papers from earlier in the evening.

Before long, I found myself jotting down notes and adding in details that I had not had time to write during the storyteller's dictation. The night wore on, and I grew more engrossed in my work. During the twilight hours, the din underneath my room died down as the guests returned to their homes. I continued to read, marking the manuscript here and there, stopping only to refill my ink or add a log to the flames. At times I felt as though the old storyteller sat in the room with me, dictating the words anew.

I did not stop at the break of dawn. Something drove me to complete the tale while everything remained fresh in my mind. A knock came to my door as the first rays of dawn shone down on my table.

"My heavens, Mr. Freeman," Benjamin Nugget, owner of the establishment, said. "Have you been awake all night?"

"Sleep has abandoned me. To what do I owe your visit?"

"Breakfast!" Nugget said with a smile and a booming laugh.

As hungry as I was, I turned him down politely. I couldn't afford to let anything distract me, and I wasn't certain I could afford the meal, either. Sometime after midday, when I finally reached the last page of the story, I set it aside with a sigh and stumbled to my bed. In an instant, I fell into a deep slumber.

When I awoke, the light of day had all but vanished. The storyteller would be returning soon to continue his tale. I sprang from my bed, threw on my clothes, and grabbed my writing supplies. I came quite close to breaking several ink bottles—and my neck—while running down the stairs. When I entered the tavern hall, I could scarcely believe the crowd. Every seat was filled, and more people stood against the walls. The noisy din sounded like a lion's roar.

I spotted Benjamin near the kitchen, watching with misty eyes as customers poured in and ordered food and drink. At the current rate, there wouldn't be enough room to fit everyone inside, standing or sitting.

"Good evening!" Benjamin said as I approached him. "A fine night, isn't it?" He rubbed his hands on his apron and offered me a handshake. "How was your room?"

"Very comfortable," I told him. "And clean."

"Of course," was his answer. "My wife used to clean the rooms when we first built the tavern, but now I have hired help for that."

"No doubt. And after tonight, you can afford to hire a king to clean your rooms."

The mistiness in Nugget's eyes grew and he smiled widely. "This may be the smartest decision I've ever made. Did you finish your work?"

"I did."

"Are you hungry?" he asked.

"In time, but at the moment I require something more urgent."

"Anything for a customer."

"Last night, when I arrived, the crowd wasn't a fourth this size, and I had no troubles finding my own table to sit and work. But I'm afraid I overslept and . . ." I nodded to the room, my hands filled with paper and ink bottles.

Benjamin leaned back on his heels. "Yes, that is a problem. How much are you willing to pay?"

"What do you mean?"

"I doubt anyone will give up a seat for free tonight. You may have to stand against the wall for the evening—unless you can pay."

"My last coins were spent arriving here last night."

"Relax, Mr. Freeman!" Nugget laughed. "It was a jest. Give me a minute to find you a place."

Nugget darted around the tables and spoke to several patrons, most of whom responded by shaking their heads. The excited chatter and laughter was too noisy for me to hear any conversation. I swallowed, wishing I had a least a coin or two in my pocket. Perhaps Benjamin would allow me to sit on the floor and spread out my papers.

Benjamin returned, wiping sweat from his brow. "You're a lucky young man. There's a woman over there—probably older than Atolas itself—and she'll let you sit by her. Her friend couldn't make it."

I followed Benjamin into the thick crowd. Wisps of pipe smoke parted around us. The smell of packed bodies, ale, and food was pervasive. I clutched my papers and ink tightly to my chest and said a silent prayer of thanks followed by a solemn oath to avoid this sort of tardiness again.

Benjamin had not lied. The woman was little more than skin, bones, and a nest of white hair on the crown of her head. She wore a lovely dress, though, and had a hearty meal sitting in front of her. She smiled when she saw me, making her wrinkled face even older, but not unkind. I returned the smile and accepted the seat across from her. It was as close to the tiny stage as I could have hoped for.

"Thank you," I said loudly as I spread out my papers.

"You're welcome," she answered, her eyes bright and cheerful. "I'm glad for the company."

"Consider me in your debt. I feared I'd be sitting on the roof trying to hear through a hole in the ceiling."

She laughed genuinely.

"I didn't see you here last night."

"I was in the back. My knees aren't what they used to be, but I wouldn't miss the story. Not this one."

My stomach growled so loudly that we both heard it.

She smiled and pushed her plate toward me.

"Oh, no, thank you. I'm here for work rather than pleasure."

"Yes, I can see." She looked at my papers and then pushed her plate even closer to me.

With her permission, I ate with as much sense of propriety as I could in my famished state. She watched me eat as though she, too, could remember being so ravenous. From time to time, she fidgeted with her hair and her clothes. It reminded me of my older sister fiddling with her gowns before heading to a banquet. Before I could remark, a hush fell over the tavern hall.

A distinct, rhythmic tapping started from the back door and slowly the crowd parted. Nearly every head in the audience turned to see the hunched figure of the storyteller. I quickly made certain one last time that all my supplies were in order. The old woman smiled again at me and turned her attention to the old man who passed her.

When he finally sat in the creaking wooden chair on the stage and rested his cane on the floor, the audience stirred, making themselves comfortable for what promised to be another fascinating night. I found my own heart beating faster. A long, deep breath helped to take the edge off my anxiety.

"Water, please," the storyteller commanded as he had the night before.

Benjamin had a mug ready and brought it forward. The old man

4

accepted it gratefully and took a sip so deliberately that I felt my own thirst quenched. His eyes passed over the crowd and briefly rested on me, as they had before. A small thrill ran up my spine.

His deep, strong voice began as a rumble and quickly became a powerful trumpet, steady and captivating. "Yesterday I spoke of love, friendship, and the powerful bonds they can forge. Many of you probably thought that this meant my story would end with those same words which you tell your children at night when you put them to bed: 'And they lived happily ever after.'

"This is not reality. In fact, the purest of loves always come with the greatest of trials, for how else can love be made pure other than by refining it again and again?

"This refinement comes in as many ways as there are persons who experience real love and deep friendship. Numerous are those who have a chance at a life of real meaning, but in a moment of weakness, set aside a priceless treasure for something tawdry, phony, or dangerous. They turn away from love, perhaps out of fear of something so great and powerful, or perhaps because they are unable to comprehend its magnificence, or perhaps, even more pitiful, they do not consider themselves worthy of an emotion so simple and beautiful.

"From what I have seen, it's as if the hand of the Lord of All Worlds reaches down and creates trials uniquely for us, so we may know the words we speak to our loved ones are indeed true and worthy of our lips. These trials come like storms in our lives, beating upon us and testing our foundations.

"I spoke yesterday of those who use the words of love and friendship too lightly. These squalls will break them down, beat them soundly, and dash them apart. But for those whose ties are strong, these moments are where those bonds become purified, hardened, and strengthened . . . in the bellows of trial and the crucibles of pain.

"Before I ended the story yesterday, we had followed Isabelle Oslan and Brandol on a six-week journey north to Neverak, taken by the Elite Guard of Emperor Ivan Krallick. Now we must go back to Henry, Maggie, James, and Ruther—the four left behind—as they crossed the Iron Forest. They had been warned by Wilson. They knew the rumors, but they did not believe them. Yet that evil forest would prove to be the first of many trials that you will hear about tonight as we continue down the path of light and shadow . . ."

ONE

Henry's Torment

Henry woke to darkness and pain. His head throbbed, his right arm was stiff and swollen, and ribs hurt every time he breathed. Why did he hurt so badly? He rolled over and looked for Isabelle, but he was alone. It was quiet, except for the turning and bumping of wheels. He closed his eyes and remembered seeing a large sword swinging at his head. Gasping, he opened his eyes and sat up, setting off explosions of pain in his shoulder, head, and chest.

"Isabelle?" he called out. "Maggie?"

The rolling stopped, knocking Henry into the carriage seats and bumping his tender body. He heard footsteps, the door swung open, and Maggie's face appeared by the light of her torch. She looked weary but relieved.

"Henry," she said, hugging him until he cried out in pain. She quickly let go. "Sorry. Your wounds. I forgot. We were so worried."

"Yeah, friend," Ruther said from behind Maggie. "Maybe you could warn us before you sleep for five days. At least James was polite and woke up after three."

"Can I have some water?" Henry asked. Ruther passed him a water skin, and Henry drank it empty and handed it back. Water dripped off his chin and down his neck. "Thank you. I feel . . . I feel so—"

"You look it, too," Ruther said. "Maybe worse."

Henry wanted to laugh but couldn't manage it. "Where are we?"

The lines in Maggie's face deepened. "The Iron Pass. Almost six days in."

"How are you feeling?" James asked. "We've fed you only water and honey for nearly a week. I don't believe you are ready to ride."

Henry's head spun at the thought. "I just want to sleep. Everything feels . . . awful."

"You were stabbed," Maggie said. "We thought you might lose your arm."

Henry began to remember. The battle at the mouth of the Iron Pass. Lots of soldiers. It had been hopeless. He had fought so poorly. "How—how did we win?" he asked.

No one answered him at first. Ruther put his hand on Maggie's arm, urging her aside. His eye was black and puffy, but his grin was still there. Not quite as large or cheery as usual, but there nonetheless.

And then Henry remembered that Ruther *shouldn't* be there. Henry had sent him away.

"What—" he began. "When did you—"

"It's a long story, friend," Ruther explained. "We didn't win. The soldiers took what they came for and let us live."

"Took what they—" Nothing made sense. Henry shook his head in confusion, but the motion nearly made him pass out. "I'm still here . . ."

It was a long moment before anyone answered him, and Henry was filled with dread. He hadn't heard Isabelle's voice. He hadn't seen Brandol.

As if reading Henry's mind, Ruther spoke, his voice breaking. "They were taken. I'm sorry, friend, but they were taken. I tried to—I tried to stop them from getting Isabelle, but my arrows fell short. There was nothing I could do. And Brandol—"

"Brandol got what he deserved," James pronounced. "The traitor is gone."

"James," Maggie said, "don't say that. He doesn't deserve to die."

James's voice was bitterly cold. "He does—he deserves a traitor's death. I hope he gets it."

Henry wasn't listening anymore. All he'd heard was that Isabelle was gone. No, that couldn't be. She would never be gone. He had to go get her. She wouldn't be far. He would ride out and fetch her. He crawled to the door and pushed past Maggie and Ruther with his one good arm. His other was still too stiff to move.

"Henry," Maggie said, "where are you—"

"Where's Quicken?" He spotted his horse as soon as he rounded the carriage. Henry's legs weren't working properly; they felt more like thick syrup than proper flesh and bone. "Five days?" he called to his friends as he ran for his horse. "How could you have traveled without her for *five days*?" He screamed the last words as a condemnation. "That means Isabelle is *ten days* from me!"

"Henry, stop," Maggie pleaded.

"You can't ride after her," James said.

"Watch me." Henry tried to climb Quicken but his right arm wouldn't move. He couldn't raise it or grip the reins or the saddle to pull himself up with his hand. Using only his left hand, he yanked at anything he could grab, but Quicken didn't like that, and responded by whinnying and stamping. "Come on, boy," Henry said as he stroked his courser's mane, "help me."

It was no use. Henry couldn't mount. He turned to his friends with pleading eyes. "Neverak. They're taking them to Neverak. We can't let them. The Emperor will make her his concubine. And who knows what he'll do to Brandol."

"He'll kill him," James said. "They think he's you."

"Why would they think that?"

"Because I told them so. He looks like you, Henry. The Emperor won't know the difference. Brandol will be executed, and the Emperor will stop hunting us."

Henry struggled to find words. His body quaked with emotion, and his good hand squeezed Quicken's reins so tightly the leather cut into his skin. "Brandol will confess! The Emperor will know it isn't me."

"Perhaps he won't believe him," James suggested. "Perhaps he wants to believe you are a coward. It makes his life easier. Isabelle will pretend he's you to protect you."

"She shouldn't have to! I'll make certain she never sees the Emperor." Henry turned and started west, back toward Blithmore, his stride nearing a sprint.

Quicken trotted alongside him, Henry still grasping the reins, but he was in no condition to outrun his friends. His legs were weak, and he soon stumbled. When his sister and friends caught up to him, Henry began to weep. "Please don't take me away from her. We have to go get her. We have to . . ."

James and Ruther pulled Henry to his feet. They carried him back to the carriage; Henry hung limply in their arms.

"He needs to eat," Ruther said.

"We've hardly moved today," James said.

Maggie silenced James with a look. Ruther sat next to Henry, ready to grab him should he try to run. But Henry didn't have the strength . . . not yet. Maggie brought a plate of food and set it into Henry's hands. As Henry ate, James spoke.

"As far as I can tell, the Emperor's Elite Guard hasn't followed us. I've backtracked a bit each day to check if they're behind us, but I've seen no sign."

"They've got Isabelle!" Henry argued.

"The Guards could be waiting. They may have spies or soldiers camped outside the Iron Pass watching, waiting for us to return."

"He got what he wanted," Henry said dully. "Why would they be waiting?"

"Do you think the Emperor is stupid?" Ruther asked. "He may well kill us if we return to Blithmore."

"Then why did he let us go?" Henry asked.

"I don't know," James admitted. "I've never seen anything so strange."

"Isabelle is your sister. How can you bear the thought of her serving the Emperor's every lust-filled whim?"

"I can't, Henry. Nor can I do something rash. How will I help her if I'm dead?"

Henry tried to think of a response, but couldn't. He turned to Ruther, his swollen eye visible in the torchlight.

"What happened to your face?" he asked.

Ruther grimaced. "James. He was out of his wits when he woke. After he saw me, he punched me. I hit the dirt on my backside, and he passed out cold again."

Maggie grinned at James. "It gave me quite the laugh."

The fact that Maggie, Ruther, and James could laugh and smile chafed Henry. But he didn't want to fight with them. He needed them to be at ease. Once he got his strength back and the use of his arm returned, he would act. "How far through the pass are we?"

The mirth in the group quickly faded. "Our pace hasn't been good," James admitted.

"No, it hasn't," Ruther agreed. The flames crackled and cast light and shadow across his face. "We stopped regularly the first few days to care for you and James. I fed you; Maggie changed your bandages. And in return I got a black eye."

"We're perhaps a fourth of the way across," James added. "It's difficult to tell. There are no landmarks other than the streams that cut across the path. Occasionally we pass abandoned wagons . . . carts—"

"Skeletal remains of travelers," Ruther said darkly.

"Ruther!" Maggie hissed as she glared at him.

A fourth of the way? It wasn't good enough. At that rate, Henry calculated, they wouldn't reach the Pappalon border for another fifteen days. "Once we cross the pass, we'll head north along the border of the forest. We'll stay away from towns and spies."

Maggie and Ruther exchanged an uneasy glance. "That might work," Ruther said. "We have plenty of time to decide what course to take."

They weren't taking him seriously. If they weren't going to listen to him, he needed to leave. He could find Isabelle on his own. Setting down his plate, Henry stretched and yawned. "I need more rest," he told them. "I'm going to try to sleep, if that's all right."

Maggie, James, and Ruther were all quick to agree. Henry listened to them as the carriage started moving again. James and Ruther must have been riding near Maggie because Henry could hear them clearly.

"You didn't tell him about the—" Maggie said.

"What was I supposed to say?" Ruther asked. "'Hey, Henry, sorry you aren't feeling well. Oh and by the way, we're all hearing strange voices.' Since when did it become my job to give the bad news?"

"He'll find out about it soon enough," James said in a tone barely loud enough for Henry to hear. "The arm worries me. He should have use of it by now."

Henry tried to flex the arm, to move it even slightly, but it wouldn't budge. Worry settled in the pit of his stomach. What if he had lost use of it forever?

The carriage hit a bump in the trail and something fell off the seat opposite him. Henry moved the blankets and found his sheathed sword. He picked it up and held it in front of him. His mind replayed the battle at the pass. He recalled how atrociously he had wielded the weapon. The Elite Guard had only spared him so they could take him back to the Emperor. Instead, they had been tricked into taking Brandol. But it was Henry's fault.

"Isabelle. Brandol. My friends," he whispered. "I am so sorry."

It had been Henry who chose to head for the pass, who had

brought Brandol, the traitor, along with them, who had not practiced swordplay well enough to defend Isabelle. How many foolish choices had he made which led to this catastrophic failure? He couldn't count them even though he saw them all. Tears fell down his face as he silently wept.

But he could still fix it. He knew what he had to do.

Henry waited until late in the night, then peeked out and saw three bodies slumbering around the remaining embers of the fire. He quietly opened the carriage door, took his sword, and slung it over his back. Securing the sheath was not easy, but using one hand and his teeth, he managed it. Next he guided Quicken over to the carriage so he could stand on the carriage step and pull himself into the saddle. No one made a sound as he worked and struggled to mount the horse.

By the time Henry started to ride away from the group, he was feeling pleased with himself. Sleep was the farthest thing from his mind; he felt a great sense of urgency to ride after Isabelle and Brandol. The three moons shone above, but the trees of the forest blocked out their light except for Hallicaf, the largest. He could barely distinguish the dirt path from the towering trees that flanked him.

In such darkness, he didn't see the three shapes blocking his path until they were almost right in front of him.

"Where are you going, friend?" Ruther asked. "If you were looking for some balm or healing herbs for that arm, you won't find anything for miles and miles."

"Get out of my way," Henry said, but James and Maggie had already taken Quicken by the reins so Henry couldn't gallop off.

"We only want to help," James said.

Henry fixed his empty gaze on James. "Then go get your horses and the carriage so we can ride for Blithmore. Right now."

"Are you certain that's a wise course of action?"

"It's the *only* course of action!" Henry said. "How you can be so calm about this boggles my mind!"

"She's safe, Henry. She's alive. I keep those two facts in here"—
James tapped his skull with a finger—"and it helps me keep a cool
head. A cool head is exactly what we need because we barely survived
the attack at the pass. We have no money, no direction, and no plan.
Do you know what we need most of all, Henry?"

"What?" Henry asked bitterly.

James held Henry's gaze until Henry looked away. "Our leader."

"You're talking to the wrong man, James. Look where my leadership got us: broken, captured, lost, and divided. An abject failure from
beginning to end."

"You led us to the pass, Henry. That was our goal."

"The goal was to get Isabelle to the pass!" he said. "I failed. Stop
trying to convince me otherwise."

James stared into the forest as though he could find some answer
there. "We need to get your arm healed."

"No."

"It must be done."

"It can wait."

"That's your sword hand, Henry! Your woodworking hand. That's
the hand you use for everything."

"You can be my sword. You and Ruther. We can look for a physician in Blithmore along the way to Neverak—"

James grabbed Henry's ankle and jerked him off the horse. Henry
tumbled to the ground and rolled in the dirt. Scrambling to his feet
took more time and effort than he liked.

"Haven't you been listening?" James asked. "We can't go back
there. We'll die!"

"The road to Isabelle and Brandol is *that way!*" Henry bellowed,
swinging at James with his left hand but missing badly.

Flecks of spit hit James's face, but he wiped them away with a
trembling hand. "Henry, calm—"

"Don't tell me to calm down! Because I can't. The same storm raging inside me should rage in you, too. By the Lord of All Worlds, she is your sister!"

"*I know that!* So you can stop saying it. The first town we find in Pappalon, we'll seek out a physician, earn some money, and get back on the road to Isabelle."

Henry dove at James, but James sidestepped him. Henry reached for his sword, but couldn't manage to draw it. He'd sheathed it for his right hand to reach, not his left.

When he looked up, James had his own sheathed blade pointed at Henry's throat. He hit Henry's neck and said, "Dead."

Enraged, Henry pushed the weapon aside, but a kick from James's boot sent him back to the dirt for a second time. James touched the tip of his sword to Henry's breast. "Dead again."

Henry snapped. He wasn't even thinking. He only wanted to inflict pain on someone besides himself. But before he could even get to his feet, James struck his good arm with the sheathed sword, then kicked Henry in the chest with the heel of his foot, and knelt on Henry's ribs. He grabbed Henry's hair and put his blade to Henry's throat.

"Dead, dead, *dead!* You are helpless until you get well. You are half a man to her and a danger to us. Let go of this foolish recklessness and see reason!"

Henry briefly closed his eyes. "I'm sorry," he finally said. "You're right. I'm not capable. I'm not fit to fight, to save Isabelle, or even to lead this group."

"Henry," Ruther started to say, but Henry interrupted him.

"No. I can't lead. I can't make the right decision. James, you're in charge. You'll make the choices. I led us into this mess. Now you lead us out of it."

Henry and James stared at each other, but Henry would not yield, would not even blink.

Finally James nodded. "I will lead until you are ready."

Henry knew he would never be ready, but at least now he would be free of the responsibility that had weighed him down since leaving Richterton.

James offered Henry a hand, but Henry did not take it. He stood on his own and walked back to the carriage, defeated and humiliated. So many poor choices . . . all his fault.

"I don't think any of us want to sleep at the moment," Maggie said. "We might as well ride."

"I'd give my right arm to be out of this cursed forest," Ruther said. Maggie shot him a furious glare, and he smacked his own forehead. "Sorry, friend, I wasn't even thinking . . ."

Henry said nothing as he used the carriage step again to mount Quicken. Even the carriage represented poor decisions he'd made, ones he had pushed far from his mind long ago, and hadn't thought of since. Perhaps even those choices had played a part in his fate. What if he was cursed to lose everything because of wrong roads he'd taken long ago?

"We're like pieces of wood," Henry's father had repeatedly told him throughout Henry's life. "The scratches and flaws we inflict upon ourselves never leave. We carry them forever. Even the unseen ones."

Henry bowed his head and started Quicken toward the east. He closed his eyes, not out of weariness, but to calm his mind. The group rode quietly with James in front. Faint breezes swished through the leaves and branches, their sounds soothing Henry's troubled thoughts. Just when he had found some measure of peace, he heard a voice. It was soft and low and came from the darkness surrounding him.

Henry, we know about the carriage.

TWO

The Voices of the Forest

Ruther had no idea if it was day or not. He didn't care. He just wanted the carriage to keep moving because the next time it stopped meant it was his turn to drive. Around him, Maggie and Henry slept, but fitfully. Maggie mumbled almost constantly. Her latest utterance, one of few that Ruther had been able to understand, had been, "No, James, don't go back. Don't go back!"

Ruther had come to the conclusion that old Barney Dentin, the man who told tales of the Iron Pass to their friend Wilson, had been full of goat dung. No one had known the true nature of the pass. No one. If they had, rumors would have spread like wildfire, and no one would have dared go through it. It was no wonder the Emperor's Elite Guards hadn't suspected the pass as a possible route or followed Henry's party into the woods. After ten days in, Ruther wished they had taken any other route. *Any.*

In the carriage, with the windows shut, he couldn't hear the voices, but somehow he could still feel them, like a silent wind pressing on his back. For him, sleep was no reprieve. His dreams were horrors, and he was often awakened by Henry shouting about a carriage or Maggie's faint protests. Between the fatigue, being holed up in the carriage, and the constant stress of the forest, Ruther's skull pounded like one of Henry's hammers. Ruther massaged his temples with the palms of his hands. His eyes watered from the pain in his head, but rubbing helped. Bit by bit the pain subsided. Then the moment he'd been dreading finally arrived. The carriage came to a halt.

"No," Ruther muttered, "not yet. Give me more time." He did not know how many hours' rest he'd had since his last turn driving the carriage, but it wasn't enough. The door opened and James stood outside. Very little light filtered through the trees, but there was enough that Ruther could see James's wide, haunted eyes set in his pale face and twin rivulets of blood flowing down his neck.

James climbed in the carriage and wrapped his arms around himself. "I went as far as I could," he gasped. "It's worse. The voices are constant. Tormenting. I don't know if I can go out there again." He wiped at his neck and stared at the blood on his hand.

"What did you do to your ears?" Ruther asked.

James shook his head. "I don't remember. They don't hurt. But the voices, Ruther . . . How do they know?"

Ruther wished he knew the answer because if he did, he might know how to block them out while he drove. With the door open, the whispers steadily grew louder.

"I can't go out there, James. What if I go mad?"

"You have to go. We need you. I already changed the horses. All you need to do is drive."

Closing his eyes, Ruther tried to summon his courage. He knew he had some. After all, hadn't he returned to his friends and helped them in battle? If he could risk death up in that tree when he had rained arrows down on the Elite Guards of Neverak, he could risk it now. Telling himself that, he got up and jumped out of the carriage door before he could talk himself into staying. A shiver ran through him when his boots hit the ground. He was climbing up to the driver's seat when the first voice spoke to him.

Remember Clarentine?

Ruther ignored the voice and urged the horses forward. How could this be? How could they all be hearing voices that no one else could hear? He knew there must be some logical explanation for it. Could it be something in the air? Or some effect the darkness had on the mind? Or perhaps the strain of the journey and the loss of Isabelle and Brandol had taken their toll on the sanity of all four travelers. Regardless, Ruther refused to believe that something supernatural existed inside the forest. There had to be an explanation.

But why had the voice reminded him of Clarentine?

Two years ago, Ruther had traveled to western Blithmore to secure storytelling engagements and receive letters of recommendation. In the town of Florron, Ruther found great success and made quite a sum of coin. As always, the weight in his coin bag had led him to the taverns late at night for drinks, dice, and dames. The three devils, as his storytelling master had referred to them.

Many people in the crowd recognized and welcomed him. The great thing about being well-known and highly regarded was that someone was usually willing to buy him a drink—or three. In his drunken state, a cute round-faced girl with chestnut-colored hair caught his eye. Her attention, however, was on the dice games.

Eventually Ruther made his way over to the tables where four other men sat rolling and betting. "May I join?" Ruther asked, glancing at the girl as he did so. She gave him a small smile, but paid him no other mind. As Ruther played, he noticed she tended to favor the men who had the hot hand. One minute she was leaning on him, whispering to him, and the next she was making eyes at another man who pulled in a pile of coin. And even though Ruther had seen her type before, she was undeniably attractive.

It wasn't long before his thoughts drifted to the pair of dice in his pocket that he kept handy for special occasions. Towns like this were easy pickings. No one ever expected a well-regarded storyteller to use fake dice.

An hour later, Ruther had cleaned out the pockets of his fellow gamblers, and Clarentine had escorted him to her small home across town, all the while laughing about the dice trick she knew he'd used. She promised to keep quiet about it if he'd split the winnings with her. Something about that disturbed Ruther even more than what he had done, but he agreed. Late that night, while she slept, he stole back the money and headed out of town to find a new place for employment.

And what about Sloppy Stuart? the sinister voice asked.

Ruther cringed and wiped sweat off his cheek. But it wasn't sweat. A thin line of blood trickled down his face. His hand shook as he stared at it. He nearly stopped the carriage and woke up Maggie to have her drive, but he knew he couldn't. Maggie needed her rest. Since the battle at the pass, Ruther had developed a soft spot where she was concerned.

Sloppy Stuart. Sloppy Stuart! Sloppy Stuart!

"I don't want to remember," Ruther whispered, but it didn't matter. The repetition of the name wouldn't go away. Rather than dwelling on the past, he tried to rehearse stories in his mind. But it seemed that the more he concentrated, the louder the voices grew.

Sloppy Stuart! they screamed. *Don't forget about Sloppy Stuart!*

Ruther slammed his hands over his ears, but it didn't dim the voices one whit. Finally he roared, "I am sorry, Stuart! I am *sorry!*"

Sloppy Stuart had frequented a dice hall in Richterton. He was a dimwitted fellow with large eyes and a long, fat tongue that often hung from his mouth despite his constant, good-natured smile. He used to laugh whenever he saw Ruther and yell, "Wuther! Wuther, tell me a stowee!" His round stomach jiggled whenever he laughed, making his stained clothes wobble and bounce.

Sometimes Ruther obliged Stuart, other times he didn't. He liked seeing Sloppy Stuart laugh himself silly, and it made him feel better about the two or three times he'd rolled the dice against Stuart and scammed him out of a few badly needed coins. Ruther had even invented a character patterned almost exactly after Stuart, down to the lolling tongue and bulging eyes. That impersonation had earned

Ruther more than a few coins, but something about it had always left him with a twinge of guilt. Maybe even more than a twinge.

Memories assaulted Ruther, one after another: the sword he'd stolen, the tavern brawls he'd started, the man he'd cheated for his good quiver, the women he'd wronged in his drunken stupors. In the distance, a square shape loomed in the center of the path. Ruther could not tell what it was, but he slowed the carriage. His first instinct was to wake the others, but what good would it do? He could investigate as easily as them.

They couldn't listen any longer, the voice in Ruther's head told him. *Their dark places drove them mad.*

The object ahead was a carriage. While its style was different from the one Henry had made many months ago, it was similar enough that Ruther felt deep apprehension as he approached.

"Hello," he called out. Swallowing hard, he continued, "I want to warn you that I am one of the top five swordfighters in all of Atolas. If you even think about scaring me, I will cut off your scalp. And if you're a woman, that means you'll receive curious stares for the rest of your life." He reined in the horses and climbed down to investigate.

Once he was a few paces away, he noticed the stench of decay coming from the carriage. He plugged his nose and took another step. "Oh . . . that's dead-people smell," he said, stepping back. "My ears are already dripping blood. I don't need to see or smell dead people today!"

Then he spotted the corpse under the carriage, clothes moldering around tight, decaying skin. It was a man, huddled under the carriage on his knees, his head bent low, hands clutching a skull without ears. The madness had driven him to pull off . . .

Ruther turned away before he retched.

You'll never make it to the end. You'll join us in here, like so many others.

"Am I going mad?" Ruther asked himself. He rubbed his forehead.

Then, balling his hand into a fist, he thumped his chest several times, shouting his defiance into the forest gloom. "I am not losing my mind! You hear me? This is just—just . . . *jungle sickness!*"

He approached the stalled carriage again. He tried not to notice the body of the woman and her young child inside, her hands pressed over the babe's ears. There were no horses, nor their remains, just empty bridles. Somehow they had gotten loose. He would need help pushing the carriage out of the way. There was only one person to ask.

He returned to the carriage and quietly opened the door. "James," he hissed. "James!"

"Vreagan!" James shouted, grabbing at Ruther's throat.

Ruther, already on edge from seeing the dead body, jumped back just as James's hand closed around the air where his neck had been.

"Do I look like someone named Vreagan!" Ruther snapped. Like an egg being tapped too many times, he was beginning to feel the cracks in his sanity.

Henry and Maggie stirred in their sleep.

"Why did you wake me? I finished my turn driving!"

"I need help moving another carriage."

"That's what we have horses for. Leave me alone."

It took a few more minutes to coax James out of the carriage and get him to help shove the other carriage through the wall of trees. As they pushed the heavy load, Ruther heard a faint hiss.

Yes. To us. Bring them to us. Ruther glanced at James, wondering if he'd heard the same words.

The moment the old carriage crossed the tree line something yanked it from Ruther and James's hands. It happened so suddenly and so forcefully that it nearly pulled Ruther into the trees, but James grabbed Ruther by the shirt and held him back.

"Did you see anything?" James asked. "Was that the *trees?*"

Ruther sat in the dirt, catching his breath. "How can trees do that? Must have been some creature . . . something tall and powerful."

"I know of no creature—"

"I don't know what it was!" Ruther shouted, trying to drown out the voice that whispered, *Thank you, Ruther. Now join them. Come to us.*

James shook his head and put his hands over his ears. "I have to . . . go. I need rest."

Ruther wanted company, but he had no right to stop James from crawling back into the carriage. Ruther drove onward, trying to ignore the voices that taunted him about the times he had been drowned in boos and sour ale as a beginning storyteller. Normally he laughed at those experiences because he had learned and grown from them, yet the humiliation he felt now was as fresh as the day it had happened. Tears ran down his cheeks. He wiped them away, not realizing he'd been crying.

Only they weren't tears. Fresh blood trickled from his eyes. Ruther gripped the reins of the horses as tightly as possible. The pain was welcome, it helped him focus, helped him retain his hold on himself.

"What is happening to me?" he sobbed.

Just think, Ruther, you're only halfway through. We still have miles and miles together. We'll get inside every crease of your brain. You'll remember EVERYTHING.

The days passed not in hours or miles, but in turns driving the carriage. At first the shifts were longer, hours at a time, and everyone only had to drive the carriage once per day. But soon it was twice, then three times. Once Henry only made it ten minutes before he begged to be let back inside the carriage, weeping red tears. "It's all my fault," he kept saying.

Another time, James buried his head into Maggie's lap and clung to her while she smoothed back his hair and mopped the blood from his ears. The four travelers grew weaker each day. Maggie seemed to be affected the least, but even she had her moments. Once she broke down, sobbing for more than an hour as she begged Ruther to forgive her for the way she'd treated him.

Normally Ruther would have laughed it off, but things like laughter and joy had become foreign. But not misery. Nor suffering. Ruther wept every time he had to drive, but he waited until he was in the seat to do it. Usually the tears weren't of blood; those didn't come until later. Same with the bleeding ears.

Ruther knew it had to be something in the air. The food didn't taste right. The air didn't smell right. No one laughed. Smiles were almost as rare. Ruther yearned to be free of the Iron Forest, and he swore to himself that if he survived—no matter how desperate he was—he would never return.

THREE

The Hands from the Darkness

Maggie trembled as she urged the horses to move faster. She knew she shouldn't be pushing them so hard, but the end was near. At least that's what James believed. "Either today or tomorrow we'll reach the end," he kept saying at breakfast.

Maggie prayed he was right. Horrible didn't even begin to describe this foul place. Nightmarish came closer, but it was Ruther who was good at coming up with words, not her. She wasn't good at much at all. She wasn't good *for* much either. That was what the voices kept telling her. Not a good sister to Henry, not a good friend to Ruther, and James still didn't seem to notice her the way she wanted him to.

They were all so weak, James particularly. He always came back from driving drained, and he always seemed to crave Maggie's touch. She caressed his head, held him, and soothed him with warm words, but such attention left her emotionally and physically exhausted. At least James felt better, and that was what mattered to her—that and getting out of this hellish place. Sometimes she imagined she could see a dim light far off in the distance, like the end of a tunnel ever out of reach.

A chilly wind blew through the trees, rustled the leaves, and whipped around Maggie's neck. She drew her cloak around her to ward off the cold. It was still winter, and while in the southern part of the land the season's bite was normally toothless, here in the darkness of the Iron Pass, where the sun had little effect, the wind had a noticeable bite. The only thing Maggie appreciated about the bitter wind was that it made the voices a little harder to hear.

But only a little.

He'll never love you. You are ugly, stupid, and foolish. You revolt him.

The thing that struck Maggie most about the voices was that despite enduring so many days of the taunting, the nagging, and the horrible memories they dragged up, their effects never dulled. Each word was a fresh knife in her soul.

Ruther was adamant it was some trick of the forest, as though the trees could cause a kind of madness. Maggie wasn't so certain. Her mother had firmly taught her that the only thing she ever need believe in was the Word of Worlds, which taught about the Lord of All Worlds and the Great Demon. Nothing else. Not the Path, not ghosts or spirits. Her mother had certainly never said anything about magical trees. So perhaps this was one of those rare moments when Ruther was right.

She thought of all the things they had passed on the trail: corpses of men, women, children, and horses, empty carriages, abandoned swords and shields, empty battle helms and armor. How many people had tried to cross the Iron Pass and failed? And how likely were they to succeed where other people, perhaps stronger and braver, had died? Had they broken the rules of the Iron Pass? Wilson had told them to follow two simple rules while inside the forest: first, keep on the path; and second, keep your weapons sheathed.

She thought of her home in Richterton, the cabbages from her gardens she sold at the market, the simplicity of that life.

You would take it back if you could, wouldn't you? You would abandon Henry.

A noise from below startled Maggie, and she shrank back in her seat until she saw Ruther's face poking out the door. "I can't sleep. I can't even hear myself think. Mind if I join you?"

Maggie couldn't think of anything she wanted more than company. "You need to rest. You need to stay out of the open."

"I don't care," Ruther said. "I just want someone to talk to."

Maggie patted the seat next to her, barely wide enough for the two of them. Ruther's stomach had grown larger from all the sitting around and riding in the carriage. He ate more than the others and it showed.

"I'm worried about Henry," Maggie whispered. "Is he awake?"

"I'm worried about all of us." The weary tone of his voice told her both men must be sleeping. "But I think it's James who scares me most of all."

"Henry never speaks. He shuts us all out."

"James almost killed me—"

"He said he was sorry. He'd had a nightmare."

"Yeah, I'm trying to remember the last person I tried to kill during a nightmare. What was his name . . . ?"

Maggie wanted to laugh at Ruther's jape, but the well of mirth inside her had run dry. James had been muttering the name Vreagan for the past few days. Well, she assumed it was a name because when she asked James about it, he'd scowled and told her it was none of her business. To be fair to James, however, none of the conversation between the four of them could be called polite.

"Would you like to play a game?"

A rare burst of sunlight shone through the trees as Maggie turned to look at Ruther in disbelief.

"It's stupid, probably, but it's the best kind of game, Mags." There was a trace of a grin on his face, but it vanished quickly. Only Ruther could muster a measure of humor in a place like this. She admired him for that, despite all his other failings. "This game doesn't have winners or losers. It only exists to pass the time."

"Nothing sounds fun. And don't call me Mags."

You deserve someone like Ruther. Fat, lazy, and—

Ruther threw his hands up. "Sorry. I forgot. Honestly, I did. Habits take time to break. But in all truth, the game is fun. Henry and I spent hours and hours and—"

"How many years ago was that?"

"Less than—umm—not that many. If Henry was talking to us right now, I'm certain he could say." Ruther offered her a deep frown and large, sad eyes. "I can't believe you don't want to play a game."

Maggie let out a long breath. "What's it called?"

Ruther hesitated. "We never exactly named it. You just describe the most disgusting thing you can think of. Why don't you try it first?"

With no idea where to start, Maggie deferred to Ruther. "There's no way I will win."

"There are no winners and losers."

"Oh, I doubt that," Maggie said.

"The most disgusting thing I can think of," Ruther began dramatically.

"I changed my mind," Maggie answered. "Can we instead—"

"Is a man so fat—"

"Don't make me ignore you for the rest of the day."

"The day is almost over." Ruther gestured at the tree branches hanging over them like a living ceiling. "Should be a beautiful night, too. I bet we'll even see a star or one of the moons." Then he took a deep breath and spoke so rapidly that Maggie could hardly understand him, "—when he sat by his wife he lost her in his blubber."

"Ugh!" Maggie cried. "And that's why I didn't want to play! Hearing that, I am clearly the loser."

An angry grunt came from inside the carriage. Maggie recognized James's low voice.

Ruther was undeterred. "I saw a man once who looked fat enough to lose a small child in his blubber. Maybe a six- or seven-year-old."

Maggie's response was a sigh.

"What is that?" Ruther bellowed, pointing into the forest.

Maggie screamed and looked, following his finger. "Where?"

"Never mind. I thought—it was nothing."

"Ruther, if you do that again . . ."

Slit his throat, the insidious voice whispered in her mind. *Kill him and he'll never bother you again.*

She had taken one of James's daggers and kept it in her pocket to help her feel safer. But if she brandished it in the Iron Pass, she would break one of the rules.

"No!" Maggie screamed and grabbed her ears. "Stop it!"

"It's all right, Mags," Ruther said, taking her hands. "Don't listen to them."

"Go away!" she told the voice.

James groaned even louder this time. He was probably dreaming about Vreagan again.

"I really am sorry." Ruther started to leave, but Maggie put a hand on his arm.

They locked eyes for a moment. "Thank you for trying to cheer me up." She turned away and stared ahead. "And just so you know, the most disgusting thing I can think of is a pig eating scraps of bacon."

Ruther stared at her, stunned, then he began to laugh. The sound was so sweet and so pure that it finally brought a smile to Maggie's face. And for a moment, she even saw light up ahead. "Look!" She pointed, but as Ruther's laughter died down, it disappeared. "Did you see it?"

"What?"

"The light. I saw something. I think I saw the end of the pass. It couldn't have been more than a mile away. We're not far!"

"Very funny, Mags. I deserved that."

"I wasn't jesting. I really saw—"

"I didn't do it!" James bellowed. Both Maggie and Ruther jumped. "Get away from me!"

Maggie stopped the carriage so abruptly the horses whinnied at her, and the ones tied to the rear of the carriage bumped into each other.

"Drive," Ruther said. "If you really saw the exit, get us there as fast as you can."

"But James—"

"Go, Maggie."

Maggie's instinctive reaction was to do the opposite of what Ruther advised. This time, however, she followed his counsel. The wind whipped at her hair as she fixed her eyes ahead, searching for some sign of the light she'd seen.

You think you will be free, but you are mistaken. His mind is already shattered. The rule is about to be broken.

Maggie didn't have time to ponder the words. A tremendous shout came from inside the carriage, the door opened with a bang, and James tumbled to the ground. He rose unsteadily to his feet.

"Come out!" James yelled at the carriage as Maggie stopped it yet again. His face was a blotchy mix of red and white, his stance weak and unsteady. "Come out and fight, coward! You taunt me day and night, but can you back up your words with the sword?"

"James," Maggie called, "get back in the carriage. It's not real."

James gave no indication that he'd heard her. "Come out, traitor!"

Maggie saw his hand twitch, and she knew what James was reaching for. His sword. The blade caught a sliver of sunlight and cast a glimmering reflection on one of the tree trunks. His arm trembled under the weight of the weapon. Ruther saw it, too, and tried to climb over Maggie to stop James. He dove from the seat, knocked James down, and probably bloodied them both, but it was too late.

The blade had been drawn.

The rustling of the trees stopped. The wind ceased blowing. And for one horrible moment, the entire world fell deathly still and silent. James, his rage gone, looked around with fearful eyes. Ruther knelt on the ground, possibly too weak to stand. Maggie didn't know what to do except tell them, "Get in the carriage! *Now!*" She looked around for some sign of attack or ambush, but the forest was as still as a pond on a peaceful day.

James pulled Ruther up and threw him back into the carriage. The instant they were both inside, Maggie snapped the horses forward, shouting her encouragement to them. Laughter filled her ears, a deep voice which came from everywhere, so powerful it made her whole body vibrate. The horses sensed it as well, and they broke into a run. As the volume of the voice grew, Maggie covered her ears, afraid her skull would burst from the noise.

The trees began to shake with violent force as the laughing reached a crescendo. Limbs fell from the branches overhead, some thin and some large. The carriage bumped over them, and Maggie heard a crunch that might have been one of the wheels, but she didn't dare stop. No matter how far they traveled, the forest remained dark. There was no sign of the sun or an end to the trees.

He is ours! the huge voice bellowed.

Ghostly hands shot out of the trees from all directions, each aimed at the carriage. They were pale and translucent, tinged with a color Maggie had never seen before. Each hand had extra fingers and spider-like joints; they moved so fast. The first hand reached the carriage and tore off the door. Others poured in alongside while the door on the opposite side suffered the same fate.

The hands ripped James out of the carriage, his arms and legs spread out wide. He thrashed and pulled, but the hands were too strong. They encircled his head and face, choking off his ability to breathe.

Ruther climbed out after him, followed by Henry. Both stared at James with terrified, stricken faces.

"Help him, Ruther!" Maggie screamed. "Cut the hands!"

"What hands?" Ruther asked. "I don't see—" But then he pulled his sword out, as did Henry. It was only then Maggie realized that this was another mistake.

"No! Wait! Put them away!" Maggie stood on the seat and waved her arms at her brother and Ruther, but the damage was done. The trees quaked again and more ghostly hands appeared, now aiming for the other two men. "They've seen you!"

Henry turned around in circles, trying to hold his sword aloft with his one good arm, but the effort was wearing him down.

Maggie moaned. How could they not see the hands? They were everywhere! The monstrous hands with extra fingers grasped Henry and Ruther and held them aloft along with James.

What shall we do with them? the voice asked. *Rip them apart? Fling their bodies miles away? Or take them deep into our lair and let them ROT?*

Henry cried out in agony. Blood began to flow from all three men's eyes and ears. They were going to die in the most horrific manner, and Maggie would have to witness it. She stretched her hands toward them, reaching helplessly. "No!"

Bright light exploded from her fingertips, solidifying into what looked like arms and hands extending from her own. How could that be? What was happening? Energy surged through her body as her new massive arms tore through the ghostly hands grasping James, Henry, and Ruther. The ghostly hands withered and shrank away at her touch, even as more of them emerged from the trees. She swatted them back, crushed them.

Maggie watched in confusion and awe, but as each second passed, her newfound energy depleted until she could barely stand. With a flicker, her extended arms vanished, leaving a tingling in her fingertips.

"Get up!" she called to the men. "Get in! Get in!"

It seemed to take every bit of their waning strength to get to their feet and climb back in the carriage.

Maggie slumped in the driver's seat and ordered the horses to run. She didn't care if it killed the poor beasts, her group had to get out of the forest. The exit was visible to her again. Sixty, maybe fifty yards ahead. Around them, the forest shrieked and shook.

Maggie glanced back and saw more ghostly hands crawling along the ground like giant spiders, gathering the fallen branches and sticks. Up ahead, the light grew stronger. She felt the warmth and freshness coming from it. Tears of joy replaced her tears of blood.

Then the forest's hands heaved the tree limbs up into the air like spears. Maggie didn't think the horses could run any faster, but she whipped them and screamed at them to try.

The sticks arced high into the air and made whistling sounds like arrows as they sailed toward their targets. So many of them flew overhead that for a moment they blotted out the sun. Maggie looked ahead. "Twenty more yards! Go go go!"

The branches began their descent, aimed directly at the carriage. Maggie could not keep her eyes open. Her heart threatened to pound its way out of her chest. She tasted blood in her throat as she gasped for air. The first branch struck the ground just behind them. She peeked again when she heard it slam into the dirt. Several more branches fell, some crashing through the carriage, puncturing it as easily as a stone dropped into water. One of the spare horses was struck deep in its flank, likely a fatal wound.

They crossed the line marking the end of the Iron Pass in the nick of time. Maggie looked back to see the rest of the branches jutting straight up in a perfect line to form a sort of fence. The path was clear of any ghostly, monstrous hands. The forest appeared to be completely empty and calm. Above them, the sun shone as they left the forest path and entered the land of Pappalon.

"We made it," Maggie said breathlessly. Then her eyes rolled back into her head and she passed out.

FOUR

The House of Concubines

Three weeks after her friends escaped the Iron Pass, Isabelle watched Brandol, pretending to be Henry, perish under Emperor Krallick's sword. Unable to stop herself, she cried out Henry's name and wept as Brandol's body slumped to the ground. As the Emperor cleaned his blade with a cloth, Isabelle wiped her eyes of the tears she'd shed for her friend. With great care, Emperor Krallick placed the beautiful weapon back in its sheath.

"For him, it is finished, but your new life begins today and your cleansing begins now." He turned to the closest servant. "Release her from the cage and take her to the House of Concubines."

As the Emperor strode from the room, accompanied by his chief servants, others hurried to unlock Isabelle's cage. They grabbed her by the arms and led her out of the throne room. She did not dare look back. She did not want to see Brandol's broken, bleeding form sprawled on the stone floor. Her body was numb as the men steered her through the palace, climbing endless stairs until they finally reached a hall lined with torches that led to a massive golden door.

The door had no window, but a thousand designs and symbols were etched into the golden plating. The servant to her right removed a ring of iron keys from his pocket and inserted one into the lock. As the door opened, he pushed Isabelle into the chamber.

She expected to enter a dark, frigid, and filthy dungeon where other female slaves might be chained, their helpless cries ringing off the walls. Instead, a rush of heated air met her at the doorway and her eyes drank in the splashes of color from ceiling to floor. Her bare feet, which had become numb to the cold stone of the palace, now lighted on warm plush rugs.

Intricate tapestries and paintings of women dancing, men on horseback fighting dragons, and scenes of passionate love decorated the walls. Lavish couches and chairs were scattered around the room, exotic scents hovered in the air, and numerous torches created a welcoming, well-lit atmosphere.

Occupying the room were beautiful women in lovely robes, many of whom regarded her with expressions ranging from curiosity to suspicion. One woman in particular, a petite blonde in a blue robe who smelled strongly of lilacs, studied Isabelle with an expression of deep dislike. She casually reached above her head to fix her hair, which was held in place by a golden clasp adorned with the largest, most brilliant ruby rose Isabelle had ever seen.

The door closed behind Isabelle with a soft clap. The servants were gone. An ominous click told her the door was now locked, leaving her alone with these strange women. She had no idea what she was expected to do.

"Cecilia," the petite woman wearing the clasp said. "See to the new girl."

Another woman stood and walked toward Isabelle. She wore a green robe, which matched her eyes perfectly. Her dark red hair didn't reach her shoulders, but bounced with each step. Although most of the women in the room were fair, this one stood out in beauty. Isabelle thought this might be the prettiest woman she had ever seen.

"Don't be frightened," Cecilia told her. "I'm going to take care of you. What is your name?"

"Isabelle." She continued to take in her surroundings with both fear and awe. Such opulence and beauty—she hadn't expected anything like it. Most of the other girls had already gone back to what they were doing before: reading books, talking quietly, or playing games.

"I'm not allowed to touch you," Cecilia continued, "not until you've been cleansed. Otherwise I would greet you more personally. If you would follow me?"

Finally, Isabelle found her voice. "Cleansed? What do you mean? The Emperor said—"

Cecilia turned with astonishing grace and walked toward the back of the large room. "Yes, you must be cleansed before you can be touched by the Emperor or any of his concubines. It's not painful, but it is exhausting. Try not to worry. I'll show you around on the way to the baths. Don't touch anything, *especially me.*"

They walked through the expansive common room toward the two exits in the back. Instead of doors, sheer drapes of lavender and blue stretched from floor to ceiling. "The exit on the left leads to our personal quarters. The right to the baths. We each have our own room. You will see yours later. After you have been bathed."

"They bathed me when I first arrived," Isabelle said.

Cecilia waved the comment away. "That was to prevent the Emperor from smelling your stench. Trust me, when you've been cleansed, you'll know it."

Isabelle stepped through the drapes that Cecilia held open for her but then stopped in the hallway, leaned against the wall, and began to cry. Cecilia backed away, as though Isabelle might reach out to her for comfort, but Isabelle didn't want to be touched. She didn't want to be looked at. She only wanted to leave this place. The idea that these girls, like Cecilia, seemed untroubled—even complacent—with their position as concubines only made it worse.

"Come on," Cecilia urged kindly, "follow me. Then we can talk."

Isabelle tried to stop her tears, but the task was too tall. She fell to her knees and placed her palms on the floor. This place was a prison.

Beautiful, yes, but still a cage like the one she'd ridden inside on her journey to the Emperor's palace. The only difference was that now she had finer furnishings and other women with her. How could she possibly escape?

"Don't cry," Cecilia said. "The maids are waiting for you."

Isabelle saw no reason to hurry, and besides, it took time for her to regain her composure. When she did, she stood proud and tall, and let Cecilia lead her.

Branching off the hallway were many rooms for bathing. Cecilia led her to one near the end of the corridor where two women in black and red dresses waited. The room was filled with steam which made it hard for Isabelle to see.

The baths were enormous. At least five or six women could comfortably sit inside one basin, and yet this room had three of such size. A dozen fireplaces ringed the room, all with huge pots filled with water. Deep, wide troughs ran from each fireplace to the bath nearest it.

"I'll be outside when you're finished," Cecilia said from the doorway. "You're in good hands."

The two older women smiled at Isabelle in a matronly way. With large brushes in hand, they guided her into the steaming bathroom. "Now don't you fret anymore," one of them told her. "Every girl goes through this, and you saw them when you came in. They all turned out all right. The cleansing process helps you rid yourself of all the unclean skin and hair you have. Now be a good girl and take your clothes off."

The maids were much more gentle than the ones Isabelle had encountered downstairs before seeing the Emperor. They led her to the first bath in the far left corner of the room. It had two steps going down into the water and was the source of most of the steam in the room.

"The water may be a bit warm," one of them said, "but nothing to worry about."

Isabelle put her foot in and jerked back. "It's not warm, it's *scalding!*" she cried, but the women responded by pushing her kindly and firmly into the water. "No, please! Let it cool!" She leaned back against them, trying to get away from the water that she suspected might start boiling at any moment.

"In you go," they insisted, overpowering her quite easily until she was completely in the water.

Isabelle tried to keep as much of her body as possible out of the water, but it was no use. It took a long time to get used to the temperature. When she finally did, her skin was red and puffy.

One of the maids entered the water with her, clothing and all, holding a large block of soap. "This may feel a little different than what you're used to, but it will help you get clean. Give me your hand—that's a good girl."

She placed the soap in Isabelle's hand while the second maid entered into the tub, too, wielding her brush almost like a sword. "You lather your body with the soap, and we'll make it nice and clean."

Together, the maids scrubbed Isabelle's skin with great vigor. Isabelle immediately noticed that the soap stung her skin wherever it touched. The women were ardent and forceful in their scrubbing, but sweet in every other way. They were deaf to any whimpers of pain and humiliatingly thorough in washing Isabelle's body. By the time they finished, Isabelle was once more in tears. Her body stung from head to foot, every nerve pulsed angrily, and her energy was utterly sapped.

"All done with that part," one of the maids said. "Now into the next bath."

Assuming that anything would be better than staying in the scalding water, Isabelle scrambled out and allowed the women to lead her into the second tub. This time, the temperature was perfectly warm.

"Sit on the top step," one of the women told her, and Isabelle obeyed. "That's a good girl. We're going to cleanse your head."

Isabelle closed her eyes and felt the women lifting her hair and moving it about. The touch of their hands on her scalp and the tenderness of their movements left her feeling the most relaxed she'd been in weeks. The calmness made her think of Henry until something fell on her arm. She opened her eyes and saw a long clump of her own hair resting above her wrist.

As she screamed and jumped up, something bit her scalp. "What are you doing?" she yelled. "Get away from me!"

The women frowned, confused. "We're ridding you of your unclean hair. Now be a good girl and sit down."

"Don't touch me!" Isabelle shouted. "You're not cutting off my hair. You're not coming near me. You're all mad. This is madness!" She felt her head and realized that half of her hair had already been cut short enough to be a man's cut. Horror struck her. Warm liquid trickled down her brow onto her nose, and she reached up to wipe the water away.

"Oh dear, you're injured," one of the women said gently, pulling Isabelle back to a sitting position. "Let us look at that."

Isabelle didn't know what they were talking about. She looked at her hand and saw that what she had assumed was water was actually her own blood. The exhaustion from the trip north, seeing Brandol killed in front of her, the scalding water and burning soap, and now her head covered in blood . . . it was too much. Her head began to pound, and she heard a distant roaring sound. Then the entire room filled up with thick, cold steam, and Isabelle fell face first into the water.

• • •

It was night when she woke. She was in a bed, her head resting on a pillow, soft warm blankets covering her body. All was still and quiet. She looked up at the ceiling unable to remember where she was. It had been ages since she'd slept in a proper bed. In fact, the last time had been the night before her meeting with the Emperor of Neverak at the Glimmering Fountain. She shuddered at the memory.

A strong gust of wind blew through the window of her chamber. Isabelle turned her head to look out. She experienced an odd sensation as her head rubbed against the cloth of the pillow. Her hand moved to her scalp and touched tender, bare flesh.

"My head," she whispered, more memories returning. "They shaved my head."

Her hands moved to her face. Her eyebrows were gone. She felt her arms. No hair there, either. There was no hair anywhere on her body. Her mouth and nose were dry. Next to her bed was a pitcher of water and a wooden, gilded cup. She poured herself a drink and swallowed it greedily, dribbling liquid down her face and neck. Looking down, she noticed that she wore a simple white nightgown, made from some kind of coarse fabric and not nearly as fine as the clothes she had seen the other girls wearing. But then, none of the other women in the house were bald, either.

"What have they done to me?"

She sprang from the bed and went to the window. If not for two iron bars running up and down its length, the window would have been wide enough for her to pass through. Even with her slender, undernourished frame, the space was too narrow. She pulled and pushed with all her strength. When she was absolutely certain escape was impossible, she stared out into the night and studied the land of Neverak under the light of the three moons.

Water surrounded the palace, and beyond that lay the capital city. To the north, the direction her window faced, the city ended at the steep cliffs of nearby mountains. Her eyes traveled along the distant cliff line and paused on two strange lights that burned like twin candles, a bright purple glow. Her eyes locked on the lights for a long time, putting her into a trancelike state. When the moment passed, she tore her eyes away from the cliff and the strange lights and left her room. The lamps in the hall were dark except for one. She took it and went into the common room.

The dozens of tapestries covering the walls made it difficult to see if there were any windows. One by one, she pulled the tapestries aside, finding four windows, each barred as securely as the one in her room. She tried the main door, hopeful that the servants had left it unlocked. They had not. Isabelle went into the baths and checked them all. None of them had windows. The place was indeed a prison despite its lavish, elegant state. She had the sudden urge to vomit. She ran back to her room and grabbed the chamber pot, but she spat up nothing except bitter water from her stomach.

"That's exactly what I did on my first night," said a voice from behind her. It was so unexpected that Isabelle gave a shrill shriek and her chamber pot clattered to the floor. "I'm sorry!" Cecilia said, clutching a robe around her throat and smiling nervously. "I should have said something. Sit down. Let's talk."

Isabelle sat on her bed, but Cecilia remained standing in the doorway. They looked at each other without speaking, and Isabelle realized how ugly she must appear with no hair and wearing such a horrid, plain gown. Yet the first thing that came out of her mouth was, "How long have you been a slave?"

Cecilia's smile held sad amusement. "Is that what you think? We're not slaves. We're concubines."

Isabelle shook her head. "The Emperor brought me here by force. I am no concubine."

Cecilia's eyes told Isabelle that she didn't believe this. "Where are you from?"

"Blithmore. Richterton."

Cecilia nodded. "That's what I thought. So am I. From Blithmore, I mean, not Richterton. I came here of my own will. Most of the other women did, too. Now that I think on it, the last girl who wanted to leave was traded not long after I arrived—about six months ago. The Emperor replaced her with a woman named Jade. Jade is in the middle of her cleansing. Two months to go, I believe." Cecilia smiled confidently. "You'll come around. It's not as horrible as you think. Look at where we live. We have books to read, horses to ride, and tomorrow . . . when you taste the food . . ."

"I don't care about the food," Isabelle mumbled. Who knew if what she said would get back to the Emperor? If all the women were willing slaves, what would stop them from giving the Emperor whatever information he requested? Her secrets had to stay her own.

"Those nightgowns are awful, aren't they?" Cecilia remarked.

"Yes." Isabelle's back begged to be scratched, but rather than giving in, she tried to hold the cloth away so the skin wouldn't be so bothered.

"I hated them. You'll be out of them before you know it. You wear it mainly so we remember not to touch you until your cleansing is done. I completed my cleansing a few weeks ago."

"How long does it last?" Isabelle asked.

"Four months."

Isabelle groaned. "I can't do it."

"By the end of the first week, you'll come to love the baths like an old friend. Your hair will grow back. See?" Cecilia combed her fingers through her own hair. "Mine is already four inches, maybe five. The maids have an ointment that helps it grow faster. The Emperor likes longer hair. And he favors newer girls. Kayla is his favorite now—she's the small girl that smells like flowers. She wears the Emperor's ruby, but he has summoned me often recently. I think he may be seeing the light."

Without realizing she was doing it, Isabelle stroked her bald head, holding back the tears for her missing hair.

"You don't look so terrible bald, you know. I was hideous." Cecilia brushed back her own short, auburn locks. "But you're beautiful—with or without hair."

"Thank you," Isabelle said, but she didn't feel grateful. And it was hard to feel gratitude toward someone she couldn't trust, even if Cecilia did seem kind. "Is there anything else I should know?"

"Kayla isn't friendly toward the newer girls until she gets a feel for them. She wants to know if they're a threat."

"A threat?"

"She wants to know how badly a girl wants the ruby rose. She sees me as competition—a few other girls, too—so she doesn't speak to us unless it's to give us orders."

"She can do that? Is she in charge?"

Cecilia shook her head. "It's all in her mind."

Isabelle yawned. These things were so petty. They didn't matter.

Cecilia gave her a friendly smile. "I should let you get some sleep. Oh, I should warn you about a couple of other things, too. If you're caught trying to escape, you'll be executed. And if a servant or a concubine tries to help you escape, you'll be forced to watch their execution first. The Emperor is a good man, Isabelle. A very gentle man, but he's not one to be crossed."

FIVE

The Four Visions

When Maggie opened her eyes, Henry, James, and Ruther were nowhere to be seen. After leaving the Iron Forest, she had caught a glimpse of a field and steep hills of green and white. Now, no matter where she looked, she saw fog. Even more surprising was the cobblestone pathway under her feet. The stones, bright and smooth, extended around her in all directions, though the fog limited her vision.

To her left, the fog grew blacker; to the right, whiter. Above her, through the fog, she spotted a brilliant sky, not of blue and white, but of stars and planets and brilliant colors. This otherworldly starscape stretched on as far as she could see. The air was cool and wet, making her skin damp.

"Margaret." It was a man's voice, old and soft but deep with an accent she did not recognize. "Margaret, I have little time before he realizes you are here. Are you listening to me?"

"I—yes—who are you? Where am I?"

"You are at the start," the man told her.

"The start of what?"

"I cannot answer your questions now, but there are four things I must tell you. You have developed late—perhaps you already know that—but it is not necessarily a bad thing."

"What are you talking about?" Maggie's words echoed as though she stood inside a vast chamber. The black fog drew closer, in small puffs and faint billows. She had the impression it wanted to swallow her up. Following this instinct, she moved toward the whiter haze, chewing her lip harder with each footstep. "Why can't I see you?"

"The danger is too great to show myself here. Listen. You must find me, but I cannot tell you where. The color lyrial will guide you. Look for it."

"Lyrial?" As soon as Maggie spoke the word, certain stones on the path glowed brighter than the rest. It was the same unfamiliar color that marked the ghostly hands that had come out of the forest. It was not red or blue or black or white, but seeing it set her heart afire with hope and gladness, so much that she smiled despite the unfamiliarity of her surroundings.

"The second is to remember that *everything has a cost.*"

"What does that mean?"

The voice continued without answering her. "The third is to remember that you may return here when you are ready. It is not difficult. When you are ready, you will be ready."

"How will I know when I'm ready? Why do you speak in riddles?"

"I must go! This is the fourth and final thing you need to know. If you remember nothing else, remember this: you must believe! You are only at the start."

A long laugh echoed. It was not a friendly sound, and it grew in intensity as the black fog surrounded Maggie. The hope and happiness she'd felt slowly siphoned out of her.

"*What* am I to believe?" she asked. She waited several seconds but received no answer. "Where are you? What start am I at?"

"The start of your death," a new voice said. It's cruel, singsong cadence chilled Maggie to the bone. "The old fool is gone. He runs and hides because he is weak." Another belt of laughter followed, even louder than the first. It rose and fell like ocean waves. "Do not put your trust in that bag of wind. He will only disappoint."

"Is this a dream? If so, I want to wake."

"Yes." The cruel voice trailed off like a snake's hiss. "Yes, wake up, Margaret. Pretend it's all a dream, a fantasy. Stay blind to your path—to this place."

"It is a dream," Maggie insisted. "It is a dream!"

"Of course it is. And while you are dreaming, there are some things you should see, events which you will find of great interest."

The black fog began to glow, and in it, she saw a man with filthy red hair matted to his dust-covered skin. The man bore chains on his feet and staggered under the weight of the rocks he carried. An obscenely fat man shouted in rage. He brandished a whip, which he used freely on the redheaded man. Maggie stared at the image for a long time before realizing that she was looking at her friend, chained and whipped.

"Ruther?" she said. "Is that Ruther?"

"It's only the beginning, Maggie. Keep watching."

An image of James appeared next. He, too, had a dirty face, pale and thin. Obscuring his face were thick bars of metal. He wrapped his hands around two of the three bars. Despair filled his eyes as he shouted words she couldn't hear. He seemed to be looking directly at her, pleading. Maggie had never seen James so desperate.

"Prison bars," she whispered. "Why is James in prison?" She spun around. "What is going on here?"

"Now behold the end of your brother."

Another vision in the fog began. Henry sat in a chair of stone, confined by ropes which wrapped around his body. The chair rested in a basin filled with water. The water level was over Henry's head. His eyes bulged and his neck and chest strained against his restraints. A look of sheer horror crossed his face, and bubbles escaped his mouth as he tried to speak.

Maggie covered her face with her hands.

Laughter filled the air.

"Who are you?" she shouted.

An eerie feeling swept through her as she stared into the black fog. It both thrilled and terrified her. She lifted a foot to step backward, toward the whiteness, but a hand the color of lyrial pushed her forward. She fought against it and tumbled to her knees on the cobblestone path.

"There is one more vision you must see. This one will answer your question."

The black mists exploded with light, and Maggie saw herself in an impossible form: huge and powerful in a room with a towering ceiling which her head nearly scraped. Another being, a man-shaped monstrosity covered in scales and spikes, loomed over her as though the ceiling was not even there. In the vision, Maggie tried to protect herself from the being of superior strength, but she couldn't. The creature pummeled her mercilessly with its fists and scales as she screamed in agony. Thick smoke filled the room and obscured Maggie's view of herself. The last thing she saw was the murderous creature pouncing on her, ready to deliver a killing blow.

"Why have you shown me this? I am no one."

"To humiliate you. And to show you your place in this new world you have discovered."

"What new world? How do you know my name?"

"It doesn't matter. You see how insignificant you are?"

"I don't believe in you. I don't believe in this place."

"Good! But before you wake, Margaret, let me give you one piece of counsel, too. I promise it will be much more helpful than what the old fool gave you."

Maggie didn't want to hear anything more, but the words came anyway.

"Fear me."

A giant shape appeared in the fog: a man who remained concealed by a long flowing cloak and deep hood. Pale white skin emerged from the sleeves as he pointed two fingers at Maggie. Yellowish-green fingernails as sharp as knives aimed directly at her eyes. Faint green spots appeared within the darkness of his hood and fixed themselves on her face.

Maggie trembled and clutched herself as she stood. "Who—who are you?"

"I am he who waits for you. I am he who will destroy you. But if you choose not to pursue this path—choose not to believe—then none of the things you witnessed will happen."

SIX

The Western Gate

The carriage bumped along unsteadily, its rear left wheel broken nearly beyond repair. Henry managed to patch it up enough to drive on it, but he was glad to see the damage. He wanted to burn the carriage to ash. James sat beside him, urging the horses onward. But with three working wheels and one badly damaged, the carriage couldn't put distance between them and the Iron Forest as quickly as they wished.

James gritted his teeth. Protruding from his right hip was a stick as wide around as his littlest finger. Blood trickled from the wound. Henry imagined it probably hurt every time James moved. Yet the soldier was the only one who could drive.

Henry had offered to do it, but they both knew he couldn't control the horses with one good arm at this pace and with the carriage rocking so badly. It shamed him to be so helpless. Maggie had collapsed the moment they'd escaped the Iron Forest. After trying twice to wake her, he and James had put her in the carriage opposite Ruther to recover.

Ruther was in the worst shape of the four. One of the branches had flown through the carriage roof and left a horrible gash in Ruther's lower right side. Without bandages or healing herbs, James had only been able to wrap a blanket around Ruther's waist.

"We'll find a town as quickly as possible," James told him. "Stay on your stomach. The ride may be bumpy."

Surprisingly, or perhaps not, the pain didn't stop Ruther from trying to be clever. "My stomach . . . is where all my cushioning is."

"He's not going to make it, is he?" Henry asked James quietly.

"I don't know. After what we just witnessed, I am not certain I know anything anymore."

"I thought we were dead," Henry muttered. "What came over you in the forest? Why did you pull out your sword?"

James shook his head. "Nothing made sense to me. I thought I heard his voice outside the carriage. He was all I could think about."

"Who?" Henry asked. "Vreagan?"

James did not answer, but Henry knew his guess was correct. If James didn't want to speak of Vreagan, that was fine by Henry. He had other matters on his mind.

"There is no logical explanation for what happened in those trees. Something grabbed us—held us in the air. It was . . . magic."

"*Magic.*" James spat out the word as though it was a curse.

"What other explanation is there? The Path, James! The Path is one of Light *and* Shadow. What we encountered in the forest was pure evil. And the moment we crossed the edge of the forest, the world was light and warm again. What other explanation could there be?"

James snorted. "The Path is an ancient myth."

"My father believed in it. We talked about it once in his woodshop. He said he knew it was real. My mother never agreed. It was something they didn't discuss because my mother so adamantly opposed it."

"How did your father know?"

Henry shrugged. "He never told me. He wasn't a man to speak much unless it was about woodworking."

"Count yourself lucky. I preferred my father not speak at all. He rarely had kind words for any of us."

They fell silent as the carriage bumped along. The terrain on the eastern side of the Iron Forest was similar to the western hills they had left behind. Tall rises surrounded them, far too steep for horses to traverse. The road wound through the valleys in a torturous route. They hadn't ridden more than two miles from the mouth of the pass when James spotted a large, unusual structure up ahead.

It spanned the length of the valley through which they rode, blocking the path. The light of the sun reflecting from metal blinded Henry. He raised a hand to shield his vision, and James did likewise.

"What is it?" James asked Henry.

"I don't know."

The giant structure turned out to be an ornate gate. It stood almost thirty feet high, metalwork forming a lattice. At the top, the lattice ended in spikes as deadly as James's knives. Henry could easily imagine some poor fool trying to climb the gate and suffering a terrible death by skewering. Flanking the gate were two towers: tall, wooden platforms built into the hillside to elevate the guards of Pappalon high above the gate. Squinting, Henry made out the shape of at least two guards per tower. Topping the platforms were purple and black canopies marked with the golden seal of the Pappalon: a quill and a sword crossed, surrounded by five stars.

When they reached the gate, a trumpet sounded from above.

"Declare your purpose!" a man's accented voice called out from the guard tower. Men at each tower were armed with bows and quivers full of arrows.

James held up his hands, showing that his palms were empty. "We are from Blithmore," he shouted to the guard. "We seek refuge in the east and ask to be allowed to pass through your borders."

"The Western Agent will meet you for inspection. Prepare your party."

Henry heard the sound of horses galloping toward them and after a few minutes, three riders reached the metal gate. A short, middle-aged man with a face as round as a dinner roll was flanked by two guards in the purple-and-black uniforms of Pappalon, complete with the quill, the sword, and the stars. The guards wore metal helmets and had sheathed daggers and swords strapped to their armor. James in his current condition would not fare well against them in a fight.

"Hmm . . . hello," the plump man murmured. "That is to say . . . hmm . . . I welcome you to the border of Pappalon. My name is Sir Asaron, Agent of the Western Gate of Pappalon. Am I to understand that you and your party have come through . . . hmm . . . the Iron Pass?"

Asaron's accent was pure Pappalonian. The word *and* sounded like *end*; *you* sounded like *ya*.

"We have," James said grimly. "And we are the worse for wear because of it."

"How many are in your party?"

"Four," Henry answered. "My friend is gravely injured. He needs to be seen by a physician without delay."

"Was he injured in the pass?" Asaron craned his neck as though he could see inside the carriage. "Pardon my . . . hmm . . . curiosity, but there are many tales of that pass. In fact, in the four years I have served as agent here, you are the first party to come from Blithmore. Very rarely, foolhardy people will leave Pappalon to travel west. A small family left a month or so ago, despite our . . . hmm . . . warnings."

Henry thought back to the carriage that James and Ruther said they had moved off the road. Had that been the small family Asaron mentioned?

"Normally we have to do a . . . hmm . . . full inspection of any party traveling through, but under the circumstances, I think we can . . . hmm . . . skip that. Your names?"

"James Oslan."

"Hmm," Asaron said, giving James a long look.

"This is—"

"Brandol," Henry hurried to say. Since the Elite Guard believed Henry Vestin was in their custody, there was no need to tell anyone otherwise. "Brandol the carpenter."

Asaron nodded. "A pleasure, good sir."

James jerked his thumb over his shoulder. "In the carriage are Margaret and Ruther the storyteller."

Asaron peeked into the carriage. "The girl is sleeping, and the man—"

"Never looked better, have I?" Ruther, covered in blood, attempted a smile.

Asaron looked at James with a solemn expression. "Your assessment was correct. This man needs to be seen . . . hmm . . . urgently. If you keep on this road, you'll reach Borderville soon. You'll find lodging, most likely at the Sheep's Entrails, also a nearby physician, and . . . hmm . . . plenty of whatever else you might need. You must go with all haste." He turned to his guards. "Open the gates at once."

James shook Asaron's hand. "Thank you for expediting our entry."

When the fence closed behind them, Henry wondered if he would ever see Blithmore again. A whole new country lay ahead, and Henry knew very little about it. The road to Isabelle awaited him, but first he had to help Ruther, James, and Maggie. Turning his eyes back to the road, he set his jaw. James spurred the horses onward down the road as fast as the carriage would allow them to travel.

"Hang on, Ruther," Henry called out over his shoulder.

SEVEN

Precious Drops of Blood

Both the towering fence and the setting sun disappeared as the group rode eastward. James and Henry traveled with all haste, speaking little except to check on Ruther, whose responses grew more and more outlandish with each passing mile. Ruther was not going to die tonight—not if James could do anything about it. He hadn't yet apologized to Ruther for the way he'd treated him in Blithmore, after Bookerton. Nor had he thanked Ruther for saving their lives and nursing him and Henry back to health after the battle. The voices in the Iron Pass had reminded James of that over and over again. But even then, James hadn't been able to face Ruther and offer a proper apology. He promised himself that if Ruther lived, James would man up and say the words.

The night's blanket of stars and inky sky felt cooler in the hills than it had on the forest path. As they rode further into Pappalon, James's mood grew as dark as the sky. Only a few months ago, after securing his release from prison, he had set plans in motion to exact his revenge on Vreagan. James had been on his way to kill Vreagan when he stopped at Richterton to bid his mother, father, and sister a proper farewell. That farewell had ruined all his plans. He'd discovered his mother was dead, stopped his father from killing Henry, and learned his sister sorely needed him. Now a whirlwind of events had brought him to Pappalon, as far from Vreagan as he could be.

Meanwhile, his sister drew nearer to Neverak every day.

He glanced back at Maggie through the holes in the top of the carriage. Her pale, fair skin glowed magnificently in the moonlight. Her dark curls framed her face and enhanced that glow. Her beauty had taken him by surprise during their journey through Blithmore. And though he wasn't certain of the depths of his feelings toward her, he appreciated knowing his jaded heart could still feel. For a time, he'd believed that Vreagan had stolen that from him as well.

The road they traveled was neither well-kept nor well-worn. Behind them, the eastern edge of the Iron Forest stretched as far as the eye could see. Gradually the hills leveled out into lush, rolling meadows, knolls, and sparse thickets of trees. James guessed if they had crossed this area in the spring, they would have seen fields of flowers, rhinelk grazing, and heard the music of birds until late in the evening. But spring was still weeks away.

He wondered how different Pappalon was from Blithmore. How well would he and his friends be able to get along with no money and no knowledge of the country? Would people try to take advantage of them? Discriminate against them? They had no maps of Pappalon or the larger region surrounding it. All James knew was that Pappalon had once been part of Avalon. The Slave Wars, however, had split Avalon into three countries: Pappalon to the south, Old Avalon in the middle, and New Avalon to the north. Since the death of Emperor Peter Krallick, Old Avalon was Neverak's strongest ally and the only country in the region that still allowed slavery.

It was well into evening when James spotted a sign along the roadside.

NEAREST BORDERVILLE LODGINGS
THE COW'S COLON, THE GOAT STOMACH, THE SHEEP'S ENTRAILS

"Is that—" Henry started to say, then shook his head. "Does that really say the Sheep's Entrails?"

"What kind of place is this where inns are given names like those?"

"It doesn't matter," Henry said. "We need to hurry. Ruther is running out of time."

"Hurry," Ruther mumbled so faintly James could hardly hear him. "The ducks are burning, Maggie."

"He's delirious," Henry said.

James urged the horses onward and minutes later, they passed another sign.

WELCOME TO BORDERVILLE
The Last Dicing Town in Pappalon

"Sounds like Ruther's kind of place," Henry said. "Keep your eyes open."

James noted differences between Borderville and Richterton immediately. The streets were not dirt, but made of stones. Despite the hour, the streets were well-lit with torches hanging from posts every twenty or thirty feet, and candles sat in most of the windows they passed. But stranger still were the many signs on the houses and shops that read either *Vote for Matt* or *Vote for Byderik*. The signs were in the windows, nailed to the walls, and in one case, painted onto the side of a wagon.

"Can you believe this place?" Henry asked.

"Is this a town full of nobles?" James wondered.

"Who are Matt and Byderik?"

James noticed that every man in town, whether walking or riding, wore a hat. The hats were by no means uniform. Some were tall and black, others short and brown. A few even had the names *Matt* or *Byderik* woven into them. The longer he and Henry rode through town, the more stares they received from those passing by.

"Excuse me, sir," James said to the first person who came near, "where might we hire the services of a physician?"

The man stared at the top of James's head as though appalled at the sight of someone's uncovered hair.

"Sir, please, my friend's life is in peril! Where might I find a physician?"

Still seemingly unnerved by James's lack of a hat, the man gave him directions. James drove through the streets, reaching their destination quickly.

Maggie woke up when the carriage stopped. "Where are we?" she asked. "What happened to the fog?"

"We need your help, Maggie," James told her. "Are you well enough to get up?"

It took a moment for Maggie's eyes to focus, but when they did she struggled to her feet, her face colorless and limbs sluggish. Henry and James held Ruther in their arms while Maggie knocked on the door of the physician's house until it opened. A man with long white hair answered the door. He wore a nightgown and a top hat, and his slippers made soft scratching noises as he walked.

"How may I be of service?" the physician asked. Then his eyes fell on Ruther. "Come in quickly. Set him down on the examining table."

The physician's wife scurried around the room, lighting a fire in the hearth and candles until the room was well-lit and warm. Maggie and James stepped back after laying Ruther on his stomach so the physician could move around without obstruction. The room was not large, especially with the shelves filled with tools and jars, each marked or labeled in neat handwriting.

"Pleased to meet you," the physician's wife said. "I am Penelope. This is Dessy."

James introduced himself then asked the physician, "How bad is our friend?"

Dessy raised a finger to them to ask them to wait, then said, "I need supplies," and left the room.

"I'm no expert on healing," Penelope said. "Dessy is. But the more he scratches his head and plays with his hair, the worse the situation."

Dessy returned with a bowl of warm water in one hand and a brown box in the other. He set both next to Ruther and went to work cleaning the wound. The more he cleaned it, the more often he scratched his head. James and Maggie exchanged a nervous look, though Penelope tried to reassure them with a smile.

"Very deep," Dessy finally said. "Very, very deep." He withdrew a needle and thread from his box and began stitching up Ruther's wound.

Watching the physician work was not a pleasant experience for James. He had never been squeamish, but a needle going in and out of skin was not something he saw every day.

Ruther never even reacted to the pain, which James thought was a bad sign.

When Dessy finished, he stood and washed his hands in the bowl.

Maggie's hands went to her dress, bunching up the fabric in her hands and twisting it. James shifted his weight from one leg to the other. He hated being so helpless.

"So very pale," Dessy commented. "He's lost too much blood."

"What can be done?" James asked.

Dessy sighed and looked gravely at his three guests. "I'm afraid there's very little that can be done. Judging by how pale he is, and how large the wound was, he's been bleeding for too long. He's hardly breathing and . . ." Dessy's words trailed off and he shrugged.

"No!" Maggie cried. "Use your herbs and bandages!"

"I don't think those will help," he said gently.

"At least try. Please! He saved my life. He's a dear friend to us."

Dessy looked to his wife as though asking silently for her thoughts. Penelope lowered her head.

"This is the best I can do," he said in a somber tone. He placed his fingers alongside Ruther's neck. "The heartbeat is far too weak. Would you like to take him or . . . wait here?"

Maggie sniffed and stepped closer to Ruther. "He can't die. We've already lost two people. We can't lose any more." She took Ruther's hand. "Can you hear me, Ruther? You can't die!"

If Ruther heard her, he gave no sign. Maggie wiped her eyes and caressed Ruther's hand and arm. "You are a fighter. You don't shut up when we tell you to, and you don't listen to anyone. You're certainly not going to let a little cut be the end of you, are you?"

For some reason, James expected Ruther to open his eyes and say something absurd or humorous, but nothing happened. His eyes stayed closed. And then his chest stopped moving.

Dessy, with his hand still on Ruther's neck, nodded to his wife. "The sheet, Penelope."

"Please," Henry said, "there must be something else you can do."

"No!" Maggie cried. She tightened her grip on Ruther's arm. "Wake up, Ruther! We want you to live!"

Dessy tried to break her grip, but Maggie held on. She shook his arm harder and harder until James thought she might be doing more harm than good. Dessy pulled at her, but he couldn't separate Maggie from Ruther. Then, without warning, Dessy fell backward and Maggie froze. Her entire body stiffened, her fingers clasping Ruther's hand with the strength of a vise.

"Maggie?" James asked. "Are you all right?"

She didn't answer or move. James couldn't tell if she was even breathing.

"Maggie, answer me."

"What's going on?" Dessy asked.

"I have no idea," James answered, but he saw what little color Maggie had in her face drain away. Her lips and cheeks grew pale. Her mouth formed an expression of mild surprise. Then, as quickly as she'd stiffened, Maggie slumped to the floor, her arms and legs trembling as though she were deathly cold.

James scooped her up. "What happened?"

Something wasn't right. Maggie had fainted twice in one day. James started to ask the physician about it when Dessy and Penelope both gasped. They took small steps away from the table where Ruther lay. James's eyes followed their gaze, and he saw Ruther stirring. Red and pink crept into his skin, replacing the whiteness that had set in.

"What is happening?" James shouted at the physician.

"I feel . . . ugh," Ruther said. "I think I—I fell asleep. How long was I out?"

"That's not possible," Dessy muttered, scratching and picking at his head.

"Did Maggie insult me again?" Ruther moaned. "I've always said her words would slay me one day. . ."

Henry laughed and rushed to Ruther's side, helping him to sit upright on the table. He gave his friend a hug.

"The best one-armed hug I've ever had, friend."

James wasn't certain if he was going to laugh or choke on his own emotions. "Ruther's all right . . ." he uttered weakly. "But Maggie? Is she all right?"

Dessy examined her while James held her, his eyes wide with bewilderment. "I—I suppose she is. Yes, I think they'll both be fine." He pointed to the stick protruding from James's side. "Would you like me to take a look at your wound?"

With some gentle, careful work from Dessy, and a lot of grimacing on James's part, the stick was removed, and the wound cleaned and bandaged.

"I suppose this means you'll be a little more relaxed around us, James," Ruther said with a wink. "Now that he's pulled the stick out of your—"

"Could you look at my arm?" Henry asked. "I haven't been able to move it for almost three weeks."

Ruther wrapped a blanket around his shoulders and moved aside so Henry could sit down. Penelope took Ruther's soiled, bloodstained shirt and went to see if she could find him a clean one.

Dessy undressed Henry's right arm and examined it thoroughly. "I don't see any real scarring except the stab wound, but that seems to have healed nicely. I suppose that's thanks to—" He nodded toward Maggie.

"Yes, the shoulder and neck look healthy, too." Dessy took a thin needle and poked Henry in the shoulder. Henry didn't react, even when a tiny drop of blood welled up from where he'd been pricked.

"Careful there," Ruther said, "every drop is precious."

Dessy poked Henry's arm again, pinched him, and finally took out a thin reed and struck Henry's arm at full strength. But Henry felt no pain.

"Normally, I would say that the arm has died, yet it shows no sign of it. I hate to say it, but I am thoroughly perplexed."

"Is there nothing you can do?" Henry croaked.

Dessy shook his head. He patted Henry on the shoulder. "My boy, not everything can be fixed. I do not know how, but tonight I saw a miracle. We all saw it, yet I wager none of you know what happened either. Perhaps that is what you need . . . another miracle."

EIGHT

The Sheep's Entrails

The closest inn to the physician's home was less than a block away: The Sheep's Entrails. Henry walked with Ruther while James placed Maggie in the carriage and drove to the inn's stables. James's gentleness in handling Maggie surprised Henry.

The innkeeper met Henry and company just inside the door. Henry tried to be pleasant, but the news the physician had given him regarding his lame arm made his guts twist and ache.

A miracle, that was what the physician had said Henry needed. Henry wasn't certain he deserved a miracle. Otherwise, why hadn't one happened at the mouth of the pass?

Like the inns at Blithmore, the bottom floor was an open, public space with tables and chairs for dining. A savory, meat-scented steam spilled out of a large kitchen in the back. To the left, a large stairwell leading to the upper floors wrapped around the corner.

The owner of the inn was a short man, no more than five feet tall. His neatly combed black hair was mostly hidden under his tall black hat. His brown eyes studied the travelers closely, first noting their clothes, then their faces, and finally resting on Henry's lame arm. His gaze lingered longest on Maggie's pale face.

"Hello, good sirs," he said in a heavy Pappalonian accent as he tipped his hat. "My name is Jessop. Welcome to the Sheep's Entrails, proud supporters of Byderik. How may I assist you? Does this woman require a physician's care?"

"No," Henry answered. "We just came from there. We are four travelers seeking lodging. Do you have any spare rooms?" The longer Henry spoke, the wider the owner's mouth opened in wonder.

When Henry finished, Jessop resumed his most polite and welcoming expression. "Am I correct in guessing that you are from Blithmore?"

"Yes."

"Splendid. It is always a treat to have guests from other nations. You must have had quite a journey traveling north from the ports. Are you here for the tournament?"

Henry looked at Ruther and James. "No, we are not. We don't plan to stay here long." He paused. "We actually arrived from the west."

The owner's mouth widened again and his voice dropped to a hush. "Did you come through . . . the Iron Pass?" His gaze flickered to Maggie. "Was she injured in the forest? Did you see anything unnatural? Anything at all? We Pappalonians who live by the forest love to hear tales of anyone traveling through the pass. It remains a great curiosity to us. Tales of such travels are incredibly rare."

"Must we discuss it now?" Henry asked. "As you can see, we're very much the worse for wear and badly in need of rest. What can you offer us for lodging?"

Jessop smiled pleasantly and said, "Naturally, I'll assist you in any way I can . . ." The lift in his voice suggested he was waiting for Henry to offer his name.

"Brandol," he said, extending his left hand for the innkeeper to shake. "And this is Ruther, James, and Maggie."

"Well, Brandol, the only remaining room I have is the grand suite. It is large enough to fit a large family or two couples traveling together. Perhaps that would be suitable?"

"You can put me in the room with the lady," Ruther suggested, giving Jessop a roguish wink and a friendly nudge with his elbow.

Jessop looked from Ruther to James to Henry and then laughed. "Ah! Ah!" He laughed again, this time harder. "I get it! Very good, then. I'm certain we can accommodate the four of you, if the three men don't mind sharing a room. All we need to discuss now is the matter of payment. Have you had an opportunity to exchange your funds into Eastern Irons currency?"

"No, sir," James answered. "We came straight from the Western Gate."

"Not a problem. I can assist you in converting your currency as well. The exchange as agreed upon by our sovereign nations is two crowns for every gyri."

"We—well—" Henry looked to James.

"We don't have much to exchange," James explained.

"How much money is in your possession?" came Jessop's overly casual question. "Between the four of you?"

Henry detected a hint of greed in Jessop's face and let out a small cough. "We prefer not to say. But we can pay you a day at a time."

Jessop raised his eyebrows so high they disappeared under the brim of his hat. "I admit I'm not familiar with the way inns are run in Blithmore, but here people pay for the entire stay up front."

"The entire stay?" Ruther asked. "This place is so backwards! No wonder everyone wears hats. It's to hide the fact that they have nothing inside—"

"How much do you charge per day?" James hurried to ask over Ruther's exclamation.

"For the one room I have open . . . two gyri per day."

"Per day?" Ruther repeated. "That's four crowns a day! And you expect people to pay it? No wonder it's vacant."

Jessop took no offense at Ruther's bold statement. "If you must know, it's normally full this time of year. The only reason it isn't now is because of a late cancellation. Not that I mind. They'd reserved it for the length of the tournament, which required a large deposit on the room. Nonrefundable, of course."

"Perhaps we should look elsewhere for a place to stay. Thank you for your time and hospitality, Jessop." Henry offered his good left hand to shake in parting.

Jessop ignored him. "Your party is perfectly welcome to look for lodging at the other inns in this town. Although, I must warn you, you are unlikely to find anything. Even the Cow's Colon is filled to capacity, if you'll excuse me saying so. The tournament, you understand. I highly doubt the grand suite will remain vacant for long. But at any rate . . . it seems your party can't afford it."

"You mentioned that people would be interested to hear our tale about our journey through the Iron Pass," James said.

"I did," Jessop agreed.

"We happen to have a storyteller with us." James nodded at Ruther. "An excellent one. If he were to entertain your guests at night with our tale, would you consider that as payment for the room until we are ready to leave?"

Jessop scratched his nose as he considered this offer. "Will he perform every night during your stay?"

"I've never worked for four crowns a day," Ruther protested. "I'll do it for free for two nights, but then you will have to pay me."

"Let's see how you perform first. If the crowds come, which I expect they will, and if you are as talented as you say, we can discuss payment then. Is that agreeable?"

As it was more than fair, no one objected.

"Very well," Jessop said once they'd all shaken hands. "Now let me find the maid in charge of that suite." He turned around, looking for someone. "Where is she?" He stomped over to the stairs and shouted, "Thirsty! Thirsty!" He frowned. "I swear she's never around when I need her. If it weren't for the fact that I'm a generous man, I'd throw her out into the street."

Light steps pattered down the wooden steps and a girl came into view. She couldn't have been more than a day over twenty-one despite the fact that her braided hair was as white as a cloud on a bright day. It was a stark contract to her dark skin. Her brown and blue dress was worn and patched, but still clean and neat.

"My apologies, Mr. Jessop," she said. "I was preparing the grand suite as you asked."

"About time," Jessop grumbled. "These guests have just rented the room."

The maid turned her attention to the new guests and smiled prettily. "Welcome to the Sheep's Entrails, Borderville's finest inn. I am Thirsty the maid, and will personally ensure that your needs and wants are met during your stay." Her voice was delicate and refined. Her smile was warm and genuine.

As they were heading up the steps, Jessop pulled Henry aside. "I'll stop by tomorrow morning to discuss what time your storyteller friend will perform. He had better impress me."

Henry tried to smile, but wasn't certain how successful he was. "He will."

By the time he made it upstairs to the room, James had already tucked Maggie into her bed. Ruther lounged on one of the sitting chairs, his feet on a bag that needed unpacking.

Thirsty met Henry at the door. "Dinner tonight will be duck and vegetables. Since I'll be managing your rooms, I'll also be cooking for you until you get tired of seeing me."

"If you cook well, that will never happen," Ruther called, rubbing his stomach.

Thirsty laughed.

"Ruther is my name. That's James, Brandol, and Maggie." He pointed to each in turn. "I'm a storyteller by trade, and I will be dazzling audiences tomorrow night and beyond about our adventures. Will you be watching?"

"I will try." Thirsty's gaze flickered to James. "What is wrong with Maggie? Is she well?"

"The Iron Pass didn't agree with her," Ruther answered. No one had told him yet that he had almost died an hour ago.

Thirsty nodded and turned her attention to her duties. As she prepared their meal, she whistled and hummed tunes that Henry had never heard before.

"Where are you from?" Henry asked her. "If you don't mind me asking."

Thirsty smiled. "My family is from Old Avalon. My brothers and parents are freedom fighters there—rebels against the Baron of Old Avalon and the slavery that still exists."

"And you are the only one in Pappalon?" Henry asked.

"I haven't seen my family since I was a young girl. My parents could only afford to sneak one of their children into Pappalon. That was me. I would have been a slave had I stayed there."

"But slavery has been banned for many years," Henry protested.

"Two hundred," Ruther added. "Give or take a few, since the Exodus."

"Perhaps that is true in Blithmore, but not everywhere. I heard the stories from my parents. When the slaves of Blithmore were freed, they left by boat, heading for the lands of their ancestors in the south across the Great Southern Sea. But many of the boats were captured by Avalonian ships and those taken were re-enslaved. When Avalon split into three countries, Pappalon became a refuge to my people."

"What a tragic story," Ruther said.

Thirsty tasted a pinch of the supper she was preparing. "The tragedies in our lives define us more than anything, I believe."

A terrible feeling twisted Henry's guts. Was this true? The voices in the forest had whispered to him that Isabelle's fate was his fault—that it was punishment for the carriage. If that was true, then he had to act. He had to rectify his mistake and undo the impending tragedy. And he had to do it tonight.

NINE

The Coffer and the Corpse

General Attikus,

With your capture of Isabelle Oslan and the carpenter, you continue to prove yourself exemplary in your service to the Throne of Neverak.

Our latest intelligence reports state that the Blithmorian Council of Nobles will convene on the tenth day of the next month. My spies report that the council will insist upon my Elite Guard's immediate withdrawal, and that King Germaine is close to bending to the nobles' desires. You are to attend this meeting and persuade him to reject these plans. Assure him that we are making progress in apprehending the criminals, and that our presence is still required. It is imperative that the Elite Guard remains in Blithmore.

To aid you in your persuasion, a coffer of coins and a condemned criminal has been sent with the letter. His description closely matches that of the hunted journeyman, Brandol. Following the meeting, you will report directly to me at the palace.

> *For the glory of Neverak,*
> *Emperor Ivan Richter Krallick III*

• • •

After Attikus, general of the armies of Neverak, finished reading the letter, he burned it. The light of the flames in his fireplace cast dark shadows in the deep creases of his face. He felt terribly old. "Ivan," he said aloud, "will nothing appease your ambition?"

Attikus returned to the meeting room where his lieutenants waited. He had three of them now: Lieutenant Kressin, his longest serving subordinate, and two new ones: Drekkler and Planok. He had known Drekkler and Planok for years and found them to be highly dependable, though he missed Wellick, who had perished in the battle at the Iron Pass.

"Sir, according to reports from our troops at the northern border," Lieutenant Kressin said without looking up from the sheets of parchment he held, "the two prisoners were escorted in secret across the Blithmore border and into Neverak without incident. They will arrive in Krallickton any day."

General Attikus rubbed his chin. He had thought often about his brief meeting with Isabelle Oslan. It had been one of the worst experiences in a long life of terrible things. He rarely felt shame for his actions, but he had that day. Reports had said Isabelle was starving herself, so he'd ridden to the caravan. By convincing Isabelle to eat and retain hope of escape, he had prevented her from death by starvation, but to what end? A life of unhappiness. She had no hope of escaping the palace on her own.

"What news do you hear from the field reports?" Attikus asked his lieutenants.

Planok spoke first. "Sir, rumors are circulating among all the battalions that the Blithmore Bandits were captured and sent north. Men are wondering why we still maintain a presence in these lands."

"We need to squash these gossipers before their words take root," Drekkler said, pounding his fist on the table.

Attikus suppressed an urge to sigh at Drekkler's dramatics. "We don't lie to our men," he reminded Drekkler. "The Elite Guard is not made up of mindless soldiers. Say nothing to them. Rumors are like fire. Starve them of fuel and they die quickly. Has there been any wind of mutiny or desertion?" the general asked.

"I've heard not a word of such heinous talk, sir," Drekkler said, clearly uncomfortable.

"Very well," Attikus said. "There may be rumors that we've accomplished our mission, but the Elite Guard who captured the prisoners have been reassigned to stations in Neverak so no one in Blithmore besides the four of us at this table know the truth. If it stays that way, the rumors will die."

"If I may, General," Kressin said. "I worry that the men no longer feel a sense of purpose."

"Thus the rise in incidents," Planok added. "Brawling, drunkenness, disobedience . . . all symptoms of the same sickness."

"If you ask me, sir," Kressin said, "we have a bigger problem. The people of Blithmore are tired of our soldiers being here. We've witnessed signs of aggression all along, but if the rumors spread beyond our soldiers, we could face extreme consequences."

Attikus sighed. "I have written to the Emperor asking for the ruse to be dropped and for us to return home, but he insists we maintain a presence."

Drekkler offered an idea. "Sir, what if the Emperor sent us an official letter stating that *some* of the Blithmore Bandits have been caught, but the others are still at large in Blithmore? That should put the rumors to rest for good, and it could help refocus their sense of purpose."

"Once again, you suggest I lie to my men," Attikus stated. His eyes remained fixed on the lieutenant until Drekkler realized his error. "And by lying to them, we create enmity." The general tapped his finger on the table to drive home his point. "One thing you never want in an army is a sense of *us* and *them*." He used his left and right hand to simulate the divide he was speaking about. "Animosity between commanding officers and those they command creates more problems than we could ever solve. It undermines authority. Most men aren't willing to die for the Emperor because they don't know him. They'll never know him. But they know us—we must be the men they are willing to die for."

"My apologies, General," Drekkler mumbled.

Attikus nodded. "Remind these men of their duty. Remind them they fight for the glory of Neverak. Remind them they are men of purpose. Lead them. Inspire them. When I have more orders from the Emperor, I'll send you word. Dismissed."

"Sir," Kressin said with a delicate tone, "permission to speak?"

Attikus nodded.

"The Emperor has captured the woman and the carpenter. The rest are likely dead in the Iron Forest. Why doesn't he send us back to Neverak? What good can we do here? Does he have bolder plans—"

"That will be all, Kressin. When I know more, so shall you. Dismissed."

The lieutenants stood and saluted the general. Attikus saluted them back. After they left, he stared at the maps and the figures upon them. His attention fell on a large map of Pappalon. He traced his finger along the Iron Pass, muttering to himself about how many miles per day a party of four could travel. He placed a tiny pin topped with a red ribbon in the town marked Borderville. If the bandits made it through the pass—and that was an enormous if, assuming the stories about the pass were true—Borderville would be their first stop.

They would be there only for a short time. Rest. Heal. But where would they go after that?

His eyes returned to Blithmore, Richterton, the Drewberry River. The Emperor intended to invade Blithmore. Attikus had suspected it almost from the beginning. He knew exactly what questions the Emperor would ask him when he returned to Neverak. He must be prepared to answer them.

The general began a letter to King Germaine, knowing that if he used the right words, the king would invite Attikus to the council and believe it was his own idea. The king was a wise man with years of experience under his crown, but his greatest weakness was how badly he wanted peace in his realm. Emperor Krallick had used that to his advantage after he had been attacked during the Feast of Kings.

Although Attikus did not possess the gift of foresight, he knew a great storm was coming that would shake all of Atolas. What scared the general—and few things scared him—was the size of his role in events yet to come. His loyalty to Neverak had never failed, never been questioned. Yet recent events and actions taken by the Emperor caused him to question the morality of his fealty.

Days later, Attikus arrived in Richterton to meet with the nobles and royalty of Blithmore. When he walked into the meeting room, the nobles glowered at him. Ignoring them, he took his seat at the long table which could comfortably seat sixty. When the king entered the room, everyone stood, Attikus included. Following the king came plates and plates of food for the feast. Each guest was served a plate of a small, roasted piglet.

Attikus fought to keep his anger in check.

He had grown up in a hovel in Kareven, the son of a foolish pig farmer and a drunken mother, and though he had worked his way to a position of honor, he still held a deep hatred for the pigs of his childhood. Even now, he would not eat pork.

King Germaine knew Attikus's history. Had he selected pork specifically to express his displeasure of Attikus and the Emperor?

Fifty nobles from all across Blithmore sat around the table. The king sat at the far end, across from Attikus. The room was finely decorated and well-staffed by the king's most trusted servants. A massive map of Blithmore hung on one wall and a flag bearing the country's colors of green and white adorned another. No one could mistake the feeling of formality in the room.

In all his years in the Elite Guard enduring backbiting, political maneuvering, and one-upmanship, Attikus had never faced a group of men with such open disdain for him as these nobles. King Germaine introduced them one by one, but Attikus only bothered to remember the important names. While he could remember every word he read, the same gift did not apply to what he heard.

The king dictated the course of the meeting, running through the regular business before turning the council's attention to the primary matter at hand: Neverak troops in Blithmore.

"Attikus," the king began, "I want you to know how grateful I am that you accepted my offer to come today. I've often said that leaders don't communicate enough. If people would communicate, so many problems would be easily solved. First, I'd like to let my nobles speak their thoughts. Then you may address their concerns and help us understand the mind of the Emperor. After we've heard from everyone, I believe I can make a decision to satisfy, perhaps not everyone, but the needs of our countries. Let's begin with Templeton."

Templeton was a man of immense girth who carried great weight both physically and politically. Attikus instinctively judged Templeton as a man who fed off the fat of the land and who disliked the idea of anything happening that he couldn't either influence or control.

"Thank you, Your Majesty," Templeton began. "It's good to finally meet the famous General Attikus. Our king speaks highly of you." Templeton's smile was neither welcoming nor pleasant. "It's quite possible that you're more trusted here than many of our own nobles." The laughter from around the table sounded uncomfortable.

The king turned to Attikus and offered his own supportive smile, then muttered, "Come now, Templeton, Attikus and I are old friends. You know what good relations we—"

"You're right, Your Majesty," Templeton acknowledged. "I know what good relations we *used* to enjoy with Neverak." Attikus's sense of etiquette bristled at Templeton's audacity to interrupt the king. "I am as grateful as anyone for the decades of peace our two nations have enjoyed. With it has come prosperity, and it's no secret that I have prospered." Templeton grabbed his belly and gave it a gentle shake. Many of the nobles roared.

"But I haven't had a good night's rest since your most unorthodox agreement with the young Emperor. Many of us considered it a folly, allowing his Elite Guard inside our lands to hunt for the Blithmore Bandits, while we stationed hundreds of our own soldiers in the capitol of Neverak to scout the area and serve as a check or a balance to the Emperor. It made no sense to me then, and it makes no sense to me now.

"I—along with the majority of my fellow nobles—have protested the welcoming of Neverak troops into our border. I have pleaded for their removal, I have pointed out the dangers in their presence, and I have employed logic in explaining that the accused carpenter had no motive to attack the Emperor of Neverak other than what rumors have suggested: that the Emperor tried to purchase Lord Oslan's daughter and make her his slave.

"Whether or not I was correct no longer matters. New evidence has come to light recently that the council must present to the king. I have the statements of two witnesses who claim to have seen the Emperor's troops escorting a female prisoner to the north, and a third witness who says she heard the cries of a woman coming from a carriage driven by the Elite Guards."

The eyes of the noblemen turned toward Attikus, perhaps to see if he would reveal the truth of the matter with a mere expression. Attikus gave them nothing.

Templeton continued to speak. "This evidence leads me to suspect that the Emperor has *not* honored his agreement to turn over any captured prisoners to our inquisitors. If my suspicions are correct, it means that his word is unreliable. I have personally transcribed statements from each witness"—Templeton held up a thin stack of parchment—"and they are all willing to come before the throne should they be summoned. So, my good king, I recognize the great work you have accomplished in your lifetime. Your wonderful friendship with the former Emperor of Neverak contributed to your success. The amicability between the sovereignties of Neverak and Blithmore during those three decades is a story that will be passed down for generations.

"However, I must voice what I have suspected for some time now: Emperor Ivan Krallick is not the same man his father was, and the same trust cannot be extended to him." Templeton's voice rose to punctuate each point he made. His oratory skills impressed even Attikus. "I have no doubt the former emperor would never have abused such power, but neither would he have requested it. We have no guarantee that the same rule applies to the son, only suspicions of the opposite! I strongly urge you, my king, to recall home our soldiers who are stationed around the palace in Neverak, and *get these Elite Guards out of our lands!*"

As Templeton sat down, avoiding Attikus's gaze, many nobles voiced their agreement by knocking on the table, some loudly, others not.

Attikus wondered which of his handpicked guards had made the foolish error of letting Isabelle be seen, and what he could say to dispel these men's suspicions.

Other noblemen rose and said similar things, though none of their speeches were quite as rousing or eloquent as Templeton's. The final nobleman chose to speak about the offense the Emperor had suffered in Richterton and the burden Blithmore carried until justice had been served. He expressed little sympathy for either Henry Vestin or Isabelle Oslan, and Attikus wondered if the man was a spy for the Emperor. After all, someone in the room had to have known the date of the meeting and passed the information to the Emperor. As a whole, the meeting proved rather anticlimactic.

When the noblemen had finished, the king turned to Attikus with great solemnity. "Serious accusations have been raised, Attikus. We recognize your loyalty is not to us, but to your Emperor. That is respected, and you are free to tell him what you have heard. Now, if you please, I turn to you, hoping you will answer these statements and report on the activities of your armies." The tone in King Germaine's voice made it clear that he planned to follow Templeton's counsel and order Attikus's men out of Blithmore.

Attikus thanked the king and, standing, took command of the room. "I express my gratitude to you all for bringing your concerns to my attention. As King Germaine said, without communication little can be accomplished, and we are all men who exist to get things done, not invent things to do. Let me address each of your items one at a time. I trust you will alert me if I omit anything.

"The Elite Guards of the Emperor have been in your lands for over half a year, and I assure you no one is more anxious for them to leave as they are." This statement brought a few chuckles from the noblemen, a good sign for Attikus. He paused, then dove fully into the mistruths he had prepared.

"One of my officers thought it would be a welcome distraction to bring . . . *working women* . . . down from Neverak. I do not stand for immorality among my men. It is an intolerable scourge. I immediately arranged for the women to be sent back, but unfortunately, one of the women and one of my soldiers had already grown quite enamored with each other. The girl refused to leave to the point where we had to remove her by force. All this happened about seven or eight weeks ago. Since, at that point, our armies had failed to apprehend any of the criminals, this altercation must be what your witnesses saw and heard. I'm told the girl was very vocal.

"Recently, however, things have changed. I am now able to report that we have the body of the journeyman in our possession." Several expressions of doubt changed to shock and disbelief. "The Emperor promised King Germaine full disclosure of all captures, and we assumed that, although this was not a capture, we are under the same obligations. The journeyman's death occurred last week in a small fishing town on the seaside—Gilly. I wrote as soon as I heard, but I am still trying to sort out the details. My lieutenants are at your full disposal to question."

Templeton stood and, without waiting for permission to speak, said, "I'd like to see the corpse. Right now."

Templeton's demand gave several other nobles their voices back, and soon eight other nobles wanted to see the body. The king ordered a recess from the meeting, and Attikus waited while the eight nobles left to perform the impromptu inspection. All but Templeton came back with handkerchiefs held over their faces.

"Ghastly!" one of them exclaimed.

"I've never seen such a thing," muttered another.

"What happened to him?" Templeton asked. His stare met Attikus's gaze with such force that Attikus wondered if he had misjudged the man's inner strength. "The bandits weren't supposed to be killed."

"It was self-defense," Attikus responded. While he considered it wrong to lie to his own men, the crime of deceiving the king and his nobles fell on the shoulders of the Emperor, who had commanded him to do it. "We were unable to interrogate the journeyman, so we don't know the entire story, but we believe he was separated from the group in Bookerton, though whether voluntarily or not, we don't know. Also, I have a letter written by his hand stating that he was willing to turn in his friends."

Attikus removed the letter he'd received from Brandol the journeyman and passed it around the table. "At some point he had a change of heart, but it was too late. He traveled to Gilly alone and unarmed. The man who owned the home where we found the journeyman agreed to give him shelter in exchange for work. On a routine stop through Gilly, our soldiers received information that a man matching Brandol's description had been spotted.

"Upon his discovery, the journeyman attacked my soldiers with a harpoon. My men reacted appropriately; thus, the injuries to the body. You should know that one of my men almost died, and two more had serious injuries. However, this body serves as proof that we are operating under the conditions we agreed to, and that our presence in Blithmore is helping to solve the problem."

The truth, in fact, was that the body had come from a thief whose taller-than-average height and flaxen hair color had matched the description of the journeyman who had aided Henry Vestin in the Glimmering Fountain. The Emperor had ordered the prisoner's execution in order to provide a body for Attikus to present to the council.

"None of this matters," Templeton said dismissively. "The King's Guard is capable of taking over the search. It should have been them all along, not foreign armies!"

Cheers rang again from men around the long table.

"They certainly are capable," Attikus said in calm voice, "but are they motivated?"

"You just said your own men want to go home," Templeton countered.

"Indeed. The farther from home a man is, the harder he'll work to finish the job."

Templeton refused to be swayed by Attikus's words. "Imagine, General, if it were the King's Guard who had access to Neverak lands. How would you react? Would you not think your Emperor had gone mad?"

"Imagine, good sir, if your king's neck had been nearly sliced open in Neverak. Would you not demand justice?"

Templeton stood, baring his teeth and seething in rage. "If the Emperor was trying to take one of our country's daughters as a slave like the rumors say, then he deserved more than a nicked neck!"

"Have you never been the subject of gossip?" Attikus asked. "Has the ugliness of slander never crossed your family's door?"

Several noblemen nodded thoughtfully. Attikus knew it was time to close the trap around Templeton, to completely undermine him.

"The Emperor is a good and generous man. His greatest crime, I fear, is being his father's son. His father, Emperor Peter Ivan Krallick, was a man so kind and beloved that no one could live up to the expectations he had set."

Templeton chortled. "When has the boy Emperor demonstrated anything but a care for himself and his own needs?"

Attikus clapped his hands and two of his soldiers entered the room bearing the enormous coffer that had been sent with the body. The nobles turned to see what might be inside the large ornate chest.

"The Emperor asked me to present this." Attikus walked over to the coffer and asked the soldiers to set it down right in front of Templeton. He opened it, filled to the brim with gold. "This gift symbolizes the gratitude and well-wishes of Emperor Krallick—twenty thousand crowns to be used specifically for the education of the noblemen's children."

The atmosphere in the room changed immediately. Templeton's face fell as he realized he had lost the fight.

"Emperor Krallick appreciates the difficulty of the situation for both parties, but believes we are on the verge of realizing our goals. With the Iron Pass sealed off, the shipyards under close observation, and the northern borders under careful watch, I am confident the remaining Blithmore Bandits will soon be caught. That is all I have to say."

King Germaine thanked Attikus and everyone for offering their thoughts, reminding them that the purpose of the council was to focus on how to best serve all the people of Blithmore. "After considering all your points," he said, "I've decided the best course of action is to set a date, three months from now, at which time I will order a withdrawal of the Neverak troops—half immediately, the other half over the next three months."

Templeton and a few others started to speak against this decision, but most of the nobles knocked on the table as a sign of support until King Germaine raised a hand for silence.

"When the Neverak troops are completely withdrawn," the king continued, "if the criminals have not been apprehended, I will order my troops to continue searching until two years from the date of the Emperor's attack. If by then they are still at large, I will return these twenty thousand crowns to Neverak during the Feast of Kings, along with my most sincere apologies for our failure. I hope the Emperor will be satisfied with these terms."

Attikus respectfully bowed. "As do I."

The nobles were not ecstatic with the terms, but it was, at least, a small victory. Attikus could appreciate that. But it was a greater victory for the Emperor. Three more months with all his troops within the borders, three more after that to slowly withdraw them. Attikus cringed to think what Ivan could do in those six months.

TEN

The Carriage and the Smuggler

A steady breeze blew through the streets of Borderville as Ruther followed Henry at a safe distance. The sun had just set, but Dronduin, the smallest of the three moons, was low and bright, outshining the lights of Hallicaf and Edowan despite its size. Ghost's white coat had a blue glint to it in the dusk. If Henry looked back from the carriage driver's seat, there was a good chance he'd spot Ruther, although Ruther wasn't worried. He wanted to make certain Henry wasn't doing something unwise. While his friend was not prone to making foolish decisions, Isabelle tended to do strange things to him. The image of Henry dancing on the back of a giant dragonox came to mind.

The carriage struggled along the dirt road north out of Borderville, bumping and swaying on its broken wheel. Ruther figured that was probably for the best since Henry would be hard-pressed to control the horses with only one working arm. He considered hurrying forward and offering Henry a hand, but he was curious about what Henry might do when he thought no one was watching.

The last day had been one of the longest of Ruther's life, and that was saying something considering some of the nights he'd spent in taverns across Blithmore, drinking, gambling, and fleeing from enraged, cheated dice throwers. During the past day he'd been attacked by an unseen monster in a forest, wounded in a storm of flying tree branches, rendered unconscious from blood loss, and stitched up by a physician. His wound was healing unbelievably well, though, and he had more energy than someone who'd been through all that should have had.

The carriage stopped under a low tree branch. In the moonlight, Ruther saw the shadow of Henry stand and climb down from the seat. "What are you doing, friend?" Ruther asked under his breath.

Henry opened the carriage door, removed something, and set it on the ground before withdrawing a box. Ruther tried to think what was inside the carriage that Henry could want while sitting under a large tree. Then he remembered the long rope buried beneath all the packs. They had used it on multiple occasions to pull the carriage out of the mud during the rainy autumn days in Blithmore. What would Henry want with the rope at this hour?

A horrible thought struck Ruther, and he spurred Ghost to a gallop. "Henry!" he shouted. "Henry, wait! Don't hang yourself!"

Henry turned, confused, and set another pack on the ground several feet from the carriage and reached back in, now holding the rope. "I didn't realize I was being followed."

Ruther hopped down from the horse. "What are you doing?"

"What are *you* doing, Ruther?"

"Well . . . what are *you* doing, *Henry*?"

Henry hadn't smiled much since the battle, but he did now. Seeing that made Ruther feel a little better. "I'm cleaning out the carriage."

"All right," Ruther said slowly, "but don't you think this can wait until morning?"

"I'm going to burn it."

Ruther blew out a long breath. "I wish you had said something before you left. I had some sausages I wanted to roast—"

"I'm not in the mood for your japes. Either help me get the stuff out of the carriage or go back to the inn."

Ruther raised his hands. "Relax. You're going to worry yourself into an early grave. Your tombstone will read, 'Here lies Henry, one-armed worrier extraordinaire.'" He grabbed two packs of clothes from the carriage and threw them aside. "Now if you don't mind me asking, why the sudden need to make your lovely work into a pyre? The inn was too cold?"

Henry shook his head, his lips pursed. "It's my fault," he moaned. Something hit the grass with a soft thump. Henry quickly tossed the last bag on top of it, but not before Ruther saw it. It was the brown leather pouch he had seen on Henry after the battle. Maggie had warned Ruther not to open it, but had never said why. "Isabelle's capture rests squarely on my shoulders. It's my fault. This carriage . . . My fault." Henry broke into sobs, covering his eyes with his left hand so Ruther wouldn't see his tears.

"It's not your fault." Ruther felt like he was trying to console a hysterical child. "Please listen to me." He placed his hand on Henry's shoulder. "You did your best against impossible odds. Now we need to adjust our strategy—come up with a new plan."

Henry grabbed his head with his good hand. "I can't think straight. I'm so angry at everyone, and I don't know why! Everything inside me is torn. I can't live like this."

"You need to pull it together for her."

Henry shook his head. "You don't understand. This is fate. This is my punishment."

"You have done nothing to deserve punishment, friend."

Henry took a deep breath and let it out in a long, hollow sigh. "You know what I want? Some rocks to skip."

"And some water to skip them on." Ruther smiled.

"Do you see any ponds or lakes nearby?"

Ruther laughed, and it felt good all the way down to his toes. When he finally stopped, he looked at his weary, worn friend. "Why are we burning the carriage? I thought it was your prized creation."

"It was." Henry cradled his right arm with his left and rubbed his bicep. "Did you know I made a twin? This was the second I made."

"I didn't know."

Henry wore an odd smile, one that Ruther had never seen before. "This carriage, this piece of wood, has brought all this ruin upon me. I should have burned it long ago. It was after my parents had passed away. You were traveling the region with that master storyteller, and I was searching for a spark of inspiration to create my masterpiece— the piece of art I needed to present to the guild when I applied for the title of master. I was only a journeyman, so work was scarce. My only project was a frame for a looking glass. I was nearly done when a large man in expensive clothes knocked on the shop door. I let him in, thinking he was a nobleman. He grabbed my hand, and said, 'You're Henry Vestin!'

"I replied that I was. He introduced himself as Theodore Trolley, and I quickly realized that he was not a noble. He acted too casually and spoke of himself too plainly. When I asked about his profession, he said he was a man of enterprise, and then he began to tell me what he wanted me to make for him.

"I had not seen a man talk about woodwork with such passion since my father's death. He knew every last detail he wanted, and he conveyed to me exactly what he envisioned: a large, sturdy carriage for the woman he was to marry in six months. And he had chosen *me* to create it! There was such an . . . an aura about him, an excitement that I almost offered to build it for free, and when he named the price he would pay, I nearly fell down.

"After we were agreed, we set an appointment to meet again, look at my drawings, and choose a type of wood. I could barely contain my elation, Ruther. My soul was on fire. This was my masterpiece! I saw the carriage as clearly as I saw Isabelle's smile. My father had told me there would be moments when the work almost made itself. It was marvelous.

"Three days later, Theodore returned. My enthusiasm hadn't ebbed, and neither had his. We sat down, I showed him my plans, and he went on and on about how much he loved them. All of his suggestions were minor, things I might have done myself. In less than an hour's time, we had the entire exterior drawn exactly as it is today. It was when we began discussing the interior that I noticed something unusual—something worrisome.

"He wanted two secret compartments installed, one under the forward seat and one under the rearward seat, large enough to stow odds and ends. That was how Theodore described it. I told him I had no experience making such a thing, and that I couldn't guarantee its quality. Instead of being dissuaded, he assured me he had the utmost confidence in my skills, and then added another fifty crowns for my trouble.

"That alarmed me. Perhaps I should have seen it earlier, but I didn't. Suddenly, Theodore seemed too excited, too agreeable. Most customers haggle endlessly over prices. They don't offer to pay me more. But the fire this man had ignited inside me forced me to look past my suspicions and do the work. I agreed to add the compartments for the additional cost, and we set another appointment for him to approve the final designs.

"Ten minutes after Theodore left, Master Franklin knocked at my door."

"Good old Master Franklin," Ruther said with a sour laugh. Most of his memories of the old silversmith who lived next door to the Vestins were unpleasant ones. Master Franklin had made it his business to report every rumor circulating around town about Ruther's activities to Henry's father.

"Yes," Henry said, "your old friend. I was so eager to continue my work, I almost ignored him. However, when I let him in, he told me he was worried about me. I asked him why.

"'That man you've invited into your shop. Do you know who he is?'

"'He told me his name is Theodore Trolley,' I said, 'and I've found him to be a most agreeable customer.'

"Master Franklin fixed me with a look. You know the one I mean. I'd seen it many times when he was about to impart to me his wisdom. 'Often times,' he began, 'our most agreeable customers are those whom we should avoid. If you want to be a respected master, you must develop a knack for spotting them. The sooner you make a reputation for yourself as a man who won't tolerate nonsense, the sooner the fools will leave you at peace.'

"Despite the strange feeling I'd had about Theodore, I wanted to give him the benefit of the doubt. I think Master Franklin saw this in my face because he pressed harder. 'He's got all the markings of a smuggler, boy. What's his story? Buying a large carriage for his mother? His wife?'

"I felt as if he'd struck my stomach with a mallet.

"'They always spot the up-and-coming craftsmen, boy,' Master Franklin continued. 'They like to see if they can persuade you while you're young, then they have you for life. You don't need to be ashamed for having been fooled.'

"I told Master Franklin I wasn't ashamed, but I needed to confront Mr. Trolley with this information before acting. After all, what if Theodore was, in fact, what he said he was? A man buying a gift for his beloved? I owed him the decency to at least find out before rejecting his business.

"'He will be very convincing, mark me on that!' Franklin warned. 'You'd be better off taking my word on this.' But he could see I was set on my decision. 'You are your father's son to a fault, Henry. Come see me after you speak to him. I want to make certain your head is right.'

"I thanked him for his advice and showed him out, then I spent the night wondering what I was to do, torn between my love of the work, my need for the money, and my fear of damaging my budding reputation as a craftsman. In the early hours of the morning I finally decided to continue my work until I was able to speak to Theodore and clear up the matter.

"Those days passed in a blur. I was consumed by the drive to complete the project to perfection. It was amazing. I made few mistakes, even though I was more critical of myself than ever before. After hours of laboring, I would step back only to be surprised at the quality of my work.

"Theodore arrived the same day I finished the exterior of the carriage. He was dressed as splendidly as the first day we'd met, and behaved just as genially. From the moment he entered the shop, he couldn't stop complimenting me. Then we began discussing the interior design. Can you guess what the first question was he asked?"

Ruther shrugged.

"He said, 'Will there be any problem installing the compartments I requested?'

"Something in the way Theodore said those words gave me the courage to confront him. I couldn't find any appropriate way to ask him, so simply asked, 'Are you a smuggler, Theodore?'

"Without a trace of guilt in his face, he said, 'Yes, I am a smuggler. And if your next question is whether or not the carriage is truly for my wife, that answer is no.'

"I was shocked. The jolly man I'd met three times was gone; in his place was one of the most humble, downtrodden men I'd ever seen. 'I know what you're thinking,' he continued. 'You want me to leave your shop and not tarnish your well-built reputation. And if you ask me to, I will leave at once. But first, please hear me out. A smuggler is not the filthy, craven criminal that many, including the nobles, would have you believe. We're not a band of thieves; we're closer to public servants.'

"Theodore spoke at length about how King Germaine placed such high tariffs on traded and foreign goods that many farmers, merchants, and craftsmen couldn't afford what they needed to survive. Smuggling helped reduce the price and relieve suffering. He spoke with such conviction I was moved with compassion.

"'I'm not asking for anything more than for you to make a beautiful carriage for me,' he said. 'But if you can't do it, I'll understand.'

"I had never faced such a difficult decision. In hindsight, it shouldn't have been so hard. I agreed to finish it for him, though to say that I did it for the starving countrymen of Blithmore would be a lie. I did it because Theodore had inspired me to create my greatest work."

Terrible sorrow came over Henry's face, so deep that Ruther could tell his friend was truly suffering. "I was selfish, Ruther. I cared less about Theodore's true motives and more about the fire in my soul pushing me to see the project to its completion. I knew that becoming a master would improve my prospects of marriage in Isabelle's parents' eyes. It was all there waiting for me to seize. I only had to complete the carriage. So I did."

Ruther had met plenty of smugglers in his travels and knew what kind of men they were. Some could talk a man into swapping a prize horse for a dead one, others would slit a man's throat for a half silver crown. But even in a gang of thieves there could be that rare gemstone, a man who actually possessed a good heart despite his occupation. Who was to say Theodore Trolley wasn't one of those exceptions?

"When I didn't go to Master Franklin's house," Henry continued, "he came to my shop. He stopped by five or six times, but I never answered his knocks. I was too captivated by my work, and I didn't want to face him. Didn't want to tell him what I had decided. Finally the old man threw all sense of propriety to the wind and barged in.

"'Henry, you'd better have a good reason for ignoring me for four days!' he bellowed. I think he would have kept on yelling if he hadn't seen the carriage behind me. His eyes narrowed, his lips tightened, and for a full two minutes, he shuffled around the carriage and inspected my work. Multiple times, he reached out his hand and, with a reverence I'd never seen in him before, caressed the wood.

"'It's marvelous,' he whispered. 'Your father would be proud.'

"The emotions I felt when Master Franklin said that were many: triumph, pride, but also shame. He saw the shame and nodded as he began to understand.

"'You made this for that smuggler, didn't you?'

"I had no words to explain my actions. He wouldn't have understood my sympathy for the smuggler, and besides, I think he would have seen through me—seen my true motivations. 'You sell your treasures for copper, boy,' he said quietly. Then he left.

"A few days later, Theodore claimed his new carriage, and I received my handsome payment. The guilt nagged at me for a while, but it eventually went away. Months later, Isabelle and I were in the market shopping. You remember how the three of us used to make fun of the posters of the Enemies of the King?"

"I do," Ruther said, smiling.

"That morning, Isabelle and I stopped to see if any new posters had been nailed to the wall. Isabelle pointed out one of a man named *Skuller.* His resemblance to Theodore Trolley was unmistakable. The King's Guard suspected him of smuggling into Neverak. Do you know what he was smuggling?"

Ruther shook his head.

Henry wiped his eyes with his left hand and cleared his throat. "Girls. He kidnapped girls and took them to become slaves to wealthy lords in foreign lands. Smuggled in the carriage that I built him!" At this, Henry lost control.

"Are you all right, friend?" Ruther asked, numbed by Henry's confession.

Henry didn't answer right away. "And now my arm . . ." He lifted his right arm with his left hand where it dangled like a heavy rope. "It won't move. I can't even wiggle a finger.

"You see, Ruther? This is my punishment. I failed to listen to Master Franklin, and I aided smugglers to kidnap girls by making a secret compartment with my own two hands. In return, everything in my life has become cursed. The woman I love has been carried away for the same purpose as those girls I unknowingly hurt. And to be certain that I can never repeat the act—that I'll never carve again—I've lost the use of my arm."

"I don't think—" Ruther began, but Henry wasn't done.

"When I realized what had happened, I tried to correct my error. For a week I hardly slept, hardly ate, until I built a second carriage, identical in every way to the original. I showed it to the King's Guard, and told them I built it for Trolley, unaware of his crimes. I lied to cover my sins. I used that cursed carriage as my presentation to the Richterton Guild of Masters to be made a member of their society."

"I recall that part," Ruther said. "They accepted you unanimously."

Henry's gaze went to the stars, and even in the faint light, Ruther saw deep lines on his friend's face. Weariness laced Henry's voice. "*Almost* unanimously. There was one vote against me. I don't know who cast it, though I suspect it was Master Franklin. I've never spoken to him about it, but I have never forgotten his disappointment. And all this time, I've hidden my guilt from Isabelle. I couldn't bear to see her disappointment. Perhaps she would have changed her mind about our marriage. Now I'll never know. But I do know her life of slavery is because of my selfishness."

"Henry, you can't think—"

"'A man is like a block of wood,' my father always said. 'Everything we do stays with us. Carves us pleasantly or scars us hideously.'" He stood and went to one of the packs, removing flint and steel. "Are you going to help me?"

"That's a lot of stuff for us to carry, friend."

"We don't need it all. It slows us down. We will need to move faster if we have any hope of saving Isabelle and Brandol."

They sorted through the packs, keeping what was necessary, discarding what wasn't. Despite what Henry thought, Ruther believed his costumes and wigs were quite necessary, so he kept them.

When they were finished, Henry struck the flint and lit the kindling under the carriage. The orange flames illuminated Henry's stony face majestically. Together they watched the carriage as the fire caught hold. Ruther reluctantly mounted Ghost and rode away, back to the Sheep's Entrails. Fire or not, he had a performance to prepare for. Henry stood a good while longer, watching as the flames ate the carriage from the wheels to the roof. Then he too mounted his horse and turned his back to the fire, its fiery tongues reaching high into the night air, hot and consuming, burning like guilt.

ELEVEN

The Tongue-Tied Storyteller

The crowds had gathered at the Sheep's Entrails to hear Ruther's story. He could hear them from the upstairs suite where he and his friends were staying. Thirsty knocked on the door not fifteen minutes after Henry had finally returned, his clothes smelling faintly of smoke. Ruther had already changed into his good clothes, creating quite the contrast with Thirsty's dress, which was so drab it should have been cut up and used as rags.

"This shirt is as tight as ever," Ruther complained.

"Your gut is as large as ever," Maggie retorted.

"Are you ready?" Thirsty asked him. "Your audience awaits."

Ruther glanced once more in the looking glass, frowning at his stomach straining against the shirt's fabric. "I eat too much."

Thirsty laughed, tossing her pure white hair. "You're a handsome man. But something *is* missing."

"What?"

Thirsty produced a hat from behind her back. "No one will take you seriously if you don't wear a hat."

"No, I don't think so. No hat will adorn *this* beautiful head of hair. Real men do not wear hats."

Just then the men's bedroom door opened and Henry and James walked out, both wearing tall hats similar to the one Thirsty had offered Ruther. Ruther shook his head sadly and clucked his tongue.

"You're both traitors to your country . . . and look ridiculous."

"They're handsome," Maggie said. She had woken late that morning, feeling refreshed but sore, wincing every time she took a step with her right leg. Ruther had felt oddly elated to see her up and about.

"Who has the room key?" Thirsty asked.

James held his hand out, a small silver key in his palm. "Here."

Thirsty went to take it, but James closed his fist. "You didn't say please."

Thirsty grinned and blushed. Maggie scowled.

"*Please*," Thirsty said.

When James opened his fist, the key was gone. Thirsty gasped and giggled. "How did you do that?"

Ruther raised his eyebrows. "Impressive sleight of hand, soldier man. I never knew you were capable of more than frowning and stabbing trees."

"We used to practice with twigs and leaves in camp when we were bored," James explained. "There were others better than me."

"I've been practicing sleight of hand since I was ten, and I'm not better than you."

James patted Ruther. "I hope you've been practicing storytelling since you were ten, because tonight is your big night."

"Please—I've been a master since I was ten. Borderville isn't going to know what hit them. I'll be known as the greatest thing around here since hats."

Jessop hadn't lied when he'd said Ruther was going to draw a large crowd. The public room was packed with people who wanted to hear about the Iron Pass. And the larger the crowd, the better Ruther performed. He fed off their interest, their energy, their laughter or fear, whatever emotion he wanted to draw from them. If there was indeed a Lord of All Worlds, he had made Ruther the Lord of Storytelling.

Ruther made his way to the center of the room and sat in a large chair provided for him. The crowd's chatter died down as their attention turned toward him. He couldn't help but smile. Jessop came through the crowd and stood beside Ruther. His head wasn't much higher than Ruther's even though Ruther was seated.

"I have a special surprise," Jessop told the crowd. "As a show of appreciation for your patronage, entertainment will be provided this evening. Tonight we have the privilege to host a renowned storyteller from Blithmore. He recently traveled here from his home country, and tonight will enrapture our minds with his tale of the mystery and horror of the Iron Pass. Please welcome . . . Robert!"

Ruther winced when he heard the name. He didn't even look like a Robert. As Jessop vacated the performance space, he clapped his hands together vigorously, but few joined him.

Ruther grinned politely and cleared his throat. Most of the crowd seemed to view him with either skepticism or great interest. Something about the idea of winning over the skeptics excited him. He cleared his throat again and opened his mouth to speak.

"Only a day has passed since—" Ruther stopped. He didn't like that opening at all. It needed to be more dramatic, more thrilling. He began again. "Many of you have heard the talk, the rumors, the tall tales of what occurs in the dark, haunted Iron Forest. Perhaps some of what you have heard is based in truth or perhaps it was all theories and fictions. But tonight I will tell you the truth, for I have crossed it. Despite great danger to myself and my companions, we finished our crossing only a day ago. Let me first tell you that the Iron Forest is as dark and perilous as they say. And something evil does indeed haunt its depths."

But what was it? Ruther wondered. What had caused his ears to bleed, his skin to quiver, and most of all, what invisible monster had lifted three men into the air as if they were made of straw?

He'd fallen silent pondering those questions. While a pregnant pause was an asset to a storyteller, unplanned silence was not. He cleared his throat again and tried to think of what to say. "The Iron

Pass is a place of blood and death. Every day we passed the bones of other travelers who had walked into the forest foolishly, unprepared for its horrors. In fact, one night—or it might have been day, it was too dark to tell, and the sun never shined its rays through the canopy of trees—we came across . . .”

Ruther remembered the carriage, the bodies inside and under it; they had died with their hands clamped to their heads to deafen themselves from the deep secrets the forest whispered in their minds. How . . . *what* had done that? What plausible, rational, natural explanation was there for such a thing? It had affected them all. Had made a man rip off his ears. What could do that? A second unplanned silence. Ruther was making mistakes not even a green apprentice would dare make. The crowd stirred unhappily.

“Did you cross the pass or not?” a man in a dirty hat asked from the second row of tables. “Because you don’t seem to have much of a *story* to tell.”

“Yes, I did,” Ruther answered in a tone that told the man it was rude to speak out of turn. “Now then—”

“Did you see anything . . . unusual? Anything in white like they say?”

Other gentlemen murmured their agreement with the filthy-hatted man’s questions. Ruther cleared his throat, placed his hands on his knees, and gave his full attention to those who sat closest to him. Yet no words came out. All he could remember was the terror, the unending depression that had accompanied him as his worst secrets, his blackest sins, had been repeated to him until blood poured from his ears. His tongue felt thick in his mouth, dry and stale. He didn’t want to speak.

“Tell us how you crossed the pass!” the same filthy-hatted man barked, banging his mug against the table as he spoke. “How you crossed the pass!” He repeated it like a chant. The men next to him joined in and their voices grew louder than Ruther could speak.

"Please," Ruther croaked, "just give me a moment to collect myself. My nerves are—" He wanted ale. And he wanted it badly. If he could just have some ale to calm himself, he could do it. But he had told himself never again after the inn at Reddings. "The Iron Pass was not a pleasant experience. No man could cross it and speak of it lightly."

"A pretender!" cackled a woman whose hat featured a stuffed raven. "That's what you are, sir. A peddler of fiction. You don't even have the decency to wear a hat in public!"

Many murmurs of agreement arose. Ruther put his hands up. "Hats aren't commonly worn in Blithmore. And I rather like my hair."

"It's indecent."

Ruther knew he had to tell a story. He had to make Jessop happy. He simply couldn't summon the courage to talk about the pass. Not yet, anyway. For the final time, he cleared his throat. "How about a funny tale? A long, long time ago—at least a week or two, that is—a man named Thurgerburder sat in the fields among his herds of sheep. It was an ugly, rainy day, and the sun shone down on him brightly. Thurgerburder was a quiet man who—"

"This is a trick. He won't tell anyone about his trip across the Iron Pass," the man with the dirty brown hat interrupted him a third time.

Ruther pressed on. "Who had more than a few quirks about him. For one—"

Something hurtled toward Ruther's head. Ruther didn't react in time, and a wet chicken bone hit him under the eye. The crowd roared with laughter. Ruther forced himself to smile good-naturedly. "Let's settle down please. Thank you."

The troublemaker stood up, his hand clenched around something else from his plate. "You said you wanted to make us all laugh!" He chucked a handful of mashed potatoes, and hit Ruther square in the chest. "Just sit there and that'll do fine."

"You want me to tell you about the pass?" Ruther shouted over the voices.

Shouts of acknowledgment followed, accompanied by the banging of mugs on tables.

"Well, I can't. It was horrible beyond imagining. Three weeks felt like three years. The forest is evil—a dark cursed garden of the Great Demon. That is all I can say. Now let me speak of happier things like Thurgerburder the Furious—"

"You mean you actually saw something in there?" a fat man with an enormous beard asked. "And you don't want to share it?"

More food flew from the tables. Ruther's protests were drowned by a chorus of boos and hisses. He stood at the same time Henry did. From the side of the room, a mug flew at his head, clanking off his skull and leaving a nasty welt behind. More laughter.

"That's enough!" Henry cried indignantly.

"This is no way to treat a guest to our city!" one audience member called. Ruther looked to see if it was Thirsty, but her long, snow-white hair was nowhere in sight. He thought that peculiar since she'd been excited about seeing his performance.

"I'm done here," Ruther said, picking gobs of food from his clothes. From behind, someone dumped ale over his head. More food pelted him as he pushed his way through the crowd. A few in the audience tried to stop the madness, but the majority either jeered Ruther or threw more food and drink. Just as he reached Henry, James, and Maggie at the back of the hall, a metal plate smacked the back of Maggie's head, cutting into the nape of her neck. Ruther cursed at the crowd, particularly the table of men who started the commotion.

"Are you all right?" Ruther asked Maggie when they reached the stairs. Henry inspected the wound.

"It's hard to say," she replied. "Everything still hurts from yesterday."

"You're bleeding," James said, pointing at the blood beginning to stain the back of her dress.

Maggie smiled bravely. "I'm fine."

Thirsty was already in the suite and looked up, surprised, when they entered. "You're already finished with the story?"

Ruther sat down with a sigh. "It didn't go well."

"What are you doing here?" James asked. "Why weren't you down there with us?"

"I was at first, but Mr. Jessop told me I had to come up here and tidy the room. Said we didn't want our favorite guests living in squalor. I wanted to be there, but he insisted. I'll go if you'd like."

She hadn't even reached the door when it burst open. An apoplectic Mr. Jessop stood in its frame, his eyes burning. "What . . . *was* that?" he hissed. "You call that a story? I call it slop! Excrement! *Farce!*"

Ruther, inspecting his clothes, found more food there and picked it off. "So do I. That was not quality work, Mr. Jessop. I apologize sincerely."

"You *apologize*! What good is that for all my customers who ordered a meal or drinks to fill themselves as they listened to your story? Many of whom now want their money back!"

"I will make amends," Ruther insisted. "I can tell other stories very well, but I simply cannot speak of what happened in the Iron Pass. Not yet. It's too—"

"I don't care. Your storytelling days are over. Either you pay me the money you owe for last night and tonight, or you leave at once!"

"We haven't got any money!" Henry cried.

"Then leave."

"Mr. Jessop," Thirsty said, "there isn't another place in town with a vacant room. You and I both know that."

James stepped forward. "We won't be treated like this," he said. "If we're not welcome, we'll leave. We can sleep in the carriage."

"Um . . ." Ruther groaned. "Actually, we don't have the carriage."

"It just needs the wheel repaired. It will work for tonight."

"We burned it," Henry admitted.

"You—" Maggie started to say. "Why?"

"It's personal," Henry said.

Jessop stamped his foot. "I don't care about your problems. I care about getting paid. I will be downstairs fixing the mess you made!" He pointed a finger at Ruther. "If I don't see *you* in an hour with either my money or your packed bags in hand, a burned carriage will be the least of your worries. And *you*, Thirsty, I gave you a job to do—"

"I apologi—" Thirsty glanced at James nervously.

"—and you ignored me. When you asked to be assigned over this room—"

Thirsty was utterly humiliated, her eyes on the floor. "Please, Mr. Jessop, not in front—"

"—I said only if it didn't interfere. You can expect to receive no wages for today. Now get downstairs and do your chores!"

"Yes, Mr. Jessop."

When Jessop and Thirsty left, Jessop slammed the door behind him.

"What a pleasant man," Ruther said.

James jammed a finger into Ruther's chest. "Why couldn't you just tell the story?"

Ruther wanted to hit him, but Henry stepped between them and said, "Really, James? Could you have talked about that place? Could any of us? We need to pack. Let's go."

"But—" Maggie said.

"We don't need to leave," Ruther stated.

"Onward," Henry said. "We have more important things to do. We leave tonight."

"But I—" Maggie tried again to say.

"Hold it," James said to Henry. "You told me—you told all of us—that I make the decisions for the time being."

"That was when I—"

"No, you'll make the decisions when the rest of us feel like you're ready for the responsibility. You were right to relinquish that."

Now it was Henry who looked like he wanted to punch James.

"I have money to pay for the room!" Maggie finally burst in.

Everyone stared at Maggie. Her cheeks went bright red, and she hurried into her room and closed the door. Ruther wasn't certain she was going to return, but she did, toting a small bag of coins.

"Were you hiding this?" Henry asked as he took it.

Maggie looked away, biting her lip. "I don't want to talk about it."

Ruther felt a cold spike in his stomach. "You—you accused me of robbing the group!"

"You did rob the group," James reminded him.

"Well . . . not like you thought—and not as much as Brandol did. I never kept any of the money. This is—how—what were you planning to do with that money, Mags?"

Maggie's eyes flashed angrily. "James said he was going to leave when we reached the pass. I—I thought it might be wise to keep some in case I wasn't wanted once Henry and Isabelle settled down."

James's mouth dropped open. "You meant to follow me?"

A long moment passed before Maggie nodded. "Henry, I'm sorry for hiding the money. And I'm sorry to you, Ruther, for accusing you. I should have trusted you."

With a deep breath, James stuck out a hand to Ruther, his eyes on the floor. "This has been on my mind—on my soul—for weeks. I was wrong to do what I did, Ruther. I beg your forgiveness."

Ruther was touched, but didn't dare show it. Instead he forced a laugh and grabbed Maggie and James, pulling them into a tight hug. "As if I could hold a grudge against you two."

Both of them pulled away and composed themselves. It was

almost comical how much Maggie could be like James. Ruther had suspected that Maggie fancied James. Now it was apparent how much she did. "So what now?" Maggie asked. "Do we give that mongrel our money?

"No," Henry said. "We leave."

James sat down heavily. "We aren't going to leave, Henry. We need maps, supplies, food . . . a *plan*. Frankly, we're not in a good position. Brandol stole our wealth, and now we have little more than a handful of gold."

"Well . . ." Ruther said, tapping his chin with his long pale fingers. "As it happens, I have an idea you might be interested to hear."

TWELVE

The Roll of the Dice

E xhausted from two long nights of bickering, James, Henry, and Ruther rode for the center of Borderville. It was early spring and the air still had a bite to it, though a weak one. The stone streets shone wetly from an early-morning rainfall. Strong gurgles and growls came from their stomachs. Breakfast had been meager as money was tight. They were taking a great chance, James knew that, but something about it excited him.

"You really think this will work?" Henry asked Ruther for the tenth time since the previous evening.

"We'll earn, friend. We'll earn." Ruther grinned and rubbed his hands together, unable to contain his excitement at the prospect. "Wait and see."

All three men wore hats. James had to admit he really liked his. Thirsty had picked them out and told them—more specifically, James—how handsome they were. She fussed with James's hat for several minutes, making certain it looked perfect. He noticed that her hands trembled the longer she fussed with it. Henry didn't seem to mind his hat, but Ruther scowled up at the brim of his every few minutes.

"Now we know the one thing Ruther will wear a hat for," Henry said when he noticed Ruther glowering. "Gambling."

• • •

Wagons, carts, and carriages filled the road, most carrying men to the tournament. Everyone wore a hat. Signs for Matt and Byderik had doubled in number the last three days. The day before, James had asked Thirsty what they meant.

"It's an election for City Guardian," she explained. "The Council of Nobles selects two lesser nobles from among us to govern the town. We vote for the person we want most."

"You vote? Why?" James asked.

"It gives the people a voice."

"And why are those two chosen for you to vote on?" Ruther asked. "Can't you select your own?"

"I don't know," Thirsty said. "All I know is that they are chosen by the Council. And we decide which among them is better."

"Who do you think is better?" was Henry's question.

Thirsty only shrugged. "I don't pay attention."

To blend in, James and Ruther wore patches supporting Matt— though neither knew a thing about him—producing some angry stares from Byderik supporters and even a few rude gestures. To James and his friends, it was something to laugh about.

Ahead they saw the Hall of Dicing Games. It was an impressive structure, larger than any other buildings Ruther had seen in Borderville. A huge sign bridged the front doorway with letters gilded in silver and gold reading

THE GREATEST
DICE TOURNAMENT
IN THE WORLD

On either end of the sign was the image of a large die. Smaller wooden signs pointed visitors to stables, registration, and other important stops. After taking the horses to the stables, the men gathered to one side of the stream of bodies heading into the dice hall.

"Remember to—"

"Stagger our entrances by fifteen to twenty minutes," James finished for Ruther. "We know. We've been through this."

Ruther nodded to James. "But don't forget to—"

"Use the hand signals if we're getting into trouble," Henry said.

"And most importantly—" Ruther started to say.

"Don't talk about it in front of Maggie tonight," all three men said together.

"I'll see you all soon," Ruther said, grinning from ear to ear and bouncing with energy. "Wait until you experience it, boys, there's nothing like it. The thrill of the game, the rattling of dice in a wooden cup, the tinkling of coins changing hands. It feels right. It feels good. This is my element. We will prevail."

James watched Ruther go, leaning against the stables next to Henry. "He's far too excited about this. Keep a close eye on him."

"I may only have one good arm, but I have two good eyes. I'll keep them both on him. If this doesn't work, we'll have to endure more of Maggie's lectures."

That thought didn't sound pleasing at all. Their planning the past two nights had taken much longer because of Maggie's continued voicing of her objections. The objections had reached a fever pitch long past midnight the night before. Maggie had become nearly hysterical, running through her list of objections at least twice. Ruther had politely listened, sipping the strawberry tea Thirsty had made. When Maggie finished, he set down his mug and asked, "How do *you* propose we earn money?"

"Find employment!"

"What can Henry do with one arm? Will someone pay him to wave at people? What trade does James excel at? Knife sharpening? And you saw how my story went two days ago. Who in this region will hire me after that debacle?"

"We can sell things!" Maggie insisted. "Starting with the horses."

"The pack horses won't fetch much," James said. "They're good for pulling a carriage and little else. We won't get far on that money. And which of us is willing to part with a beloved steed? Not me. Ruther? Henry?"

"What about my necklace? Ruther, when we first entered the pass, you said a jeweler told you it was worth quite a sum."

"That's true," Ruther reluctantly agreed, "but that was when it had been repaired. Now it's broken, though I'm not going to name names as to why that is." Then Ruther coughed something that sounded very much like *James*.

"That necklace is the only thing you have of Mother's," Henry said sternly. "You're not selling it. James is the leader, and he has decided on Ruther's plan."

"It's cheating!" Maggie cried. "We're above that, or we should be!"

"I'm not," Henry said so quietly James hardly heard him. "My betrothed was taken from me by the sword. By the sword, Maggie! Up until this point in my life, I have tried to live uprightly every way I can. Look where that's gotten me! Spare me your righteous indignation, and let us do what we can to help Isabelle. If rolling the dice is the fastest way to get to Isabelle, then I will roll the dice."

"Besides," Ruther added, "if you really think about it, only James is cheating."

"This is a mistake," Maggie pleaded, near tears. "It will come back to haunt us."

That had been the end of the conversation the previous night. James pushed the memory away. He had to focus. His hand slipped into the pocket that held Ruther's dice, waiting for the time to pass until he could go inside the hall and join his friends. He made the two cubes disappear up his sleeve and passed them from one hand to the other, switching them out with the other pair in one deft move. Ruther possessed several pairs of weighted dice, some white and some black. James held two pair of each color. After practicing the trick for hours over the last two days, James was confident he would perform well under pressure.

Five gyri each was all Maggie had allowed them. The coins bounced in his pocket with each step. He enjoyed the jingling, the roughness of the metal on his skin, and their weight in his pocket. When he reached the main hall, two large men greeted him. One wore a patch on his sleeve that read *Vote for Matt*; the other's hat displayed *Vote for Byderik*. The man supporting Matt tipped his hat to James. The other did not.

Just inside the building's entrance was a large sign which read *MONEYCHANGING*, pointing toward a long table behind which sat several women all wearing an identical style of blue dress. A short line had formed behind it. James took his place and moved slowly along until he stood in front of one of the women, who smiled prettily at James.

"How much money would you like to change today, sir?"

Rummaging in his pocket until all five gyri landed on his palm, James presented the money to her. "Five gyri, please."

The woman's smile faltered as she surveyed the paltry sum. "Is that all?"

"For now." James winked, something he knew Ruther would do. "I like to start small. Luckier that way."

The woman giggled politely. "Do you have your unique bet marker?"

James reached into his pocket and showed her a medal he'd received during his service in the guard. Ruther had brought a small copper Blithmorian coin. Henry had a wooden top that he'd carved himself as a child. The woman surveyed the medal, then changed James's five gyri into ten red wooden circles that had a complicated symbol seared into both sides. James picked them up and examined one curiously.

"I suppose I give these back and receive money for them?" he asked.

The woman shot James a look of disbelief. "What else would you do with them? You can't spend them in the markets."

James thanked her and went to find Ruther and Henry. It didn't take long, despite the hundreds of tables thronging the great hall. Ruther's tall frame and pale blond wig stood out among the crowd. Only the storyteller and James wore disguises; Ruther had argued that there was no need for Henry to wear one. His lame arm was something no one would forget. It was a liability that couldn't be helped.

Ruther's plan was to search for tables populated by easygoing gamblers—rich men in a laughing mood playing low stakes were generally the best targets for using false dice. According to Ruther, such men never seemed to mind losing a bit of their extra money and were slow to suspect any foul play.

"Starting with such a crowd will be good for you," Ruther had explained the previous night after Maggie finally gave up and went to bed. "Many people are quite good at their talents until they have to perform under stressful conditions. My uncle was an amazing juggler, but anytime he tried to show off beyond his circle of friends, he got 'the fumbles,' as he called it. We have to be certain you don't get the fumbles."

James approached his friends' table with eagerness. "Pardon me," he said in his best Pappalonian accent. Ruther had made both him and Henry practice it. "Might I join you?"

Ruther and Henry sat with five well-dressed gentlemen around a dice table. Though he was well-traveled, James had not seen anything like it before. In Blithmore, dice games were played around inn tables, whether smooth or rough or littered with dishes from the gamers' meal. The tournament tables were everywhere, and seemed nearly identical. Each was about dinner-table height, six feet long and about three feet wide. Each had a long, straight half-circle-shaped trough about six inches deep and five feet long running through the middle. On either side of the trough two words were painted in large, yellow letters: *SUCCESS* and *FAIL*.

All seven men looked at him. "What's your name, son?" Ruther asked in a perfect Pappalonian accent.

"Jipper Ornestfell."

"Morning, fine man, my name is Rumps Liggit. This is my friend, Hask Vornbit." He pointed to Henry. "How do you do today?"

James replied that he was well, then greeted the other men at the table. The gentlemen all welcomed him warmly. The man at the head of the table introduced himself as Fossy Barnic. James noted the name—and the vapid smile adorning his face. Ruther gave James a sly wink and leaned over to hiss in James's ear.

"Easy pickings."

"I've been having the worst luck today," Ruther complained. "Here's hoping that your presence changes that, Dipper."

"Jipper," James corrected him.

Fossy spoke up. "If your luck is that terrible, maybe we should send Jipper away!" Everyone shared a generous laugh at Ruther's expense, including Ruther. "And you, Jipper? Are you feeling lucky today?"

Ruther looked at James skeptically. "I'll wager he's the type that always breaks even!" Then he placed a hand on Henry's shoulder. "And poor Hask's wife just left him for his best friend, and his stable burned to ash with his prize horse inside."

The men laughed again and invited Jipper to join. "Do you share dice or play your own?" Fossy asked James.

"I brought none," James answered.

"Not a worry! You can use ours."

"I'll share the pairs I brought," Ruther said, reaching into his pocket and showing the men the pairs of white and black dice. These were standard six-sided dice, not the identical weighted pairs James had hidden. The five men barely more than glanced at Ruther's dice, and Fossy spoke for them: "Rumps, Jipper, or Hask, which of you would like to roll first?"

Ruther, or "Rumps," pointed at James. "Let Jipper roll first. We'll test his luck."

Fossy Barnic took the dice from Ruther, put them in a wooden cup, and handed it to James. "Place your bets, gentlemen," he said. Each player had to place a bet by stacking his wooden token on either the success side or the fail side and covering it with his marker: some initiating the bet, others accepting the bet. No dice were thrown until everyone had initiated or accepted a bet. Multiple people could bet against one man, giving him the chance to win or lose big. It all depended on the dice.

For the first toss, as planned, Henry placed a half-gyri on the fail side. James bet a half-gyri on his own success, while Ruther bet three half-gyri on a success. Two of the men around the table took Henry's bet. Only one man bet against Ruther and James. Once all the bets were placed, James surreptitiously swapped his dice for those in the cup and shook.

"Come on, Jipper," Fossy said, "throw me a seven!"

James released the dice. They thundered down the trough. His hands were clammy, and his heart pounded faster with each inch the dice traveled. They bounced off the backstop and lay still.

Seven. Fossy, Ruther, James, and the men who had bet against Henry all cheered. Ruther shook his fist in triumph while Henry grimaced. "And the bad luck continues," he groaned.

Fossy had a stick with a crook at the end. He used the crook of the stick to gather the dice and pull them back to James. Ruther and James bet on the fail line for James's second toss. Henry bet heavily on the success line. Again James tossed the weighted white cubes. All sixteen eyes followed them down the table.

Another seven—a six and a one. Cheers and groans followed. "Curse my luck! It followed me here!" Ruther exclaimed.

Outwardly James remained his stoic self, but inside he was beaming. He was good at this. He was good at something besides soldiering and killing. Who would have guessed that it would be cheating in dice games? Henry received eight half-gyri from the men who'd bet against him, while James and Ruther paid what they owed. Once the table had cleared, new bets were placed. Henry bet for James to succeed, and won again. Then, for James's fourth toss, Ruther took the bet opposite James, so that when James lost, Ruther had only to pretend to receive his friend's money. After five throws of the dice they had earned a net of one and a half gyri, and James passed the cup to Ruther.

And so it went the first day, the eight men playing dice for hours. James found the game exciting: he watched Ruther for signals, placed bets, waited to see the outcome, lost intentionally sometimes, cheated others, made careless mistakes by not correctly following Ruther's directions . . . All in all, the day gave James an odd sense of satisfaction as he and his friends slowly accumulated money. With their advantage, the three men garnered fifteen gyri altogether. James had no doubt that they could have earned more, but Ruther had warned them not to raise suspicion. Earning an average of five gyri apiece was a very good start. Before they left for the day, they exchanged their tokens for coins. When added back to the five gyri they had each started with, it gave them a total of thirty to their names. Ruther kissed each gyri on the ride home, and James understood why. Never had thirty coins looked so beautiful.

THIRTEEN

A Pampered Life

S pending a month in the palace had given Isabelle many insights into the women around her. From what she had observed, her fellow concubines fell into one of two categories: those born and bred into wealth and luxury in lands both far and near who aspired to marry the Emperor, and those lesser-born women who entered into this service to live a concubine's lavish lifestyle. Almost every evening a servant came to escort the chosen concubine or concubines to the Emperor's chambers. Those girls in the first group were usually thrilled to be chosen and devastated when passed over, while those in the second group didn't seem to care whether the Emperor selected them or not.

Isabelle kept a close eye on her fellow concubine, Jade, who was nearing the end of her period of cleansing. Months ago, Jade had been traded from a southern kingdom called Hax. Her real name was much longer and difficult to pronounce, but since Kayla thought her eyes were the color of jade, they called her that. Jade had tanned skin the color of oiled wood and hair like fresh cream. The Emperor wanted her because she had never known a man despite having spent two years as a concubine in a palace of the Sultan of Hax, whose harem of over a thousand women encompassed twenty palaces. Jade told the other girls stories of her nomadic people, who hunted sandsharks, giant creatures who lived in the dunes of the Great Desert of Hax.

The Sultan considered sandsharks a delicacy for which he paid the nomads who hunted them a premium price.

While Jade had at first been counted among Kayla's friends, the closer she got to the end of her cleansing, the more Kayla and her small clique shunned her. This was how Isabelle learned about the hierarchy of concubines. The Emperor had his favorites, and it was no secret which ones they were. While all were given access to the royal stables to ride the Emperor's prized horses once they were cleansed, some were invited on boat rides with the Emperor on the lake near the palace. Others were given access to his library or were asked to accompany him on short journeys to neighboring towns.

But the pinnacle of his favor was wearing the ruby rose, the large gem set into a clasp which Isabelle had seen in Kayla's hair on her first day. One responsibility of wearing the rose meant meeting with the Emperor regularly to discuss the other concubines' concerns. Kayla also seemed to think this meant bossing others around.

Isabelle much preferred Cecilia's tactics. She was the Emperor's other current favorite. Though she was still new compared to others, a majority of the concubines respected Cecilia. With her deep auburn hair, white skin like fresh milk, and pale green eyes, her beauty was more than apparent. She also had a knack for brokering peace among quarreling girls. Many believed Cecilia was next in line for the rose. She was taller, prettier, had more friends than Kayla, and lately was the Emperor's most requested concubine.

Isabelle, on the other hand, was instantly unpopular. It had only taken a few days for word to spread throughout the house that Isabelle claimed to be held against her will. Long stares and even longer un-comfortable silences followed whenever she entered the common room. Cecilia insisted that the reason the girls distrusted Isabelle was because, like Jade, Isabelle was a novelty. Cecilia claimed that she, too, had been treated poorly her first weeks. She attributed this to the Emperor's tendency to show preference for a new girl after her cleansing. Cecilia assured Isabelle that once the novelty wore off, the animosity would end.

As much as Isabelle hated to admit it, there were some tangible benefits to her life. She enjoyed wonderful foods every day: exotic and delicious fruits and vegetables, succulent meats and ripe cheeses. Food cooked to perfection was at her fingertips any time she wished. Chambermaids cleaned her room, washed her clothes, and submitted Isabelle to a lengthy massage each afternoon. And as Cecilia had predicted, Isabelle grew accustomed to the baths, and now found them extraordinary.

Yet a deep malaise gripped Isabelle's stomach every time she thought of the day her cleansing would end. None of these luxuries made up for what she'd lost. A day didn't go by without thinking of Henry, his hair covered in wood dust, hands calloused and worn from work, his lips pressed against her forehead. These memories almost always came with tears. She missed James, Maggie, and, when she needed a laugh, she missed Ruther, too. Isabelle thought often of Brandol, his unexpected bravery, his trembling kiss and grateful gaze before his death. She wished for a way to thank him for that.

After spending hours during her first month wondering where her friends were, what they were doing, and how long it might be before they found her, she had given up that exercise. But she hadn't given up praying for their safety.

She longed for human contact. None of the other concubines were allowed to touch her, which meant no hugs, no friendly pats on the arm or hand, no physical contact at all. Even the masseuses and the maids wore gloves during her massages and baths, making them relaxing but soulless events.

The lack of emotional connection was even worse. While Jade and Cecilia cared enough to listen to Isabelle's woes and offer words of comfort, Isabelle got the distinct impression that the others weren't certain if they could trust her, and that their conversations were more about extracting information than they were about sympathy.

"What happens to the slaves—excuse me—the concubines if they are dismissed from service to the Emperor?" Isabelle had asked Cecilia one day while they lay side by side having a massage. She had quickly learned that Cecilia and the others preferred the term *concubines* to *slaves*.

Cecilia's gaze became distant and she lost some of her color. She continued to smile but stiffly. "Those who stay in the Emperor's service long enough can become servants such as our maids." Cecilia gestured to the women rubbing their legs.

"It's quite an honor," one of the maids remarked, "to continue to live here in the Emperor's employ."

"Both of you were concubines?" Isabelle asked.

"Yes, but we didn't serve the current Emperor; we served his father."

"I had heard that Emperor Peter didn't have concubines."

The maids giggled into their hands, leaving streaks of oil on their faces. "That's a little known secret. King Germaine frowns upon such things, so Emperor Peter kept our existence hidden. But we were there. In fact, the Emperor fell in love with one of his concubines. What was her name, dear?" the first maid asked the second.

"Kathryn . . . Karolyn?"

"No, those are the names of the twins. Who was the one he *married?*"

"I can't remember."

"Well, it doesn't matter. He married her. But she fell ill and died. Very tragic. Emperor Peter was a kind man."

"Not all become palace staff," Cecilia explained. "Some are sold to noblemen in different countries. I've heard of some sent to Old Avalon or southern lands where older, experienced women are prized. Those who can't be sold and don't wish to remain as servants, if the

Emperor is no longer interested, receive a house and a small plot of land in Widowton."

"What's that?" Isabelle asked.

"A small town set aside for widows and former concubines. Somewhere in the north, I think."

"Neither of you wanted a piece of land of your own?"

"Oh, no," one of the maids said. "I prefer living here. This has been my home for decades. It's what I know."

"Besides," said the other, "our meals are cooked for us. Our rooms are cleaned for us. All we have to do is pamper you."

"And the women who leave and go to Widowton?" Isabelle pressed. "They don't marry?"

The two maids gasped quietly, and Cecilia gave Isabelle a belittling stare. "Is that supposed to be funny?"

Isabelle regretted the question. "No."

"Who would want to marry one of us?"

"Cecilia, you are the most beautiful woman I have ever seen. You're likable and kind. I can't imagine a man not showing interest."

Cecilia's normally calm demeanor almost broke as her eyes narrowed at Isabelle. "Please don't ever say that again. Excuse me." She quickly left the room, leaving Isabelle to wonder how she had offended her friend.

"I wasn't finished with her massage," the maid complained. "She's not going to be rested enough for the Emperor."

Isabelle didn't have much time to ponder Cecilia's emotions. Most of her energy, when not submitting to her daily baths and massages, was spent searching for ways to escape. She took great pains not to be obvious about paying close attention to every detail about the concubines' quarters: noticing what times the servants came and went, listening for the sound of locking doors, always keeping an eye out for a miscue or mislaid tool she might be able to put to use. But after four weeks, her efforts had been futile.

The servants *always* locked the door. They *never* forgot a knife or sharp object. In fact, they rarely said anything to the slaves beyond their names, and when they did say something more, it was to Kayla, because she wore the ruby rose. Every night Isabelle left her bed to hunt through the many closets, drawers, and cabinets. By torchlight, she rummaged through spare robes, games, brushes, slippers, and cosmetics. She found nothing to force open the gold plated door.

This meant that her only other option of escape was the window. Peering through the bars, she calculated the distance from her window to the moat below. She was no expert, but she estimated the drop at nearly two hundred feet. Such a fall would kill her. And coupled with the iron bars, she had no choice but to accept that her prison was inescapable.

Isabelle asked the maids once why the bars and locks existed. The maids glanced at each other knowingly, giggling stupidly. "To keep men out, of course. There are more than a few stories of women being carried off against their will, kidnapped by brave, bad men who want the Emperor's prizes for their own."

"Surely concubines have run away, haven't they?" Isabelle continued, keeping her voice light and casual.

"Not that I recall. I've been here over forty years and have never heard of it. Who would want to leave?"

"Well, there was that one girl from Gaddano," the other maid said. "She tried, remember? Grabbed the servant's knife and tried to force her way out. Poor thing lost her head—literally, I mean. I've never seen Emperor Peter so angry. Emperor Ivan is more like his father in that regard, isn't he?"

On the morning that marked the end of her first month as a slave, Isabelle, finishing her baths, donned her robe to return to her bedroom for a nap. As she walked down the hallway, Kayla, enveloped in her familiar scent of lilacs and roses, nearly walked straight into Isabelle out of one of the other baths. She shrieked and clutched herself as if she'd been burned. "Don't touch me! Do you realize what you almost did, you stupid girl? Watch where you're going!"

Isabelle tried to apologize, but Kayla continued yelling until Cecilia, Jade, and several other concubines poked their heads into the hallway to investigate. Kayla turned to them and cried, "This filthy— ugh!—tramp is trying to sabotage me! Stay away from her, Jade. Your cleansing ends tomorrow, doesn't it?"

Jade didn't answer. Isabelle didn't know whether to be angry or amused at Kayla's overreaction. She knew that if Kayla's skin had even brushed against Isabelle's, it would mean a month of cleansing for the flower-scented slave, even though Isabelle bore no fault. But Kayla's tantrum, combined with looks of disdain from the other slaves, made Isabelle feel like a mangy mutt prowling about a pristine home.

Rather than trying to explain, Isabelle fled the hallway. When she reached the knot of girls at the end of the hall, they moved aside to let her pass. She spent the rest of the day alone in her room. That night, when all was quiet except the sounds of more than twenty girls softly slumbering (except for one with a decidedly unladylike snore), Isabelle resumed her search through the nooks and crannies of the house.

"What are you doing?"

Isabelle almost screamed in fright, dropping a handful of pins. It was only Jade, an empty water pitcher in hand.

"Sorry," the cream-haired slave whispered as she pulled her robes tightly around her. Jade spoke with a thick Haxite accent, which Isabelle often struggled to understand. "Haxites are known for their ability to walk lightly. When on the dunes, we have to tread with great care to not attract sandsharks."

"It's fine," Isabelle said. She held one of the hairpins up to the light. "Sometimes I can't sleep when my hair gets in my face."

Jade glanced at Isabelle's head. Only a month's growth, roughly two inches in length, covered her head. "I don't believe that's a problem for you."

Isabelle sniggered. For some reason, she remembered what Ruther would do in a moment like this. "I was teasing."

Jade smiled softly. "This isn't the first time I've heard you poking around. Do you have trouble sleeping at night or do you just like to snoop?"

Isabelle gestured to the open drawer. "I still don't know my way around here, so, yes, I snoop. The dark only makes it worse. What about you? Do you have trouble sleeping?"

Jade looked over her shoulder to make certain no one was behind her. Then she moved closer to Isabelle and said, "Yes. I'm nervous."

"Tomorrow is your—"

Jade nodded.

"Did you want to be a concubine?" Isabelle asked. "Was that your ambition?"

Jade stared at Isabelle curiously. "I should go to bed. My strength—I'll need it tomorrow."

"Jade . . ."

"Goodnight, Isabelle. Please don't lose any sleep over Kayla. Her strings are wound tightly, if you understand me. She's had the ruby rose since I arrived here, and for good reason. But the Emperor is close to giving it to Cecilia, and Kayla won't surrender it easily."

Jade retired to bed, leaving Isabelle with a drawerful of hairpins all over the floor. Isabelle started to pick them up one by one. About a minute later, someone touched her robed shoulder.

It scared Isabelle so badly she dropped them all again. "Is everyone planning on sneaking up on me tonight?"

Cecilia giggled. "Just me. At least, I think I'm the last." She bent down and helped Isabelle pick up the pins. "How many of these do you need?"

"None, really, as you can see. But I couldn't sleep, so I was going through this drawer, and had picked up a handful of pins when Jade surprised me. And now they're all over the floor."

"You're lonely, aren't you?" Cecilia asked. "Have I invited you to play Stone Jump with my other friends?"

"No. I've seen you and the others playing it, but I've never joined in. I don't know the rules."

"Tomorrow after your baths I'll teach you. Then we can organize a game. If they get to know you better, they'll be more friendly. What do you say?"

"That won't be a problem? Playing a game together? I don't want to—"

Cecilia shrugged dismissively. "Not if we're careful, and believe me, we will be. If someone touches you, her re-cleansing only takes a month, but it would be enough to displease the Emperor. If it happened to me, I'd lose my chance at getting the ruby rose."

Isabelle laughed because it seemed like she was supposed to, but her laughter fell flat when Cecilia did not join her.

"I appreciate the kindness you've shown me," Isabelle said sincerely.

Cecilia blushed, but patted Isabelle on the leg where her gown covered her skin. They bid each other goodnight, and Isabelle was soon in bed, asleep. The next morning Cecilia made good on her promise, for which Isabelle was grateful. After her baths, her skin felt particularly raw and sensitive. If Cecilia and her game hadn't taken Isabelle's mind off the itching, she might have gone mad.

Stone Jump was one of the games the girls played regularly. Some played it every day. The game board was a heavy cast-iron slab dimpled with dozens of small hemispheres which formed a six-pointed star. Each player had a number of colored stones which could only move by jumping over another one. The goal was to get all your stones to all the other points of the star. Isabelle learned the rules easily enough, but lost consistently.

The best part of her day was not learning or playing the game but getting acquainted with the other girls. Jade, Jessika, Nikole, and Joyful all adored Cecilia, and once they got to know Isabelle, they were full of compliments and stories about themselves and each other. Each of the girls had something unique about her. Joyful, for example, had very dark skin—far darker than Jade's—and had been sent to the Emperor as a gift from Baron Verkozy, the ruler of Old Avalon, three years ago. Apparently her black hair was a rarity among her people, most of whom had hair whiter than Jade's. Nikole was the oldest of all the slaves, and feared that the Emperor would release her from his service soon. Jessika was the best at Stone Jump and won the first three games. The fourth, however, was won by Kayla, who invited herself to play, while disinviting Isabelle. When Kayla's last stone dropped into the hole, she jumped up and cheered loudly in Cecilia's face.

"Here she goes," Joyful remarked.

"I hate it when she wins," Jade added under her breath.

Kayla certainly made a show of it. When she finished cheering, she unclipped the massive ruby rose from her hair and turned the board over, spilling the stones onto the table. On the back of the iron board were several small but deep scratches, all in a neat row. Using the ruby rose, Kayla made another scratch and began whooping again. Isabelle stared at the deep scratches that Kayla had made so effortlessly with the large gem.

"Won't that ruin the ruby?" Isabelle asked Cecilia.

"No, of course not," Cecilia answered as Kayla clipped the flower back into her hair. "It's a dragon-ruby. My father was a gem collector and taught me all about Atolas's minerals. Dragon-rubies are extraordinarily hard, almost magically so. Forged in the stomach of a dragonox for many years, they can cut nearly anything without damaging the stone. Ready for another game?"

Isabelle said she was; so were the other girls. Kayla, victorious, wandered away to other pursuits. Nikole won the next game, and Isabelle didn't mind. Her mind had left the game and was focused on the iron bars on her window, wondering how she could get possession of the ruby rose.

FOURTEEN

Henry's Wager

Henry sat alone at the dining table in their suite at the Sheep's Entrails, sipping a mug of hot cider to warm him against the chilly, late morning air. His right hand rested on his lap, where it always rested when he ate. He enjoyed being alone. Maggie was at the market, James and Ruther at the dice hall. Henry went with them less and less, choosing to spend his time searching for a cartographer who might sell them maps and information, or someone who might know of a healer for his arm. So far, his efforts had been as worthless as his right hand.

A knock came at the door. Henry knew it was Thirsty, so he got up and let her in. She smiled brightly with white teeth that matched her hair. Her bright blue eyes danced. "How are you, Brandol?" she asked, entering with her broom. Henry and his friends continued to use the journeyman's name around anyone but themselves.

"I'm well enough." He sat back at the table and set down his mug. "Come in."

"Is Maggie back with the dinner supplies?"

"Not yet," Henry said, picking up a small chisel and a block of wood. He was determined to teach himself to carve with his left hand. "She takes her time at the market. Even as a young girl she was like that."

A troubled expression stole over Thirsty's face, but it quickly vanished. "I didn't realize you two have known each other for that long."

"Oh . . ." Henry struggled to come up with a believable lie. "Mostly stories . . . her brother told them . . . when I worked with him . . . in his woodshop. Do you, um, plan to work at this inn forever?" His attempt to change the subject was clumsy and poorly concealed. He moved his right hand to the top of the block of wood to try to stabilize it while he carved.

"No. I'm saving my money to go on an adventure of my own someday."

Henry fixed her with a curious stare. "Why would you want to go on an adventure? Look what happened to me."

"One day I want to buy a small inn on the coast in Panautica. I hope to have lots of adventures getting there." Thirsty sighed and toyed with her fraying dress. "But that won't happen for a very long time. Mr. Jessop doesn't pay well, and anytime I do something wrong, he takes away a day's wages."

"Then why do you stay?"

"It's the best job I can find. Although—at times—I make a little money on the side. So for now, my little inn is the dream that gets me through the day."

"Well, a dream is one thing," Henry told her as he tried to push the chisel into the wood. Because his hand wasn't heavy enough to hold the wood still, each scrape pushed it farther away. "An adventure is much different. An adventure is getting chased by people who want to kill you, starving for days, getting trapped in a blizzard, or being hopelessly lost."

Thirsty laughed. "Sounds exciting to me. Although now that you mention it, none of you have ever told me where you're headed. Why is that?"

There was something off in her voice. Henry didn't know what it was, so he chose not to answer. He made a few more halfhearted attempts at carving the wood before shoving the block and the chisel away from him in disgust.

"Where does a name like Thirsty come from?" he asked testily.

Thirsty swept the room as she spoke. "In Old Avalon, mostly among my people, it is customary to name a child based on her most prevalent characteristic. My mother said I constantly wanted to nurse. Hence my name."

"Are you serious?"

Thirsty nodded. "I have three brothers: Smiles, Stinker, and Furious. I never realized my name was strange until I came to Pappalon. At first I thought everyone else had the odd names. And what about you?"

"What about me?"

"I answered your question, so what about mine? Where does your adventure end?"

Henry liked Thirsty, and he believed she sincerely cared for him and his friends. She'd even asked to be assigned to clean their rooms. He didn't have any reason to mistrust her. But something told him not to tell her where they were going.

"I'm not certain," he finally said. "The road is long and winding. It ends where it ends. You know what would help me find the road, though?"

"What is that?"

"Maps. Now that we've earned some money, we can afford them. Do you know where I can make such a purchase?"

"Maps of what lands?"

Henry thought for a second. "The Eastern and Western Irons. All of it."

Thirsty shrugged and began stabbing at the dust in a corner with her broom. "Not around here. I haven't heard of any mapmakers in Borderville. I can ask Mr. Jessop if you'd like."

The door handle rattled, and Maggie entered with her marketplace purchases. When she saw Henry she gave him a half-smile. "Hello, He—Brandol," catching herself as she spied Thirsty in the corner with the broom. "Hello, Thirsty."

"Good afternoon, Maggie!" Thirsty said. "Would you like me to help you with those?"

"No, thank you. I've got it."

Thirsty went back to her sweeping. "So, Brandol, as I was saying. Do you want me to talk to Mr. Jessop?"

"No, no. It's fine. Forget I asked." Henry had a sudden urge to leave, so he grabbed the money purse and took twenty gyri out of it. Maggie shot him a venomous look, which he ignored. Even now, days after their arguments regarding the dice games, she carried a grudge about Ruther teaching Henry and James to cheat. "Ruther and James are waiting for me at the hall. I'll be back tonight."

Every morning James, Henry, and Ruther left a portion of their gold at home and returned with double what they'd taken with them. After five days, Ruther had taken himself, Henry, and James to the shops and bought them each a set of well-tailored Pappalonian clothes so they could mix in at higher-spending tables. The idea paid off. The next day they returned with over fifty gyri in earnings.

The drawback to gambling for more money was that the high rollers were more wary of cheaters. The day after they earned the fifty, two men wearing *Vote for Matt* badges appeared at their table and stood watching, refusing to bet. Ruther signaled to James and Henry to lose repeatedly. Between the scrutiny and the panic it induced, they ended up losing all the money that they had brought with them that day. But this was their only setback. They spent that night tweaking the mechanics of their operation until Ruther was satisfied it would work better and more covertly than before.

The sound of dice rattling in cups and troughs had become as familiar to Henry's ears as that of saws, chisels, and sanding cloths. Over a thousand men crowded around tables in the great hall, all intensely focused on the random fall of two small spotted cubes. Henry spent twenty minutes searching the hall for his friends. He finally found them at a corner table with several wealthy men, laughing as they exchanged money.

Ruther watched warily as Henry approached. "Hello . . . Hask, isn't it?" he said in a pleasant tone, still using that perfect Pappalonian accent. "How nice to see you again, you unlucky, one-armed devil!"

"Certainly an unexpected surprise!" James agreed. "Won't you join us?"

"We're already at eight players," Ruther said. "Unfortunately that means—"

The man at the far end of the table interrupted Ruther. "Actually, my friend and I are leaving. Mr. Hask is welcome to take one of our spots."

"May I join, too?" a voice said on Henry's right. It was Fossy Barnic, a man they'd rolled dice with on their first day of gambling. He seemed to remember Hask Vornbit quite well and greeted him like an old chum. James and Ruther, however, he didn't recognize, as their disguises changed every day.

"How have you fared since we last played?" he asked Henry.

"Alas, my bad luck continues!"

Fossy Barnic stroked his graying mustache. "Oh, trust me, I know. All my friends have left. Lost all the money allotted to them by their womenfolk. Very unfortunate. One more bad day, and I might be packing my bags, too."

Ruther nodded sympathetically. His talent for performance never ceased to amaze Henry. Rather than take his turn at throwing the dice, Ruther offered the cup to Fossy, and stepped aside. "I refuse to believe your good luck has run out, Fossy," he said. "Indeed, I will even risk my own money to bet that your good fortune returns now."

As Fossy shook the cup, Ruther motioned to James to give Fossy two tosses of sevens and then switch the dice for the normal ones. Meanwhile, all three bet heavily on success as Fossy tossed the cubes.

Fossy had an excellent start to his day, and grew talkative as the afternoon wore on. He chatted about his travels all over Eastern Irons. The more he spoke, the more Henry realized how wealthy such a man must be to travel so extensively. Fossy had even sailed the Great Southern Sea to visit the southern lands—places Henry had never even heard of.

"Have you ever been to Blithmore? Neverak?" Henry asked.

"Oh no, never crossed the Iron Forest. Too afraid of it, to be honest. And those areas don't interest me. Not nearly exotic enough. Why, if I tell a man I've been to Scortussin, Judica, or Hax, they're all ears, they buy me a drink. But Blithmore? Neverak? No . . ."

"I'm interested in maps, particularly—"

"I dabble in cartography, too," Fossy boasted to Henry and another man on his opposite side. "Indeed, I've worked with some of the most knowledgeable cartographers in all of Atolas, sharing my travels and maps with them."

"Anyone with extensive traveling through Neverak?"

Fossy hesitated for a moment, then answered. "Yes, one in particular. Though he's not familiar with just Neverak. He's probably the most well-traveled man I've met."

Henry's ears perked up. "I'm looking to acquire maps of Neverak. It's a place I've always wanted to see. I don't suppose you could help?"

Fossy scratched at his mustache and fiddled with his nose before finally saying, "I don't think I can enlighten you on that specific region. However, if you're interested—"

"Then might I ask the name of this cartographer?" Henry cut in.

Fossy regarded Henry for a moment. "Yes, well, you see—the thing is—I simply can't give you that information. The man values his privacy above all else. It isn't my place to betray the confidence of a friend."

Henry nodded, pretending to understand Fossy's dilemma. But if this man actually knew the location of a cartographer as he claimed . . .

"Is there any way I could pay you for—"

"Mr. Vornbit!" Fossy exclaimed to Henry. Henry could see that Fossy was trying to be polite, but Henry had crossed a boundary. "One does not sell his friends' secrets. If one does, one has no friends left. Please respect that."

"I do. I truly do. Yet if you knew of my plight—if you knew why I am in such great need for this information, I think you would agree to help me."

"Regardless, it's not my place. But since I can see that you have no intention of letting this settle, I will take my leave of you. Good day, sirs." Fossy tipped his hat to Henry and the rest of the men at the table, cleared his debts, and walked away.

A flame ignited inside Henry as he watched Fossy disappear into the crowds. How could something so fortuitous appear within his grasp and slip away so easily? He squeezed the edge of the table with his good hand until he had no strength. What more could he have done? Not paying attention to Ruther's signals, Henry placed his money on the fail side of the table. James threw the dice and rolled a seven. Henry groaned when he realized that his carelessness had canceled out James's and Ruther's winnings.

"Pardon me, gentlemen," he told his fellow gamblers, "my luck seems to have run out." He left the table. As he stormed across the floor, he saw Fossy Barnic about twelve feet ahead of him, also leaving. Henry glanced back to see if Ruther or James had followed him, but they were still at the table, paying him no mind.

Henry followed Fossy from a distance, careful to avoid being seen. He had apparently made many friends over the course of the tournament, stopping multiple times to chat. Each time Fossy stopped, Henry found something nearby to inspect studiously until he was on his way again. Finally they reached the stables. Fossy mounted a grand horse with a magnificent saddle. Henry waited only a few moments before exiting the stable on Quicken.

Fossy rode to a large inn called the Decapitated Horse on the other side of town. The atmosphere inside had a different air about it: more refined, subdued, and chatty, not rowdy. Henry stood in one spot, searching for Fossy's face. When he didn't see him among those at the dining tables, he turned about and caught a glimpse of him disappearing up the stairs. Henry walked quickly to the stairs and climbed them quietly. Three flights up, Fossy walked to his room. Henry peered around the corner. As soon as Fossy's door closed behind him, Henry crept up, checked the number carved into the door, and hurried back downstairs.

James and Ruther still hadn't returned when Henry reached the Sheep's Entrails. Maggie and Thirsty were in the kitchen preparing dinner. Thirsty waved and asked how his day had gone. Henry ignored her, going to his bedroom and locking the door. Rummaging through James's and Ruther's packs, Henry gathered what he needed. Once finished, he donned his traveling cloak and shoved one of Ruther's costume pieces deep into his pocket.

As he walked quickly from his bedroom to the main door of the suite, Maggie asked, "Where are you going now? Don't you want dinner?"

Without answering, he headed down the stairs, hoping not to run into James or Ruther on their way up. The afternoon was turning into evening. Henry wanted the cover of night before carrying out his plan.

He rode Quicken back to the Decapitated Horse at a leisurely pace. The atmosphere in the public room hadn't changed. Henry sat by himself and ordered dinner with plenty of ale. When he'd had his fill, he sat back in his chair sipping from his mug and watched the other guests, paying close attention to the couples. He noticed the way they looked at each other, the gentleness when fingers interlocked or a hand trailed down a lover's arm. More than once, he closed his eyes and pretended that Isabelle sat next to him, her arm resting on his, her warm smile fixed intently on nothing but him.

He sat drinking for over four hours. Long after the moons came out to dance with the stars in the night sky, he got up from his chair, left money on the table to pay for his food and ale, and headed for the stairs. His heartbeat throbbed in his ears, growing louder each step he climbed. When he reached the last step, he nearly abandoned his plan. Then he remembered the scenes of love and tenderness he had witnessed downstairs: men and women conversing, laughing, savoring each other's company. Fossy Barnic held the information that could get Henry closer to Isabelle.

"Isabelle." He hadn't said her name aloud in days, which made him ashamed. He crossed the hall and took the doorknob to Fossy's room in his grip. "For you, Isabelle."

Taking great care, Henry removed one of James's throwing knives from his belt and jammed the point of it into the space between the door and its frame, applying steady pressure until the door popped open, then he put the knife back in his waistband. Before entering the room, he tied a black handkerchief over his nose and mouth, a difficult task with one good hand. Then he pulled his cloak over his head so that even his eyes could barely be seen. As he entered the room, he unsheathed Ruther's sword from where he'd hidden it under his cloak.

Fossy was asleep in bed. Henry raised the sword until the point touched Fossy's throat, and increased the pressure of the blade on Fossy's skin until his eyes opened. Henry's right hand useless to gesture, he shook his head in warning and whispered, "Shhh . . ."

Fossy gasped. His eyes widened and reflected the dim light from the hallway outside. The fear in them gave Henry no satisfaction.

"What do you want?" Fossy spat. "Money? Take it and go."

"Shhh . . ." Henry repeated. He lowered his voice enough that it sounded menacing and unlike his own. "Get out of the bed."

Fossy blushed. "Will you at least spare me some indignity and hand me my trousers?"

Henry shook his head.

Fossy sighed, climbed out of bed naked, and put on his pants. All the while, Henry's sword remained pointed at the man's neck. When Fossy had made himself more decent, he fixed his cold, angry eyes on Henry. "Well . . . what do you want from me?"

"Turn around and face the wall."

When Fossy did as directed, Henry quickly sheathed the sword, removed the throwing knife from his belt, and placed it against Fossy's throat. Again the man gasped, but now it sounded more like a whimper.

"My dear fellow," he begged, "there must be something I have that you want. Why come into my room just to kill me? Let me help you. I'll give you what you want, but please, spare my wretched life!"

"Keep quiet. Do you have parchment, quill, and ink?"

"I do. In the nightstand drawer." Fossy raised a trembling hand to point.

"Walk to it. Not too quickly. You might slice your neck open on my blade. Be warned . . . it is *very* sharp. Do you understand?"

Fossy understood. Once the requested items had been set out on the table, he waited for instructions. This was the part Henry had dreaded since the idea popped into his head.

"Write down directions so I can find the cartographer."

"Which cart—"

"The one that knows about Neverak."

Fossy flinched. "It's *you!* Hask . . . Hask Vornbit." Though he didn't know Henry's real name, Fossy knew what Henry looked like.

"Write it down!" Henry's hand shook as he hissed furiously in Fossy's ear.

A nervous laugh tumbled from Fossy's mouth. "Good sir, put the knife down and let's discuss this like men."

"Don't interpret the trembling in my hand for a lack of willpower. You might think you can overpower me because of my arm, but I assure you any attempt will cost you your life."

"Mr. Vornbit . . . there is no—"

"*Write!*" Henry whispered as loud as he dared, pressing the blade against Fossy's throat until a small cut appeared.

Fossy picked up the quill. For a long time, the only sound in the room was the scratching of the quill on the parchment. Henry paid close attention to Fossy's hand, noting the pauses, the hesitation in some of his movements. Finally, Fossy put down the quill.

"There. You have it. Leave me be."

Henry read over Fossy's shoulder. What he saw did not satisfy him. "Reach into my cloak pocket, Fossy. The one on my left."

"There's nothing but dice."

"Take the dice."

Fossy did as he was told. The dice in his hand were black with white spots. Ruther didn't like to use them because they were difficult to read from a distance.

"What do you know about dice, Mr. Barnic?"

Fossy choked back a chortle. "My dear fellow, they have six sides and six numbers. What else is there to know?"

"That pair of dice was bewitched by a sorceress from the land of Scortussin. They will only roll a seven if someone answers a question truthfully and then tosses them. If that person lies, they will never roll a seven. Never."

"What has this got to do with me?"

"Are the words on the paper you just wrote accurate?"

"Why—of—yes, of course they are!"

"There. You've answered my question, now roll the dice. If you get a six or less, I will remove your left ear. Roll an eight or more, and I take off the right. Roll a seven and you win."

Fossy could barely shake the dice in his hands. He managed a few feeble shakes before he broke down, quaking. "Don't do this. I've done what you asked!"

"Roll the dice!"

"I can't."

Henry pressed deeply enough that he made another small cut on Fossy's neck. Red drops trickled down his skin and fell onto the table. Three landed on the parchment.

"This is madness!"

"Yes. Now fix what you wrote until it is correct."

Fossy picked up the quill once more and scratched out four lines, rewriting them in a hurry. Then he added a few more lines at the bottom. Henry noted that the hesitancy in his writing was gone. When Fossy set down the quill a second time, Henry knew that the instructions were accurate.

"Get back in bed," he told Fossy.

Fossy set the dice down and climbed back into the bed.

"Pull the sheet over your head."

Again Fossy did as commanded. Henry slipped the dice back into his pocket, gathered up the parchment, and returned the knife to its sheath. Then he slipped out the door and left with all possible haste. Before he knew it, he was at the stables and mounting Quicken. He set off for the Sheep's Entrails. The streets nearly empty, Quicken's hoofs sounded like thunderclaps, and Henry worried that he'd soon hear Fossy sounding the alarm behind him. His thoughts were as dark as the sky above. He came upon a black alleyway between two tall shops, and pulled Quicken's reins to guide him into the small street. There, Henry dismounted and knelt on the ground. The dice in his pocket rattled. Henry pulled them out and let them roll off his hand to the dirt.

One landed as a six, the other a one.

They were weighted; they would roll a six and a one every time.

Henry had tested them before bringing them. He picked them up and squeezed them so hard that his hand hurt. Thick tears streamed down his cheeks as he gasped for air between sobs.

"Isabelle, I'm sorry," he wheezed. "I'm sorry. There was no other way."

FIFTEEN

Maggie's Wish

The food on Maggie's plate sat untouched. It smelled divine, but her appetite had vanished in Henry's absence. She glanced at the door, chewing at her tightly pursed lip until it began to bleed. Ruther pointed at her plate with his fork and spoke through a mouthful of veal.

"You're wasting perfectly good food, Mags. You're not going to let this poor bird die for nothing, are you?"

"Veal isn't a bird," Maggie said tonelessly.

"Yeah, I knew that," Ruther said with a cough.

"He left without saying anything?" James asked for the fourth time.

"Nothing," Thirsty said as she pointed across the room. "She and I were both standing in the kitchen when he came in. He didn't say a word. He went into the room, locked the door, and left not long after without a hello or goodbye."

"Strange." Ruther shoveled more food into his mouth. "He was acting odd at the dice tournament today, too. Didn't pay attention to my signals."

"But where would he go?" Maggie declared.

James rested his hand on Maggie's. Maggie noticed Thirsty's brief and unsubtle glance at the gesture. "Let's avoid drawing baseless conclusions," James suggested. "I bet he'll return any moment. Probably with a good explanation of where he's been."

Images of Henry drowning in a basin of water were stuck in Maggie's mind. She thought of that vision, along with the others: James in prison, Ruther in chains, herself battling some monstrosity. What did they mean?

Thirsty tried to take the dishes, but Maggie shook her head. "I can clean up, thank you."

"Maggie, I must insist. This is my job. It's bad enough that I eat with you, if Mr. Jessop discovered that I let you do your own washing, I'd have to find new employment."

"It's the principle," Maggie explained. "I don't like having someone clean up after me."

Ruther leaned over the table and spoke to Thirsty in a fake hushed voice. "Truth is, Thirsty, Maggie gets like this when she's anxious or worried . . . or tired or awake or happy—"

"No," Maggie said, ignoring Thirsty's polite laughter, "it's simple. I'm not lazy."

"And I've got to keep my job," Thirsty finished. "But I appreciate your willingness to help."

Ignoring Thirsty, Maggie collected and washed the plates, mugs, and cutlery. Having something to do was better than sitting around fretting. Thirsty, a bit put out by Maggie's stubborness, busied herself dusting around the fireplace. James and Ruther sat near the fire talking about dice while Maggie worked. Staying in the kitchen let her keep an eye and ear on them. The gambling still bothered her, and the more time James spent around Ruther, the more her irritation grew.

"How much coin do we have now?" Maggie asked, scrubbing a plate.

"A little over two hundred gyri," Ruther answered.

"How much more do we need?"

"I know it sounds mad," James said, "but I don't think I'd be comfortable with less than a thousand."

"A thousand?" Maggie repeated. "Is that even possible?"

"With what we have now," Ruther said, "a thousand is reachable. But we would have to play at some of the best tables, and at those tables, they practically roll for blood. If we're caught . . ."

James nodded. "And you think *I'm* good enough to fool even the most experienced players?"

"James, if you weren't good enough, I'd tell you."

"Even the best cheaters can get—" Maggie began, but the door to the suite opened and she forgot what she was about to say.

Henry entered briskly and hurried into his bedroom. He shut the door and locked it, exactly as he'd done earlier. Maggie knocked on it and called to him. He didn't answer. All she could hear was him rummaging around in his traveling pack and sniffing as though he'd inhaled too much wood dust. She knocked a second time.

"Henry, please come out. We were worried."

"I wasn't worried, Brandol!" Ruther hollered. It was plain from his tone that he was reminding Maggie to use Henry's *other* name around Thirsty. "I knew you were fine."

"So did I!" James said, in a very Ruther-like tone.

The lock clicked, the bedroom door flew open, and Henry stepped out. He strode into the main room, wearing a forced smile. He held a piece of parchment in his hand which he waved as proudly as he would have the Blithmorian flag. "Does anyone want to guess what this is?" he asked.

"Another writ of passage?" Ruther guessed. "A pardon from King Germaine? The recipe for the best pie ever?"

"Directions to the home of a cartographer," Henry answered. He placed it on the table for all to examine. Maggie noticed that parts had been scratched out and there were red splotches near the bottom of the page. "Is that blood?" she asked.

Again he smiled that very un-Henry-like smile. "I had to venture into a nest of thieves to get this. No one gets out without spilling some."

"With that arm of yours," Ruther commented, "you couldn't make it out of a nest of birds. What really happened?"

"I had some wine. And the man giving me directions got more than a little tipsy."

James, Ruther, and Thirsty looked over the document next. "And you're certain these directions are accurate?" James asked.

Henry shrugged. "Not until I follow them. And I plan to do that tomorrow."

"Tomorrow?" Maggie repeated.

"What about the dice tournament?" Ruther asked.

Henry sat down heavily. "I'm done with that. I can't go back there. If anyone asks if you knew me, pretend that I was a nuisance who liked to tag along."

"That's not pretending, friend," Ruther japed.

"I'll persuade this mapmaker to sell me maps and advice. While I'm gone, you two earn as much money as possible so that when I return, we can leave Borderville for good. We'll head whichever direction the mapmaker recommends. I'll need a hundred gyri."

"A hundred gyri?" Ruther repeated, standing up. "That's half our earnings! James and I plan to play at the high stakes tables. We need more than a hundred to do that."

"Then it sets you back a few days!" Henry shouted, all trace of his phony smile gone. "So what? Isabelle is the property of the Emperor of Neverak. Quit worrying about a little bit of money!"

Ruther sat down. "You're right, Henry. I apologize."

"How much money do you think you can earn during my absence, assuming I'm gone for at least two weeks?"

"Our goal is to earn a thousand gyri," James answered. "We might make more if you'll be gone that long."

"As soon as I return," Henry said, "we leave Borderville. So make certain we have enough money."

Maggie couldn't stay silent any longer. "I'm going with you, Henry."

"No, you're needed here," Henry shot back.

Maggie let out a sardonic laugh. "For what? Watching Thirsty cook and clean? Listening to Ruther and James's bragging about cheating others out of their money?"

"I need to do this alone."

"And I need to come with you."

Henry shrugged. "Okay, okay. Fine. But you had better be ready to go first thing tomorrow, or . . ."

Maggie had hoped that resting in Borderville from their long journey would help her calm and organize her mind. But the opposite was happening. Her world was slowly unraveling like a tapestry with its threads pulled every which way. Henry was lying about bloodstains, James was cheating and stealing, Thirsty was constantly interfering with—well, everything. Maggie missed Henry's leadership, Isabelle's quiet strength, and most of all, James's unflinching morality. Traveling had been, ironically, her only constant.

At dawn the next morning Maggie and Henry said their good-byes to James and Ruther and headed to the market for supplies. Everything happened so quickly that it surprised Maggie when, taking the main road south, Borderville was slowly disappearing behind them. Maggie rode Fury while Henry took Quicken. She trailed Henry for a time, watching to see how well he rode with his bad arm.

Finally he turned to her and said, "I'm not going to fall off my horse, Maggie. You can relax."

The road took them through a prairie of tall grass, brown and somewhat dry, bent under their own weight. It was too early in spring for flowers. To the west, a dark line on the horizon marked the tree line of the Iron Forest. The sooner it disappeared the better, in her opinion.

"Would you ever go back in there?" she asked Henry.

He stared off to the west, and his face paled a little. He shook his head. "If it meant the difference between finding Isabelle and not, then yes. Otherwise I would prefer to find a different route."

Maggie didn't think she could go back in the Iron Forest for any reason. "Is that why you burned the carriage? Because of what you heard in the pass?"

A cold gust of wind blew across the road, almost spilling Henry's hat off his head. He caught it, but almost fell off his horse in the process. "Can we talk about something else?"

"Why can't we talk about it? Aren't you curious about what happened in there? The hands that came out of the dark?"

Henry looked at her with a puzzled expression. "What hands?"

"The hands, Henry . . . The hands that grabbed you, Ruther, and James. They were monstrous things."

Henry's confusion only grew. "I didn't see any hands. I didn't see anything. It felt like the air itself grabbed me. Truthfully, Maggie, I thought I was a dead man."

Again, Maggie saw the image of Henry drowning in a stone basin. "I saw hands attack you. Then another pair reached out and helped you."

"And then you passed out for several hours. We were all exhausted, scared . . . even delusional."

Maggie felt her face flush. "Are you saying I imagined it?"

"I don't know. I don't know what happened. It was an awful experience, Maggie. One I don't want to repeat."

"No. Listen, Henry, that wasn't all I saw. After we escaped, I didn't pass out—"

"You did," Henry insisted. "We couldn't wake you."

"I went somewhere! A place of fog and stones and there were two voices." When she saw Henry's grin, she said, "I know it sounds like madness, but it's true. Someone spoke to me about how everything has a cost and that there is a color called *lyrial*—"

"Lyrial," Henry repeated. "I've heard that before. I think Isabelle had a friend named Lyrial. Or was it Laurielle . . ."

"Henry . . ."

"Maggie, I promise you didn't go anywhere. You were there the whole time. I checked on you through the holes torn into the carriage."

Maggie was about to retort, but Henry made a good point. What if she had simply passed out and had a lucid dream? It made more sense than thinking she had magically appeared in some foreign, foggy place. But it had been so clear, all of it: the voices, the fog, the stones, and the visions. All four visions. She remembered them perfectly. Almost too perfectly. Dreams weren't like that, were they?

Late that evening, Maggie set up her bed underneath the darkening sky. The air was cool, with a gentle wind. After a light dinner, she and Henry lay side by side under their own blankets, staring up at the stars that dotted the darkness like dazzling diamonds.

As a young girl, something about the sky's vastness had made her anxious. Her mind couldn't fathom such a large, mysterious thing. Now, as a young woman who had traveled hundreds of miles and faced real terror, the secrets of the stars didn't seem so daunting. They mesmerized her.

A shooting star flashed brightly for the briefest of moments. Its color caught her eye—it was lyrial. "Did you see that?" she asked Henry.

"Hm?" Henry's response told her he'd either been asleep or nearly so.

"That star. The color. You didn't see it?"

This time all she got from him was a soft snore. Minutes later, he whimpered. Maggie called out, but he didn't answer.

"Please," he said with a small sob, "*please.* I'm so sorry, Isabelle."

His pleas and whimpers continued for a long time. Even when they stopped, his breaths came in ragged gasps. Maggie had been so wrapped up in her own troubles—her own anger—that she hadn't given much thought to what her brother must be experiencing, how hard it must be for him to put on a brave face day after day.

She reached over and brushed his hair. He twitched in response. "Isabelle," he muttered, "I'm sorry."

Maggie rested a hand on his shoulder. "I wish I could take away your pain," she whispered. "I wish I could help."

The fingers resting on his skin grew hot, then started to pulse. The heat spread to her palm and wrist, coursing through her in rapid waves. As it went up her arm, the sensation began to frighten her, and she tried to pull her hand away. It would not budge. Somehow her skin was attached to Henry's. No matter how hard she tried to remove her fingers, they remained bonded to him.

When the heat finally reached her chest, the pulsing stopped and the bond between them broke. Maggie's heart thudded rapidly; her lungs gasped as though she'd run a race. All at once a profound sense of sadness overwhelmed her. It made her heart ache and her chest constrict so tightly that she moaned in pain. Her vision darkened, and she clutched at the ground.

"Henry," she said in a wheezing, small voice. It was all the sound she could manage to make. "What's happening to me?"

The loss of Isabelle filled her thoughts like a black poison. A terrible dread fell over her, convincing her that happiness would never be familiar to her again. She was a prisoner of despair, barred from anything sweet or wonderful or good. Tears dripped from her eyes. Guilt, depression, and loneliness filled her. She grabbed at her chest as it grew tight and cold.

Next to her, Henry sighed and laughed at something in his dreams. Maggie reached a trembling hand toward her brother and tried to rouse him. He mumbled and tossed about, but continued to sleep.

"What is wrong with me, Henry?" she whispered.

Four words appeared in her mind. *Everything has a cost.*

A hooded man waited for her in her dreams. His hand out-stretched, he pointed at her heart. His long, dirty fingernails kept perfectly still until he crooked one finger, summoning her nearer. She tried to escape, but digging her boots into the ground did not help. She rose from the ground, and as she hovered in the air before him like a leaf, she stared into the black depths under his hood and saw nothing but two glowing eyes and the hint of a face covered in scars. She dared not speak. When he opened his mouth, a thick stench of decay filled her nostrils.

I still wait for you, Margaret.

SIXTEEN
A Thief in the Night

Maggie woke the next morning with a terrible headache. Her body protested as she got up to fix breakfast. Bitter feelings coursed through her as she contemplated having to cook for her brother. A smell greeted her, something savory. Salted pork. Henry sat over the fire cooking, a subtle grin on his face.

"Morning, sunshine."

Maggie grunted. Her eyelids felt fat and heavy. She wanted to go back to sleep.

"Hungry?"

"I can't remember the last time you cooked."

Henry laughed. "I know. What's come over me? I woke up this morning feeling better than I've been in weeks. I thought to myself, 'I bet Maggie would love it if someone else made breakfast besides her.'" He gave her the first plate of food, which helped improve her mood only a little. Why she felt so glum, she didn't know. "I had the strangest dream last night. Would you like to hear about it?"

Maggie shrugged and blew on her food to cool it. "I guess."

"Oh . . ." Henry's face fell a little. "If you don't, just say so."

"Fine," she muttered through a mouth full of food. "I don't want to hear about it."

The rest of breakfast passed in silence. Dark clouds gathered in the sky like clusters of black grapes. Maggie helped Henry clean the cookware only because she knew he couldn't with his lame arm. Yet all she thought about while she scrubbed was how he should do it since he had cooked the meal. After all, she'd always cleaned up after cooking the meals.

"Maggie, you're not yourself," Henry commented. "What's going on?"

"What's going on is I don't want to talk!" The words came out like acid from a Gaddanian spitting flower.

Henry nodded kindly. She both hated and envied how impervious he seemed to her words. Last night he had been so forlorn, he'd wept in his sleep, now . . .

Cost.

"Today we're headed straight south until we reach a bridge over Deep River. Then we take a southeastern road for the rest of the day. Should make good time if we keep a steady pace and the rain doesn't slow us down."

"Think you can manage that with your arm?" Maggie asked bitterly.

Henry chuckled as though she had meant it as a friendly tease. "I wonder how Ruther and James are faring today. Can you imagine if they actually earn a thousand gyri? That would be astounding. We'd have as much money as we ever had. Can you imagine, Maggie?"

She said nothing.

"Maggie?" Henry asked. "Are you listening to me?"

"No."

Henry didn't say another word until nightfall. Though the rain continued to threaten, and the sky grew ever darker, no drops fell from the sky. Maggie's thoughts weren't on the weather, but on everything wrong in her life. She could not summon a single happy thought into existence. "What is wrong with me?" she asked herself more than once.

When they finally stopped for the night, Henry offered to cook dinner.

"Do you think I'm helpless?" Maggie asked him.

"I'm trying to help. I haven't been the kindest person since—since everything happened—but today I finally feel . . . hope, happiness. I feel like the sun is finally shining."

"All right," Maggie answered, "I heard you. You're happy. Great."

As they ate dinner, he tried speaking to her again. "How's the food?"

Maggie only shrugged.

"Will you please stop ignoring me?" He reached for her hand until she pulled hers out of reach. "I don't want to travel like this."

"Don't you dare talk about ignoring people! You hardly spoke to me inside the Iron Pass. You refused to make any more decisions for the group. You've been almost worthless since the battle! No, you were worthless even before that. Against those Elite soldiers, I wielded a frying pan better than you did your sword. It amazes me that you didn't end up stabbing me or Isabelle, you were so pathetic."

Henry stared at her with a stunned expression. He looked so stupid that she picked up a bit of potato from her plate and hurled it at his face. It hit his forehead with a wet slap and stuck there until Henry reached up and threw it into the flames. His eyes blazed bright with fury as the potato sizzled and popped. Maggie sat and met Henry's gaze with her own.

"Maggie, I want you to take that back and apologize."

The first raindrop fell from the sky, landing squarely on Maggie's nose. She looked up as more fat raindrops hit her face and arms. Henry didn't seem to care about the rain. He was waiting for Maggie to say the words he'd requested.

Maggie opened her mouth to say them. He deserved to hear them. She'd been cruel to him all day. Something had happened last night when she touched him, something she couldn't explain. As her brother's face grew wet from the rain, it reminded her of her vision of him drowning.

Choose not to pursue this—choose not to believe—and none of the things you witnessed will happen.

Maggie couldn't—*wouldn't*—admit her suspicions. If she said nothing, it wouldn't be true. Still Henry waited for her apology. Without a word she stood, hopped onto Quicken, and rode off, not giving her brother a backward glance. He shouted after her and ran for Fury, but Maggie had a head start, pushing Quicken hard despite the poor condition of the road. Quicken was the faster horse and put plenty of distance between Maggie and her brother.

The water continued to fall, soaking her cloak, but not getting through to the pack she wore underneath. She wanted to scream, she wanted to rage, but what good would it do? Her frustration mounted only to more tears that she couldn't feel on her cold, damp cheeks.

Hours passed before the rain let up. Maggie's hair hung in sheets over her face, and she struggled to keep her eyes open. Atolas's three moons were small and dim behind the clouds. She couldn't see far ahead, but she spotted a small hill where the ground might be less muddy at the top. It took some effort to start a small fire with the mostly-dry wood stowed in the horse pack, but once it was crackling and warm, her spirits rose. She spread her blanket out near the fire and curled up inside it. Before falling asleep, her last thoughts were of Henry, wishing she'd never tampered with his emotions.

The sound of movement in the mud and grass below the small hill woke her. "Henry?" It was too dark to see properly but she thought she saw him rummaging through her packs hanging from low branches at the bottom of the hill near Quicken. She stood and started down the hill to where Quicken was tied to the tree. "Henry, what are you doing?"

As his head jerked in her direction, he hastened his movements, throwing things out of the bag onto the wet ground. She looked closer at the dark figure and her pace slowed. It was too short to be Henry. She noted a black cloth tied around the lower part of his face.

"Thief!" she screamed. "Get out of here!"

The thief didn't run, instead he turned and crouched. A large dagger appeared in his left hand. In his right hand, he carried the sack of gold he'd just pulled from the horse pack; it contained the one hundred gyri Maggie and Henry needed to purchase the maps. "If you follow me, I'll kill you," he said in an odd, whiny voice that sounded as though he had too much air in his nose.

The thief turned to mount his horse, but Maggie grabbed his leg and pulled him to the ground. He swiped at her with his knife as he fell, but only the back of his hand connected with her head. The blow was hard enough that it knocked her into the mud. Next to her, the knife hit the dirt with a soft thud. Both she and the thief scrambled to get it. He pinned her down just before her fingers could brush the handle of the weapon.

The thief's breath blew across Maggie's neck, hot and pungent. She grunted as she flung her arm out a second time to grab the knife. The thief reached out, too, and as he did so, gave Maggie enough room to wiggle out from under him. Two hands grabbed the dagger; one belonged to Maggie, the other to the thief. Maggie tried to grab it with her other hand, but the thief locked his spare arm around hers. Slowly he wrenched the knife from her grip. Maggie used all her strength to maintain her hold on the handle, but she couldn't match her adversary.

"*HENRY, HELP!*" she screamed.

With his dagger firmly in hand, the thief put the blade to Maggie's throat and twisted her around by her hair until she lay on her back. Maggie never stopped fighting. She pushed the hand with the knife away, holding it back while scratching at his face with her other hand. In the process, she pulled down the black handkerchief, exposing his nose and mouth.

His upper lip looked as though it had been cleaved in half, a scar extending up to his nostril. His nose hung abnormally crooked on his face. Maggie's obvious disgust made him angrier. He brought his arm back beyond Maggie's reach, then brought it down again to stab her. Maggie raised her hand to block him. Incredible pain blossomed as the knife struck her hand. The sound of a galloping horse interrupted their scuffle. Maggie screamed again. The thief paused to look up, and Maggie jammed her fingernails into his eyes as a hot wet sensation trickled down her arm. Hissing in pain, the thief scurried away with the sack of coins.

The thief mounted his horse and spurred it on. Seconds later, Henry and Fury came into view. Maggie jabbed a blood-soaked finger in the direction of the thief. "He's got our money!"

The masked man tried to get away, but was not quick enough to escape Henry. When Henry and Fury caught up to the assailant, Henry rode close, wrapped his good arm around the thief, and drove both of them to the ground. Henry landed on the thief, whose head hit the ground first with a nasty crunch. For about twenty seconds, Maggie heard nothing from their direction except breathing, then came the jingling of coins. Henry walked toward her, limping, the sack of coins in his hand. He panted for breath and rubbed his right leg. Then he sat down next to Maggie.

"I—I think he's dead. He started to—to shake really fast. Then he stopped. I think he stopped breathing."

Maggie held up her hand so she could see it better. The exquisite pain in her hand brought tears to her eyes. "There's something wrong with my hand, but I can't see it very well."

"Does it hurt?"

"Yes—it's throbbing—" She gasped and clenched her teeth as a fresh wave of agony washed over her hand and up her arm.

"Let's get back to the fire and look at it."

Maggie cradled her left arm in her right. Her legs ached as they limped together up the hill back to her camp. Something was wrong, her hand felt too small. She dreaded what she would see in the firelight. When she reached the top of the hill, she extended her hand outward and saw the damage: her smallest left finger had been completely severed. Blood covered her hands, arms, and dress.

"No," she sobbed. "Please no. My hand! Henry, my hand!"

Henry wrapped his arm around her. "It's all right. It's going to be all right."

"I can fix it," she said. "I can make it better!"

"Maggie, it's gone."

"I can fix it!" she shrieked. "I fixed you. I took your sickness away from you. I—I think I fixed Ruther. I can do it!"

"Maggie, you're talking madness. You can't."

"I *can*!" A black rage filled her, and she broke away from her brother. Sprinting back down the hill, she nearly lost her balance more than once. She returned to the spot where the thief had attacked her and felt around in the wet grass for the missing finger. Unable to find it, she held her left hand and said, "I wish I could fix my finger."

Nothing happened. There was no bonding, no heat, no pulses. Just more bleeding.

"I need to find it!" she sobbed. "Help me!"

Henry grabbed her and tried to her hug her, but she wrenched away.

"Where were you?" she yelled. "This is your fault! You should have come after me! Why didn't you?"

"I'm sorry. I tried to follow you in the dark. I tried."

Maggie pounded her fists on his chest. "I hate you!"

Henry hugged her again and cried with her. "It's all right."

"I hate you," she moaned. And as he held her, she felt his heart beating and his own tears mixing with hers. "I'm sorry, Henry. I'm sorry. Forgive me." She wiped her face, but the tears hadn't stopped. "I don't hate you."

"I know, Maggie."

"Why is this happening to us? What did we do to bring this on ourselves?"

Henry didn't answer. His chest rose and fell rapidly as he shared her emotions. When they broke apart, he opened his own pack and took out supplies to clean and dress her wound. After he finished, Maggie surveyed his work. It didn't seem real, even when looking at the wrapped hand. Henry went off in the darkness. A little while later, he returned with her missing finger wrapped in a handkerchief. "Should we bury it? It just doesn't seem right to leave it laying on the ground."

Maggie looked at it for a long moment. "I guess we could."

Using the thief's dagger, Henry dug a modest hole in the hilltop near the fire. With a surprising amount of respect, he laid Maggie's finger in the ground and covered it, patting the dirt until it was smooth. Then he found a large flat stone and carved in shaky, awkward letters:

Here rests the little finger of Maggie Vestin

When Henry showed it to her, she laughed and cried. It wasn't really funny, but the injury could have been much worse. Maggie knew she would manage without her finger just fine. Henry had not only lost his fiancée, but also the use of his right arm.

With no desire to rest, they packed up and rode onward. Dawn broke a few hours later, bringing with it clearer skies and a fresh scent in the air. Cloudless skies, greening grasses, and warm breezes greeted them as they set out on the last half of their journey. The aching in Maggie's finger grew steadily throughout the day until the pain became nearly unbearable. Changing the bandage and cleaning it again did little to help.

Though she tried to hide the agony, Henry knew she was suffering. He rode beside her and talked to her to keep her mind off her hand. She thought about telling him about the strange occurrence where her skin had bonded to him and she'd helped him heal from his despair, but she couldn't find words to explain it. She didn't understand it herself. Then the pain became so overwhelming that she didn't want to speak at all.

"It's going to hurt worse before it gets better," Henry commented in a soothing tone.

Maggie didn't know if she could handle a second day of such torture. Sometimes it got so bad that she would have cut off her whole hand if that would relieve the agony. Those two days passed not in hours or minutes, but eternal seconds of gritted teeth, salty tears, and silent prayers for strength. Henry helped all he could, doing whatever it took to keep her mind occupied. On the night after the second day, Maggie dreamed of the place with colorful stones and fog. A dark voice laughed at her, taunting her for the missing finger. But the older man was there, too. He spoke to her from the white fog. His words brought comfort to her.

"You see, Margaret? Everything has a cost. You took the pain from your brother and bore his grief. You made his pain yours. You became its owner. Be careful what you take from others, because some people are better equipped to deal with their own pain. Learn the rules before you wield the gift."

SEVENTEEN

The Death Pact

Emperor Ivan Krallick had few complaints these days. His health had never been better; he had killed the carpenter; and Isabelle was now a full month into her cleansing. According to reports from Kayla and Cecilia, currently his favored concubines, Miss Oslan's spirits were steadily improving as she settled into her new life. The Emperor's plans for the invasion of Blithmore moved forward, led by General Attikus, who continued the charade of hunting the bandits.

Emperor Krallick listened as two noblemen disputed land ownership in the new town the Emperor planned to build near the Iron Forest when his chamberlain interrupted, as previously planned, with the Emperor's post. One envelope in particular caught his eye, and he sat up with sudden interest. It was dark yellow with a black seal, the colors of Old Avalon.

"Excuse me, gentlemen," he said, leaving the throne room for privacy. As he closed the door behind him, he told the chamberlain, "In five minutes go back in, pick one of the noblemen, and tell him I have ruled in his favor. Tell the other that the matter is closed."

"Which one shall I choose, Your Majesty?"

"Whichever I most desire to owe me a favor. Do not make me repeat myself."

"Yes, Your Majesty." The chamberlain excused himself as the Emperor opened his letter.

Emperor Krallick,

Much has changed since our last correspondence. One week ago, the armies of Old Avalon dealt a crushing strike to the slave fighters, forcing them out of hiding and scattering them beyond our borders into the Farmlands and Pappalon. With the rebel leaders gone, the fervor of the slaves has all but vanished. Order is being restored to our country. Public executions of the prisoners will serve as warning for any imprudent thinkers. Rather than pursuing these insurrectionists to the ends of Atolas, we now turn our attention westward to Blithmore. I told you in my last letter that your patience with this matter will pay us large dividends, and I have not failed. You will see my gratitude when my armies arrive by ship and march with yours to conquer King Germaine's lands.

Let us construct a new timetable by which we will achieve our goals. As for Lord Tippetts, while he assures me that he is still my ally, he does not wish to join the forces of the United Farmlands to our endeavor. He does not understand ambition or that the nations of Atolas stand at a crossroads. I align myself and my forces with yours and trust the intelligence that you and your spies have gathered regarding tactics. When you have made your plans, send General Derkop to me, and my armies will hasten to join yours. Quelling the slave rebellion has only whetted our appetite for conquest. I await your general's arrival.

Baron Verkozy, Sovereign Lord of Old Avalon

"Such a dramatic man," the Emperor muttered to himself as he reentered the throne room and sat, deep in thought.

The Emperor's chamberlain entered again. "Your Majesty, the Seer has arrived."

The Emperor had not seen the Seer since the vile magician had visited him in his southern mansion. On that day, he had warned the Emperor that two obstacles stood in the way of his plans to conquer Blithmore, but that Emperor Krallick need only remove one or the other to guarantee Neverak's victory. One of those obstacles had been separating Isabelle and Henry, which the Emperor had accomplished the day he slew the carpenter. If the Seer's prophecy proved correct, nothing could prevent him from expanding Neverak's borders southward. After months of silence, Emperor Krallick had received a letter from the Seer a week previously, begging an audience. Despite his revulsion, the Emperor did not deny the request, and a letter was sent with an appointed date and time.

"He has brought four guests with him, Your Majesty," the chamberlain continued. "Shall I show them in?"

"No," the Emperor of Neverak answered. "Set some guardsmen around the room to watch them. And I want them armed and ready in case the Seer has hatched some foul plot. I want only to see the magician."

The chamberlain bowed and left. The Emperor shifted his weight uncomfortably on the throne as the Seer entered. As he approached, the Emperor noted that he did not seem to be walking but gliding toward the throne. He wore a shimmering green robe which dragged along the floor, far more impressive than the rags he'd worn on his last visit. The same chain bearing a chalk-white stone hung about his neck. His robe had a hood which covered his head and face, leaving only two pale blue lights shining from his eyes for the Emperor to gaze upon.

The torches in the throne room flickered and dimmed. A chill settled upon Emperor Krallick, raising goosebumps and causing him to shiver ever so slightly. He hated the effect the Seer had on him, involuntary though it was. The thought of killing him crossed his mind, and he entertained it longer than he knew he ought.

"Emperor Krallick," the Seer announced in his light, dancing tone. "How I appreciate the audience you have granted me. I promise to make it worth your time."

"Speak, Seer. You have my ear."

From inside his shining emerald robe, the Seer revealed his hands. His skin was pale as the white stone hanging over his breast, the nails as long and filthy as ever. When he interlocked his fingers, the nails dug into the flesh of his hands. The light that shone from his eyes changed from blue to red. "Word has reached me that you captured a woman—a woman from Blithmore. She resides here now as your slave."

Emperor Krallick narrowed his eyes at the Seer. "It troubles me that you are intimately aware of my affairs. They do not concern you."

"I beg to differ, my Emperor. I am tied to the prophecy which I gave you months ago. To peer into the future . . . there is a cost, and I paid it. Now I have come to warn you that the obstacles you seek to remove still exist."

"That's impossible," the Emperor said. "The girl is in my tower with the other concubines. Her betrothed died on the very spot where you stand. I could summon her and she would confirm every detail."

"Both obstacles exist," the Seer continued in his annoying sing-song tone. "While it is true you captured a woman who traveled with the carpenter, I peered into her eyes from afar. She is not the one. You did not separate him from the woman who endangers your plans."

Emperor Krallick gripped the armrests of his throne and leaned forward. "The sister?"

The Seer lifted one finger. "*Is* there a sister?" Despite his response, the Emperor could tell that the Seer knew the truth.

Seething rage flooded the veins of the Emperor. "But the carpenter is still dead! I fulfilled the terms of the prophecy."

The Seer shook his head. Though the Emperor could not see the magician's hideous face, he knew if he pulled back the hood of the robe, he would find a smile.

"If I did kill the wrong man, why not tell me weeks ago? Why come to me now?"

"It was not known to me until I saw her the first night she arrived. I studied her well, my Emperor, although from afar. She is not the one. The man you killed was not the carpenter. The threat still exists."

The Emperor pounded his fist into the golden throne. "No! I killed the carpenter. It was the same man. My soldiers verified it. He asked to kiss her just before I cleaved his head from his neck. She wept as I did it!"

"You are mistaken."

"Not I. You—you are the one who is mistaken!"

The Seer took a step back and made a gesture of peace with his hands. "Perhaps I am. But it costs you nothing to consider the possibility that the wretch you killed only looked like the carpenter. Is this not possible?"

Emperor Krallick pondered the question. Certainly it was possible, however unlikely. Then he shook his head. "No, no, that man was the carpenter. He spoke like him, had his courage, his face. I know what this is! This is a trick."

"You paid me for a service—to reveal to you events that may come to pass. I am only here to help you fulfill them. The obstacles still stand."

"Curse you, Seer! This is your fault. You gave me no reason to believe the woman was anyone but his betrothed. Every word you spoke implied that separating him from Isabelle was the action I needed to take. I could have had the sister killed as easily as an ant."

Laughter came from within the hood. The eyes changed to bright golden spots that flickered each time his laugh peaked. "Curse me? Curse *me*?" The laughter turned into howling. The torches dimmed to the point of extinction. A few completely died, leaving only vines of smoke curling toward the ceiling. "Curse *me*? My Emperor, can you not see that I am already beyond cursed?"

"Are you trying to intimidate me?"

"The thought never crossed my mind. When one walks the Path, emotions can be difficult to control. Forgive my outburst, great Emperor."

The Emperor did not forgive it. Instead, he used the insult to remind himself how lethal the Seer could be and how dangerous it was to allow him so near the throne. To defeat a man or woman who walked the Path took not strength or steel, but intellect and heart. Attikus had taught him this years ago, but Emperor Krallick had never tested himself against one who walked the Path . . . nor did he wish to now.

"Since you have brought me bitter news," the Emperor said, "perhaps you wish to restore yourself to my good graces. Though I do not believe the news you bear, let me presume for a moment that you are correct—that the carpenter lives. How shall I rectify your error?"

"The sister will not be so easy to kill." The lights in the Seer's eyes changed from gold to gray. "Not now. She has seen . . . things. Her power is growing."

"Have you any counsel for me?"

"Your wisdom serves you well. I indeed have counsel for you. More than that, in fact—I have bounty hunters."

The Emperor recalled the chamberlain telling him that four people had accompanied the Seer to the palace. He had assumed these four were acolytes, younger pupils learning to walk the Path of Shadow like the Seer. "Bring them in," he ordered the chamberlain.

"If I may, my Emperor," the Seer said, "I would also suggest ordering five chairs and a table to be brought in for our use. I will not require a chair."

The Emperor nodded at the chamberlain, a silent order that the

Seer's request be fulfilled. One by one the bounty hunters entered the throne room, but stayed out of earshot at a gesture from the Seer. None of them looked at ease. The chairs and table followed quickly. The Emperor took his seat first at the head of the table, his chair higher than the rest.

"Using a combination of my own powerful methods of persuasion," the Seer explained as he stood just behind and to the right of the Emperor, "and your intricate network of spies, prisoners, and informants, I have gathered the best hunters both east and west of the Iron Forest."

"How did you happen to use *my* network?" the Emperor asked.

"Those who walk the Path of Shadow are not strangers to the criminal underworld," the Seer answered. "Your network and mine share similar branches. To extend my reach through yours was not difficult. My prescience told me weeks ago that these lowlifes would be needed, though for what purpose I knew not. Trusting that sense as I would my eyes, I began the work of gathering them together. Allow me to introduce them."

The Emperor merely curled his lip, perturbed at the audacity of the Seer.

"Bonesy," the Seer called, beckoning the first forward.

The bounty hunter took the seat at the table across from the Emperor. She was a ghastly, skeletal woman who wore her sickly yellow hair in an odd, twisted arrangement. Her masculine clothes looked clean, but worn. Her boots were as black as death, with silver points on the toes that could gut someone if she kicked them in the stomach. "Bonesy's real name is unknown to any living creature. Born in Old Avalon, her father began training her to hunt bounty when she was five."

"The next man is Ivory," the Seer reported, still using his maddening sing-song tone. White teeth, white shirt, white pants, and white hair. His eyes shone a pale red, and his skin was a soft pink. Ivory was an albino, but a sharply dressed one. "From Blithmore, a former Guardsman."

"Can he be trusted?" the Emperor muttered to the Seer.

"I would not have contacted him otherwise."

Ivory came forward and took his seat at the table.

"Kelric is another Blithmorian," the Seer told the Emperor. "A nasty, brutal bounty hunter with a reputation that precedes him among all the criminal underground. Rumors claim this man's methods are more diabolical than those he is paid to capture."

Emperor Krallick cared nothing about this. All that mattered was the man's effectiveness in accomplishing his designs. The man's shrewd, tomcat-like eyes glanced around the room, surveying everything, including his fellow bounty hunters. Kelric seemed to recognize Ivory, but not Bonesy.

"The last man is named Skuller. Whether he is from Neverak or Blithmore, no one knows. He has used several aliases over the years: Eugene Gunter, Frederick Koffee, and—"

"Theodore Trolley," the Emperor finished. "I know him well. He was a smuggler then, and helped me and several other nobles procure many fine slaves from Blithmore, New Avalon, even Panautica."

"It was a pleasure serving you, my Emperor," Trolley said.

"Why you? How does a smuggler become a bounty hunter? I thought you were dead."

"I left the smuggling business more than two years ago after I was arrested in Northern Blithmore by the King's Guard."

The Seer's eyes changed to a bright yellow as he pulled his hands back into his sleeves and folded his arms. As the four guests settled into their seats, the Emperor's footmen brought in trays of drink and refreshment. Goblets and plates were passed around. The Emperor stared at the hands of the bounty hunters, increasingly disgusted by the unwashed filth under their fingernails and in the creases of their skin. He took out his gloves and slid them on, instantly feeling much more at ease.

"I believe you all know the purpose of our meeting," the Seer said.

Four different heads nodded. Emperor Ivan took a long draught of his wine. The Seer turned to him. "Only the great Emperor knows about the movements of the Blithmore Bandits. His network of spies has no equal. I shall defer to him to inform us of his latest reports."

Emperor Krallick set down his goblet. "Ten weeks ago the five so-called Blithmore Bandits reached the Iron Pass. Two were captured and brought to me. Almost three weeks later, my spy at the West Pappalon Gate sent me word that *four* travelers, three males and a female, entered the borders of Pappalon. This information was inconsistent with what we had assumed for months: that the band of criminals was composed of five travelers, not six.

"However," the Emperor continued, "we know this was their party because three of them matched the descriptions of the guardsman, James Oslan; the journeyman, Brandol; and the sister, Margaret Vestin."

"You've had it all wrong for months, Emperor," Kelric announced in a gruff, surly voice.

"Pardon me?" the Emperor said.

"The group was six from the beginning. The tall blond man who attacked you at the Glimmering Fountain was a storyteller wearing a wig, not the journeyman. The storyteller is the sixth member of the party. His name is Ruther. He's a fat, lazy, stupid slob. All along there was six: the two Vestins, the two Oslans, the storyteller, and the journeyman."

Emperor Krallick's lips tightened at the thought of a bounty hunter knowing more than all his spies.

"Naturally, after the two were captured, you were left with four. Your arithmetic problem has been solved."

"I have to know how you came by this information."

"I ran into them bandits in Fenley. Didn't recognize them at the time because their descriptions hadn't been posted yet. But I was already hunting 'em. Can't say I expected 'em to be in a drinking hole in Fenley with a writ of passage, neither. But once I dug into the matter, I realized I'd let 'em slip through my fingers. Won't happen again."

"Of course not."

"But to my point . . . the storyteller is a tall, fat, red-headed monkey. I'll kill him myself if I get the chance."

"You will have use of my stables to get yourselves to Pappalon as quickly as possible. You should be able to make the trip in three weeks. Once you reach the pass, my soldiers will await you with fresh, strong horses for your journey. The horses are yours. A gift of faith, of course. I expect regular reports to keep me updated on your progress. Use my well-placed spies in other countries. I assume you each have resources as well. Find the four Blithmore Bandits. Today I was informed that it is possible, however unlikely, that Henry Vestin may still be alive and among the group. If this is true, he must be dealt with."

"You want him brought to you?" Trolley asked. "Alive?"

The Emperor's gaze met Trolley's. An understanding passed between them. "Kill him. Kill them all. Especially Vestin and his sister. I want heads."

Ivory leaned forward. "The reward?"

"Of course. I forgot to mention the most important part. One thousand crowns per head." He looked into each of their eyes. "Are we agreed?"

Each of them stated their agreement to the proposition, but the Emperor wasn't satisfied. He needed something more, some way to be certain they would complete their task. Everything rested on the life of one girl; to put all his ambition into the hands of four bounty hunters would be an incredible folly.

"I may have forgotten to mention one other thing." He paused to suppress a smile. "Since we have the Seer here, each of you will enter into a death pact with me."

All four bounty hunters stirred uncomfortably in their seats at the Emperor's request.

"The oath will be administered and sealed by the Seer. If any of you object, you may leave at once."

Ivory looked like he wanted to do just that, but the other three didn't budge. Ivory glanced at them, then at the Seer, and kept his objections to himself. Satisfied that no one planned to refuse, Emperor Krallick turned to the Seer. "Proceed with the ceremony."

"The lives of the four bandits will be tied to yours," the Seer said. "You shall not escape the burden of the pact until their lives are extinguished." He held up his loathsome hands, quaking with power, and made signs of his magic in the air, then stood and placed his hands on each hunter's shoulders. Then he stood behind the Emperor and placed his hands on both of Ivan Krallick's shoulders. The Emperor's flesh recoiled at the touch and a ice-cold chill ran through his body.

The Seer's illuminated eyes locked on the bounty hunters and asked each for their name. After they each answered, he called them by name and said, "Do you understand what the Emperor has commanded you to do?" Then he waited for their answers. "Do you swear on your life to accomplish it?" Again each answer came in the affirmative. "And if you should fail or abandon the search, what should you expect?"

Ivory was first. "Death shall pursue me until I am vanquished."

Then came Kelric. "Death shall pursue me until I am vanquished."

And next, Skuller answered, "Death shall pursue me until I am vanquished."

The Emperor turned to Bonesy, who did not speak. She nodded to the Seer and the Emperor. It was good enough to be binding. The Seer took his hands from the Emperor's shoulders and addressed him. "They have all taken the oath. If you, Emperor Ivan Krallick the Third, should fail to complete your end of the agreement, what shall be the punishment?"

"Death shall pursue me until I am vanquished," said the Emperor as he took the glove off of his right hand.

"Your palm." The Seer accepted Emperor Krallick's hand in his own. Contact with the Seer's skin was almost unbearable for the Emperor, but he gritted his teeth and closed his eyes as the Seer drew a small blade across his palm. With a swift, steady stroke, he cut the Emperor's skin and collected his blood in a small glass vial.

With a twitch of his eyebrows, the Emperor gestured to his chamberlain to make certain the vial of blood was not kept by the Seer. One by one, the magician placed a drop of the Emperor's blood on the head of each bounty hunter. "By this oath, I bind you to one another. May darkness enshroud you in your efforts and conceal you until you are ready to strike."

Finished, the Seer's hands disappeared into the folds of his robes with a clinking sound. The chamberlain approached him and requested the vial of the Emperor's blood. His eyes now glowing fire red, the Seer's hands reemerged with the glass container. The Emperor noted the reluctance with which the Seer relinquished his prize.

Without another word, the Seer left the room. Emperor Krallick signaled a footman who brought a clean napkin which the Emperor wrapped awkwardly around his wounded hand. He addressed the hunters: "As I said before, find the bandits, kill them, and bring me their heads. I will send letters with you detailing your mission and demanding assistance from anyone you find who is loyal to me. Go swiftly."

In less than a minute, the room was empty save for the Emperor and his chamberlain, who brought bandages and hot water to clean and dress the Emperor's hand. "Your Majesty, General Derkop is here."

"Show him in."

Dressed in his black and red Neverak uniform, the general whose place Attikus had taken entered the throne room. Emperor Krallick had reassumed his place on the throne. Behind Derkop, several footmen also appeared to clear away the table and chairs. General Derkop approached the throne with wariness, no doubt still unsure why he had been removed from command and his position given to his predecessor. His mannerisms amused the Emperor.

"General Derkop, thank you for so promptly answering my summons. I am pleased with the way you've conducted my affairs on the northern border. General Attikus tells me that security has never been tighter in that region. I commend you."

Derkop's graying mustache twitched at the compliment. His eyes stayed fixed to the floor. Clearly he still operated under the assumption that his demotion from General Superior was due to some failure on his part. The Emperor had no desire to correct this so long as it drove the general to excel at his duties. "Thank you, Your Majesty. I am always at your service."

"Your commitment to my service is why I have summoned you. My plans for the future of Neverak include you, General. It is time you received a new assignment."

"I am yours to command, my Lord."

"I am sending you to Old Avalon." This statement surprised the general. The Emperor also noted disappointment. "Come now, Derkop. Wait until you know my purpose before making a judgment. Baron Verkozy and I are planning a joint invasion of Blithmore. Your duty will be to meet with the Baron and prepare his armies for the invasion. You will take our strategies with you and counsel the officers who lead the Baron's forces. You will report back regularly to me."

"Invasion?" Derkop looked as though the Emperor had said one of the moons had fallen from the sky. "My lord, when is this to take place?"

"When we are ready, but the time isn't far. Go make your preparations. Choose two lieutenants to take with you. You depart first thing tomorrow."

General Derkop saluted Emperor Krallick, who returned the gesture and watched him leave. Then the Emperor motioned to his chamberlain. "I want two slaves in my chambers tonight. It's been a long day, but much has been accomplished. A celebration is in order."

"Yes, Your Majesty," the chamberlain said.

Emperor Krallick crossed the room to the door leading to his chambers. Before exiting, he gazed around his throne room with the odd feeling that something was amiss. His hand ached where the Seer had cut him, though the bleeding had stopped.

"The bleeding . . ." he muttered as he massaged his palm.

The blood froze in his veins.

"My blood."

EIGHTEEN

The Maker of Maps

By the end of the morning on the seventh day of their journey, Henry noticed Maggie gradually returning to normal. He still wasn't certain what had come over her, only that she claimed to have fixed him, which wasn't true. His arm was just as lame as ever. But he was glad to see her back to her usual happy self. Plus her hand was healing nicely and they were making excellent time toward their destination.

After breakfast, he reviewed the last of the instructions Fossy Barnic had written. "The cartographer has discreetly marked the point on the road where those seeking his services are to turn off. So it must be marked well enough that someone looking for it can find it."

"A sign, maybe?" Maggie massaged her injured hand as she spoke. He had noticed that she often did this lately when her mind was elsewhere. "Perhaps a small one?"

"I doubt it. Heading southeast, we'll come to a crossroads at the northern point of Silver Eagle Lake, and head directly south. That road continues all the way to the Southern Sea. If we reach that point, we've gone too far."

They rode for most of the morning at a steady pace, a sense of excitement between them. Around noon, they reached the lake. The silver eagles had not yet migrated north, and he and Maggie observed hundreds of the majestic birds soaring overhead, diving into the water, and swooping back skyward with fish trapped in their massive talons or beaks. When the sunlight reflected off their silver feathers just right, the eagles looked like streaks of light shooting through the daytime sky. Maggie suggested they stop for lunch by the lakeside to watch.

After the meal, they reached the crossroads and headed south. A forest of thick, brambly bushes bordered the road on either side, broken up by tall thin trees that allowed plenty of light to shine through and illuminate the road.

Focused on finding a hidden mark, they inspected anything that seemed even remotely out of place. At one point Maggie got off her horse to examine the shell of a mocking tortoise, thinking it might be the sign they were seeking. The toothless tortoise's head emerged from its shell and its jaws clamped down on her hand so hard that Henry had to pry it off her fingers. As it scooted away into the bushes, the tortoise cackled oddly.

As soon as Maggie got back on her horse, she gestured with her good hand and asked, "What's that?" She pointed to a towering tree whose roots had started to encroach on the road. A thick wall of bushes surrounded it, stretching on for countless yards in each direction. About ten or twelve feet up, on the north side of the trunk, someone had carved a perfectly symmetrical star with sixteen points. At the tip of the highest point was a small letter N.

Maggie stared at it. "Do you think his name starts with an N?"

"You've read maps, haven't you?" Henry asked. "It means north."

"So we go north?"

"That's the mark of a mapmaker. We'll find the path not far from here. I'm certain of it."

Through the bushes, a tiny trail stretched on for miles, though often covered by thick growth which made it difficult to follow. Squirrels as black as night chased each other across the treetops. Firefoxes with bright red tails scampered away, emitting clouds of gray smoke from their paws. A majestic rhinelk, white as the moon, horns the size of Henry's arms, chewed grass and bark while it stared at Henry and Maggie as they navigated along the faint trail.

Just as Henry was beginning to question his decision to follow the trail, he spotted a large house a few hundred yards off, surrounded by an orchard and plowed but empty gardens. The homestead was made of red brick covered in thick vines. Henry thought it was one of the most magnificent homes he'd ever seen, not because of its size, but because in his mind's eye he saw the orchards and gardens in full bloom. He saw children playing with sheep and goats in the yard while he and Isabelle watched from the doorway.

He wiped his brow and sighed. "We found it. Seven days and we found it."

Henry rode the last few yards with birds flapping around in his stomach. His hands shook as he tied up their horses to the post. The door was made of thick decorated wood that hurt his knuckles when he rapped upon it. He ran his fingers lightly over the wooden carvings.

"This is quality workmanship," he announced to Maggie. His pronouncement came with a sharp feeling of sadness. "I miss it, Maggie. I miss the work. And I might never do it again."

Creaks from inside the house told him the owner was approaching. Unseen hands fiddled with the doorknob before it clicked and the door opened to reveal the wizened, wrinkled face of a man with almost no hair and keen brown eyes that studied Henry and Maggie untrustingly.

"Who are you to come here and make judgments about the quality of my door?" he asked sharply. His voice reminded Henry of a saw cutting through a thick block of wood. It was low and scratchy, but still pleasant. His expression, however, was not.

"We are travelers who want to buy maps," Henry told the man.

"I'm not in the mood to sell maps this month," came the reply in the same tone. "Please leave. Thank you!" He withdrew his face and slammed the door with a tremendous bang.

Henry knocked again, this time with more force. "Won't you at least hear what we have to say? Our need is dire."

This time a peephole in the center of the door opened. The old man's eye stared, fixed and unblinking. "I'm sorry. Maybe in the spring—an excellent season for map buying . . . and selling. Thank you!" The man's voice was dim through the door. The sound of creaking wood told them he was walking away.

"Please, sir!" Henry pounded on the wood with his good hand. "We've come too far! We can't wait that long!"

"Please," Maggie added while Henry caught his breath and rubbed his sore hand. "We've come from Blithmore. You're our best hope for survival."

"All I do is make maps!" the man replied, still unseen. "I'm not giving you food, shelter, or anything else of the kind. So unless you eat maps, I don't see how I have anything to do with your survival. Thank you!"

Henry shouted back. "Stop saying thank—"

Before Henry could say more, Maggie rested a hand on his shoulder and silently told him to shut his mouth. "Sir, my name is Maggie Vestin. Please let us speak to you. We want to pay you for your services. Is that too much to ask?"

There was no reply from inside. Maggie and Henry stood still, afraid that even moving might spoil their chances. Finally the mapmaker spoke. "I see you are trying to use the beautiful voice of a young girl to soften my heart and open my door." Once more, creaking noises approached the door. For a moment, Henry thought it would open. "Well, you're wrong! It won't work."

"You're wrong, too," Henry responded, "if you think you can get rid of us so easily. We will sit on your porch until you let us in."

"What do I care? I go to bed early."

"We will sleep on your porch, if need be. We've slept on worse."

"If you fall asleep, I may sneak out and slit your throats. Well, not the lady's because that would be impolite, but you, sir, had best sleep with an eye open!"

Henry and Maggie looked at each other quizzically. Neither of them believed the old mapmaker capable of such a grisly act. Making as much noise as possible, Henry dropped his pack on the porch and kicked off his boots. Then he crossed the lawn to Quicken and removed his horse's packs as well, lugging them over and dropping them on the porch. "I can start a fire while you prepare our dinner," he fairly shouted at Maggie.

Maggie gave Henry a mock curtsy. Little time remained before evening fell, so they worked quickly and efficiently to build their camp and start supper. Henry kept an ear out for the mapmaker, and occasionally he heard the old man approach the door and then retreat. As the sun went down, a quaint fire crackled only a few feet from the porch.

"You're not helping your cause!" the elderly man called through his door. "I haven't had a decent meal since my wife passed, and now I have to smell that delicious food . . ."

Henry held up his plate, offering some to the one eye he knew was peeping through the door. A rude sound came in response. After their dinner, Henry and Maggie laid their blankets out on the porch. Henry was exhausted but determined to rise early the next day and reason again with the mapmaker.

"He won't try to hurt you, will he?" Maggie asked.

Henry shook his head. It dawned on him that this man might be more scared of Henry and Maggie than they were of him. But what would an old hermit have to be afraid of? He pondered this question, gazing up at the stars as he did so. His thoughts roamed to what it must be like to map the world. He and his friends had traveled a great distance, yet Atolas was much, much larger. How much of it could one man see?

Henry's eyelids grew heavy. Rather than dozing off, he got up and rested against the old man's door. Being so close to his goal and yet so far was maddening. If only the cartographer knew how much his maps meant to them.

"I'm searching for a way into Neverak," Henry said, hoping the old man could hear. He had heard no movement from inside the house in a while. "We came from Blithmore—fled from there, I should say—chased by the armies of King Germaine and Emperor Krallick. My betrothed, Isabelle, was taken from me six weeks ago. Taken to where, I can only guess. Wherever the palace of the Emperor is, I suppose." Henry stood on his feet and faced the door with his back straight and his chin set. A new energy filled his body.

"Her father sold her as a concubine to the Emperor, and I took her back. We spent months trying to reach the Iron Pass without being caught, but it was all in vain. They found us, and now she's gone. You can't imagine what that's like. All you do is make maps. I used to make wood into beautiful works of art. Now I can't even move the hand with which I once carved." He picked up his right hand with his left and put its uselessness on display to the door and the man he hoped was still behind it. Then he let it drop and swing back down. "That, too, was taken from me by the Emperor's Elite Guard. I have nothing left but a small flame of belief that somehow, someway I can reclaim her, that I can make some kind of life out of what once held such promise of happiness. But I don't know these lands. I don't know the way. If you do, sir, I need your help."

"You—you say your woman was taken from you," a tired, croaking voice came from behind the thick wooden door, "but who is the woman traveling with you?"

"My sister."

"Why does she accompany you?"

"She has helped me since the beginning. Now she, too, is wanted by the Emperor."

A long pause followed Henry's answer. Then the mapmaker said, "Such loyalty in a sister. I have never seen it. My sisters would never—*never*—have done such a thing."

"I am lucky in that way. But unlucky in others."

"And you crossed the Iron Pass?" the old man whispered. There was fear in his voice.

"I did. But I would only ever do it again to save Isabelle."

"Go to sleep," the mapmaker sighed. "I will consider what you have said and decide by morning whether or not I will help you."

This wasn't good enough. "I won't leave this place until your decision is to help us."

"I guessed as much. Now go to sleep. Thank you."

Henry pulled his blankets over himself. He thought of Isabelle as he fell asleep, remembering her face and her smile, imagining her soft voice whispering tender affections. The fantasy was real enough that if he had dared open his eyes, he would have expected to see her. Under the twilight sky, the vision turned to a nightmare—he heard her scream his name, beg him to help her, to save her. He woke up shaking, his right arm aching, and vain promises falling from his lips.

Rest came in spurts after that. When dawn broke, Henry was still tired but unable to fall back asleep. Maggie got up first, rebuilt the fire, and prepared breakfast. Henry said nothing about the brief conversation he'd had with the cartographer while Maggie had slept. A few bites into the meal, the door opened. Both Henry and Maggie stood at the sight of the bent and wrinkled bald man. He pointed at the meal Maggie had prepared.

"Do you have enough to share?"

"I do." With that answer, he gestured for them to follow him indoors. When Maggie reached the porch, he turned back to her. "Aren't you going to bring me some breakfast?" She hurried back to the fire.

Holding his plate of food in one hand, the old mapmaker led them into the main room of the house. A few chairs were scattered about; there were no windows—the walls were covered, top to bottom, with shelves. On those shelves were hundreds of maps. Everywhere Henry looked was a map either rolled up into a scroll or mounted in a frame with a clear glaze coating it. He couldn't see any of them properly, but the sheer number was staggering. When the mapmaker saw Henry and Maggie's wonder, he showed his first genuine sign of pleasure.

"You're impressed?" His keen brown eyes twinkled beneath his wrinkled brow. His accent was familiar, but not anything that Henry could place right away. "That's good. Maybe we will get along. Sit down and tell me what you want. And don't ask me for anything to drink, because I'm not offering."

Maggie and Henry took a seat on two rickety chairs in the middle of the room. The cartographer took sat in a plush chair facing them at an angle. He watched them closely, then ran his fingers over his head as though he still had hair to slick back. After a short pause he said, "So go on. Speak."

Maggie looked to Henry to tell the mapmaker what they needed.

"First of all, sir, allow me to introduce ourselves."

The man clicked his tongue impatiently, but didn't object to the formality.

"I'm Henry Vestin. This is my sister, Maggie. We're from Richterton, capitol of Blithmore, the children of a highly regarded carpenter and his wife, an educator."

The mapmaker nodded to tell Henry he knew exactly where Richterton was and had no doubt his parents were respectable to some degree or other.

"We're not certain exactly what we need. Maps, yes, but also advice from someone who knows the Western and Eastern Irons very well. We're prepared to pay you for your help."

The mapmaker stopped rubbing his head and placed his fingertips together just under his chin. "That's usually what people come to me for, thank you, but first you have to tell me where you want to go. You mentioned Neverak last night."

"Yes, sir. Neverak, sir. We want to go to Neverak."

The mapmaker snorted air out of his nose in long bursts. It took Henry a moment to realize that he was laughing. "Tell me more about your . . . adventures."

Henry began in Richterton with Isabelle and her father. When he reached the point in his tale where Isabelle was invited to dinner by the Emperor of Neverak, the ancient mapmaker no longer seemed impatient, but eager to listen. As Henry told of how he rescued Isabelle at the Glimmering Fountain from the Emperor, the mapmaker looked happy. By the end of their story, he sat on the edge of his large, comfortable chair, giving Henry his full attention.

"And so, even now, Ivan Krallick has the woman you love in his possession?" the mapmaker asked.

Henry nodded, his trembling left hand wiping the dry corners of his mouth.

"I think you are going to make a liar out of me, then. Thank you," the mapmaker said, getting up from his chair.

"Why is that? Did I say something offensive?"

"No, I'm going to offer you refreshment after all. My name is Markus Finkley. I was once the Imperial Cartographer of Neverak. There is no one in this world I curse more than Emperor Ivan Krallick."

NINETEEN

High Stakes

James took the cup and placed his bet. The other men followed suit. Ruther bet heavily on James to fail. James voted on his own success. He threw the dice down the trough and watched as they hit the backstop. Double twos. The dice returned to him. James subtly switched them for the loaded pair and dropped them in the cup. Then he rolled them down the lane.

Seven.

Ruther clapped his hands and let out a merry laugh as James cursed his bad luck. And so the day went until James and Ruther had amassed another four hundred gyri by evening, most of it won by Ruther with James's help. It brought their total to over fifteen hundred gyri. It was more money than Isabelle had dug up in their late mother's coffer.

"Lucky devil," one of the gamblers said to Ruther with a groan.

"I wish I was so lucky," James replied in a near-perfect Pappalonian accent. "I lost today, and will likely lose more tomorrow."

"Then I hope to see you tomorrow!" another gambler said with a hearty guffaw.

Thirsty was nearly finished preparing dinner when James arrived at the Sheep's Entrails. She hummed to herself a tune he had heard her sing many times, though he had never thought to ask its name.

Her welcoming smile showed off her white teeth, and he couldn't help but return it with one of his own.

"Another good day, I see," she commented.

"How can you tell?" he asked.

"Your face." Thirsty beamed with such an adoring look in her eyes that James blushed. "It's extra handsome on the days you do well."

"It's not me, it's Ruther," James said. "He could make money from dirt if he had to."

"I'm certain those talented hands of yours had something to do with it," Thirsty said, still grinning. "When's Ruther going to be back, anyway? I've got his favorite meal almost ready."

"Probably a half hour behind me. We can't leave together or it will look suspicious."

Almost exactly a half hour later, Ruther arrived home. "Why don't you join us, Thirsty?" he asked as he sat down to eat.

"Oh, no," Thirsty quickly answered. "Mr. Jessop would fly into one of his rages right in front of you. Then he'd refuse to pay me. I daren't even consider it."

Ruther took a big bite and chewed it slowly, savoring its flavor. "Mmm," he said through a full mouth. "You certain? The food is marvelous."

Thirsty looked at James. "What do you think, James? Should I?"

"Um . . ." James's neck grew warm. "I wouldn't turn you away. But I don't want you to get into trouble, either."

She laughed prettily. "I'll grab a plate."

All James and Ruther talked about was dice. As they spoke, Ruther practiced the sleight of hand trick which James performed so easily. James never thought he could be so gripped by something as simple as a game, but he found himself thinking about it constantly.

"I don't mean to interrupt your conversation," Thirsty said after listening to them go on for fifteen minutes, "but shouldn't Maggie and Brandol be back soon? It's been two weeks."

"I hope tomorrow or the day after," Ruther answered.

"So will the two of you be going out again? Because by the sound of it, you've earned more than enough money. If it was me—which it's not, but I'm offering my thoughts anyway—if it was me, I'd let things be. You know, take my money and walk away."

James looked to Ruther to say something, but Ruther stared at his food with a blank expression. "Well . . ." James finally offered, "we haven't decided yet, but you make a good point. Thank you."

"Er, yes, Thirsty, thank you," Ruther added.

"What will you do when they return? Stay a little longer or leave at once?"

"Leave at once," James said grimly. "We have important matters in faraway lands."

"Your sister?" Thirsty asked quietly.

The men both stared at her. James spoke first. "What do you know of that?"

"I've overheard things. She was taken, right?"

It shamed James that he'd been so consumed by the dice games he hadn't thought of Isabelle much lately. Thirsty reached across the table and took James's hand. Ruther made it a point to look away, but a trace of a smirk adorned his lips. The touch of her hand sent a hot feeling from James's throat to his gut, but he pulled the hand away.

"I'm sorry, James," she said, and he felt the sincerity of her words.

The dinner table was quiet for a long minute, and then Ruther launched into a story about a time he saw a gambler badly beaten by his wife after losing all their money in dice games. James nodded and made approving noises at all the right parts so Ruther thought he was listening, but his thoughts were elsewhere.

That night, as James lay in bed, he could not help but think back on Thirsty's advice. What need was there to gamble again? They had more than enough money to finance their journey. Why risk it? But the thrill of winning, the sound of the dice tumbling down wooden troughs, and the exchange of tokens all called to him.

James could not remember the last time he'd had so much fun. Fun was a word he had almost forgotten during his career in the King's Guard. And he was having fun with Ruther, of all people.

"We have more than enough gyri," he whispered to himself. "We have plenty. Nothing good can come of greed." By the time he fell asleep, he had convinced himself that Thirsty was right. Tomorrow, he and Ruther would stay in and enjoy a quiet day at home. Maybe they could find a secluded wooded spot nearby and practice throwing knives.

But throwing knives was the last thing on James's mind the next morning as he ate breakfast with Ruther. And from the look in Ruther's eye, they shared the same thoughts. Neither wanted to say anything, however, with Thirsty darting around cleaning dishes and utensils. When she asked about their plans, they both hemmed and hawed until she quit asking. The moment she left, Ruther asked James. "What do you want to do today?"

James shrugged, trying to appear indifferent.

"You want to, uh . . ."

"Only if you do."

"I asked you first."

Thirty minutes later, they were out the door, riding to what they assured each other would be their last day of dicing. They took care to avoid the places where the Matt and Byderik supporters congregated most often, and arrived at their destination without trouble. To ease their consciences about playing when they didn't need the money, Ruther came up with two stipulations: first, they would not use the special dice. And second, they would only play with two hundred fifty gyri each. When they arrived and changed their money into tokens, Ruther surprised James by removing a golden token from his pocket.

"What is that doing here?" James hissed. "You told me yesterday you had it changed back to gyri."

"I was going to, but I'm in love with it." Ruther rolled the large, gilded token around in his fingers, grinning at it like a little boy with a toy. "I just wanted to see it and touch it one last time. It really is a beautiful thing."

"It's a piece of wood coated with gold paint, and much easier to lose than a bag full of coins."

"I know," Ruther said, pocketing it with a sigh, "but it has stolen my heart. Gyri are so thin and small. The tokens remind me more of the fat, heavy crowns back home."

"I'm holding onto it," James said, slipping the gold token in his money bag. Each colored token represented a different amount of money: red for a half gyri, green for a full one, white for five, and so on up to gold, which represented one thousand gyri. The day before, Ruther had said he would exchange it for coins.

Forgoing the use of their special dice not only made James apprehensive, but also brought a new thrill to the game. He could no longer rely on having better odds. Ruther chose a table occupied by a crowd wealthier than one James would have preferred. He even recognized one of them, Fossy Barnic.

After a round of greetings and introductions, Ruther received the dice to roll. James decided to bet against his friend. Ruther tossed a two and a one. His next roll was another two, but this time accompanied by a five. Ruther lost. James had bet big on Ruther to fail, and so he won almost a hundred gyri.

From there on, everything went downhill.

They occasionally won, but every time they bet large sums, they lost, especially when James rolled the dice. Ruther started to grow testy and then disappeared for a short time, only to reappear with a flask of ale. Each time James handed the dice to one of the other men in the group, they laughed about how cold the dice felt. Everyone at the table was having a great time except for James, Ruther, and Fossy Barnic, who smiled rarely but cast furtive looks at James and Ruther.

Eventually Ruther sidled up next to James and quietly asked, "How much are we down?"

"Nearly everything we won yesterday. About four hundred."

Ruther hissed angrily. The scent of ale was strong enough to make James hold his breath.

"We should leave," he told Ruther. "We have plenty of money. Let's cash in the golden token and go home."

Ruther stared at James as if he were a rabid dog. "Quit as losers?" He laughed, then hiccupped obscenely. "Not on your life. I'm not leaving until we're up *five . . . hundred . . . gyri.*" He punctuated the amount by poking James in the chest.

"Ruther . . ." James put his hand on his friend's shoulder. "We're fine. Why risk it?"

"We have barely eleven hundred. I'm not leaving until that number is two thousand."

James shook his head, his eyes closed, and forced himself to remain patient. "I'm going back to the inn now. You're coming with me."

"I'm not." Ruther's tone told James that the storyteller wouldn't leave the dice hall without making a scene. And a scene was the last thing he wanted. He started to walk away but realized what a terrible mistake that would be. To leave Ruther alone in the hall, drunk and angry, would be utterly foolish. How many times had he seen Ruther make inexplicably poor choices under the influence of ale?

He turned back. "Fine. We'll make back the money with the dice."

"You brought them?" Ruther asked.

"Of course I did. Just in case."

Ruther pinched James's cheeks with mock adoration. "I could kiss you! Maybe I will!"

"If you do, I'll knock you out and drag you home. How does that sound?" James gave Ruther his iciest stare.

"Fine, I won't kiss you."

"Bet against me on the first roll."

The game began again, and the gods of the dice smiled on them once more. Even on bets where they had no control over the outcome, James or Ruther still managed to win the majority. Within two hours, they were one hundred gyri away from Ruther's goal of two thousand. James gave Ruther a look telling him that it was time to quit, but Ruther took a deep swallow of ale and rolled again.

Across the hall shouting erupted, drawing all the eyes in the grand room in that direction. At least six men, possibly more, were brawling. James got up on his tiptoes to see what the commotion was all about. It only took a moment to see that the pro-Matt and pro-Byderik supporters had decided to settle their arguments with their fists.

"Those Matt supporters are the worst, aren't they?" one of the gamblers asked.

"I'm sure it's Byderik supporters who started it," countered another. He regarded the Matt supporter as one would something stuck to the bottom of his boot.

Fossy Barnic leaned in close to James. "I abhor violence, but was recently the victim of somebody with whom you and I rolled dice not three weeks ago."

James stared at Fossy, perplexed. "I am not from Borderville, Fossy. The chances of you and I knowing the same person are quite slim."

"Believe it." Fossy's tone became angry. "This man stole into my room at the inn where I stayed—I no longer stay there now, as you can imagine—held a blade to my neck and demanded to know—"

"Excuse me, Fossy," Ruther interrupted. "It's time for Jipper to throw the dice."

His attention more on Fossy's story, James tossed his dice down the lane and rolled a seven. He had bet on a success, so he took his winnings and placed his tokens on the same space.

"—demanded to know the location of a mapmaker!" Fossy finished.

James's head jerked back to face the older man. "Excuse me?"

"Yes, this madman broke into my room and put a blade to me for the sole purpose of finding a mapmaker. He was a lunatic! Threatened to kill me."

"And it was the man we threw dice with?" James asked. "Hask Vornbit? You must be mistaken. He seemed like a gentle, good-natured man."

"Roll the dice again, please," Ruther insisted.

James tossed the dice down the lane, eager to let Fossy continue his tale. "At first I resisted him," Barnic said. "What can I say? I value the trust others place in me, especially that of my friends. However, I had no choice but to do as he said."

"You don't really believe he would have killed you, do you?" The table was cleared again as James had rolled a second success.

"Take your dice, Jipper," Ruther said, coughing loudly as he dropped the cubes into James's hand.

James accepted them as he watched Fossy's face for signs of lying. Could Henry be capable of such an act?

"I—I thought so at the time," Fossy stammered. "I won't lie, he scared me."

"And this is the same man with whom you and I rolled dice?"

Fossy nodded. "That man was there, too. Rumps." Fossy pointed at Ruther. "Twice. The four of us rolled together twice."

Fossy's words reminded James that he still had to toss the dice. He pulled his attention away from Fossy long enough to stare down the trough. What had he just rolled, a success or a fail? Which dice were in his hands? He couldn't remember. He looked to Ruther for a sign, but Ruther was taking a long drink from his flask.

"Hurry up," one of the gamblers said.

He placed his bet on success and threw the dice. His mind was filled with the image of Henry holding a knife to someone's neck. It didn't seem right. Henry was no aggressor, and with one good arm, how dangerous could he be? But Henry had disappeared that night and come home under strange circumstances. He'd even insisted that should anyone ask about him, James should pretend that they barely knew him.

"Remind me what the man looked—"

Fossy's attention had left James and turned to what was happening at the other end of the dicing table. One of the other men had picked up James's dice to inspect them. He hefted them between two fingers, glancing sidelong at James as he did so. Then he dropped them and rolled a one and a six.

"That's the same roll you've had four times in a row." His tone was nothing but accusatory. Then he picked them up and dropped them. "Five in a row." He repeated the action again. "Six."

Everyone's eyes were on James, none of them friendly, not even Ruther's.

"You thought you could cheat us?" Ruther asked James. "I say we take all his money and divide up amongst us."

"Gentlemen," James began to say as he looked at Ruther for help, not accusations, "Please allow me to explain what—"

One of the other gambling men gestured to someone behind James, and before James could count to three, several hands seized him roughly by the arms and legs, rendering him helpless. Cries of "cheater," "scoundrel," and far worse echoed in his ears as his gambling friends' faces transformed from furious to apoplectic.

"Wait!" James shouted, but a bag was pulled over his head, blocking out the sunlight streaming in from the tall windows. The bag was tightened against his face so that his cries were muffled. Then they dragged him away.

TWENTY

A Tale of Two Emperors

Markus Finkley returned to the sitting room with large mugs of tea, a plate of fresh bread and soft cheese, and three bowls of steaming soup. Maggie and Henry accepted the meal gratefully. They ate quietly for only a few minutes before Markus began peppering them with questions of his own. Henry answered them truthfully, sensing deeply that Markus was trustworthy and willing to help. Most of his questions related to what they were doing in Pappalon and their immediate plans.

In a moment when his curiosity got the better of him, Henry asked the mapmaker, "Why do you loathe the Emperor so much?"

Markus set his mug down and his brow furrowed into a myriad of wrinkles. He sighed deeply as though a hundred years of memories were passing before his eyes. The color of his nose changed from peach to purple, and he wiped it with a handkerchief from his pocket. When he began speaking, his hands went back to his hairless head, his fingers stroking the leathery skin lightly.

"As I said, I was the Imperial Cartographer for many, many years. My father held the post before me, and his uncle before him. I was named to it when my father died, which was a few years after the coronation of Emperor Peter Krallick. That's Ivan's father, if you didn't know. He was a good man. And he was very popular because he eased generations of hatred between Blithmore and Neverak. He and King Germaine were great friends.

"I don't want to lead you on that I was a close friend of the Emperor like the King of Blithmore. I wasn't, but I knew him better than most ever get to know such a man. We only spoke whenever he summoned me, but he entrusted me with some very, very important projects. I spent much of my life in his service, mapping the Eastern Irons. I traveled through every country south of the River of Ice, west of the Sea of Kings, north of the Great Southern Sea, or east of the Towering Mountains. It was an enjoyable time of my life. I had no family attachments, no obligations to anyone but the Emperor, so I wandered around Atolas for months at a time, learning the land and making maps. When all was said and done, I spent more than twenty years at it. I picked up all the various dialects so I wouldn't be considered a stranger in any place. It was a glorious, glorious time. That was when I first found this property."

Markus gestured around the room at the dozens of shelves decorating his walls. "I'd guess that almost three-quarters of these maps were made during those years. I'd walk or ride with my quills and parchment doing what I loved most. In Greenhaven, where I spent two years, I met Ginger. She was the only thing I ever loved more than mapmaking. Oh! You should have seen her when she was just a young lady. She had a way about her that made every young man stare at her at least twice when she rode by. I wasn't a young man by then; I was in my forties, but even I was caught in her net.

"I don't know what Ginger saw in me, but she wanted to marry me. I still had duties to perform for the Emperor, so she came with me to Neverak. It was a long journey, and both my parents had passed on, so we married in Greenhaven before we left. It was a beautiful, beautiful ceremony. Her mother cried through the whole thing. When we returned, the Emperor threw us a feast. I think he did it for two reasons. He claimed it was to celebrate my wedding, but he was also thrilled with the extensive maps I'd made of the Eastern Irons. It was a sizable addition to his library.

"During the feast I told the Emperor I didn't want to travel as much without my wife. My family was a priority now, and he understood. So he gave me the duty to examine my father's and great-uncle's maps of Neverak for half the year and make corrections. During the coldest months in Neverak, I traveled to the southern lands to continue my work. At first I took Ginger, but when she bore children, I went alone. After I finished my corrections, he assigned me to make plans of the palace. That was one of the greatest experiences of my life. His most trusted servants showed me every room, and I drew plans of each floor. Some of the things I saw—rooms and passages and secrets—only the Emperor himself knew. I did that work until the old Emperor died.

"It's customary to continue your assignments from the former Emperor until the new one gives you something else to do. So I continued to make plans of the castle. By then, Ginger had given me two sons and a daughter. When my oldest boy was ten years old, I could already tell he would excel at the family profession. For months he begged his mother to let him accompany me on my trips, and when he turned twelve she finally agreed.

"That same winter I was summoned to the palace. I brought my plans of the castle with me and presented them to Emperor Ivan. This took place about six months after he'd taken the throne. I knew at once he wasn't like his father. He hardly looked at my work. He was impatient, disrespectful; it seemed as though he found my work boring. He gave me an assignment to map the inside of the northern Iron Forest, concentrating on the most northern, mountainous areas. My first reaction was to tell him that I'd been specifically ordered by his father to stay away from the Iron Forest. When I did so, he pretended not to hear me. I thought it best not to repeat it a second time. As you would guess, I'd heard all the rumors of those cursed woods during my travels, but had, on the Emperor's orders, never actually set foot in that cursed place.

"My wife and I discussed it at great length. She asked me more than once not to go, but I insisted that I had to obey the Emperor. I waited until the weather turned warm and set out with my son. After three weeks of hard travel, we reached the border of the forest."

Markus paused to drink from his mug. His chin trembled as he did so. Henry wasn't certain if the trembling was from age or emotion, but it affected the old mapmaker quite badly, and he spilled tea on himself. After hastily mopping his face and neck, he continued.

"Never in my life have I feared spirits or ghosts. I'd never seen any sort of phenomena, and I'd traveled more than almost anyone I ever knew." He raised a bent finger of warning to Maggie and Henry. "*But that forest is haunted.* For two days my son and I walked the border of the northern forest looking for any kind of landmark: a trail, a river, rock formations, but we found nothing. My mind was filled with the most awful memories. Voices in my head telling me things, reminding me of things, taunting and mocking . . .

"Then the third day we found a trail, narrow and dark, that went straight east through the trees. Against every instinct, we took it. My son wept as we rode in. Symbols had been carved into the trees every few yards. We walked that path for hours with the feeling we were being followed or watched. Taunting voices filled our heads more and more the deeper we traveled."

"You heard them, too?" Maggie asked in a voice so low Henry hardly heard her. He noticed for the first time that his sister was trembling and her face bone white. She chewed her lips so hard he thought they might bleed.

"Then my son started screaming that we had to get out. His ear was bleeding. I couldn't calm him. He begged me to go back. His eyes—I've never seen that kind of fear in anyone's eyes before—so we rode and rode and rode. We heard crashes in the woods all around us, but never saw anything. My boy was in hysterics by the time we made it clear of the forest. We swore we'd never go back in again, no matter what the Emperor said, even if I had to resign my post. At the end of the summer, I returned to the palace and told Emperor Krallick everything that had happened. He became very, very agitated. He asked me question after question about what had spooked my son and myself. So I answered them as best I could.

"'I want you to return to the forest,' he said. 'I need this done, and I need it done soon.'

"I had a distinct impression that there was something in that area—what that could be, I still don't know—but something he wanted, perhaps a long-forgotten treasure or something of extraordinary power. He never told me what it was, but I adamantly refused to go back. If that doesn't tell you how frightened I was, I don't know what would. When I offered him my resignation due to my inability to serve, the Emperor shook his head and said, 'Your offer is refused. You will map that area. If you fail me again, the penalty will be severe.'

"I couldn't believe his words. I asked humbly if he was threatening me, and he laughed as though it were all a cruel jest. 'I expect detailed maps from you in a year's time,' were his words. Then he looked at me like I was a dog and said, 'Now get out.'

"That was when I understood how different the two Emperors were. It was not only their character and mood, but even the way they governed. Emperor Peter was, in essence, a good man, a father to his people. Until that time, I had thought his son was a bully. I found out he's a tyrant. For days I struggled with the decision to go back to the forest. My wife told me she would support whatever I chose, bless her heart, but that didn't make it any easier. In the end, I broke my vow to my son and went back to the Iron Forest. This time, I went alone. I didn't ask my son to come with me, and I don't think he would have.

To make things worse, I didn't go in spring. I kept finding ways to put it off.

"It was a terrible journey. I was ill the entire way. The summer's heat burned like the Great Demon's oven that year, but when I reached the edge of the forest, I don't know if the sweat drenching my clothes was from the heat of the sun or from my own fear of death. I—I couldn't do it. I couldn't step foot into that forest again even though I stood at the edge of that tiny, narrow path for hours. There I was, a man in his sixties, sobbing like a five-year-old, petrified with fright.

"I went home. My wife told me she understood and didn't blame me. We didn't have much time before the year expired, so we got ready to return to her family in Greenhaven. I couldn't leave without my maps. They represented half my life, and I couldn't leave them in the hands of the Emperor. The night before we left, I returned to the castle. I knew all of its secrets; I was able to go in and out without anyone ever knowing I was there.

"We had planned to take two wagons to Greenhaven, one carrying my maps, the other with the rest of our possessions. The second wagon was never filled, unfortunately."

Markus's deep, scratchy voice suddenly broke. Henry felt a stab of pain in his dead arm that spread to his heart, making breathing difficult. Markus's eyes reddened, but he never cried. "I saw smoke—too much smoke—from miles away. I pushed the horses so hard that they nearly collapsed in exhaustion. My home was in flames. I ran into the house. It was an inferno, but I ran in. I couldn't find Ginger or my children; I could barely see. So I ran back out again; they weren't there. The heat was too much. I was nearly trapped inside, but I got out. My clothes had caught fire, and I had to put them out. I still have scars on my leg from that. The flames singed my head, and my hair never grew back."

His fingers went back to his scalp and rubbed it.

"Your family?" Maggie asked. "What happened?"

The cartographer shrugged with a sad smile. "I came here by myself. I've been here now for eight years or so, making maps and growing food. I don't need money. It's a good life. Lonely, but satisfying. And now you're here, and I'll do whatever I can to help you keep your family together."

"Thank you," Henry replied.

"But you must promise me one thing."

"What is that?" Henry asked.

Markus's eyes narrowed and his kind face transformed to one of deep and unmistakable malice. The effect unnerved Henry. "Kill him."

Henry looked at Maggie, who stared back at him in doubt. With a lame arm and utterly no skill in swordsmanship, they both knew it was impossible for Henry to accomplish such a task. But Henry squared his jaw and faced Markus again. "I will," he said solemnly.

Markus nodded and began rummaging through maps. "Obviously, you don't want to go back to Blithmore. And that's really unfortunate because there are so many wonderful routes that would take you into Neverak and directly into Krallickton without being noticed. You could take a small army to or from Blithmore without being noticed if you knew what you were doing. But the risks are far, far too great . . . especially through that cursed forest. You really only have a few options of getting into Neverak without entering Blithmore. Is anyone in your party qualified to operate a sea vessel?"

"I don't think so," Henry answered.

"Yes, that's probably for the best. You wouldn't want to travel by sea for a year or longer. After all, you've probably only got four months before your lady's cleansing is complete."

"Cleansing?" Henry repeated.

"What are you talking about?" Maggie asked.

Markus glanced up from his maps to read Maggie and Henry's

faces. "You don't know about the cleansing? I apologize, I thought—well, why would you? The Emperor has some strange habits, Henry. He likes everything clean. Very, very clean. Nothing more so than the women he takes into his bed. Now don't get me wrong, concubines are a normal part of an Emperor's retinue. Even Emperor Peter had them, though hardly anyone knows it. But Ivan takes his obsession with purity to the utmost extreme. He puts them through a stringent cleansing process. Shaves off all their hair. No one can touch them for four months—"

"Four months?" Henry asked. "He won't even touch them?"

"Yes, it's believed that four months is the amount of time it takes for the body to replenish itself in one full cycle."

"Then we only have three—" Henry corrected himself, "nearly two!"

"No, Henry," Markus reminded him, "she had to be taken from southern Blithmore to northern Neverak. That's no quick jaunt. If she was taken near the pass six weeks ago, she is probably only just arriving in Krallickton."

"How could you know that?"

"I traveled those roads and lands for years and years. Distances and travel times from one point to another are second nature to me. My guess is that you have almost exactly four months before her cleansing ends."

A small ray of light grew in Henry's chest as he experienced something he hadn't in weeks: hope. It was like a warm bath, washing his heart, mind, and soul of the filth of despair he had been wallowing in since Isabelle's capture. He felt a little more like his old self again. There was still a chance that he could prevent Isabelle from becoming the Emperor's possession in every sense of the word. If he could protect her from that terrible ordeal, he might still be worth something to her after all.

"There are no easy ways into Neverak," Markus said. "Your best option would be to hire a ship to take you westward, down the River of Ice that runs north of Neverak, New Avalon, and so forth to the east . . . it is a nasty, nasty river. Only a large vessel can get you to the river ports in Northern Neverak."

"Why can't we just travel on foot along the coast?" Maggie asked.

"Neverak isn't on good terms with its northern neighbors, and the northerners patrol the border with great diligence. On the southern border of the River of Ice, the Iron Forest goes right up to the cliffs overlooking the water. It's impassible."

"Would hiring a ship be dangerous?" Henry asked.

"Could be," Markus said, "if the Elite Guard stationed at the ports become suspicious of you. But your other options are worse. You could take a boat from Pappalon westward on the Great Southern Sea, sail past Blithmore, and to the Western Lands. From there you'd need to travel north and cross the Towering Mountains into western Neverak. That would take you months, up to two years, depending on how severe the winters are. Your other choice is to find the northern trail through the Iron Forest, which will bring you into Neverak."

"No," Maggie and Henry both said together.

Markus nodded. "No one option is optimal, but if you get into Neverak, I can all but guarantee you safe passage until you reach the castle. And I can get you inside without difficulty. I know where the house of concubines is, and you can find your beloved woman, kill the Emperor, and take all the jewels you'll ever need without anyone knowing you entered . . . except the Emperor himself. But if you kill him, he won't be telling any tales."

"I have another question," Maggie said, glancing nervously at Henry. "What do you know of—of a healer? Someone who can perform wondrous acts or—or even miracles?"

Markus's eyes fell on Henry's arm as he took a long sip from his mug. "There is a place I know of—never actually visited, mind you— where you can find a healer. A real healer, too, not one where you pay an exorbitant sum just to drink muddy water and roots, and wake up with bowel problems . . ." Markus cleared his throat. "Not that I've had experience with that kind of healer. But this one is in a valley in Greenhaven. I will give you directions. To navigate the secret places of Neverak Palace you will need both hands, Henry."

They talked late into the night about their upcoming journey and the knowledge they would need before going into specific areas. The third day they spent poring over maps of Neverak and Pappalon. Before sending Henry and Maggie to bed, Markus told them he would give them maps of each Eastern Irons country, one of Neverak with the best routes traced for them, and a map of the palace. He stayed up all night performing this work. When Henry awoke, he had only barely finished.

"Your sister woke up early and helped me," Markus said. "She's got a steady hand and a keen eye. But it's her brain that you should heed. She has quite a mind."

Maggie blushed. "Now I know how you convinced Ginger to marry you. Flattery."

Markus refused to accept any money for his maps. After ensuring that his guests had enough food and drink to get them back to Borderville, he saw them off. As Henry mounted Quicken, an idea struck him. He turned back to Markus and asked, "Would you like to come with us? For one last adventure?"

Markus smiled and raised a hand. "If you had asked me five years ago, I would have said yes, but I've aged much faster than I should have. It won't be long before I'm reunited with Ginger and my three children."

They said their goodbyes, and he and Maggie rode away. It was the first morning of an early spring as they rode, and all Henry could see was the bright sunlight. The world was a better place. He knew there would yet be dark days ahead, but today—today was a good day.

TWENTY-ONE

The Royal Trainer

During breakfast, the Emperor discussed the day's agenda with his chamberlain. "What reports do we have from the spies watching the Seer's lair?"

"Still no sign of him, Your Majesty."

The Emperor scowled. "That's not good enough! I've had him watched before and he's never been this difficult to track. Now you're telling me there's been no sign for two weeks? It's no coincidence that the moment he gets near my blood—"

"Your Majesty, we have no proof that the Seer took your blood."

This was true. The Emperor of Neverak had nothing but a vague foreboding, perhaps just a suspicion, that when the Seer had returned the vial of blood from his pocket as his chamberlain requested, it somehow held *more* blood than before. In that briefest of moments, was it possible that he could have switched them? The possibility made the Emperor uncomfortable. While it was not uncommon for the Seer to disappear for weeks or even months at a time, it seemed awfully convenient to vanish immediately after he had administered the death pact to the bounty hunters. Regardless, the Emperor had other important concerns begging for his attention.

"General Attikus arrived in the city last night," the chamberlain reported.

"Expect him first thing this morning. Escort him to the training room when he arrives and tell him I wish to spar. I think it will be fun and . . . nostalgic."

"Will you bathe after, Your Majesty?"

"Yes. I want two guardsmen posted outside the room so nothing gets out of hand. The general is not pleased with me right now. I don't want to take any chances. But be wise about it. I don't want him thinking he's not trusted."

The Emperor often thought of his first sword lesson with his mentor. As a spoiled, petulant child, he had fought against the rigid discipline Attikus forced on him.

"Bow to me," Attikus said before they began the instructions.

But young Ivan bowed to no one. He crossed his arms and stiffened his legs.

Attikus's hard brown eyes and tanned face became stern. "Bow to me!"

"The Prince bows to no one!"

Attikus struck Ivan in the face with the flat of his sword.

"You can't do that to me! I'm the crown prince!" Ivan ran off for his father. Emperor Peter sent him straight back to Attikus, who served him with another dose of pain while Ivan screamed, "*I hate you, Attikus!*"

Despite his hatred, he quickly but reluctantly adapted to Attikus's method of teaching. From age ten to fifteen, Ivan Krallick spent more time with Attikus than with his mother and father. Despite his duties leading Neverak's armies, Attikus had been asked by Emperor Peter to teach young Ivan swordplay, military tactics, and all things related to the art of war. Attikus had even been invited to live in the palace during those years.

Over time, Prince Ivan let go of his hate for Attikus, though he rejected nearly everything he'd taught him about principles, morality, and compassion for weakness. Swordplay and the art of war, those things he kept. He revered Attikus's perfect fighting technique, brilliant mind, and demanding character.

An hour after breakfast, the Emperor met Attikus in the training room. The room held a great history between them. This was where Attikus had spent countless hours teaching young Ivan all the movements, stances, and tactics of swordplay. As soon as Ivan had mastered them, Attikus made him practice outdoors: in grass, on rocks, uphill, downhill, and standing in water up to his waist. The Emperor could still hear Attikus barking orders.

"Thrust! Dodge left. Parry high! Kick! Parry high! Dodge right! Torso thrust!" Then, at some point during the exercise, Attikus would yell, "Where are your elbows supposed to be?"

The last time they had crossed swords was on Ivan's seventeenth birthday—nearly twelve years ago. Despite all the training he had received from his swordmaster, the crown prince was still handily defeated. "Your skill is quite adequate," Attikus had told him.

"It's not *adequate*!" The prince threw down his sword, disgusted and embarrassed at defeat. "I lost!"

"I am a grown man. You are a boy."

"I'm no boy!"

"You lack my strength. It will come with age and training."

The Emperor guessed that Attikus recalled that day with even more clarity than he, given his mentor's brilliant mind. Attikus was already in the training room, dulled sword in hand, wearing light chain mail. When he saw the Emperor enter, he stood at attention.

"Why am I not surprised," said Emperor Krallick, "to find you already here?" He nodded to his trainer. "I've looked forward to this for a long time."

"Why is that?"

"You are my measuring stick, of course. If I can beat you, I can beat anyone." The Emperor crossed the room to the sword rack and chose his favorite blade while Attikus waved his own blunted sword around to teach his muscles its weight and flexibility, a technique he had taught the Emperor in their earliest lessons.

"Allow me a moment of modesty, please, Your Majesty. I can assure you there are better swordsmen in the world than myself. If you must know, I once competed in a contest in Hammond and didn't even make it to the highest round of play."

The Emperor laughed and waved the comment away. "My father told me about that. If I remember correctly, you were made a noble so you could compete. He also said you insisted on using a poorly-made sword in only your left hand to be fair to the other fighters."

"Shall we begin, then?" Attikus asked briskly, standing at the ready near the center of the large room.

The Emperor smiled at Attikus's commitment to humility, then became sober as he focused on the task at hand. It was no secret that the Emperor longed to defeat Attikus. It was the reason Attikus had agreed to spar on the prince's seventeenth birthday. Ivan's father had insisted it was the only thing his son wanted. It was the same reason the Emperor continued his intense daily training.

"Let us begin," the Emperor replied, meeting Attikus and preparing himself mentally for the challenge. Both men assumed their natural, aggressive stances. A nervous thrill went through the Emperor's body as he met the same hard stare from Attikus which he still found to be as intimidating as at age ten.

For the briefest of instances, the swordsmen stood perfectly still and held the other's gaze, two warriors whose sole desire was to put a blade into the other. Then the Emperor moved, darting forward with a quickness Attikus no longer possessed. Attikus spun right, barely avoiding the Emperor's thrust, countering with his own swipe.

This first moment dictated how much of the sparring match went: the Emperor using his superior strength and speed to dominate Attikus, but never able to finish the task. Several times Attikus escaped with no more room to spare than the width of a few hairs, and each time the Emperor became more certain of his victory, more relaxed and focused. Still, Attikus hadn't given up. As they moved about the room, Attikus did whatever he could to disrupt the Emperor's concentration: knocking down suits of armor, tumbling the sword racks, smashing the furniture. Three times he threw nearby objects at the Emperor, forcing Emperor Krallick to dodge and then counter yet another attack. The whole time it felt like yet another lesson from the older man.

"Still teaching me? After all these years?"

"Hah!" Attikus cried and lunged powerfully at Emperor Krallick, but found his attack swept aside.

The Emperor's counterstrike was equal to his trainer's, but once again Attikus avoided defeat with precise maneuvering.

"You can't lose, can you?" The Emperor shook his head, incredulous.

"Can you, Ivan?" Attikus asked. Sweat streaked from his hairline to his chin. His eyes stayed locked on the Emperor's, moving and shifting his weight in reaction to where his student's eyes moved. "Have you learned that lesson yet? It is the most important of all."

"Losing?" Emperor Ivan clucked his tongue with a mirthful, jeering grin. "No, I think not. The most important lesson of all would be how to never lose."

"Only if you live in a world of your own fantasy."

The Emperor pressed his attack, trying to use his brute strength and speed to beat Attikus into submission, but Attikus beat back the attack and stood his ground, effectively parrying everything the Emperor threw at him. The Emperor grew awed at how Attikus could fight harder the longer the contest lasted. His confidence waned, forcing another of Attikus's lessons back into his memory.

"If you don't believe you can win, you'll never be wrong," Attikus had often told young Ivan.

The usual reply from Ivan had been, "How can I believe I can beat you if I know I can't?" The Emperor hated how, even now, Attikus made him feel like a ten-year-old. He channeled this anger into his technique, letting it focus rather than distract him.

The battle grew in ferocity. Steel clashed against steel like bolts of lightning streaking a night sky. Shouts of frustration and determination rent the air. The Emperor yearned to prove once and for all that he had banished all traces of the raw boy that Attikus had so harshly molded into an *adequate* young man. But Attikus matched every bit of the Emperor's intensity, drawing from some deep, hidden well of strength to repel his pupil, and eventually gained the upper hand. The Emperor tried to hide his astonishment as his swordmaster pushed him back, pressing the attack. Attikus's blazing brown eyes were filled with the powerful emotion of fury. Then, in a mighty stroke, Attikus bellowed loudly and swept the sword clean out of the Emperor's hand. The Emperor backed away to find something to defend himself, but stepped on a broken chair leg and stumbled to the ground. Attikus advanced, his sword leveled at the Emperor's chest, and the Emperor was certain that Attikus intended to kill him.

He meant to call his guards, but the command caught in his throat, and all he could croak out was "Yield!"

Without hesitation, Attikus lowered his sword as the guardsmen came into the room, hands on the hilts of their own weapons. The Emperor held out his hand to them. "Stand down. Our sparring match became spirited, that is all. Leave us." His face burned in shame as he realized how powerless he appeared in front of these men of arms. But nothing was more humiliating than to see Attikus standing above him, offering a hand to his beaten foe.

The Emperor got to his feet without Attikus's aid and faced him. He tried to appear calm, even jovial, but the bitterness in his stomach made him want to wretch. "By far the best fighting I've ever seen," Attikus said, not quite smiling. Attikus never smiled, so perhaps the Emperor should have felt grateful, but he didn't.

"If you'll excuse me," the Emperor said as he pushed past the general to the door, "I'm going to get into a bath, then we can discuss other matters. Have my servants bring you whatever you desire."

A few minutes of soaking in a piping hot pool improved his mood sufficiently to continue his business with Attikus. Jade, a beautiful concubine with caramel skin, snow colored hair, and green eyes stood behind him, rubbing Emperor Krallick's shoulders with careful attentiveness. He had recently released her from her cleansing and taken her into his bed. He appreciated her gentle touch and attentiveness to his needs. His chamberlain brought Attikus in. He was given comfortable seating and food and drink. "Tell me about the council in Blithmore."

Attikus set aside the plate of food. He had hardly touched it. The Emperor could tell his general would rather be standing, but the setting was so informal that the Emperor preferred he sit. "King Germaine's decision was to begin withdrawing all Neverak troops in three months. A complete withdrawal within six."

"How much of that time remains?"

"We have a month and a half until we begin the exodus of our men."

"King Germaine and his nobles were perfectly predictable, of course," Emperor Krallick stated. "Was it the gold?"

"They were nearly swayed by a nobleman. Templeton."

"Templeton Marsh." The Emperor nodded. "I've had an eye on him for a long time. He plots to get his blood seated on the throne. Has a daughter a year or two younger than King Germaine's son, the crown prince. He would see them wed. But he's very loyal."

"The affairs of Blithmore nobles mean nothing to me," Attikus replied.

"But they mean a great deal to me. I must know which houses will fall in line and which will be problematic when Blithmore is joined to Neverak."

The Emperor reflected on his most recent letter from Baron Verkozy. It was highly unlikely that his plans for war could be executed in such a short time. General Derkop would not arrive at Grettinah, the capitol of Old Avalon, for at least another week.

"We will need to use deception to keep our troops in Blithmore. The entire point of the arrangement was to have my men strategically placed to act the moment the invasion begins."

"And why invade Blithmore, Your Majesty?" Attikus asked wearily. The Emperor was not at all taken back with Attikus's forwardness. He knew that Attikus had understood the Emperor's intentions for some time now. "Do you fully understand the scope of this undertaking? The years of uprisings you'll have to deal with? The damage it will do to our relationships with other countries?"

"I thought it was the duty of the Emperor to make his empire as strong as possible."

"That doesn't always mean making it as large as possible."

"How am I to interpret your objection, General?" Emperor Krallick sat up in the water, curious to know Attikus's response. "Are you unwilling to lead my armies? Each time you salute me, you say, 'For the glory of Neverak.' Are you not willing to increase the glory of my empire?"

"Invading our allies doesn't bring us glory!" Attikus said, losing some of the great control he normally had over his emotions, fascinating the Emperor. "The kingdom of your father's best friend. Your Majesty, do I need to remind you of the history between our countries? Or why your father was never as popular as when he and King Germaine ended the hostilities?"

"Of course not, but there are still many in Neverak who dislike Blithmore and its people. Very many. Now answer my question: Are you unwilling to lead my armies into war?"

Each man looked into the eyes of the other; finally Attikus averted his gaze. The Emperor had known his general would be reluctant, but this was a much stronger reaction. Attikus spoke quietly. "I wish to caution you, Your Majesty, against forgetting everything you've been taught about diplomacy. If the rumors are true, then you have already sent General Derkop to Old Avalon to formulate plans for war. But you are betraying your most powerful ally for Old Avalon, a land torn by slavery. The Baron's rule is as unstable as a child's tower of wooden blocks."

"Attikus . . ."

"Verkozy is a tyrant, Ivan. How should I react to your decision? You're rejecting everything I taught you because you hate King Germaine. You hate him for being closer to your father than you were."

"I've heard enough." The Emperor did not bother to hide the menace in his voice, nor the pain and anger on his face at the words Attikus had dared utter. "Get out," he told his servants and the slave girl.

Attikus's face showed neither fear nor remorse, but he still would not look at the Emperor. When the servants had left and the doors were closed, Attikus spoke first. "You would be better served focusing your attention on other tasks, Your Majesty. Strengthening the northern borders, better strongholds in the western mountains, the robbers plaguing the southern swamplands . . . or your project in northeastern Neverak."

The Emperor did not respond immediately. He was fuming over his general's audacity to speak down to him as though one were still teacher, the other still Ivan, the crown prince. But it was a difficult situation. He needed Attikus, but he couldn't let him get away with such brazen behavior. It would be a grave sign of weakness. He allowed Attikus certain informalities in their discourse, but not this, not such blunt—and personal—objections.

The best thing to do was to wait and watch, he decided. A rash decision—demoting Attikus, or executing him, of all people—could prove disastrous. Finally the Emperor responded. "Which task do you think most requires my attention?"

"One in particular, Your Majesty," Attikus answered. "You have a small band of outlaws somewhere out there." Attikus gestured to the east. "We still have no idea how large or small this band might be, but we know they are very capable. They repelled our Elite Guard at the Iron Pass—"

"My Guards were under orders not to harm them. They did precisely that."

"—which means they are still alive. And if you were them, what would you do now?"

"I've taken all this into consideration already. Four of the best bounty hunters have been sent to find and kill them."

"Bounty hunters?" Attikus practically spat the word.

"You heard me."

"Lowlifes. You are above such actions, Your Majesty. The bandits repelled the Elite Guard; they can fight off bounty hunters."

"We shall see. In the meantime, I want you to remain in Neverak for a short while, be with your family. It will do your health some good."

"But Your Majesty—"

"That's an order, and I will not change my mind. I want you to think about the question I've asked you twice now. If I decide to invade Blithmore, will you lead my armies?"

"I will give it my full consideration," Attikus replied with a bow.

"I expect nothing less. You are excused." The Emperor watched him leave. Then he was alone in the bath. He thought about Attikus, and the brilliance inside that man's head. He needed Attikus by his side for the invasion. Having the Baron's armies reinforcing the Elite Guard gave the Emperor great comfort, but having Attikus guiding them would give him far greater. Then after the war ended, if need be, he could deal with Attikus's insolence. Of all the things the Emperor had learned from Attikus, the most important was how to read and manipulate him.

TWENTY-TWO

Vote for Matt

A long time passed for James as he sat in a dark, quiet room with no other sound but the coarse breathing of the men flanking him. The smell in the room was horrendous, worse than the rotten onion powder he'd used when he'd rescued Henry in Bookerton. James had never smelled anything like it. He tried to breathe through his mouth, but the thick, decayed stench pervaded his sense of taste, causing him to choke and cough.

He wanted to cover his mouth with a cloth but couldn't. Shackles around his wrists and ankles prevented him from doing anything. He sat on a chair with one short leg that wobbled when he shifted his weight. After what seemed like hours, he heard the sound of others entering the room.

The bag came off his head, and James looked around the small room, lit by a single candle on a table made of some reddish-black wood he couldn't identify. As his eyes adjusted to the flickering, faint light, he realized that five other people were in the room with him. James was not small, yet all but one of the room's occupants were larger than him. The man who was smaller in stature stepped forward, flanked by the giants.

He wore finely tailored clothes which matched his impeccable grooming. His own straw hair was neatly styled, and he wore brown pants and a matching brown vest over a blue shirt. Perched on top of his head was a small brown hat which hardly dented his hair, and he held a cloth, perfumed, no doubt, over his nose and mouth.

"My name is Rudolfos," he said. "I am the owner of this establishment."

"I can't say I'm pleased to meet you," James said. Talking made the stench of the room worse, and James coughed reflexively to expel the bad air from his lungs. "Why the shackles and the room of death?"

Rudolfos smiled pleasantly. "You cheated." His pleasant, almost lilting voice reminded James of a parent gently scolding a child for being naughty. He pulled a pair of dice out of his pocket and shook them with his free hand. "Tell me what number you think I'll roll."

"If I could do that, I would be a rich man."

Rudolfos laughed. Then his hand curled around the dice and flew out, smacking James across his face backhanded. Despite Rudolfos's small size, it left James's cheek smarting and his pulse pounding in anger.

"The rules state that the dice of a thrower may be inspected at any time," James stated, "but there's no rule or law about using dice that are weighted, only that if any player objects to a pair of dice they must be discarded. Those are the rules!"

"The rules assume that all parties agree to one set of dice being rolled throughout the game, and that all parties act like gentlemen. It's my job to ensure the game stays fair."

"Then apparently you aren't doing your job."

Rudolfos's hand flew out again, hitting James on the other cheek—and harder this time. He grinned merrily and said, "You're right. Now I have to do something to ensure no one will act as ungentlemanly as you have. A gentleman has to protect his business."

Suddenly James heard Maggie's warnings clearly in his mind, as if she were standing next to him. She had warned him, Ruther, and Henry about the dangers of their choice, but they had ignored her.

"Why don't you stop blabbering and tell me what you want?"

James said. Without giving himself away, he observed the other, larger men carefully, waiting for the moment when one of the beasts would give him an opening to strike.

"For starters, you will forfeit all your tokens."

"You can't do that!" James struggled to stand as best he could with his limbs shackled to the chair, but the other men quickly subdued him while Rudolfos dumped the tokens from James's bag into his hand and then shoved them into his pocket. After making certain the bag was empty, Rudolfos threw it back at James's face.

"Quite a sum you accumulated," Rudolfos stated.

James snorted at the tiny man. "I didn't win all of that by cheating! Not even half of it. I shouldn't have to give it all back."

"Since you're the one in shackles, I don't think you have a place to argue. There's one more thing we need to do to teach you a lesson."

"What more can you take from me?" James asked. "My clothes?"

"No, no, no," Rudolfos said. "Nothing like that . . . We'll take your hand."

Before James had time to register what Rudolfos had said, one man pinioned his arms while a second unlocked the shackles binding his right wrist. The other men turned James's chair so it faced the table. After his arm was free, the man who'd unshackled it placed James's hand on the reddish-black wood. Facing the wall, James finally discovered the source of the terrible smell.

Over a dozen dismembered hands in various states of decomposition were nailed to the wall in a straight line. To one side a filthy, bloodstained cleaver hung on a metal hook.

"Wait!" James yelled.

Rudolfos crossed the room and removed the massive knife from the hook with great care. The candlelight reflected off the few unstained spots on the blade. "Like you said, I have to do my job. If I let you get away with cheating, pretty soon others cheat, too. I don't want that. It's bad for business." Rudolfos's eyes were cold as he advanced toward James. James struggled to loosen his arms from the thugs' grasp, but they were stronger than him.

"You're making a grave mistake!" He jerked each and every way to free his arm.

"Hold him tight," Rudolfos ordered as he raised the blade.

"This is madness! You can't use that on me! On whose authority are you carrying out this punishment? You don't even know who I am!"

His words had no effect on Rudolfos, whose lips curled back as he ground his teeth together. The small man's eyes fixed intently on James's arm.

"Don't do this!" James roared.

Just as Rudolfos raised his arm to separate James from his right hand, the door burst open. Light flooded the room, and Ruther stood in the entrance. In one hand he held his flask, in the other was a piece of parchment.

"What in the name of the Royal Committee are you doing to my partner?" he cried in a thick Pappalonian accent.

Everyone turned to face Ruther.

"Rudolfos, have you any idea who this man is whose hand you plan to remove?" Ruther covered his nose as he stepped further into the room. "And what is that awful stench?"

Rudolfos glanced from his men to Ruther. "I haven't any idea who you are, sir, other than that you were at the dice table with this man."

"Yes! I am with him. I've thrown dice with him every day for the last three weeks because both of us were sent here by *Matt* to raise money for his efforts!"

James looked around the room and noticed for the first time that everyone, including Rudolfos, was sporting Matt patches. Rudolfos seemed even more confused. None of his thugs knew what to do, either, but they had all let go of James.

"Is this how you reward someone working for Matt?" Ruther

asked. "We were sent here with those dice to roll against Byderik supporters. And now you've obliterated our disguises!" Ruther jabbed a finger at the Byderik patch on his sleeve.

"I knew nothing—"

"Matt said he sent you a letter regarding this matter three months ago!" Ruther stuck three fingers in Rudolfos's face. "Three men would be coming to your establishment to raise money for him: Rumps Liggit, Hask Vornbit, and Jipper Ornestfell!" Ruther shouted each name louder than one before it as he ticked down his fingers one at a time. "And that man is none other than Jipper Ornestfell."

"A letter?" Rudolfos frowned and looked to the men with him.

Ruther slapped his own forehead and cursed. "You think this is a game, Rudy? We've raised over two thousand gyri from Byderik supporters in the last three weeks. *Two thousand!* How else do you explain his ability to so vastly outspend Byderik? You think he plucks gyri from cherry trees?"

Ruther slammed a worn piece of parchment against Rudolfos so hard that the little man nearly fell over.

"Here's a copy of the letter! Honestly, you'd think a man who runs a place like this would have more brains. Let's go, Jipper. Maybe if we lay low for a couple of days we can get back onto a decent table, but I wouldn't count on it."

"I'm sor—" Rudolfos was quickly interrupted.

"Not as sorry as you will be if Matt loses the election."

"Why didn't you say anything?" Rudolfos asked James.

"You—you—you had a bag on my head!" James sputtered. "And you were about to cut off my hand!"

The tiny man dug in his pockets for the tokens he'd taken from James. His hands trembled so badly that most of the tokens spilled onto the floor and rolled across the room with a clatter. "Here! Here! Give these to him—to Matt—with my apologies."

Ruther picked one up that had rolled next to his boot. Then he flipped it back to Rudolfos; it hit him square in the nose. "You keep them. Tell Matt yourself what you did when you give them to him. And get those shackles off Jipper!" Ruther ordered testily.

Rudolfos's men hurried to obey Ruther. Rubbing his sore ankles, James stared at the money scattered all over the floor. Had Ruther gone mad? Why would he allow Rudolfos to keep their tokens? Perhaps Ruther noticed James's confusion because he tapped his boot twice on the floor. "Mr. Ornestfell, please, our business is urgent. Move quickly."

Still shaking and sweating, James followed Ruther out the door as Rudolfos persisted on apologizing for his mistake. He stopped after Ruther insisted that no *permanent* harm had been done. Ruther wouldn't say a word to James until they'd reached the stables, and each time James tried to speak, the storyteller waved his hand to tell him to shut his mouth. Finally, when they were on their horses and headed for the inn, James was allowed to talk.

"The money, Ruther!" he spat. "Rudolfos threw the money at you and you turned it down! What were you thinking?"

"His men pulled you away before you could clear the table of your tokens, so I picked them. You made two hundred gyri on that last throw. And I made one hundred fifty. I scooped it all up. That plus everything else I kept is in my pocket right now. What Rudy threw on the floor was barely more than two hundred."

"That's—" James paused to calm himself down. He wanted to punch Ruther in the face for so many reasons. "You fool! The gold token was in that bag! It was twelve hundred gyri!"

Ruther let out a sputtering laugh, filling James's nose with the scent of ale. James leaned over and punched his friend in the side of the face. Ruther, surprised, fell off Ghost and landed in the dirt road. James hopped off Sissy's saddle and grabbed Ruther by his shirt collar. Ruther's face was streaked with dirt and a trickle of blood ran down his cheek from his forehead where a rock had scraped him, but he still beamed as though nothing was wrong.

"You stupid drunk!" James bellowed. "This is all your fault!"

Ruther still snickered. "We'll have more tomorrow. Stop worrying."

James exploded, shaking Ruther violently with his left hand, and slapping him on both sides of the face with his right. Several people stopped to stare at the scene. "I'm not going back there. If you hadn't arrived when you did, my hand would be nailed to a wall! Did you see those hands on the wall? *Did you?*"

"Of course I did, you dolt," Ruther giggled.

"And you think Rudolfos won't figure out that you lied to him?"

No matter what James said, Ruther only laughed harder. "I'm certain he will. But that's not what I meant. I mean after breakfast tomorrow, we'll have more money . . . much more—because when everyone laid hands on you, I swallowed the golden token. Lifted it right out of your bag. We still have over seventeen hundred gyri, friend. Most of it here!" Ruther patted his large stomach, and laughed until tears ran down his face.

James let go of Ruther's collar and let him hit the dirt. He sat down next to him and wiped the sweat from his eyes. He pictured Ruther in his mind, washing the golden token down with a large mouthful of ale, and soon he couldn't stop laughing either.

When their mirth finally died, James pulled a throwing knife out of his boot, grabbed Ruther's hand, and placed the hilt in Ruther's palm. "I want you to put this into my stomach," James said.

With his hand still open and the blade resting on it, Ruther frowned at James. "What? Why?" He threw the knife into the dirt next to James. "That isn't funny."

James wiped more dirt off his face and pants. "You're right, it's not."

"Then why—"

"Because you're going to get me—or someone else—killed if you keep drinking that poison. First it was Henry at the Friendly Fenley. This time it was almost me. Who will it be next, Ruther?"

"It was one time! I haven't touched it since—"

"Then it was one time too many."

"I've seen *you* drink." Ruther got to his feet sluggishly and slapped the dust from his clothes. "What makes you so special?"

"I can control myself!"

"So can—"

"You can't, Ruther. You just can't."

Ruther extended a hand to James and pulled him to his feet. They regarded one another for a moment. James hadn't been particularly fond of Ruther until recently. The last few weeks had helped him understand that Ruther was a man of vices. He climbed back on Sissy, and Ruther remounted Ghost. They rode side by side, ignoring those who had gathered to watch them.

"Fine, James. Fine. You're right. No more drinking for me."

James exhaled softly through his nose. "Thank you."

TWENTY-THREE
Thirsty's Choice

Even though the tournament still had a few days left before closing for the year, neither Ruther nor James returned to the dicing hall. As soon as the golden token was back and washed the next day, Ruther discussed with James how they should convert the tokens back into gyri. They had no idea if Rudolfos had discovered that their story wasn't true, but they couldn't go back to the dicing hall in case he had. James suspected they'd be in danger of losing more than a hand.

"Give them to Thirsty," Ruther said, helping James sharpen his new set of throwing knives. "She'll get the money for us."

James thought for a moment, then shook his head. "I like Thirsty," he said, "I really do. But that doesn't mean I trust her with that much money. I'd rather wait until Maggie and Henry come back. Let them do it."

"I trust her. She's served us every day since we've been here, even though she wasn't supposed to. Can't you see that she loves us? Well, at least she loves *you*."

James felt his neck grow hot. "What makes you think that?"

"I know it." Ruther wiped the blade he was working on and returned it to its pouch, then selected another. "I have a sense for these things."

James tapped a knife on his knee as he reconsidered Ruther's suggestion. "I don't know. Something about her worries me. Why not just wait?"

"The tournament ends in three days, and we'll be lucky if Rudolfos doesn't try to confirm our story with Matt by then. What if Henry and Maggie don't return in time? We'll be stuck with worthless tokens! We need to make certain we won't have any problem getting the money. Just ask her."

"*You* ask her."

"I beat you in the knife throwing contest that one time. You should have to ask her."

"It's your token," James said.

"We both earned it."

"Trust me, Ruther, after where it's been, that token is all yours. If you trust her that much, you ask her." He tapped Ruther on the chest with a finger. "But you had better make certain we get our gold back."

Ruther summoned Thirsty. She agreed to do it without hesitation. Ruther instructed her on exactly what to do and reviewed everything several times. James watched her closely for any sign that she might betray them, but she seemed enthusiastic, even excited, at the chance to help. When she left, Ruther grinned at James and patted him on the back. "See, you need to relax. All those years as a guardsman made you paranoid. I'm going to the market to pick up supplies. Anything you need? More knives perhaps?"

James took a knife from his belt and cocked his arm as if he was going to throw it at Ruther. "Fair enough," Ruther said, tipping his hat, and left the suite. James's thoughts were on Thirsty. He couldn't shake the feeling that there was something amiss with her. Then he recalled all the times Thirsty had helped them. Maybe Ruther was right . . . maybe he was paranoid.

About an hour later, the door burst open and a red-faced Jessop entered. "Where is she?" he bellowed. "Where's Thirsty?"

James bit back a laugh. "Why do you ask me?"

"She's always spending time here when I've told her not to. She keeps switching chores with other maids so she can be around your lot. Fancies one of you, I suspect. So where is she?"

"She changed the linens this morning and took her leave, same as every day," James lied. He supposed Thirsty hadn't asked permission to leave work and run their errand, which made him feel a bit guilty. Why hadn't she told them she might get in trouble?

Jessop waved a piece of parchment at James. "You're behind this! I know it. I've seen her, the way she acts so happy—getting ideas into her head—running away from me." He turned around and stormed off muttering to himself. "I'll show her who resigns and who doesn't . . ."

James jumped to his feet and ran after Jessop. "Give me that!" James scanned the letter and realized his fears had been well-placed.

Everything was a blur until he was flying down the road to the dicing hall on Sissy. Thirsty was probably long gone by now. She'd had plenty of time to exchange the tokens for money and leave, but Sissy was fast, and James had to catch her.

"How could you be so foolish?" he asked himself. "Trusting a woman—again? You deserve every punishment you get."

Experience had taught him better, but apparently his skull was too thick to learn the lessons of the past. He had disappointed himself. The dicing hall came into view. James rode Sissy near, eyes peeled for a woman with dark skin and hair whiter than the clouds. She usually wore drab, patched dresses, and most everyone near the dicing hall was well-dressed from head to foot. He thought to tie Sissy to a post and enter when he noticed the two men standing at the main doors. Both were from Rudolfos's goon squad, men who had held him down and threatened to cut off his hand. He turned away before either could notice him watching them. He checked a side door and found two more familiar faces there.

Cursing, he rode away from the hall. Where would Thirsty go with a bag full of coins? Which direction would she go? James turned Sissy around and headed for the town square. From there he took the main road north. The longer he rode, the more panic welled up in his chest. James remembered well the rage he'd felt when he'd believed Ruther had stolen the chest of gold from the carriage.

When he reached the northern outskirts of Borderville, he eased up on Sissy's pace; her ribs were heaving with each breath. Seeing her so labored, James dismounted and walked next to her. "Sorry, girl," he told her, "I forgot how long it's been. You're not used to riding so hard."

James stopped at a stone watering trough to let Sissy rest and drink. Around him were some of Borderville's smallest and most dilapidated buildings. The meager shops offered second-hand hats, suspect potions, or rusty swords and daggers. James heard sobbing from an alley between two of the stores. He left his horse and peered around the corner. There, wearing the same worn, patched dress he'd always seen her in, her head tucked between her knees, two bags of gold at her side, was Thirsty. She gasped when she saw him.

James expected her to jump to her feet and try to run, but she didn't. Instead she got down on her knees and clasped her hands together. "I'm sorry, James. Please don't kill me."

"You betrayed us," James said, kneeling in the dirt and grabbing her wrists. "I trusted you, and you tried to steal our money."

"I know! I—"

"Why?"

Thirsty started to sob again. "I'm never going to make it out of here. I'm never going to earn enough money to do what I want. I told myself I was justified because you stole the money from other people."

"We need that money to rescue my sister!"

"I know. I know." Fat tears rolled down Thirsty's cheeks. Her bright blue eyes swam as she searched James's face. "Forgive me, James, please. I made it this far, and I stopped because I wanted to turn back, but I was afraid you might already know. I wanted to turn back, James!"

Her hands sought his shoulders as though she wanted to hug him, but he continued to hold her at length. She was beautiful, even in such a pitiful, wretched state.

"You've lied to us more than once, Thirsty. What else are you hiding?"

If Thirsty had been crying before, it was nothing compared to what she did next. She shrieked in pain and wept as though her very soul was in agony. "I've spied on you!"

"For whom?" James asked. When she didn't answer, he shook her. "Tell me!"

"I don't know!" She pulled away from his grip and covered her face. "I send letters to the border agent . . . Asaron. He tells me to watch people. A pigeon brings me notes and I return them."

James recoiled from her. "Who is he spying for?"

"I don't know! I'm so sorry! I need the money. I'm desperate. I never meant to hurt anyone."

"What have you told him?"

"I report to him every two days. I tell him if you are still here, if I've learned anything new, and anything else of interest I've noted."

"What sort of questions has he asked?"

"I—I—I—"

He shook her again. "Tell me!"

"What—what you look like . . . what you plan to do . . . where you plan to go. Things of that nature! James, you're hurting me!"

James let go of her before he attracted unwanted attention. "Stay away from us, Thirsty."

"No . . ."

"Go back to your job."

"No . . . no . . ."

"Tell Jessop you don't want to resign."

"James, I beg you, don't do this! Let me help you. This can be fixed!"

Those last four words stuck in James's mind. He remembered

similar words written to him in a letter months ago, only they said, "This can't be fixed."

"What do you mean?" he asked Thirsty. "How could you possibly—?"

"Let me go with you! I'll cook, clean, anything."

"Why would you want to come with us? Why would I let you?"

Thirsty stared into James's eyes for a long time before answering. "For years I accepted that my life was over. I was stuck at the inn, stuck spying for Asaron. My dreams have faded into nothing. Then I met you four. You, Henry, Maggie, and Ruther. You all have such purpose, you're *alive*. I want that! I want to live! I want to be more than a maid who listens at doors and writes letters. And you four have been my friends—you let me eat with you! No one has ever done that in all the years I've worked there. It means something!"

"You have a poor way of showing your gratitude."

"I know, and I'm—"

"Stop saying you're sorry. You know Henry's name. Did you reveal that to Asaron, too?"

"No. I heard you say his name, and I suspected, but I never wrote it. I swear I didn't!"

"You're a thief and a spy." James spat the words from his mouth and turned away, but Thirsty grabbed his knees and clung to them.

"I will follow you. I will sell everything I have and follow you to the ends of Atolas."

"Do what you like. We will not help you, feed you, or accept you."

"I swear by everything I love. My family, my life . . . my freedom, I will not betray your trust again."

James's first thought was that this was a decision the group should make, but then he reconsidered. Maggie would say no. For some reason, she didn't like Thirsty. Ruther would say yes. And Henry . . . James didn't know. But if the vote was two and two, Thirsty would never come along. And that would be that. Did the others even need to know? Other than confirming what the Emperor already knew, Thirsty hadn't really harmed them. And what Ruther had said earlier in the day was true—James did like her. She was a delight. Despite her horrible employer and her impoverished state, she found a way to be happy and spread that to others. Maybe the group needed such a spark.

He offered her his hand. "One chance. You do anything even remotely—"

"I won't." Thirsty smiled and hugged him, kissing his cheeks and neck. "Thank you, James. Thank you. Thank you. Thank you."

James sighed, pulled away, and picked up the gold. "You're not going to be welcome back at the inn. You know that, right?"

Thirsty grinned sheepishly. "I know a way to sneak inside without being seen. Do you think Maggie will let me share her room?"

When James and Thirsty returned to the suite, they found Henry and Maggie back from their travels with an armload of maps. Everyone fussed over Maggie's injured hand, then over James's announcement that Thirsty would join them in their travels. Finally their attention turned to the journey. Long into the night, the five travelers studied maps and discussed the routes to Greenhaven and Neverak that the mapmaker had shown to Henry and Maggie.

Soon after dawn, James woke. Thirsty was already cooking breakfast. When their eyes met, she nodded to him gratefully. He nodded back, knowing he had made the right decision.

The group's first stop was at the market for supplies. Then they took the road east out of Borderville. Maggie rode Fury, Henry rode Quicken, James was on Sissy, and Ruther had Ghost. With her saved money, Thirsty had purchased her own steed, a fine animal named Chance, though she thought that *Sissy* was the most adorable name for a horse she had ever heard. Ruther snickered loud enough for James to throw him a dirty look. And in that moment, everything was as it should be.

TWENTY-FOUR

The Soldier and the Storyteller

The party's swift travel across Pappalon was quite a different experience than their flight from Blithmore. They stayed on the roads rather than seeking out hidden paths. Without the carriage, they moved faster and had less trouble crossing treacherous spots, and on nights when they reached a town, they slept at inns, providing needed relief from the weariness of sleeping under the stars.

However, the journey through Pappalon did allow each of them to learn new skills. Henry asked James to teach him swordplay for an hour a day. Maggie swallowed her pride and let Thirsty teach her some tricks with cooking. Even Ruther had an opportunity to acquire a different skill. Since the last gift Ruther had received from his dying uncle had been a bow and quiver, he'd always wanted to learn to hunt. Before leaving Richterton with Henry, his hunting experience had been limited to searching for storytelling work at public houses and inns.

"You'll need to look after yourself, Ruther," his uncle had said. "Best you know how to use a bow and arrow properly so you can eat if work is scarce." Though Ruther developed a respectable skill in archery, he had never hunted for food. Traveling through Blithmore, he had always preferred to let James do the killing while he stayed by the campfire drinking ale he'd purchased in passing towns.

But it was no surprise to Ruther that when he volunteered to accompany James on his next hunt for rhinelk and spiny boars, everyone else acted shocked.

"Did you bump your head?" Maggie questioned.

"Because you do realize," Henry began, "that the boars don't just walk up to you. You actually have to go and—"

"Find them," Ruther finished. "Yes, I'm aware. James explained it all to me last night about where the pointed ends of the arrows go. I think I can manage."

Maggie kissed James on the cheek in front of everyone. "Show Ruther how a real man hunts, James."

James blushed and patted her arm. Ruther's stomach felt like a stone had been dropped in it. He wasn't certain if that was because he felt awkward for James or for Thirsty, who turned her head away from the sight of Maggie kissing James.

"You ready, Ruther?" James asked quickly.

"Yes," Ruther said, "just waiting for my kiss from Maggie." Ruther turned his cheek to her, but only received a firm but friendly pat on it instead. "Thirsty?"

Thirsty laughed. "Oh, go on then."

She put her hands on his cheeks, and then kissed her hands. Ruther gave her a wink and grabbed his hunting gear. Armed with knives and bows, the two set off into the wilderness of eastern Pappalon. Ruther was glad to leave camp. Something in his mind hadn't been right lately. When Maggie and Henry had returned from the cartographer, and he'd seen Maggie's damaged hand, Ruther had felt a surge of rage at whomever had done her harm. And ever since then strange thoughts about her bubbled up in his mind. Though try as he might to push them away, they crept back, distracting and unsettling him.

He figured the best thing he could do was get away from camp for a few hours. "Unseen, unheard, unthought," was, after all, how the old saying went, and Ruther wanted more than anything to unthink some of his thoughts. James seemed the perfect person with whom to spend some quality time. Ever since the dice games in Borderville, Ruther had come to enjoy James's company. It reminded him of the passage in the Word of Worlds about the lamb and the sabre-tiger becoming companions. Although Ruther would never call James a lamb to his face.

James and Ruther rode Sissy and Ghost deep inside the woods two miles north of the main road eastward. The trees of the forest were tall, thin, and sparse enough that plenty of light shone through the canopy. The sounds of birds and other creatures were plentiful in these woods, which meant that having a quiet conversation would not scare the animals away.

After they had ridden far enough that Ruther had lost all sense of where they were in relation to their camp, they heard a thumping sound and followed until they spotted a large buck nearly fifty yards off. The sound reminded Ruther of when Maggie banged her spoon on her pot to call everyone to eat. When she did it, she always made the same stern expression that made Ruther laugh.

Ruther shook his head angrily and chased the thought away.

The horn on the rhinelk's nose stood at least a foot high. The beast was using it to ram the trunk of a tree to knock down twigs and leaves for food. James gestured for Ruther to shoot it. The buck's attention was solely on the trunk. Ruther felt a sense of power as he pulled an arrow from his quiver and nocked it. His hand stayed steady as he aimed and released. It was a good shot, but a little high, and sailed less than a foot above the beast.

"Again," James mouthed.

Unfortunately, the arrow's whistle had alerted the rhinelk to their presence, and it turned and ran for cover in the denser forest. Ruther moved much faster this time, taking no thought to his shot or his aim, moving by instinct. In less than two seconds, his hand flew from his quiver to the bow, then he pulled back on the string. When he released, he knew the shot was good, and he wasn't wrong. The buck jerked when the arrow struck him, nearly stumbling, but then sprinted off into the green.

"Let's go!" James cried in exhilaration. "That's our dinner!"

After a half hour of chasing the rhinelk, Ruther wished he had shot a smaller, weaker animal. "How can it have any blood left?" he asked. "We've been following its trail for a thousand miles."

"Should be dead by now," James answered, craning his neck to see ahead. "I don't see him. He must have dropped."

They followed the trail of blood another two hundred yards before finding the fallen beast. Ruther had to look away as James cleaned out the animal on the spot, but even the sounds and smells of James's work proved enough to make him sick. James chuckled as Ruther vomited behind a tree.

"You think this is humorous?" Ruther asked huskily between retches. "My boot just came out my mouth."

"Oh, yes, it's humorous."

"Believe me, I know humor, and this doesn't qualify."

"Ruther has a weak stomach," James said, still laughing. "And all this time, I thought you didn't hunt because you're lazy."

"Laziness *is* why I don't hunt. I didn't know I had a weak stomach until today."

James laughed even harder as he finished his work and hoisted the carcass of the deer over Sissy's back, carrying the saddle in his arms. "Long walk ahead, better get going before it gets dark."

Ruther surveyed the sky and noted that the sun was well along its way into the afternoon. It reminded Ruther how Maggie sometimes called the late afternoon "sundrop," and laughed at her own made-up word.

"Stop it," Ruther told himself.

"What?" James asked.

"Oh . . . nothing. We'll be lucky to be back at camp by sunset."

Ruther considered riding Ghost at a slow trot, but decided against it. Instead, he walked beside James, leading Ghost by the reins.

"Who was the last girl you took a fancy to?" James asked.

Ruther peered at James's face to see if the soldier was asking this in jest or in seriousness, but James's expression was set in stone. "Funny you should ask," Ruther mumbled.

"What was that?"

"Oh . . . nothing."

James grinned slyly at Ruther. "Come on, tell me."

"I don't know," Ruther answered as best as he could. "As a storyteller, I never had time for women. Of course, I've *known* women, I suppose that goes with the work I chose, but only a couple of girls ever really caught more than my eye."

James looked at Ruther as if he was seeing him for the first time. "You—you've known a—a woman? Really?"

"You're a guardsman. Haven't you known your fair share?"

"I've never bedded a woman, Ruther," James admitted. He didn't seem at all ashamed of this fact, which surprised Ruther.

"Well, that's . . . fine. There's something to be said about the nobility of chastity." Ruther still couldn't believe that James was so naive about women.

"There's much to be said about it," James countered. "But you've never been in love?"

"No, I can't honestly say I have."

"So all those women, and not one spark of genuine affection? I think I pity you."

"I don't think it earns me any pity," Ruther said, "but if you choose to look at it that way . . . Like I said, I never had time for those things."

He had never been a religious man, though he had read the Word a few times, mostly to glean material for storytelling. Nor was he a man strict in morals like his friends. He had, in many ways, become much like his uncle. Sometimes that fact bothered him, but only if he dwelled on it.

"What about you, James?" he continued. "Have you ever loved a woman? Anyone I might know from Richterton?"

James adjusted the rhinelk carcass on Sissy's back as they walked. Ruther started to wonder if James had heard him, though he didn't dare repeat the question in case James had but didn't want to answer. Instead he waited, trying to pretend as if he'd said nothing and the trees had suddenly become very interesting to stare at.

"I loved a woman once," James stated quietly. "I met her in the market in a town where I was stationed. It was one of those moments where the instant I saw her . . . anyway, it wasn't . . . well, events happened . . . and now I'm here . . . but I cared very deeply for someone for a time."

"That was the worst story ever told!" Ruther laughed. "Where's all the interesting information? Her name, the color of her eyes . . . the size of her bosom . . . and most important of all: what happened to force you apart?"

James shook his head. "That's why I was a soldier, not a storyteller. Her name isn't important."

"Of course it is."

"I haven't spoken it in a long time."

Ruther saw the faraway look in James's eyes and interpreted it easily. James was usually a man of little emotion, but when it was there, it was plain for anyone to read. "You still love her."

James didn't respond

"Does anyone know? Henry? Maggie?"

"It doesn't concern them." The familiar stoic tone crept into James's voice, but all it did was make his poor attempt to conceal his emotions more glaring. Perhaps James wished he hadn't brought up the subject, but Ruther's interest was too great to let it go. "Henry and I don't speak about such things. And Maggie . . . is a very complex woman. I realize that the two of you have never gotten along well, but I see many desirable qualities in her. I didn't know her very well before we left Richterton, but as I've come to know—"

"Have you kissed her?"

James's face turned red. "No."

Ruther let out a burst of laughter so loud that Sissy neighed in annoyance. "I'm sorry. I just thought—"

"How are you supposed to know if you want to spend the rest of your life with a woman?" James's gaze was on the cloudless, darkening sky. "My mother and father hated each other. I look at how they lived, and it makes me ill. I don't know much about love. I knew that I was in love once, but I haven't felt that way since."

"Not even about Maggie?"

"I—I—I don't know. Should I even be comparing two different women?"

"Of course!" Ruther cried, perhaps too enthusiastically.

James surveyed Ruther with skepticism. "You seem awfully confident about these matters for a man who's never been in love."

"It makes sense to me, is all. I've been watching you and Maggie for weeks. Don't be offended, but I think Maggie is worried about your feelings toward Thirsty."

Ruther had expected more laughter from his friend, instead all he got was contemplative silence. "Thirsty, James? Do you fancy her?"

"No." James shook his head weakly. "I don't know. I admit that I have an eye for Maggie. Even when we were children I found her attractive, but she's seventeen—"

"Eighteen now."

"Exactly. I'm six years older. I've seen so much, and she so little."

Ruther didn't agree. In the past few months, Maggie had seen and endured as much as anyone twice her age. And for the most part, she'd handled things well. However, he felt no need to point these things out to James. Instead, he nodded and gestured for James to continue. "The age difference *can* be a problem for some people."

"Thirsty is different. She—she—"

"She's almost three years older than Maggie."

"She is."

"And she adores you."

"Yes."

"And makes no effort to conceal her attraction toward you."

"None!"

"And she's also quite beautiful, isn't she?"

"I . . . she, yes, but . . ." James took a deep breath. "There's no denying Thirsty is very attractive."

Ruther agreed, but didn't find Thirsty nearly as attractive as . . . He shook his head again to clear his thoughts. "Do you love Thirsty, James?"

Again there was a pause. James kicked a broken branch out of his path and several stinkrabbits hopped away in fright, leaving a faint foul odor in their wake. Ruther savored watching James confront his own passions. It was like watching a newborn goat take its first wobbly steps.

"No. I don't know, Ruther. I *can't* know. Any attempt to spend time with Thirsty is met with jealousy from Maggie, whom I also enjoy being around. And right now we can't afford ill feelings in the group. This isn't the time or place to court a woman or decide whom to love. Isabelle . . . I have to focus on her. How selfish would it be if—"

"Are you worried about what Henry or I will think of you if you develop feelings for someone? Because you don't—"

"I'm not worried about that at all. It's . . . for the last few years, I've had one plan in mind."

"To find this other woman?" Ruther asked.

James spat with excessive force. "No. It has nothing to do with her. I've—I've completely forgotten about that. I've had a plan, and now I don't think I'll ever be able to fulfill it . . . and women only complicate things."

"James, you have to give me more than a vague notion of what this plan is . . . or was."

"No, I don't. We're far from what I wanted to speak to you about. I wanted to—the point is—I'm not good with feelings. They frustrate me. And I frustrate Maggie. I've never understood them well enough to trust them."

"You've never trusted women?"

"No, no. My feelings. The only time in my life I was certain of something was one time with one woman. It's different with Maggie and Thirsty. I feel attraction inside, I feel caring, but I don't feel the same as I did with the first woman I loved. Why is that?"

Ruther snorted. "How should I know? Maybe because women are different, we feel differently about them. Maybe you don't care for Maggie or Thirsty the way you did this other woman. Nothing wrong with that."

"Perhaps. But as I said, this isn't the time or place for those feelings."

Ruther wasn't so certain about that, but preferred silence rather than voicing his dissent. The sight of flowers and trees awakening from winter was a welcome distraction from the conversation. As they emerged from the forest with their prey in tow, the first splashes of orange and purple could be seen as the sun dropped toward the horizon. Ruther wondered why his uncle had never settled down. Was there something in his family's blood that set them against marriage? The notion of settling down had once repulsed him, but after spending months with Henry and Isabelle and seeing what a powerful bond love could forge, Ruther's feelings had evolved.

"One of the things you must never ever do if you wish to be successful," his uncle had often advised, "is fall in love. Women are good for breeding, not for loving. They're like leeches. They suck the joy of life right out of you."

Like most things his uncle had taught him, Ruther had believed this and taken it to heart. Yet it was hard to deny that his uncle had been wrong about many things. What if it was just another error passed down from uncle to nephew?

Not long before nightfall, they reached the camp. Thirsty was the first to see them. When she saw the buck, her eyes lit up. "My goodness, James, did you kill that?" Maggie and Henry's heads turned to see the kill. "That's incredible."

"Actually—"

"Impressive, but not surprising," Maggie said, hugging James and pecking him on the cheek only a foot away from Thirsty. When Ruther saw this, he imagined himself, not James, receiving a peck from Maggie. He clenched his teeth together in hope that the image would flee his mind.

"Don't get too excited," James said, "it was Ruther who made the kill."

"Oh. Really?" Maggie said.

"Indeed it was, Mags," Ruther chimed in. "I told it one of my best stories, and it died of boredom."

Maggie burst out in giggles. Another stone dropped in Ruther's stomach as he noted how her smile wasn't too big or too small; her red lips framed her teeth nicely. He had noticed before that Henry's sister was attractive, but recently he had realized it was more than that. She wasn't so much attractive as she was beautiful; and sometimes, depending on her mood, *radiant* described her even better.

"He killed the rhinelk as well as I might have," James remarked. "Cleaning it didn't go as well, though. Did it, Ruther?"

"If by 'going well' you mean me puking my guts up behind a bush, then I think it went incredibly well."

Maggie laughed again. So did Thirsty, James, and Henry. But making Maggie laugh had the greatest effect on Ruther's spirits. He hated the way her laugh made him feel.

"Not Maggie," he told himself. "Anyone but Maggie."

TWENTY-FIVE

The Library of the Emperors

With a deep sigh, Emperor Krallick left his throne room after a long, tedious meeting with Sir Grellek regarding the cursed town he was trying to establish in Eastern Neverak. The Emperor had finally ended it by giving Grellek full authority over naming and planning the town, more power than he wanted to bequeath, but necessary at this point to get things done.

"That should keep him out of my hair for a few months," he said as he and his chamberlain strode, several footmen in tow, down a long hallway lined with torches and portraits of his ancestors. "This process has taken too long. That town should have been planned years ago."

"You could not have foreseen the prophecy, Your Majesty."

"The Seer's prophecy only makes it more expedient. If Henry Vestin is truly alive, the bounty hunters may not find him. I need to focus on the second obstacle." Emperor Krallick's expression turned dark. "Eastern Krallickton is far more important than Grellek understands. But he's so frustratingly *particular* about everything!"

"Yes, Your Majesty," the chamberlain responded.

"What appointment do I have now?"

"Your Majesty has lunch today with Cecilia. You ordered the kitchens to prepare whatever she chose."

"What did she choose?" the Emperor asked.

"A green salad with kappertrot."

"Change that. I don't want fish. Do we have chicken pie?"

"The cooks know it is your favorite, Your Majesty. It will not take long to prepare."

The Emperor stopped in front of the portrait of his father and ran a handkerchief-covered finger along the gilded wooden frame, then examined the handkerchief. He saw several specks of dirt that made him feel slightly ill. As he handed the handkerchief to the chamberlain, he said, "I want every portrait in the palace dusted by the end of the day. When was the last time our door handles were cleaned?"

"Last week—late last week, per the schedule Your Majesty has ordered."

The Emperor didn't like this at all. "Who is in charge of cleaning now?"

"You have Kristian in charge, Your Majesty. A month ago you commended him for his exemplary work."

The Emperor growled and began walking again. Now he remembered Kristian. A good servant. "Tell him I'm not pleased with his recent efforts. If he wants to stay in my service, he'll need to do better."

"About the lunch—"

"Chicken pie. Of course, if Cecilia wants salad, put the chicken on her salad. If she wants to earn the ruby rose, she should learn to select things that I will enjoy." The Emperor turned his thoughts to more important matters. "Tell me about the archiving of the palace records."

"The last report stated it should be completed ahead of schedule."

A smile formed on the Emperor's lips. This was good news. He loved the way everything ran efficiently in his palace and in his kingdom. In the end, Blithmore would be grateful when he conquered them.

"What news do we hear from General Attikus and his lieutenants?"

"His latest letter came yesterday, Your Majesty. He is carrying out your orders, sending the Elite Guard north under the watch of

King Germaine's soldiers while sneaking more men south through hidden routes. The Elite Guard arriving from the south will be ready for battle by the time they reach Neverak Palace. Do you wish to read the letter?"

"I do. After the meal."

"Your Majesty," an arriving footman said, bowing, "Cecilia awaits you in the dining room. Are there any other concubines with whom you wish to dine?"

Many of the palace staff knew that the Emperor contemplated inviting Isabelle for a meal, even though her cleansing was not yet complete. The only question was when he would finally give the order.

"Since lunch will be later than planned, I will visit the library and observe the archivists in their work."

"Your Majesty, what shall I do with Cecilia?"

The Emperor sniffed at the air. For a moment he thought he'd caught a whiff of an unpleasant odor. "Leave her there until the food is finished. Perhaps she will learn a lesson from the long wait."

When they reached the library, Emperor Krallick found almost a dozen archivists combing through the thousands upon thousands of books, papers, and other documents stored within the towering, dusty shelves. One of his most trusted servants oversaw the work within these walls, where the writings of the nobles and rulers of Neverak over hundreds of years and dozens of generations were stored.

"Your Majesty," the chief librarian said, "how may I be of service?"

Knowing that the library was filled with dust and other filth, the Emperor did not want to venture too far into the room. Already his skin had begun to crawl and itch as he thought of all the dirt stirred up into the air. Quickly he pulled out his handkerchief and pressed it to his mouth and nose. Several deep breaths into the cloth helped to calm his nerves. His entourage pretended not to notice his behavior, but he could see a mixture of concern and wariness on their faces.

"What have you found so far from my father?" Emperor Krallick asked.

"Nothing, Your Majesty. No signs of journals or other writings. We know they're here. It's only a matter of time before they are discovered."

"My father wrote voraciously," the Emperor reminded the librarian impatiently. "He kept meticulous journals. How can all those papers and books have disappeared without a trace?"

In them, the Emperor knew he would find answers to his most burning questions: what secret lay hidden in the northern Iron Forest, what had transpired between Emperor Peter and his first wife, and why he had appointed General Attikus as his superior general so quickly.

The Emperor's eyes were drawn to the colossal library surrounding him. He disliked touching the filthy tomes. Anything he read had to be thoroughly dusted, and even then he handled it with gloved hands. And the room—he hated it, too. It made him feel insignificant. So much knowledge in the world; so little time to acquire it. In all the years of his life, if he were so lucky to read a few hundred of these tomes, he might gather the tiniest drop in an ocean's worth of wisdom. It wasn't fair. An emperor should be endowed by the Lord of All Worlds with greater intellect than that of his peers. Thus he might rule perfectly.

"So little time," he whispered to himself, keenly aware in that moment of his mortality. Somewhere in this room his father had stored an important piece of work. It needed to be found.

"Your work is commendable," he told the librarian. "But I will not be satisfied until I have those writings from my father."

"It is lamentable that my predecessor passed away without being able to train me. He could have helped me understand his archaic system of storage."

"How long will it take you to sort through the remaining collections?"

The librarian gazed around the vast room with a doubtful face. "Your Majesty, I will make all haste. I will work—"

"How long?"

"Weeks . . . maybe months, Your Majesty."

"That is not good enough! My chamberlain here will supply other servants; train them if you must, but I need those journals sooner. Do not disappoint me."

The Emperor and his chamberlain left the library. "How many men will Your Majesty allow the librarian to use?" his chamberlain asked.

"As many as it takes without letting the palace's day-to-day operations suffer. It's imperative that I find those writings. Their disappearance is strange. Almost as though they've been hidden from me . . . Write a letter to King Germaine. Ask again if any of my father's journals or papers made it into his library. Request that he check a second time. Make certain he understands that the writings are of great significance."

"As you command, Your Majesty. Are you ready to dine? I was informed that your meal is nearly prepared and Cecilia awaits you."

The Emperor was indeed ready to eat, but he couldn't shake the library from his thoughts. If the legend was true that Attikus knew of a way to conquer Blithmore with such ease and swiftness, the information was vital to his plans. Especially if Attikus could not be trusted to do the job himself. And the Iron Forest . . .

"*He who was lost must be found and vanquished.*" Those were the words the Seer had spoken in the throne room months ago. Somehow all these things were connected. But how? The Emperor's father had kept his secrets well-concealed. But Emperor Ivan also knew he had written them down. He wrote everything down.

The chamberlain opened the doors to the dining room. Cecilia stood the moment she saw him. "Good afternoon, my Lord," she stated sweetly but humbly, bowing her head in graceful reverence.

"You look radiant, Cecilia," he replied, taking her hand and placing his lips on the back of it. "Forgive me for my tardiness. While I didn't want to be apart from you for a moment, the library needed my urgent attention. I sometimes think this palace would not last a day if I weren't here to run it."

The Emperor of Neverak kissed her hand a second time. He savored the sensation of touching his concubines. Due to his concerns over touching unclean persons and things, he rarely touched people without gloves, but his concubines were the exception. Grasping the flesh of Cecilia's hand was marvelous, and a kiss was extraordinary. She was adorned in a simple gown that accentuated her green eyes. Her auburn hair had been elegantly styled, and if the Emperor had wished, he could have led her straight into a ball where she would have fit in with all the daughters of the noble families. Knowing the proper etiquette expected of her, she waited until he sat before resuming her place at the table.

The footmen arrived carrying trays of food, and a pleasant odor wafted over the table, but the Emperor did not order it placed on the table just yet. He had not seen Cecilia in nearly a week and wanted to converse before eating. Her wit was one of the things that made him fond of her. She was educated and naturally clever. With some of his concubines, especially the dim-witted ones, conversation always felt forced or one-sided. Not so with Cecilia.

"Every day you grow more beautiful," he told Cecilia.

She grinned prettily. "Thank you, my Lord. And you are handsome as always. I sincerely appreciate the opportunity to dine with you."

After their short chat, the Emperor rang the meal bell, and the footmen answered the call. They poured drinks, distributed napkins, and sprinkled herbs and spices when requested. Only after the Emperor took a bite of his food was Cecilia free to eat. The Emperor kept to these rules very rigidly, as had his father. If decorum wasn't observed, respect was lost.

"How is Isabelle adjusting to life in the palace?" the Emperor asked. He was rather curious, but tried not to show it. "Is she happy?"

Cecilia set down her salad fork and took a sip of wine to clear her throat. Then she dabbed her face with the cloth. The Emperor appreciated how she always wanted to look her best around him. The little things mattered. "She's beginning to come around, my Lord. The first several days she seemed miserable. I've done my best to cheer her up, introduce her to other girls, offer her comfort."

"No problems between her and my other concubines?"

"None of concern, my Lord, other than a small spat with Kayla. Isabelle has a kind disposition despite her reluctance to get acquainted with us."

"Tell me about the spat with Kayla."

"A misunderstanding is all, my Lord. Kayla nearly bumped into her and got very upset. It was nothing. Any problems Isabelle has in the house would be those caused by others. She doesn't seek quarrels."

The Emperor wiped the grease from his pursed lips. This was good to hear. Isabelle's beauty was an astounding acquisition to his collection, and hopefully would be well worth the effort of bringing her to Neverak. "Has she said anything about me? Anything negative?"

"Nothing at all, my Lord. She hasn't said anything in your favor or otherwise. She mentioned briefly that she was here against her will." Cecilia laughed as though such a statement was absurd. "But I think it was the jitters on her first day. I don't think she knew what would be expected of her—in terms of the cleansing and the isolation. She was overwhelmed."

"Yes, that must be it." But the Emperor knew the truth: Isabelle's last memory of him was watching him slay the carpenter, a man for whom she held strong feelings. This needed to be remedied as soon as possible or her thoughts of him would turn to poison. He couldn't have that. To his chamberlain he said, "I want Isabelle to dine with me soon . . . after my journey north. All the standard precautions will be met."

Cecilia, who was halfway through a bite of her salad, turned a shade paler and began to cough. "Excuse me, my Lord," she croaked out in a hoarse voice that the Emperor found rather unattractive.

"Is something wrong?"

Cecilia shook her head quickly and offered a fragile smile. The Emperor watched her carefully, intrigued by the reaction.

"Yes, Isabelle is to dine with me. It is rather sudden, as I normally wait until a concubine is closer to the end of the cleansing, but this is a special circumstance. She is nearing her halfway point, and I am anxious." The Emperor watched Cecilia's face as he spoke. Cecilia was currently his favorite concubine, but he had not given her the ruby rose . . . not yet. He enjoyed making the girls crave it before he rewarded them.

All traces of Cecilia's usual pleasantness were gone, replaced with something that looked like deep concern.

"Are you certain that you're well, Cecilia?"

"Yes, my Lord," she quickly answered. "I was merely surprised. Like you said, it is sudden."

No, the Emperor decided. It was more than concern. Cecilia's reassuring smile was not at all reassuring. Her eyes were too shifty. *Jealousy.* Emperor Krallick grinned, amused at his own cunning. This would be a good test for Cecilia. He would make her more jealous and watch how she responded. The ruby rose was nearly hers to wear. The Emperor was growing tired of Kayla but had not ruled out favoring Jade. Changing the bearer of the rose regularly ensured that his slaves did not become too complacent. He planned to choose a wife from among the women in the house, and whoever he decided on would have to learn to *use* jealousy, not let it use her.

"Isabelle is a very stunning woman," he remarked offhandedly. "Of course, like you, she comes from noble blood. I'm not certain how her future will play out here, but if she comes to feel fondness for me, who knows . . . I have several women who are worthy of being an empress someday. I include you in that group."

Cecilia blushed and looked away.

"How badly do you want to wear the rose, Cecilia?" the Emperor asked.

Once again her eyes met his gaze. "More than anything, my Lord," she said.

"And why? You already live a privileged life. You have whatever you want."

"It is not the jewel itself I seek, my Lord, but your favor. That means more to me than all the jewels in your empire."

The Emperor smiled, but wondered at her statement. Cecilia's circumstances were most unusual. She came from Blithmore, a broken, lost thing, and offered herself up as his property. Could she be a spy? Was it possible she had been planted by King Germaine? The notion intrigued him. "I would have you prove your worth to me, Cecilia."

"Anything, my Lord." Her eyes shone brightly as she leaned toward Emperor Krallick. He liked the hungriness he saw.

"Watch Isabelle. Report to me on her activities. Let me know if she is happy."

"I will, my Lord. I will do whatever you ask."

The Emperor sipped his wine, still watching her. She was a rare beauty, like Isabelle, Kayla, and Jade. "You do have ambition, don't you?"

Cecilia did not hesitate before answering, "My ambitions are limited only by your desires, my Lord."

Emperor Krallick smiled at that answer. They continued to eat and talk, but it took effort not to laugh at Cecilia's blatant discomfort each time Isabelle was brought up. His mirth wasn't from cruelty, but surprise. He had believed Cecilia was the most confident concubine he had owned. What was it about Isabelle that put her on her guard? He needed to find out. It made his upcoming dinner with the new slave all the more interesting. He even had ideas on ways to increase the entertainment of the meal exponentially.

TWENTY-SIX

Crossing the Avalon River

James had never known a place to rain so much. With spring came clouds, wind, and then rain. Some days it sprinkled, other days were a downpour. But it always came. The weather slowed their travel and forced them on the worst days to take refuge at inns rather than risking mud and washed-out roads. However, there was reason to be optimistic. Each day brought them nearer to the Avalon River, which marked the border of Pappalon and the United Farmlands. According to their maps, once they crossed the river, two weeks of travel would see them across the Farmlands to the border of Desolation.

"Oh rain be gone, oh rain be gone," Ruther sang with the hood of his cloak over his head.

"And don't fall 'til we've moved on," Thirsty finished. James laughed politely.

"Or perhaps for a month or two," Maggie added in a sing-song voice, but only drew a half-chuckle from Ruther.

Ruther looked over his shoulder at Thirsty. "I told you it was going to be like this, didn't I?" he called to her. "I'm certain you didn't imagine you'd be stuck in all this loveliness."

"This is the best day of my life," Thirsty laughed. "I love the rain!"

James admired Thirsty for keeping her spirits high. "How do

you stay so cheerful?" he asked, bringing Sissy up next to Chance, Thirsty's horse.

Thirsty shrugged, still smiling. "What's there to be unhappy about? Water from the sky?"

Before he knew it, James was smiling, too. "I've never been good at finding things to be happy about," he said.

"My philosophy is if I have nothing to be sad about, I may as well be glad."

"Your mother misnamed you. She should have called you Happy."

In the distance, James saw the large blue expanse of the Avalon River, the eastern border of Pappalon. Henry stared at the river for several seconds, his hand shielding his eyes from the rain, though the hand did very little.

"I didn't expect it to be so wide," James commented. "The rains have filled her banks to the brim."

It was late morning when they reached the banks of the river and found the ferry operator's home. The ferry owners were bunkered down in a wooden hovel on a short pier, keeping out of the rain. James and Henry knocked on the door twice before it was answered.

"Whatcha want?" came the answer from a small, bearded woman with skin so red she looked like a human partially transformed into an apple. "You can't be wanting a ferry ride in this weather."

"We can and we do," Ruther answered.

"Come back tomorrow!" cried someone behind the door in a shrill voice. "Maybe the rain will have quit by then."

"Or at least lessened," the bearded woman added.

"It's rained every day for a week," James said. "There's no telling when it will stop."

"You can wait one more day," the woman said.

Henry stepped forward, nudging James aside. "We will not wait another day. Nor will we wait another hour. If you want to earn our money, get out here and ferry us."

The woman scowled and then said, "Let me grab my cloak." Behind her a tall, skinny bald man emerged.

"How many's in your party?" the bald man asked. No sooner had he stepped outside than he saw the size of Henry's party. "Good night! You wants us to take all y'all across the river? That'll be three trips each way with all your horses! Have you seen the state of the river this morning? She's as angry as a zapperbee trapped in a jar, and more swollen than my mother-in-law's ankles."

"What's your normal charge?" James asked.

"A half gyri," the bearded, apple-like woman said.

James reached into his traveling bag where he always kept a few coins in case he needed some quickly. He snatched out five gyri. "You get us all across in one piece, and these are yours. Anything goes wrong, we pay the normal amount. Sound fair?"

The bald man put out his hand, and James shook it. Soon there were handshakes all around. While Mrs. Beard and Mr. Bald got the ferry ready, James and Henry discussed with Maggie, Thirsty, and Ruther how they wanted to proceed across the river.

"Only two horses per trip," Mrs. Beard said. "I won't budge on that. Except the last trip. You can take three horses then."

"I'll go first with Ghost and Quicken," Ruther volunteered. "Then we send Henry and Maggie with Fury and Gopher. Then James and Thirsty with Sissy, Kicker, and Chance."

"Why not let me—" Maggie began.

"Don't make things difficult, Mags," Ruther said. "That's the easiest way."

A half hour later, Ruther and two horses were well on their way across Avalon River. The ferryman and his wife each had a pole at least twenty feet long to help move the ferry along. Stretching across the width of the river—more than two hundred yards—was a thick, tight rope. Two tall posts, one on the front and one on the back of the ferry, had rings atop them where the rope fed through, enabling the ferry to cross the river without drifting downstream.

James wondered how well the rope and posts would work with the current moving so swiftly. The river was indeed swollen from all the rain over the last few weeks. Secretly, he was glad that Ruther had volunteered to go first. Maggie held James's hand in a death grip while the ferry operators worked their long poles like feet, steadily, slowly across. Ruther waved to his friends on the shore and shouted, "Tell my children that I love them!"

Thirsty laughed nervously and looked at the others. "Was he serious? He doesn't have children, does he?"

It was a tense several minutes. James caught himself squeezing Maggie's hand as well until Ruther made it to shore. Then the four friends all gave a cheer. Thirsty even hugged James, but she quickly let him go under Maggie's unhappy gaze. When the ferry returned, Henry and Maggie climbed aboard with two more horses, but not until after Maggie had hugged and kissed James's cheek. The kiss was a soft, lingering peck that James guessed was as much for him as it was a reminder to Thirsty.

"Wish us well," Maggie said.

James watched the Vestins with the same concern and worry he'd had for Ruther. The wind and rain whipped his hair and sprayed his face. Next to him, Thirsty looked like she'd just climbed out of the river, her hair and clothes drenched. She had a faraway look in her eyes as she watched Maggie and Henry gradually drift away.

"What's on your mind?" he asked her.

Thirsty blinked and locked eyes with James. Her bright blue eyes glowed in the gray rain. "The last three weeks have been the happiest I can remember since—since I was with my family. You mean so much to me. Thank you for giving me this chance."

James nodded.

She giggled nervously. "I'm actually terrified right now. This is my second time crossing a river. The first was when I escaped from Old Avalon."

"Tell me about that."

Thirsty's bright blue eyes stared off across the river. "Well, we had an abnormally cold winter that year. A cold that seemed like it would never end. I hated it. I cursed it. It was terrible . . . walking all those miles with little to keep me warm. We had a group of almost a hundred slaves trying to escape to Pappalon. I lost count of how many times I asked myself why, of all the years, the Lord of All Worlds had to send such a bitter winter. Seventeen in our group died in the cold, but more were caught by bounty hunters. It was terrifying. Every morning we'd wake up and find someone dead from the cold, or missing—just gone. All we could do was heap snow over the dead bodies and move on."

"That's awful."

"Not far from the river, bounty hunters picked up our trail and chased us south. They tried to corner us at the river. Not many slaves can swim, myself included. The only water I can tolerate is when it's shallow, warm, and in a bathtub." A twinkle returned to her eyes at her own bit of humor. "The wind and cold was so cruel that the river froze. When we reached the river, we ran right onto the ice. None of us fell through, but the bounty hunters didn't dare ride out onto the water on their horses. When we reached the other side, we were free. Pappalonian Riders had been expecting us. They guarded us. I should have been happy, but my toes were so numb. Some of the others thought I might lose them." She shook her head. "Like I would give up a toe. I sat right down on the ground and rubbed each one until I could feel it again."

"You are amazing," James said.

"Why is that?"

"You're such a strong person. All the things you've been through, yet you're so happy and optimistic. You know what you want and go for it until you get it. That's admirable."

Thirsty grinned so widely that her face almost cracked in half. "There's still one thing I want that I haven't gotten yet."

James stared back at her but said nothing. Finally Thirsty looked back at the river where Maggie and Henry neared the opposite shore.

"Besides," she added, "I'm not certain I should be called *strong*. Those bounty hunters scared the wits out of me. I still have nightmares about them."

"I've met several bounty hunters. I can't say that they scare me."

"When we reached the ice of the river, I looked back as they considered pursuing us. There were three teams of them . . . two men and a woman, who looked like death itself. As we watched, one of them, the leader, he took his knife out of his belt and put out his own eyes. The second man put a knife to his ears. And the woman . . . I've—I've never seen anything so horrible."

"You mean she—" James motioned to his own throat.

Thirsty couldn't speak for moment, as though the air had gotten stuck in her lungs. "No, no. She didn't kill herself. *Her tongue!*"

"That's ghastly."

"I later found out it's the Baron of Old Avalon's custom. He always sends three hunters. And if they fail . . . the punishment is always the same. See no evil, hear no evil, speak no evil."

The ferry was returning to their side now. James shielded his eyes from the rain to help him see better. The longer he stared, the more certain he became that there were three people on the raft, not just Mrs. Beard and Mr. Bald. The long, dark, wet hair told the rest of the story. Maggie had come back. When the ferry reached the pier, James helped her off.

"I thought you might need an extra hand keeping the horses settled."

"You didn't think Thirsty and I could handle three horses?"

"Now it's one horse each," Maggie said with a grin. "Why take the chance?"

"Great!" Thirsty exclaimed. "The more the merrier."

James saw through this, and Thirsty probably did, too. Maggie didn't want him to spend any more time alone with Thirsty than was necessary. They loaded the horses onto the ferry. James took Sissy's reins in hand and Thirsty held onto Chance, which left Maggie to watch Kicker, the orneriest of the three.

With a great heave from the ferry operators' two poles, the large raft set off from the pier. Rain and hail pelted down, slamming into the ferry like thousands of arrows. The wind blew, forcing cold rain into James's ear. The bald ferryman turned back to chat while he worked the long pole to guide the craft.

"Must say I feel as though we've earned every bit of the wage you promised us," he yelled over the wind.

"We appreciate it," James responded. "We don't exactly have time on our side."

"Haven't we heard that a lot lately, ma'am?" Mr. Bald asked his bearded wife. "Mind if I ask your name, miss?" He looked at Thirsty now.

"Thirsty."

"Don't see many folk of your type in these parts. Not until recently, that is."

"What do you mean?" she said over a loud groan from the ferry as it rocked against the rope guiding it across the river.

"A bunch came through not a month ago."

"Not three weeks ago," Mrs. Beard corrected.

"Yes, not three weeks ago. Raggedy lot, if you don't mind me saying. Some injured in their group. Reason I bring it up is because they all had funny names, too. We never get much darker folk, and now all of a sudden we get them and you."

"Were any of them named Smiles, Stinker, or Furious?"

Mrs. Beard and Mr. Bald both guffawed. "Can't say I remember any particulars," Mrs. Beard said.

"Me, neither. Just remember they all had funny names."

At that moment a powerful gust of wind slammed into the ferry. The rope groaned under the strain. James looked ahead to see how far they had to go to reach the opposite pier. His best estimate was that they were only about halfway across.

"That didn't sound good," Mrs. Beard said. "Let's go faster."

"Anything I can do to help?" James asked.

Mrs. Beard's breathing was labored as she struggled to support the ferry with the pole and take the strain off the guide rope. "Do you . . . by chance . . . have . . . a really long . . . pole with you?"

Another gust of wind thrashed into them, ripping Maggie's scarf off her neck and swirling it into the air until it wrapped around Sissy's leg. James let go of Sissy's reins and knelt down to retrieve it. Only a second after, the rope gave the worst groan of all, followed by a loud *snap*. James turned to see the rope fly high into the air and land in the water. In the distance, Ruther and Henry shouted to them, but the wind muffled their words into nothing more than vague sounds. They were less than a hundred yards from shore, but the raft was now at the mercy of the current.

"Hang on!" Mrs. Beard shouted to her passengers. "We'll be all right."

James quickly grabbed the scarf and stood, taking Sissy's reins back in hand. The horses were getting jittery from the motion and the yelling. James stroked Sissy's nose and whispered comforting words in her ear while Thirsty rubbed Chance's neck. Then a blast of wind smacked into them, startling Kicker enough that she whinnied and reared up on her hind legs. Thirsty was knocked off balance and began to fall over the edge. James tried to reach her, but Maggie got there first. Her foot slipped on the wet wooden surface and she slid into Thirsty's legs. Both women fell into the churning water.

James froze. Maggie's head breached the surface first, only a couple seconds after the fall. Thirsty's head took about four times longer to appear. He looked at Maggie, then at Thirsty, and then back at Maggie. "Get the horses to the shore!" he shouted to the ferrymen. With only a moment to decide, he heard Thirsty's words again in his mind: *"Not many slaves can swim, myself included."*

He shrugged off his cloak and dove into the water after Thirsty. The current pulled at him, dragging him downstream regardless of how hard he swam. Maneuvering around Thirsty wasn't easy. She clawed and grabbed at him desperately. Finally he got an arm wrapped across her chest and hooked under her armpit. Then he searched everywhere for Maggie, but knew he couldn't spend much time looking, or they'd all drown. He kept an eye out for her while kicking his way to shore. Thirsty's thrashing made the going much more difficult.

"Calm down or we're both going to drown!" he told her. It helped a little, but Thirsty was still fitful. Struggling for air, James tried to not breathe in the river water. "Maggie!" he cried out, swallowing a mouthful of water. "Where are you?"

He continued to make his way toward shore when Maggie's scarf drifted by. James reached for it, snagging it with the crook of one finger, but there was no Maggie. His foot hit something in the water and his heart stopped. "Maggie!"

But it wasn't her; it was the riverbed. Still some thirty or forty yards from shore, the river reached to his lips. If he craned his neck, he could still breathe and walk. Another ten yards closer, and Thirsty could walk, too. James had his hand behind her back, pushing her along so they could hurry to shore. He still saw no sign of Maggie. He tried to run through the water toward the shore. It reminded him of nightmares he'd had where he couldn't run fast enough to escape some faceless monster.

Water poured from his hair, his face, his heavy clothes. Everywhere and everything was wet, even the air. He finally reached the riverbank, well downstream from the ferry dock where Ruther and Henry were. He stopped pushing Thirsty and ran onward, trying to climb the slippery slope. The soggy grass made his ascent difficult. A sharp rock sliced through his pants and into the skin on his knee. Another opened a cut on his finger. Behind him, Thirsty had just as much trouble. When James had finally made some progress, he gave her his hand and pulled her along with him until they reached solid ground.

Panting for air, they ran up the shoreline, James's eyes on the water for any sign of Maggie. The ferry was even further downstream, its owners fighting to get it to shore to deliver the last three horses. James searched everywhere for Maggie as they sprinted through the grasses toward the pier. A thicket of trees blocked their view of Henry and Ruther. James yanked on Thirsty's arm, willing her to go faster. "Where is she?" he called out. "Did you find her?"

The sound of footsteps tearing through the grass told him that Henry and Ruther were running over to help. "Where is she?" James called again.

"We don't know!" Ruther shouted. "We lost her!" He shrugged off his cloak and kicked off his boots.

James turned back and slid down the river bank. Just as he and Ruther waded into the water, a cloaked head breached the surface a hundred yards away near the middle of the river. The hair was dark and matted to pale skin.

It was Maggie.

Her head rose completely out of the water, her eyes glowing a faint blue, like twin moons, head slightly bowed, dark hair dripping, and a look of serenity on her face. Then her neck appeared, the skin taut and white from the frigid river.

"Is she . . ." Ruther's voice trailed off as Maggie's shoulders and chest appeared. Her arms stayed tight against her sides, her fingers fanned out with her palms facing behind her. James tried to understand what was happening. Why were her eyes glowing? Her torso showed next, framed and outlined by her soaked green and blue dress which looked as though it had been painted on her. Then he saw her hips and legs and feet.

"James," Ruther whispered, "What's happening?"

James couldn't find his voice, so he just watched.

Maggie's full body was visible; only the soles of her feet still touched the water. She turned in the air and glided gracefully upstream toward where Henry and Thirsty stood. James and Ruther ran toward her. James thought she looked like a water spirit, if such things existed. She looked so peaceful, droplets of water raining from her fingers, nose, hair, and sleeves. But the light from her eyes made the hair on James's neck and arms stand up straight.

"What's happening?" Ruther said again as they reached the river bank once more. "How is this possible?"

James shook his head, still unable to speak. Henry and Thirsty jogged over to where James and Ruther stood. When Maggie's toes touched solid ground, her body crumpled. Everyone rushed forward to help her. James reached her first. The instant their skin touched, Maggie grabbed James's arms with a grip so powerful he couldn't break it. The scarring around her missing finger began to grow, spreading around the sides of her hand and reddening angrily.

He had never felt such cold as he did when she touched him. It seemed to penetrate through his skin, muscles, and bones, severing them from his body. He gasped her name in shock, but her eyes stayed closed, her face as angelic as ever. Before he could say more, his lungs filled with water and he coughed it up in waves. The more liquid he choked up, the warmer her hands grew until some small measure of feeling was restored to his limbs.

The light in Maggie's eyes faded and her gaze locked onto James, who continued to cough and sputter up water. His lungs burned in agony even as he stared at her. Her irises changed color from a bright blue to her natural brown. He jerked his arms out of her grasp and stepped away. Maggie fell to the ground on her knees, hands over her face, sobbing.

"You saved *her*." Maggie's words were a moan of condemnation.

"What?" James croaked through another cough, water still coming up from his lungs.

"You went after *her*."

He looked at Thirsty. "No, no." He coughed again. "It wasn't like that."

"Maggie," Henry said, "you just—something unbelievable—you practically flew!"

"It was incredible," Thirsty said. "A miracle."

Only Ruther had nothing to say. He sat on the ground with his head in his hands, muttering under his breath. James knelt down and wrapped his arms around Maggie. The act of it felt oddly wrong, being surrounded by other people watching them. He wanted them to look away so he could fix this without their eyes on the scene.

"Why did you go after her?" Maggie shouted. *"You picked her!"*

"I didn't, Maggie. She needed—"

"You did. You did! *You did!*" Maggie was hysterical. James had seen men get like this before, most often during a battle. They couldn't be reasoned with, no matter how hard one tried. They just had to be kept out of the way until the madness passed. But even knowing his words would make no difference, he still felt compelled to explain himself.

"She can't swim, Maggie. Thirsty told me she can't swim. You can. The pond. You grew up and swam at the pond in the woods. We all did. Thirsty can't—she's never . . ."

But, as he already knew, the words didn't matter. Maggie continued to sob, and her tears were just more water falling to the ground.

TWENTY-SEVEN

To Walk the Path

By crossing the Avalon River, the group of five had passed into the southern tail of the United Farmlands of Sam, or "the Farmlands," as most people knew it. Henry found the ferry operators downriver, paid them five times the agreed-upon amount, and rejoined the group. By then the winds and rain were lashing down so violently that it forced the group to move on rather than argue about what had happened.

They rode another ten miles in the howling, streaking rains before arriving at the first town, Sammich. Maggie wouldn't speak to anyone, though she probably wouldn't have been heard over the winds anyway. Henry spotted an inn between a pottery and a blacksmith's shop. James and Henry went inside and haggled with the inn owner. The inn had only three rooms. One was available. Neither Henry nor James liked the idea of sleeping on the floor, but they took the room rather than go back out into the gale to find other lodgings.

Once settled, they gathered around the fireplace to warm and dry their clothes, their chairs set in a semi-circle with Maggie on one end and James on the other. Thirsty sat in the middle of the group between Henry and Ruther.

"I feel like my head is full of water," Ruther complained, smacking the side of his head with his hand to get the fluid out of his ears.

Normally Maggie would have turned such a comment right back

at Ruther. In fact, sometimes Henry wondered if Ruther intentionally set himself up so she could do so. But tonight Maggie was quiet and withdrawn.

"How long did the owner's wife say we have to wait for supper?" Henry asked.

"An hour or more," James said. "We're last to arrive, so we're last to eat."

Ruther beat on his ear again. "Just as well. I'd rather eat in dry clothes. Maybe I'll just go to the back of the room and change, if everyone promises not to look."

Again Henry waited for Maggie to say something, but she remained silent. He cleared his throat and said in the most pleasant voice he could summon in his cold, miserable state, "While we're waiting, perhaps we can talk about what happened at the river."

Maggie gave Henry a grin so wide, it showed off almost all her teeth. It was so unlike her that he found it unsettling. It reminded him of Thirsty's smile, but several times creepier. "It's in the past." Even her voice was too cheery. "Let's forget it happened."

"Great!" Ruther said. "Next topic of conversation: if it rains any more, should we consider buying a small boat or a raft?"

Maggie giggled and slapped her knee. "Oh, that's funny! Ruther, you are too funny."

James and Henry exchanged a glance of bewilderment.

"Maggie . . ." James said, leaning forward, his face grave. "When you and Thirsty fell in the water, I had only a half a second to make a choice. It came down to knowing that Thirsty can't swim and you can. It had nothing to do with—"

"It's in the past," Maggie said, still wearing that horrible smile. "Let's move on."

Henry threw another log on the flames. "I think I'd like to talk about it more. I don't know what happened when you—"

"James saved Thirsty," Maggie said pleasantly. "That's all that happened."

"Well . . ." Ruther said, "that and your eyes glowed like giant, evil fireflies."

"My eyes didn't glow!" Maggie's attempt at laughing off Ruther's comment fell flat when Henry, James, and Thirsty all said, "Yes, they did."

Maggie shook her head, her smile all but gone now.

"Look into my eyes, Maggie," Ruther said.

"No."

"Look into my eyes."

"No." But Maggie looked anyway.

"Are they glowing?"

Maggie pursed her lips and narrowed her eyes at him.

"Because my eyes are the opposite of what your eyes were doing a few hours ago."

Maggie's lip and chin began to quiver. "Don't lie to me!"

"It's you who has been lying to us," Thirsty said. "Your fake tears aren't fooling me."

Maggie sprang from her chair and sprinted at Thirsty, her hands outstretched. Henry and Ruther darted forward to grab her. Henry caught an arm and Ruther a hand. It wasn't easy to hold onto her with her clothes and skin still quite wet.

When they finally secured her, she screamed at Thirsty, "I've never been anything but honest with James, you, and everyone else!"

Thirsty retorted, "Then why haven't you told anyone that you walk the Path?"

Maggie stopped struggling and stared at Thirsty for such a long time that Henry began to feel uncomfortable. Her face was just as pale as when she had emerged from the water. "Is that how you intend to do it?"

"Do what?" Thirsty asked.

"Drive a wedge between James and me? By insinuating that I perform magic? I want you all to know," Maggie stated, "that I have nothing to do with magic, sorcery, the Path, or anything else like that. It sickens me to think that you would conjure up such a notion to make James afraid of me."

"You walked on water," Thirsty said. "How do you explain—"

"I didn't."

"You did. I saw you. We all saw you."

"Technically, she floated," Ruther said, raising a finger.

"*Stop it!*" Maggie yelled. "I do *not* walk the Path. It—it—it was the wind. Something. Some phenomenon . . . a miracle of nature."

"That's ludicrous, Maggie," James said. "We all know what we saw."

"I don't know, James, but it was not the Path! The Path does not exist! It's an ancient myth. My mother told me so."

"It's real," Thirsty said.

"Then it's long dead. Older than the Word of Worlds, older than time. It's gone."

"But we saw—" James began again.

"I don't know what you saw!" she shouted. "But consider the idea that you might not know what you saw either!"

"Why are you so angry?" Thirsty asked.

"Because you have no proof! No evidence! Nothing! You saw something you can't explain, and now you've grabbed onto an impossible conclusion."

Despite Maggie's claims, Henry suddenly remembered several strange events happening around Maggie since she was a girl, and he couldn't shake the memories away. She'd once thrown him clear across a room when he'd startled her. Another time when he'd teased her about a boy, a wooden plate had flown at his head. When confronted by her parents about it, she'd sworn she hadn't touched it. The more he thought on it, the more instances he came up with, and the more convinced he became that Thirsty might be correct.

"Mags," Ruther said, "I know you're upset about this. We're all under a terrible strain. But remember the Iron Forest? Things didn't seem to affect you the way they did the rest of us. And you were the one that—"

"Ruther, I said I don't want to talk about it!"

"But everyone else does," Henry said. "We all care about you. Something happened in the water. You should have died."

"Because of James!"

Henry ignored this and pressed on with his point. "We couldn't see you for several minutes, and then you suddenly appeared and forced James to cough up all that water—water he hadn't swallowed. *Your water.*"

"I didn't—" Maggie moaned, clutching and rocking herself. "I'm not—I don't . . . Please stop saying it, Henry. Please?"

"Why are you so averse to the Path?" Thirsty asked. "It's a wonderful gift. In Old Avalon, among my people, those who walk the Path are held in very high esteem. They are a force of good and light."

"No!" Maggie replied. "It's not real!"

"It is as real as the water and the sun," Thirsty said. "I've witnessed it. A woman in our village walked it. She taught me and three other girls about it, always telling us that one day she would die, and when she did, she would give the Path to one of us."

Something sparked inside Henry at these words. Something buried very deep.

"Give someone the Path?" Ruther asked. His raised eyebrows and buried smirk told Henry that he believed little of what he was hearing. "Like you give someone a prized horse? Or a black eye?"

Maggie jumped to her feet. "There! See? That proves it. I've never been given any sort of gift. No one ever passed that along to me. I would've known!"

"It often happens when you're very young," Thirsty explained, "and the person who walks the Path is very old. You might not remember it."

The image of an ancient, wizened man standing in the Vestin living room appeared in Henry's mind. He tried to remember details, but couldn't.

Maggie glared at Thirsty. "You're determined to sway everyone against me."

"I like you, Maggie," Thirsty responded. "I like you very much. Since the day I met you, I've found you to be kind, beautiful, and strong. Why would you think I dislike you?"

Ruther snickered. "Wait! You mean it's not obvious?"

"Shut up, Ruther," Maggie said.

Thirsty put her hands together and softened her tone as she spoke to Maggie. "Let me explain what I've learned about the Path. This is not a terrible thing. It's a blessing."

"I don't want to hear anything because it doesn't matter."

Henry sighed. "Please let her speak, Maggie. It won't hurt."

Maggie pursed her lips and folded her arms tightly, but raised no further objection.

"The Path has two directions . . . Light or Shadow. There are multiple gifts that are granted to those who walk it. I only know of two, but I have seen you display both."

Maggie snorted in disbelief and looked around at the men in the group, as though she wanted someone to agree with her that what Thirsty spoke was utter nonsense. No one said a word. Henry felt like he'd heard some of this information before, but couldn't remember where.

"The first power is the simplest. Projection of self."

"I don't know what that means," Ruther said, "but it sounds painful."

Thirsty scratched her head, a look of frustration on her face. "I don't know everything, but I believe it has something to do with making yourself bigger or extending yourself. The woman who walked the Path in our village, she would sometimes hover in the air, make her bowl levitate, tap us on the shoulder without moving. She did this to capture our attention so we would listen better."

"Maggie, tap me on the shoulder," Ruther said. "Or better yet . . . make me levitate."

"How about I levitate you onto the fire?" she asked.

"What's the second power?" James asked.

"To heal. Cure sickness, rebuild broken emotion, strengthen the human spirit."

Maggie stirred in her seat uncomfortably and glanced at Henry.

Henry thought of his arm. "Is the healer in Greenhaven someone who walks the Path?"

"I don't know," Thirsty answered. "But one who walks the Path of Shadow can heal for money or favors or power. But mostly he would want to heal himself. While a healer of Light can imbibe a portion of the pain or wound in himself, the healer of Shadow will give the pain or wound to another. Everything has an opposite. Everything has a cost."

"Like when Maggie drowned," James said, "but made me cough up water."

"Yes. The powers always carry a cost. To project one's self requires energy or life force. It will leave she who walks the Path fatigued. At least at first—but the stronger she becomes, the less drained she will feel. The healing also carries a cost. To heal someone else means the healer will accept the pain, or share a portion of the wound to make it less lethal. To heal himself, the healer will be scarred. The mark is the cost of forcing his own pain onto another."

Maggie shook her head furiously. "This is madness. You're making it up." But Henry noted how she wasn't looking Thirsty in the eyes anymore.

"When Ruther was all but dead on the physician's table," James said, "Maggie, you touched him and brought him back to life, and it took a toll on you. You were pale and faint for two days."

"I was tired . . . the forest . . . I fainted after we escaped the pass."

"You floated above the water!" James cried. "How can you not even consider the possibility?"

"Because she doesn't want to," Henry concluded.

Tears ran down Maggie's face as she stared into her lap. Thirsty got out of her chair and knelt in front of Maggie. When she touched Maggie's hand, Maggie flinched.

"You have nothing to be ashamed of. Walking the Path is like wielding a powerful blade. You can use it to help people and defend life, or your power can be twisted and you may become an agent of darkness. One of the first signs of having the gift is that you see a new color. Have you seen a color you didn't recognize?"

"No!" Maggie answered, wrenching her hands from Thirsty's grasp.

"Yes, Maggie, think!" Henry told her. "You asked me about that on the road to the mapmaker. You mentioned something about a color."

Maggie shook her head furiously. "I didn't."

"If you can heal," Henry pressed, "you could save us the time of traveling to Greenhaven. We could go right now to Neverak. It would save us weeks!"

"When you came up out of the water," James said, "you grabbed my arms. It was like you were made of ice and steel. One moment I was strong, and then I was coughing up water as though *I* had drowned. And the scar on your hand turned red and—and it grew a little."

"It—it—it looks perfectly fine," Maggie stated. "Same as it did yesterday."

"I know what I saw," James said, his tone both weary and impatient.

"I have never healed anyone!" she pleaded. "Why won't you believe me?"

"I believe you," Ruther said. To Henry's surprise, his friend sounded sincere. "I don't believe in the Path. I never have, and I never will."

Seconds passed in silence. Only the fireplace made noise with its popping and crackling. The seconds turned into a minute. Maggie broke the solemnity with a sniffle. Thirsty, still kneeling, patted Maggie's knee. Silence reigned in the room once more. Another minute passed.

Finally Henry spoke. "Lyrial."

Thirsty blew her snow-white hair out of her face. "Lyrial," she said. "Yes." Her eyes snapped back to Maggie's face. "*Lyrial* is the name of the color. How did you know that?"

Henry's eyes met his sister's until Maggie looked away. "She said it to me. I knew I had heard it before. Remember?"

Maggie did not respond.

"I was a little boy, Maggie. I couldn't have been more than five. It was night. Very late at night. I wanted water so I got out of bed and found my pitcher dry, so I had to go to the pump. Father was still awake, and I heard him talking. I stopped at the bottom of the stairs to listen. He was excited or scared, I couldn't tell. He kept saying it had to be kept a secret. That Rachel, our mother, could never know."

"Know what?" James asked.

"I didn't know what my father meant, so I sat there. Then I heard an old man speak. 'Her actions will bear a cost,' he said. 'A serious cost.'"

"I caught a glimpse of the guest, a man so old he looked as though he might have witnessed every war, every major event in the history of Atolas. I remember his eyes changing color. They went from . . . blue to gold. And they shined so brightly, it wasn't natural."

"And you're just now telling us about this?" Ruther asked. "You've seen someone's eyes change color and you never mentioned it to me?"

Henry placed his hands on his head. "It's like the memory was buried in my mind until now. *Lyrial.* My father was worried. He asked if he could change his mind.

"'It's too late,' the old man told my father. 'I already gave it. She will know lyrial. She will know the cost. The burden. All of it.'

"I was tired and didn't understand it. I went back to bed, back to sleep, and forgot."

The next memory was harder for Henry to relive, but he closed his eyes and told it anyway. "When Father and Mother fell ill, I did my best to care for Father while Maggie cared for Mother. One day Maggie was at the market, Mother was asleep, so I sat by Father's side and kept him abreast of the business of his woodshop. Until that—until that day, I still believed they were going to get better.

"Father put his hand on mine and pointed to his old desk where he kept all the receipts and orders. 'Bottom drawer,' he said. 'Open it.'

"I did as he asked. Then he instructed me to press down on the bottom panel. It activated a spring, revealing a secret space underneath the drawer. All I found in it was a brown pouch. When I gave it to him, Father clutched it to his chest.

"'I love your sister,' he told me. 'I have protected her from what I fear was a terrible mistake on my part. Now you must do so. You will be the man of the family. It will be your duty. You must never open this pouch. Swear to me you will obey.'

"I swore to him that I would. Then he raised a finger. It was so weak and fragile. It was then I knew that he would not recover from the illness.

"'Unless she discovers her burden . . . only then. Never lose this. No matter what.'"

Henry removed the small pouch from around his neck where it hung on a chain. It barely covered his hand. It was so light, it might contain nothing at all. "I took my promise seriously. I don't know why. Even the night the guardsmen chased us from the Glimmering Fountain, I risked the time it took to save this."

"And you never opened it?" Ruther asked. "You weren't even a little curious?"

Henry held up his hands. "It was my dying father's final wish, Ruther." Then to Maggie he said, "I didn't know what he meant! He was feverish and—and delusional half the time. And I still don't know if this is it . . . but what else could it be?"

He handed the pouch to Maggie, feeling rather foolish. Judging by her expression as she took it, she seemed to be feeling the same way. Maggie undid each of the tiny clasps one at a time, an expression of cold fury carved into her face. She stared inside it and removed a folded piece of parchment, frayed and worn as though it had been stored in the pouch for many years. When she unfolded the parchment, another piece fell out, this one much smaller and newer. Maggie caught it and held it up, reading it silently.

"Would you mind reading it aloud . . . please?" James asked.

Maggie's head jerked up as though she'd forgotten her friends were there at all. "Fine." She cleared her throat and read the note.

> Be it known to all who traverse the Path, the Way of Lyrial, the ancient and mystic art and gift from the Lord of All Worlds, that I, Rimnel Urrath, have bestowed mine greatest gift, the Path, to a young girl on the third day of the tenth month of the twenty-first year of the reign of King Sedgwick Germaine. I did this with the full knowledge and agreement of the girl's father, indeed, in his sight I laid mine hands upon her and spoke the words taught by Chimel Kzeed, my mentor, teacher, and friend.
>
> I chose this girl because of her strength which burns like a bellows. Her heart, which knows no bounds. Her mind, which is keen and bright like the very star Lyrial. Mine heart did confirm my choice to me that it was good, and so I may now rest in the

eternities with a peace of mind that the Path has been preserved in a worthy vessel. The holy magick will live on so long as one worthy vessel carries and walks the Light. And that vessel's name is Margaret Vestin, daughter of William and Rachel Vestin.

"Maggie," Henry said, "it's real. You can heal my arm."

Tears in her eyes, she whispered, "I can't."

"You healed Ruther. Yourself. You can heal me. We don't have to go to Greenhaven."

Maggie was hesitant. "Won't that make *my* arm go lame?" she asked.

"Ruther was almost dead, but you recovered in a couple of days," James said. "Maybe the same will happen now."

Maggie agreed to try. Biting her lip, she used her trembling hands to roll up Henry's sleeve and ran her fingers lightly down his arm. "It's thinner," she remarked.

"That happens to muscles when they aren't used," James commented. "The muscles grow weak and thin."

Henry felt shame at this comment, though he knew it wasn't his fault. "I know you can do it."

Maggie nodded and put her fingers back on his arm. Then she closed her eyes and mouthed silently, "I wish I could heal Henry's arm."

He waited for something to happen—they all did—but he felt nothing unusual. Maggie's eyebrows bent and her nose wrinkled in concentration as she mouthed the words a second time. Still Henry felt nothing. Maggie opened her eyes and stared into Henry's. He nodded to her determinedly. "I know you can do it."

Maggie tried again. Mouthing words more distinctly. Yet the arm remained dead. After three more attempts, Henry's arm was still as useless as ever.

When her fifth try ended, everyone watched Henry to see if there was any change. He tried not to let her see his disappointment, but it was difficult. He had genuinely believed she could do it. Finally he shook his head.

"Nothing to see here, folks," Ruther declared. "Just as I suspected."

His jest fell flat. James turned away, disappointed. Thirsty sighed and patted Maggie on the shoulder, but Maggie sat back in her chair, frustrated, and, if Henry read her expression correctly, somewhat relieved that it hadn't worked.

TWENTY-EIGHT

The Thirsty Thief

The days ticked away one by one. Each sunset reminded Henry of how far he was from Isabelle, and how far he had yet to go before he could wrest her from the Emperor of Neverak. The only thing that distracted him from these thoughts was swordplay. He didn't even have to ask James if they could practice during their spare moments. James already knew they would spar, so he prepared accordingly. Henry let the clash of sword on sword absorb him, savoring the brief respite from the regret that followed him every step of their journey.

The crossing of Rocky River from the Farmlands into Desolation was far simpler than crossing the Avalon River. It was more like stepping over the Rocky Stream. The farther east Henry and his friends traveled, the more barren and arid the land grew. Not a day passed when Ruther didn't say, "They don't call it Desolation for nothing." Trees grew sparsely, and dry, ugly bushes and cacti became more common. The tall grasses gave way to stiff yellow reeds that grew in patches in the shadows of shrubbery. Henry had known they would travel through the desert; he just hadn't known it would be so miserable.

Though they rationed their water, they spent valuable time finding places to fill their water skins. The sun rose earlier and fell later each day, and the hours spent unsheltered under its punishing rays were hard on everyone. They woke later in the day and rode longer into the night. Henry felt like he spent half his days licking his lips to keep them moist, but they remained cracked and parched. Ruther predicted that before long they would all turn into leather and wear each other as belts.

Desolation was a wild land, unruled by any sovereign entity. Robbers and thieves were common, especially near sources of water. According to the advice given to them by Markus Finkley, thieves would hide and wait to plunder or kill lone foolish travelers not on their guard. Fortunately James was always on his guard.

The first town the party came to after crossing into Desolation was Tiller's Thain. It was located near the halfway point from the Rocky River to the Valley of the Healer in Greenhaven. The mapmaker's instructions said that Tiller's Thain was an essential stopping point for water and rest when crossing the desert. Seeing the houses and shops on the horizon brought small cheers from Thirsty and Ruther. Even Henry didn't dispute spending a day to recover from the hardships of the desert.

They arrived in Tiller's Thain in the early evening. It was bigger than Henry had guessed it would be, though not as fancy as Borderville nor as large as Bookerton. Homes and shops were not made of wood, but bricks. Henry supposed that the brick helped keep dust and sand out. Very few establishments had windows, and no buildings were taller than one floor. Henry and James stopped at the first inn they saw, the Sandman.

The thought of a soft bed and fresh water called to Henry. After stopping at the stables to have their horses watered and fed, Henry and his friends entered the inn. The owner searched the faces of each party member, his eyes pausing on Thirsty. "I got two rooms available. You want 'em both?"

"That'd be fine." Henry dropped coins on the countertop. "How much will that get us?"

"Two nights."

"Perfect."

The owner pointed to Thirsty with a fat, leathery finger. "Yer lucky you came here, Miss, and not to my competitor. He wouldn't have let ya stay in his establishment. 'N fact, he turned away a whole company of yer kind a few days ago. Chased 'em out with a pitchfork. They came here, but didn't have no money. I let 'em sleep in the stables."

"How thoughtful of you," James said grimly.

"Don't mean no offense by it." The owner chuckled in a deep, growling tone. "Just sayin' I don't give out freebies to nobody. Not even my own mudder. But, Miss, I'd keep yer face out of sight so ya don't attract no trouble. Lots of unfriendly folk toward yer kind here."

The next morning they disregarded the innkeeper's advice, and the group spent the day in the town market taking care of errands so they could leave early the following morning. Thirsty received several ugly stares and a few vulgar comments, but by and large people left her alone.

While in a shop, Henry saw a woman about Isabelle's height with similar hair color. When he saw her face, he realized that they looked nothing alike, but something else reminded him of her. She had a quiet grace about her, a beautiful soul. He didn't know how he knew that, but he felt it deep in his bones. Not an hour later, he ran into her again in the market. This time she had a man on her arm. He, too, was tall and handsome. Their glow of happiness was unmistakable, and though it filled Henry with a bitter pain to watch them, he couldn't stop. He wanted to leave Tiller's Thain immediately, and he said as much to Ruther and James.

"We haven't done everything we need to, friend," Ruther said. "A few hours won't make a difference."

"I don't care about the errands!" Henry responded, struggling to control his tone. "These delays are just making it worse."

James put his hand around Henry's shoulders. "Relax, Henry, I know you're anxious, but these things are important, too."

Needing to be alone, Henry returned to the inn. Ten minutes later he realized he didn't want to be alone, but he didn't want to be around his friends, either. He really only wanted to be around one person.

Following dinner, the five friends left the Sandman and found a good drinking hole where the ale came highly recommended. The tavern was called the Thirsty Thief. Thirsty and Maggie weren't much for drinking, and only had a mug apiece. Ruther, despite his sighs of deep longing, refrained from partaking. Henry, however, was intent on emptying the Thirsty Thief's stores of ale in one night. The more he drank, the better life seemed. And James tried his best to keep up. They laughed, sang, and drank. Even sober, Ruther joined them. When Maggie and Thirsty announced that they were ready to leave, James and Henry were both unwilling to go. So Ruther volunteered to escort the ladies back to the Sandman.

Watching them go, Henry and James clanked mugs, drank, and roared with laughter. Four men sat at a small table across the tavern hall. Two of them looked like they might be brothers. They watched Ruther lead the ladies out and catcalled them as they departed.

"Oi!" one man shouted at Henry and James's table. "Which one of you is in love with that devil-woman?"

Henry peered over to see which one had yelled at them. It was a tall man with balding carrot-colored hair and a mustache the size of Quicken's mane. He wasn't particularly mean or strong looking, but he had a nasty glint in his eyes that Henry had seen before among men who turned ugly after too much ale. The other men at his table weren't much better. Henry turned his attention back to James. They looked at each other for about three seconds, and then started laughing again.

"Do you think his mustache has its own name?" Henry asked.

James spit his ale all over the table.

"Did I say something funny?" the same man called. "Because I see nothing funny about devil-folk. Nor about those who choose to associate themselves with them. My uncle owns an inn in this town. Bunch of devil-folk came past not a week ago. You know what he did? Chased them off. Speared one of them. Exactly what they deserved."

"Devil-folk?" James snickered into his mug. "He's talking about Thirsty."

"Devil-folk!" Henry bit his lip to stop from howling in his mirth. With his good hand, he pounded on the table. Both his and James's faces threatened to turn so red that they put ripe tomatoes to shame. "Obviously he's never met your father!"

"To the man who is *devil-folk* if ever anyone was!" James cried as he and Henry clanked their mugs together once more.

The four men huddled together at the table while James and Henry went back to their own conversation. "Maybe it's time to go," James slurred.

"Just one more." Henry swirled the last drops of ale, tipped back the mug, and drained down every drop of delicious drink. He grinned with all his teeth and belched so deeply that he felt it in his toes. "Well . . . maybe two. But no more than three."

James laughed heartily and refilled both his and Henry's mugs. About four swallows later, the two similar-looking men from the other table approached Henry and James. Henry wiped the froth from his upper lip. "Canna help you, shir?" he asked.

"Indeed, you can," said the tall, red-haired, balding man. "You can leave."

Henry let out a long, dramatic, "Har-har-har," and then fixed his eyes on the man's receding hairline. "And why would I do that?"

"You aren't welcome here. See, we get your kind all the time. Let me guess. You're on your way through Desolation, either east or west, and this is a watering stop." His eyes fell on James. "You're a man who looks decent enough, but then I see you escorting a devil-woman around town like she's the Lord of All Worlds. Even drinking with her. Makes me sick. They're slaves and workers for a reason. One step below man, one step above animals."

In his drunken state, Henry could not help but laugh at the absurdity coming from this man's mouth. "I can't tell! Is he serious, James? Because with that mustache, I can't—"

Quick as a spit, the balding man slapped Henry on the cheek three times: right cheek, left cheek, right cheek. Then he picked up Henry's mug and threw its contents into Henry's stunned face. Nothing was funny now. James stood up, but so did the balding man's two friends. The last thing Henry wanted was a situation that got out of control. He put up his one good hand and backed away.

"Look, shir, I'm shorry." One more step back and he bumped into the brother. He wasn't quite as tall, nor quite as bald, but his hair was equally orange and his expression equally angry. "Shorry to you, too. We may not agree on things, but that doesn't mean we can't drink this fine ale in peace."

The slightly shorter brother pushed Henry toward the taller brother. James yelped a warning and drew one of his knives. Other heads in the room now turned toward the commotion. Henry tried to defuse it all by yelling, "Shtop! Shtop. We'll leave. All right? We'll leave."

The older, taller brother caught Henry by his shirt. His breath on Henry's stinging, wet face was sour from ale and meat. "That mean you'll leave town right now? I follow you back to wherever you're staying and watch you pack and leave? If so, you have a deal."

"Firsht thing in the morning." Henry couldn't understand how things had escalated so quickly. "How'sh that shound? You won't shee me. You won't even know I'm here. We leave the tavern right now."

"I don't want that devil-girl in this town another second." Each word he articulated caused flecks of spittle to land on Henry's cheeks and nose.

"I guess you'll just have to live with that." James's voice was ice. Henry saw in his friend's eyes a burning anger, hot and dangerous, something he hadn't seen since James believed Ruther had robbed them. Each hand held a knife, ready for use. The taller brother let go of Henry's collar and took two steps back. "That's better." James looked to the tavern owner. "We'll be paying for our drinks now."

The smaller, younger brother took advantage of James's distraction and tackled him from behind. The older brother had the same idea and rushed Henry full on. Henry dropped to his knees, his hand covering his head, the other hanging useless. The older brother, uncoordinated in his inebriated state, tripped over Henry and slammed his head into the table where James and Henry had sat not two minutes earlier.

There was something unnatural about the sound of the older brother's head hitting the table, or perhaps in the way his body fell to the floor like a lifeless puppet. A sick chill ran up Henry's spine. He opened his eyes and saw a red pool forming under his assailant's head. Then he noticed that the chest of the man was still too.

"Help!" Henry cried. "He's hurt! Help him!"

After those words left Henry's mouth, the world seemed to speed up in motion. The younger brother who'd wrestled James to the ground got up and scrambled over to his brother. Erupting from his mouth were the most vile obscenities Henry had ever heard, all directed at Henry and James. The brother screamed until his face turned purple as he shook Henry and tried to punch every inch of him. Henry could hardly ward off any of these blows with one arm. James tried to help, but the two other men from the injured man's table restrained him.

Others approached, most of them shouting. Henry thought this might be the end. He was going to die in a lousy tavern in the middle of the desert. Instead, one of them yanked the younger brother off Henry. Two more grabbed Henry's arms. Before he realized what was happening, he and James were being carried out the door. The posse of men hauled Henry and James through town like two sacks of pota-toes. One of them had a torch to light their way through the streets. Henry struggled against them for about a minute, then gave up, but James fought his assailants the whole way.

They came to a square brick building no larger than a horse stall. The man carrying the torch opened the door and almost a dozen men squeezed in behind him. The shanty was empty except for a chair and a table, but one of the men fiddled with something on the floor. Henry twisted his body to see what it was. A trapdoor opened into a pitch-black hole.

"No!" Henry cried. "We did nothing wrong! Don't put us in there!"

No one listened to his pleas. James and Henry were dropped into the hole, and the trapdoor above them shut with a clang.

TWENTY-NINE
The Ruby Rose

O ne bright spring morning after her morning baths and breakfast, Isabelle realized she had been the Emperor's prisoner
for two months. This sudden awareness was accompanied
by a shame that she had started to lose track of time in her pampered
palace life. As Cecilia had predicted, the baths were no longer torture,
but enjoyable. It was hard to *not* enjoy being scrubbed and massaged
by women who existed solely to make her body as perfect and relaxed
as possible. If there was one thing the house of concubines had in
abundance, it was looking glasses. Isabelle had watched as her skin
changed from its weathered and callused state, born of weeks of travel
with Henry, to the smooth, flawless beauty she had known as a young
woman. Her complexion had never been fairer nor had her hair, short
as it was, ever been so shiny that it sparkled in the light.

Two months remained before her "night of blessing," as the other
girls called it. The thought of any form of intimacy with the Emperor
made her want to tear out her hair and scratch her perfect skin. She
stopped pretending that her day of liberation was at the doorstep.
Henry might never come for her. He might not even be alive. But
Brandol's sacrifice would not be for nothing. Isabelle had already set
into motion her plan for escape.

That same day, Jade returned from a short trip with the Emperor.
Cecilia, Kayla, and a few other girls had been extremely displeased

that they were not chosen to go; Kayla especially because she, not Jade, wore the ruby rose. When Jade was escorted back into the concubines' quarters (it required two footmen just to carry all the clothes and accessories she'd brought), several girls converged on her to find out all the details of the trip. Jade beamed as though she'd been named Empress.

"You think the Emperor favors her now?" Cecilia asked, leaning against the wall next to Isabelle, her arms folded and a suspicious expression on her face. "Kayla has had the rose for weeks. I doubt she'll have it much longer."

Isabelle struggled to sympathize with Cecilia. "I can't say. The Emperor may now have grown tired of Jade. You always say he enjoys variation."

Isabelle's suggestion seemed to bring a glimmer of hope back to Cecilia. All the girls were aware that Jade received most of the Emperor's favor recently, despite Kayla having the rose.

Cecilia turned to Isabelle. "Let's do something fun today. How about trying our hand at painting a canvas?"

Isabelle had noticed that Cecilia was spending more time around her than she had the previous weeks. It gave her hope that they were becoming true friends. "Will they let us do that?"

"I think so." Cecilia winked. "I may not wear the rose yet, but the Emperor still favors me above most."

After lunch the footmen brought up a large canvas, bottles of paints, and a dozen brushes. Isabelle had never tried painting, but she enjoyed it. She and Cecilia chose to paint a sweeping landscape of the Towering Mountains in Western Blithmore and Neverak. A few other girls wandered over to watch them, including Jade.

"That's very good, Isabelle," Jade said.

Cecilia nodded. "She's a natural painter. Who'd have guessed? Makes me wonder what else she's a natural at . . ."

"Have you painted before?" Jade asked Isabelle.

"This is my first time."

Jade watched them paint for a while longer before commenting, "The Emperor is so generous. Letting us explore our talents and skills. We truly are blessed to live in this house, aren't we?"

"How was your trip?" Cecilia asked. "Where did you go?"

"It was wonderful," Jade said, her Haxite accent still quite thick, but improving. She smiled brightly as she spoke, and her eyes lit up. "The Emperor took us north. He had the most luxurious carriage. He had business in Widowton and two other towns. Meeting nobles, observing conditions, lots of important errands. It was lovely. He was so doting."

"It sounds like you had a great time," Cecilia said, wearing a forced smile. "It must have been splendid having him to yourself. Did you feel like his Empress?"

Jade's eyes narrowed at Cecilia. "I know you wanted to go. I hope you don't bear me any ill will. Truth is I *did* feel like an Empress. And it was everything I hoped it would be."

At that moment, Kayla walked by, preceded by the thick scent of lilacs and roses. Her expression was one of pity. "You don't really think the Emperor would marry a sandshark hunter, do you? He'd have to fill the palace with sand just so you felt at home. And the Emperor can't tolerate even a speck of dust."

"Don't belittle me because you're jealous," Jade sneered.

"Jealous?" Kayla gave a long laugh, but there was no mirth there.

Cecilia pointed a brush at Kayla's face. "I don't think Jade was far off. Your cheeks are even rosier than your ruby."

Kayla poked a finger at Cecilia. "We all know how much you covet the crown. You came here for the sole purpose of becoming his bride. How will you handle the crushing blow if he chooses someone else?"

"You don't know anything about me," Cecilia said, eyes narrowed on Kayla. "You think you know why I came here? You think you understand me?" She shook her head slowly. "Don't fool yourself."

"Leave us alone, Kayla," Jade said.

Kayla turned her belittling stare to Jade. It amazed Isabelle to see someone so pretty and yet so ugly at the same time. "So the Emperor took his sandrat out and showed her around the north. Remember that the Emperor recognizes that Neverak blood is superior to any other nation, especially one filled with sand. If anyone becomes an Empress, I can assure you it will be someone from Neverak."

"You?" Cecilia asked.

Kayla raised an eyebrow. "My noble bloodline goes back seven generations. I was born and bred for the life. Think about that while you play with your paints." She spun on her heel and walked away.

That night, it seemed to take the girls longer than usual to get to bed. Cecilia had not been requested by the Emperor that night, so she chatted with two fellow slaves in the halls, her tone muted and dull, which Isabelle guessed was from disappointment. Cecilia had expected to be chosen the night the Emperor returned home from his trip. Instead it was Jessika, her tall, regal friend, a dark-haired beauty of noble Neverakan blood.

Finally the torches were extinguished and the girls went to bed. Isabelle had no difficulty staying awake, though her mind wandered. She found herself thinking often of her mother and what she would say to Isabelle now. It seemed an eternity ago when she had been in her mother's chamber, holding her hand and crying as her mother took her last breath, muttering those strange last words to her daughter: *"Tell James to climb on the windy side."* Not a year had passed since Lady Oslan's death. She had given Isabelle her fortune to prevent a disaster from her father, and yet the very thing she had tried to prevent had still occurred.

Steeling herself to act, Isabelle muttered the words of a song her mother had often sung to her and James when they were small, words she in turn had sung to Henry when he was troubled:

When I am gone 'cross distant lands,
Lonely though your walk,
Save a place for me within your heart,
And we shall soon clasp hands.

The words gave her strength. She pretended her voice was her mother's, and that the blanket wrapped around her was her mother's arms enfolding her. When enough time had passed, Isabelle silently rose from the bed, lit a torch from the embers in her fireplace, and left her room. The thick fur rugs throughout the hallway muffled her steps.

Kayla's chamber was the farthest from Isabelle's. None of the girl's rooms had doors. For privacy, strips of velvet hung across the door frames like curtains. Isabelle entered Kayla's room and listened to the soft whispers of her breathing.

"Kayla?" she breathed. Kayla made no movement, nor gave any sign that she had heard Isabelle. "Kayla, I'm going to touch your face." Though this wasn't her first time taking it, Isabelle's hands were clammy and quaking as she stole the ruby rose from Kayla's bedside table and carried it back to her room with all the care she would give the King of Blithmore's crown.

Standing on her bed, Isabelle donned a pair of gloves she'd nicked from the old maids who scrubbed and massaged her. Nothing scared her more than the thought of dropping the ruby. As she worked, she gripped the ruby tightly in her padded hands and rubbed the pointed end against the iron, slowly cutting through it. She'd realized the need for gloves after the maids had discovered the first evidence of her nightly activity.

"My goodness!" a maid had exclaimed one morning more than a week ago. "What have you been doing to your hands?"

She held Isabelle's hands at the wrists, looking at them as if they were made of horse droppings. Other maids gathered, muttering to each other with disapproval. "Blisters forming here and here . . ."

"Oh my—"

"Yes. Look at her fingernails."

"How did she do that?"

"Chipped!"

"What will the Emperor say?"

"I haven't been doing anything!" Isabelle face grew hotter than when she emerged from the scalding baths.

"Calm down, Isabelle," her maid said. "This is why we're here. We'll bring it up with Kayla. She'll know whether or not she should inform the Emperor."

Isabelle stood, assuming an air of offense. "There's no need to discuss it with Kayla. I'll find out what's causing it and end it myself. Do you think I want my hands to look like a nervous child's? The Emperor would discard me like an old glove."

The words *old glove* had stuck with her. Since she'd begun wearing the gloves, her hands had healed. But that wasn't her only worry. During the first few nights of cutting, Isabelle had stopped and checked the ruby more than a dozen times to be certain it hadn't been damaged, but each time she wiped away flakes of metal, the ruby looked the same underneath. Cecilia had been right. Nothing could damage a ruby hardened in the fiery belly of a dragonox.

The noise worried her, too. In the quiet of the concubines' quarters, the sound of the ruby digging into iron seemed like a trumpet. While she was fortunate some of the girls slept loudly (one in particular, Joy, had a peculiar high-pitched snore), anyone outside her chamber could hear the scratching sounds and might investigate. But it couldn't be helped.

As she toiled, she daydreamed. It was easy to slip into thoughts of Henry while she worked on the bars. She imagined his words of assurance and love, his fingers clenched tightly around her waist, his warm lips pressing against hers. Other times she thought of James, wishing for his strength and intellect. Her thoughts also went to Cecilia. It wasn't uncommon for Cecilia to, late at night, peek in for a chat, but lately Cecilia was more concerned about the Emperor's seeming disinterest.

The nights passed in waves of deep thought broken by moments of terror whenever she heard a slight sound. When Isabelle's arm grew too tired to work any longer, she silently stole back through the chambers and returned the ruby as carefully as she'd taken it.

• • •

The next day, while eating lunch with Jade in the common room, Isabelle received a visit from a member of the Emperor's staff. He was a friendly-looking man with gray hair in patches like a quilt. He entered and peered over his tiny spectacles at the slaves dispersed throughout the room, and asked, "Which one of you is Isabelle?" pronouncing it *Eezabella*.

Kayla dropped her empty plate on the floor. "You're making a gown for *her*? She's only been here two months!"

Cecilia, on the other hand, did not seemed surprised, but glanced at Isabelle with a look of distrust as the man approached.

"Isabelle, my name is Derrick. I am the personal tailor of Emperor Krallick. I expect Isabelle is already aware of her dinner appointment with the Emperor in one week?"

Isabelle sat in place, stunned. The tailor was slightly alarmed. Cecilia stepped forward. "This is my fault, Derrick. I forgot to pass along the message. I'm sorry."

The tailor smiled graciously and turned his attention back to Isabelle. He reached into the pocket of his vest and removed a long piece of string for measuring. He grinned at Cecilia and said, "I forgive, I forgive." With his string, he began measuring Isabelle while muttering numbers under his breath. "Please stand up straight,

Isabelle. Now sit, as Isabelle normally would while eating. Now stand again. That's a girl."

As quickly as he'd arrived, he finished and politely excused himself. Isabelle did not know what to do or say. She looked around at the other girls questioningly, but none of them offered advice. Finally she broke through her shock and asked, "What am I supposed to do? Dinner with the Emperor? What does that mean?"

Although this was really her second dinner with the Emperor, Isabelle thought it best not to mention the first. After all, having dinner as an invited guest was different than dining with a man who thought himself her owner.

"I don't know what he sees in her," Kayla whispered loudly. "She's ugly *and* stupid. This cannot stand."

"His servants will come and get you a half hour before the meal," Jade informed Isabelle. "They will prepare you for the etiquette expected of you."

"I'll kill myself before I see that pig wear the rose," Kayla said.

Isabelle ignored Kayla and left, coming out of her room only for dinner and then returning to wait for nightfall. By the light of the low half-moon through Kayla's window, Isabelle snuck in again and lifted the ruby rose. The work left her satisfied and feeling more hopeful than she'd been in weeks. She returned the ruby rose and slept soundly.

The week slipped by until Isabelle had only a day left before her dinner with Emperor Krallick. Each night Kayla slept in the concubines' quarters, Isabelle took the rose. Her work went slowly but steadily. Significant progress had been made on one bar: she had ground deep cuts in both the top and bottom, leaving little more than a sliver of metal holding it together on either end. The second rod, however, had not been touched.

The night before Isabelle's dinner, to Kayla's chagrin, Nikole was chosen to entertain the Emperor. So, with the intent of working on the second bar for two to three hours, Isabelle took the ruby and went to work. She had been whittling away at the bar for only a short while when she heard a sound from down the hall. In an instant, she untangled her arms from the window bars, stuffed the ruby rose underneath her pillow, and crawled underneath her blanket.

Isabelle listened for the faint sounds of muffled footsteps or the soft swishing of another slave's robes. She heard nothing, but waited anyway. Once she was certain that only sound was her own breathing, she left her room in the darkness to return the ruby. No sooner had she entered the hallway when something slammed into her face just below her eye. It took Isabelle a moment to realize that what she'd felt was a gloved fist. The scent of stone filled her nostrils as her face met the floor. But there was another scent—something faint.

Lilacs.

The ruby rolled out of Isabelle's pocket onto the floor. She heard the soft sound of someone reaching for it, picking it up, feeling it. The silence that followed filled Isabelle with a terrible dread that reached her bones and ate at her gut.

"You want this?" a hoarse whisper asked. "You want to be his favorite?" The gloved hand grabbed the short hairs at the back of Isabelle's neck and pulled until Isabelle's ear was next to unseen lips. Isabelle's strangled cry was lost in a sharp hiss. "Don't you *ever* touch the rose. I don't care if the Emperor has taken a fancy to you. You're nothing special."

Isabelle snapped. She didn't want to hurt anyone, but she wouldn't tolerate being manhandled in such a way, either. She reached up and placed her bare hands over the unseen face. Isabelle's hands muffled the girl's scream as she tugged on Isabelle's hair, producing a searing pain in Isabelle's scalp. Isabelle stifled her cries, determined not to wake anyone, but bit her lower lip trying to do so.

Padded feet ran down the hall, away from Isabelle. She lay on the floor for a while, letting the cool stone ease the heat in her face.

Finally Isabelle got up, a dull ache throbbing in her right cheek. She tentatively reached there and gently probed the spot. The pain was enough to make her wince.

Isabelle climbed into bed and pulled the blankets completely over her. "Henry," she whispered. "Where are you?"

THIRTY

Ruther's Efforts

W hat would you do if it were your sons?" Ruther asked
the tavern owner of the Thirsty Thief. "Would that change
things?"

"Your friends aren't my sons," the owner, Morvin, responded testily. "They're strangers. So are you. I will not help you."

It was early morning in Tiller's Thain. Ruther had found the tavern owner scrubbing tables and dishes, preparing the tavern for the
first customers of the day. He was a tall man, taller even than Ruther.
But he was also thin, clean-cut, and wore a spotless apron. Ruther
held a broom, trying to earn Morvin's good grace by sweeping.

"Do you believe in fate?" Ruther asked Morvin.

Morvin shrugged and started wiping another table. "I don't think
about it much."

"Some believe that those who do good, honest deeds are blessed
by the Lord of All Worlds with good fortune. Perhaps if you help,
good fortune will come to you."

"Maybe so. But can you guarantee that?"

"No, I can't, but—"

Morvin stood up straight and pointed a tall, thin finger toward the
ceiling. "Let me tell you what I can guarantee. If I come forward and
state what I saw that night, customers will stop coming through my
door. Which means my ale will go undrunk, my chairs will go unsat,

and I'll be out of business. *Or* . . . one night I'll wake up and find that my tavern has caught fire, and I'll be out of business. That I can guarantee. That's how things work here, especially when the son of the town leader ends up dead."

It was true. The brothers who had attacked Henry and James were Matthew and Michael Erwick, sons of Marcus Erwick, the town leader. Michael, the elder brother, had died almost instantly after cracking his head open on a table. With a trial forthcoming, Ruther was trying desperately to find a witness to cooperate and give testimony.

"But, Morvin, will you sleep well at night knowing two innocent men were—"

"I'll sleep fine if their heads roll or not. Day after day you bother me about this. How many more times are you going to ask? I am not helping you."

Ruther set the broom down and headed toward the door. Before leaving, he stopped and turned back. "Is there any help you can offer me? They're my friends. I'm desperate."

Morvin stopped polishing the table and stared at Ruther. His expression changed from one of annoyance to pity. His jaw moved side to side as though he were deep in thought. "There is a physician you may wish to consult: Scotty Brittamon. Lives in Miner's Moore, about twenty miles northeast. He might assist as you prepare your arguments. He's wise and respected. Word around town is that he's the physician Erwick called to examine his son. Came to town, but wouldn't give testimony the death was a killing."

Ruther thanked the tavern owner and left. As he rode Ghost through town, he stopped next at the bladesmith's shop. The bladesmith, Ruther had learned, had been seated at the table next to where James and Henry had sat inside the Thirsty Thief. He'd seen the fight with an unimpeded view. Ruther had spoken to him once before, and decided to try again.

There was one other customer in the shop, a massive man with arms the width of Ruther's head and a chest like a dragonox. He gave the smith a powerful sword that made Ruther's own blade look like a dagger. His voice was deep and rich.

"I don't want a new blade," the large man complained, "I want this one sharpened!"

The bladesmith handed it back. "I can't do it, Hector. Look at how badly you've notched it. How many times have I told you that you can't use your sword to chop wood?"

Hector ran a meaty paw through his long black hair. "I ain't got an axe! They don't pay me enough for killing folk to buy one!"

"Being the town executioner isn't a time-demanding job, Hector," the blade smith muttered but warily, as though afraid to pick a fight with the giant.

"I got work coming up in two weeks. A double execution. I'll have enough money then to pay for the new blade. How about you give me the blade now, and I'll pay you then."

The bladesmith shook his head. "You pay when you get the blade, or you don't get the blade. That's always been my rule, and it's not changing for you. Even my own father has to pay for his blades."

Hector growled. "You remember the last execution? How many swings—"

The bladesmith made a face of disgust. "I just ate breakfast. Don't bring that up."

"Four swings!" Hector yelled. "Four swings to behead that horse thief. You know how that embarrasses me! People come to these executions expecting a nice, clean severing. The suddenness of it makes it entertaining. They don't need to see me hammering away like a carpenter. It scares the children."

The bladesmith remained firm that his policy wouldn't change, and Hector finally left in a huff. As the smith watched Ruther approach, he narrowed his eyes and frowned. "Not you again. I'm not going to help."

"Were you listening to that beast of a man?" Ruther argued. "My friends aren't even going to get a fair trial. He thinks the execution is going to happen regardless of my arguments. They need to hear from someone they know—someone they trust."

"If I help you—" the bladesmith started to say, but Ruther cut in.

"Let me guess . . . people will stop buying your swords or they'll burn down your shop."

"Indeed they will."

"Is there another bladesmith in town?" Ruther asked.

"No."

"Then where else will they buy new blades?"

Nothing would persuade the bladesmith. Ruther slammed the door as he left the shop. Then he opened it again and slammed it a second time for good measure. Rather than returning to the inn, Ruther went to the market and asked for directions to Miner's Moore. Once he was certain he knew where to go, he paid a boy to send a message to Maggie and Thirsty at the inn, and set out to find the physician named Scotty Brittamon.

Pushing Ghost hard, the journey took him until early in the evening. When he finally rode up to the house of the physician, he saw a woman outside tending a newly planted garden. Ruther waved at the woman, and she waved back. After he introduced himself, she asked, "Are you looking for Scotty?"

"I am."

"He's not here yet. I'm Pippynn. I don't expect him back until nightfall. But you're welcome to stay and wait if you'll help me prepare supper. I like having company while I cook. And anyone who helps me cook helps me eat."

Ruther thought that sounded like a fair trade. Pippynn took him inside and instructed him to wash vegetables for stew. While Ruther rolled up his sleeves and started scrubbing potatoes, she prepared a chicken.

"So you're from Tiller's Thain?" she asked.

"No, ma'am," Ruther answered. "Blithmore."

"Really? I've never met anyone from across the Iron Forest. What brings you all the way out here? Certainly not the scenery!"

Ruther laughed courteously before relating a shortened version of how he'd ended up so far east. When he got to the part about his friends being arrested, Pippynn gave a loud gasp and set down her chicken.

"You know, I've heard talk about that. Scotty would kill me if he knew I told you this, but he's helped out the Erwick family many times. Marcus Erwick's boys used to get the most unusual rashes. Purple and green, full of pus and bleeding. Oooh, nasty!"

"Thank you for telling me about that in such remarkable detail," Ruther said. Then he changed the subject. "So how did you and Scotty meet?"

The physician's wife smiled and wiped her eyes. "Oh, you want to hear that story, do you?" She set down the knife she was using to cut and peel the potatoes and wiped her hands on a cloth. "I was always a romantic girl. Wanted to marry my childhood friend the day I turned eighteen, a boy I'd always loved, Tippy Dinker. Tippy and Pippy, that was always our little saying. He was the neighbor's son. Tall, handsome, and so polite. His father raised cacti for glue and sold it in the Farmlands. He did quite well with that business until he accidentally swallowed some and glued his tongue to the back of his throat. Poor thing. Tippy and I were in love. And Scotty was Tippy's best friend.

"I always thought Scotty was a nice boy, but never felt any sort of attraction to him. Then he went away to school to become a physician in Grettinah, the capital of Old Avalon. And I sort of missed him, which I thought was odd. And then, months later when he came home, he came to visit me. I was a month shy of eighteen at the time."

A gleam appeared in Pippynn's eyes and she raised her eyebrows. "He asked me to take a walk with him."

Ruther wasn't certain why, but he found Pippynn's story fascinating.

"He took me to the desert oasis, where a little pond flows up from the ground with flowering cacti that grow around it. The flowers bloom three or four times a year, and it's very lovely. We sat on a rock and talked and looked at the flowers. Then Scotty confessed his love for me. I must admit that it caught me off guard. He told me he'd loved me for years, but had been too scared to tell me. He went on and on—it was so beautiful. I realized I loved him, too. And that was that. We've had our spats over the years, but we've had a good life."

The story made Ruther think of Maggie. Perhaps he needed to confess his feelings to her. But how would Maggie react? How could he be certain if the time was right? What sort of things had Scotty said that changed Pippynn's mind? Before he could ask more questions, Scotty came home. Pippynn greeted him with a small kiss and then introduced Ruther. Scotty was a little shorter and fatter than Ruther, but had a kind face, shaggy gray hair and a matching mustache. He looked Ruther over twice before offering him a hand to shake.

"Can't say I enjoy coming home and finding a younger, skinnier man than myself talking to my beautiful wife. What brings you here, mister?"

"Dear," Pippynn told her husband, "this young man is friends with those two boys arrested in Tiller's Thain. He needs your help."

"Ah yes, the Erwick boy. I examined the body after he died at the request of his father." Scotty scowled and scratched his gray mustache. "Don't know what I can do to help. None of my business as I didn't offer an opinion on the body."

Ruther squeezed the carrots he'd been peeling so hard that they slipped from his hand back into the pail. "It is your business," he argued. "It's everyone's business. I have to help my friends defend their lives, and I need help. In Tiller's Thain I was told you're a respected man around these parts. Isn't that true?"

"Well . . ." Scotty's wife fixed him with a stern gaze that told him exactly how he should answer. "I suppose that's true."

"And do you think a respected man has a duty to tell the truth?"

"But I wasn't even there!" Scotty protested. "What do you expect me to say?"

"You're a man of logic and reason. I would like you to come down, talk to people, and help argue for my friends at the trial. When you examined the body, what did you find?"

"Well . . . like I said this isn't my—"

Pippynn cleared her throat and crossed her arms.

"The evidence did not substantiate the claims of the accusers."

"So you came to the conclusion that my friends are innocent?"

Scotty raised a finger. "Well . . . just because the evidence . . . It doesn't mean that your friends are without guilt. As I said, I wasn't there."

"I'm trying to find one person who is brave enough to stand for the truth. One man. One woman. And would you believe I can't find that person?"

Scotty grunted something while avoiding his wife's gaze. Despite the physician's reluctance, Ruther refused to give up. And if there was one thing Ruther was good at, it was his ability to painfully, obnoxiously erode the resistance of anyone who opposed him. And so he talked and talked and talked until the physician finally broke down.

"I simply can't speak in front of the town. That's for my wife's safety." He raised his hands and wouldn't let Ruther interrupt. "But I will help you prepare your own argument so that you can make it perfectly clear that your friends are innocent."

THIRTY-ONE

The Story of the Scar

Henry had heard stories as a boy about the Endless Abyss, the final resting place for the wicked, a place so terrible it twisted and deformed the souls sent there. If this wasn't the Endless Abyss, he would gladly welcome it because it couldn't be worse than being imprisoned in a dark, cold, damp hole, falsely accused, and vilified by an entire town. Each day in prison was a day lost that he could be moving toward Isabelle. Each day was torture. Screaming, pleading, and begging did no good. No one would listen to reason. Twice he and James had gotten sick from the darkness and cold. They could barely stand to full height, and when they did, James's head pressed against the ceiling, while Henry's brushed it.

With no king, no soldiers, and no government, Tiller's Thain was ruled by the community as a whole. They had no paid guards to watch the prison. Instead, people volunteered their time in shifts. Some of them seemed to genuinely enjoy their duties. Others came and sat in silence until the shift ended. The people of the town provided no food or drink to James and Henry. Any sustenance they received came from Ruther and Maggie, who were not allowed to speak or pass messages.

To help occupy their time, James begged two thick sticks from one of the more cordial guards to work on Henry's swordplay stance and form. For a few hours a day—when the sun was brightest and Henry and James could see each other well enough—they practiced.

It was all they had to release their aggression and frustration at the injustices inflicted upon them. Henry's improving skill was the only thing that kept his growing madness at bay.

The two men went through fits of conversation: hours of talking followed by hours of silence. It was strange hearing James speak so much. He had always been the quiet one when they were younger.

One night, while the guards softly slumbered, Henry asked, "Maybe it's time we try tunneling through the wall. If nothing else, it will give us something to do."

"Is it worth the risk?" James asked. "If they catch us, we'll look guilty."

Henry sighed. "You think that we'll be acquitted? In this town?"

"It's all I have," James said.

"All I have is Isabelle. All she has is me. I can't die here, James."

"They said if we try to escape, they'll kill us without a trial."

Henry let the idea go, sighing again. "I'm losing my mind in here."

"When did you first know you were in love with my sister?" James asked.

The question stunned Henry. James had never asked him anything so personal. Henry didn't have to think about the answer. "Your mother, for a long time, insisted that Isabelle not spend any time around me and Maggie outside of school. After you left, she became even more strict. It was to protect her, you know, since you weren't around. Isabelle was only thirteen, I think."

"Thirteen sounds right," James said in the darkness.

Age thirteen seemed like a hundred years ago. "I can't remember a time when I didn't think she was beautiful or just wanted her to notice me. I chased her around and teased her because I didn't know how else to express that. The day I realized I was in love . . ." Henry scratched his forehead absentmindedly. "I was fifteen. She was thirteen. Ruther and I were walking through the market with a couple other friends. We turned the corner on Shop Street going to

Havisham's blade shop, and there was Isabelle with a swarm of girls around her. We almost walked right into them. One of her friends pointed at me. I hadn't washed after working in the woodshop. From my hair to my boots, I was covered in dust.

"The girl next to Isabelle mocked my appearance. All I could do was stare at Isabelle, and all she did was stare back. Then a second girl joined in and a third. It was humiliating to be insulted by a group of pretty girls. Ruther kept prodding me to say something back, but I couldn't. Then Isabelle stepped forward and took my arm. She turned to her friends and said, 'This is the smartest, bravest, and most handsome boy I've ever known.' And she kissed my cheek." Henry touched the spot. Even in the cold and dark he recalled the moment with brilliant clarity. "I thought that my chest was going to grow a hundred times bigger. Everything inside me was hot and wonderful."

Henry had no more to say, but the memory brought back so much emotion that he was content to sit in silence and relive it. He heard James shifting his weight against the wall. "I know the feeling you described, Henry. It is wonderful."

"When did you experience it?"

"It's such a—it's so powerful. In a way, it's life-threatening, isn't it?"

At first Henry thought James's statement was absurd. Then he realized his friend was right. How often, in recent weeks, had he struggled to contemplate a life without Isabelle? How often had he wondered if life was worth living if he couldn't get her back? He had wanted to charge the Emperor's palace blindly—alone if need be. "James, I never knew you felt so passionate about my sister. How long ago did this happen?"

"Not—not Maggie. I *was* in love. Now I'm terrified of it. It was a mistake to reciprocate Maggie's feelings. I'm not ready to love someone."

"Why not?"

"My promotion to First Guardsman was a surprise, but one I

deserved. With it came orders to transfer to Severn. That's in the Towering Mountains in Western Blithmore. My first day in town, I went to the market. One of the junior officers had been assigned to show me around. The market was packed because the town was holding a ball that night. Severn held a ball whenever new officers came into the area. Everyone in town came. While in the market, I recognized my new commanding officer: Senior Guardsman Logan Vreagan. I recognized him because his reputation preceded him. Everyone said he was a man who cared deeply about his appearance— never a hair out of place or a smudge on his clothing. And he looked younger than his age because of his thick black hair and his tanned skin. On his arm was a beautiful woman.

"I still remember what she wore that day. It was a light green dress that made her auburn hair stand out. She wore emerald earrings that matched her eyes. When I say matched, Henry, I mean literally—her eyes were the same color as the emeralds. Our eyes met, and my heart thumped in my chest like I'd run a footrace. It was new to me, the feeling of such intense attraction, and it scared me.

"That night at the ball, I saw her again. I watched her dance with Vreagan and I wanted her. Have you felt that? Where you would do anything just to have someone look at you?"

"I know the feeling," Henry answered.

"When I saw her dance with other men, I knew she would be open to an invitation. So I asked her, and we danced. I loved every-thing about her, her beauty, her voice, her scent. We introduced our-selves, and it was as though we already knew each other's names. We only needed to be reminded. Three or four songs went by in our first dance, and then we were interrupted by Vreagan. I could tell in her eyes and her voice that she wanted to keep dancing with me. And I made it clear by the way I looked at her that the feeling was mutual. Everything about life excited me in that moment.

"That night she told Vreagan that while she appreciated the time he had spent courting her over the last year, she did not want him to pursue her any further. He was cordial and gave her his blessing in finding someone more suitable. The next day she came to our camp and asked me if I could help train her filly. I told her I could help, and that was how we became acquainted. The horse and I bonded, too. She gave me the horse—Sissy. I named Sissy after her."

"You named your horse after a woman you loved?" Henry asked.

James chuckled at himself. "Not the highest compliment a man can give a woman. I realize that now. Fortunately she didn't mind. A week later she and I kissed for the first time, and I began courting her.

"Her father, a nobleman, owns a mining operation. Unlike my father, he's quite wealthy. Her mother died giving birth to her, leaving her an only child. She was . . . I've never met someone with such joy for living, an ambition about everything. As I courted her, my life seemed to be going so well, even my career looked bright. My superior officers often commented that they expected great things from me. Vreagan said he believed I'd become the youngest Premier Guardsman ever, and he wanted to do everything in his power to make it happen. We got along well in those days. He was so quick to laugh and smile. I counted him among my best friends despite him being my commanding officer.

"He had a passion for people, for laughing, for dancing. He also had a strange obsession with collecting artifacts with supernatural stories attached to them. Sometimes, when he acquired a new piece to his collection, he'd summon us into his quarters to show it off—tell us stories about its history. Have you heard the tales of the underwater dwellers in the Great Southern Sea?"

"I have. They're not true, are they?"

James laughed again. "No. But he claimed one of his daggers had a handle made from the bone of the chief of the underwater dwellers. Honestly, though, I thought it looked northern . . . Frolian probably. Another was an arrowhead cursed by a self-proclaimed sorcerer from

Gaddano. I can't remember everything he told me. Each of them had a history and some special property he believed in. But as strange as he was, I liked him. And as I said, we got along well.

"Then orders came from the King. A band of robbers had taken refuge in caves thirty miles west of Severn. Vreagan was ordered to flush them out. He ordered two battalions, one which I led, the other under his charge. His team would set up ambush points to snare them after we drove them out of the caves.

"On our way to the caves, three of my men got sick. I told them to return to camp, but they insisted on going with us. Our battalion had only twelve men, and they thought if we only had nine, our forces would be insufficient to capture the robbers. None of us wanted to ride the three days back to base because we didn't know if the robbers would still be in those caves by the time we replaced the sick men. So we pressed on, and the three seemed to get a little better. When we reached the caves, the robbers ambushed us. In the middle of the battle, two of the three sick men collapsed. The third could hardly stand. At that point, not only did we have to protect ourselves, but we had to protect the other men. The rest of us fought valiantly, hoping that Vreagan would come to our aid. I barely survived, a couple of my soldiers didn't."

Henry finally understood why James had been so adamant that Henry see a healer before going after Isabelle. James had experienced what happened in battle when there were liabilities.

"Finally Vreagan came and we defeated the band of thieves. I was indebted to Vreagan for saving us, but when praise and awards came from our superior officers, most of the honor fell to me. I wrote to our superiors and insisted that had it not been for Vreagan, my battalion would have died. They responded with words about valor and bravery in the face of death. I later learned that one of the generals in the guard had a personal grudge against Vreagan, but this didn't matter.

Vreagan's opinion of me changed. I'd already stolen his girl, and now I'd robbed him of his accolades.

"Our friendship grew cold despite my efforts to fix it. So I made arrangements to transfer my assignment. My plan was to travel to Richterton with my betrothed and announce our intent to marry. Then we would return to Severn and marry. When I went to Vreagan to inform him of my plans, he asked me to meet with him privately. When we met, another officer was in the room with us—First Guardsman Nathaniel Codley. I hated that man: a fat, balding sycophant if there ever was one. Some men earn their rank; others attain it by less than honorable means. Codley was of the latter sort.

"Before I'd even sat in my chair, Vreagan launched a tirade of accusations against me: that I had lied to the generals, falsified reports from the field, stolen money from the Guardsmen coffers to pay for gifts I'd bought my betrothed. At first I found it comical . . . then I realized he was serious. I defended myself, heatedly at times. When I got up to leave, Codley blocked the door. As my back was turned, Vreagan approached me, and I reacted unwisely."

Henry remembered the scar James had shown him while journeying through Blithmore, a nasty, twisted thing that traveled three or four inches across his scalp.

"I drew my sword, though I stood little chance against two well-trained guardsmen. We fought with steel, but they beat me back until I was against Vreagan's desk. Codley disarmed me, but I grabbed the cursed arrowhead from Vreagan's desk and stabbed Vreagan with it. Vreagan brought the blade of his sword down on my head, cutting my scalp open. Blood poured into my eyes until I passed out, the sound of Vreagan's screams in my ears.

"Being imprisoned in Severn was the most humiliating experience of my life. Some of my men stood by me, but most thought me a traitor. Word spread through the town and reached *her* ears. She received permission to visit, and I told her everything that had happened. At the time, I thought she believed me. It was my word against Vreagan and Codley's. When a Supreme Guardsman heard our arguments, Vreagan told him he wanted me hanged for my offense. Those words stung as much as the day my father kicked me out of his house on my seventeenth birthday.

"The Supreme Guardsman told me privately that he believed me, but politics prevented him from ignoring the testimony of two officers. The best thing he could do was offer me a dishonorable discharge from the Guard. As for Vreagan, he would be reassigned to a southern post, and Codley north.

"I accepted his offer and asked him to deliver a letter to a woman for me. He agreed to do so. I begged parchment, quill, and ink from my guards, and wrote to her. I implored her to believe my innocence. If she would still have me, I offered to take her to Richterton, introduce her to my family, and then return to Severn for our wedding. I pledged to her my love and my loyalty in the strongest words I knew. Then I sent the letter.

"Everything went exactly as he said it would. I signed a declaration of my innocence and a willingness to forego trial in exchange for a dishonorable discharge. This stripped me of my rank and any chance of rejoining the King's Guard. I can't really describe how hard that was for me. Six years of my life wasted. I told myself that at least I had love—a lifetime of love—to look forward to. After my release, I rode to my betrothed to take her to Richterton.

"She met me on the road leading to her father's homestead. The moment I saw her, I knew something was wrong. It was her . . . but it wasn't. That makes no sense, but I don't know how else to describe it. She had a strange expression on her face. Anger or pity perhaps. But I didn't see sadness. Then she spoke to me and things became perfectly clear."

There was a long pause, and Henry began to wonder if James was going to tell him what she said. It wasn't until he heard the soft sounds of sniffling that he realized James was crying. He had never seen nor heard James cry before. Not even as children.

"She was ashamed of me. A man who would not defend himself against lies could only be guilty. She told me to leave; our problems could never be fixed. That line stuck with me. I can't . . . nothing . . . it was crushing. Crushing. My life was pointless. I argued with her, begged her, but she sneered at me, mocked me. I took her hand but she slapped it away and spat in my face. I decided it was time to go home to my mother. I traveled weeks across Blithmore and . . ."

"And she was dead."

"Everything changed the night I found you fighting my father. If you hadn't been in that situation, I would have hugged Isabelle, gotten back on my horse, and set out to find Vreagan. There are still days I want to leave you so I can hunt him down and put my sword in him."

Henry's mouth was dry, but he would not receive food and drink for hours. "Hearing this makes me all the more grateful for your help, James. We would not have survived if you hadn't come along. Your arrival at the manor was fate."

"I don't know what fate is anymore. You say I was fated to save you, but look what happened to Isabelle and Brandol. Brandol, whose hand got caught in a saddle strap, and is probably locked up in a prison in Neverak. Or dead! Look what happened to me. Look at us now. Is *this* our fate?"

These thoughts dampened Henry's spirit and left him silent. Above them through the barred trapdoor, he could hear the guard shuffling around the room, probably stretching his legs. Henry's back ached, so he shifted from a sitting position to a lying one. The ground was hard, but soothed the muscles around his spine.

"I should have gone after her, but it was too late. I knew how desperately you and Isabelle needed me, and I couldn't leave then. Traveling through Blithmore, I grew fond of Maggie. She's beautiful and spirited. When she kisses my cheek, I feel something in my chest, something good. But I'm not certain if it's her I love or if I simply miss being loved."

"I can't fault you for being confused. Have you considered trying to find your former love? Rather than hunting down this Vreagan, why not seek what you truly want?"

James stirred in the dark. Henry wondered if he had stopped crying. "I've thought about it, but I am afraid of reopening a wound that is now nearly closed."

"Do you think that she—Sissy—is with Vreagan again?"

A sigh came from across the room. "I don't know. I'm not certain I want to."

Henry closed his eyes. "We are blocks of wood," he said. "Once we are touched by a chisel and hammer, the marks are permanent." The distance between himself and Isabelle seemed insurmountable, the weight of his decisions infinite. They affected not only himself but the people he cared about. What was his destiny? Did he control it? Was he truly meant to accomplish certain things, or did everything depend on making the right choice at the right instant? The notion that his choices mattered terrified him, but so did the idea that they didn't matter at all. His arm had never felt so dead. "I hope you find Sissy . . . if you are meant to."

"Her name wasn't Sissy." James said in a smaller voice than normal. "That was the nickname her father gave her. I didn't call her that."

"Oh. Then what—?"

"Her real name was Cecilia."

THIRTY-TWO

Lunch with Cecilia

I t's hideous!"

"And on the day of your dinner!"

"The Emperor—what is he going to think? How did this happen?"

"I have no idea," Isabelle told the maids. "I woke up this morning in pain."

"You poor thing!"

As the maids washed and scrubbed Isabelle, they discussed how best to hide her disfigured face. Neither of them bothered to ask if she was all right, they only tittered on about how her face could be made presentable as soon as possible. Isabelle had received more than enough scrapes and bruises to know that this one, too, would go away on its own.

After an hour of their best efforts, the maids left in a state of disgust, infuriated at their inability to hide the monstrous bruise. Isabelle found the situation silly, though she was in no mood to laugh. Her mind was elsewhere. Had Kayla attacked her? Another girl? And if it was another, would whoever it was tell Kayla that Isabelle had stolen the ruby?

Not long after her baths were over, Derrick, the Imperial Tailor, returned to the concubines' chambers with assistants carrying over a dozen gowns for Isabelle to try on. He made her put on each gown in the privacy of her room, then display them for him. He gave her orders, "Isabelle turns slowly. She walks toward me. Isabelle is about to sit. Now she smiles. And now she closes the eyes." More than once she caught him staring at her bruised face.

The process took much longer than expected. In the end, he chose for her a splendid light blue dress which he said suited her perfectly so long as she ate a light lunch. He advised her to not don the gown until just a few minutes before her escort arrived to take her to the Emperor. If she needed any more advice beyond that, she should ask the other concubines. In parting he added, "Oh, yes . . . Isabelle should do something about that eye."

That evening, Isabelle waited in her room until the escort arrived. On her way out of the quarters, she noticed how all the concubines had gathered in the common room except for Cecilia. Kayla, in particular, seemed particularly displeased, and her glare followed Isabelle out the door.

Isabelle had not set foot outside the house of the concubines since her arrival two and a half months prior. It amazed her how quickly it had become her entire world. True, the space was large enough to house several women quite comfortably, but it was not genuine; it was not a home. The lavish decorations and workmanship of the palace did not impress her nor soothe her tormented emotions.

On the way to the dining room they crossed a magnificent courtyard, completely indoors. It was the first place in all the palace that Isabelle found interesting. The domed ceiling overhead was painted to look like a brilliant summer sky. Lining the walls were beautifully manicured fir trees, tall rosebushes, and flowers. A waterfall created a pleasant cacophony as singing birds flew from tree to tree. Connected to the waterfall was a pond of water lilies and a stream that ran the length of the courtyard and exited via a conduit under the wall. Trimmed lawns and smaller flower gardens in various terraced shapes were scattered about. As a whole, it was a magnificent sight.

Before she could admire the gardens long, she was whisked through the opposite side of the courtyard where her escort introduced her to a grand dining hall. The table stretched several yards down the length of the hall, adorned with bouquets of roses, tulips, and other flowers. Dozens of chairs surrounded the massive board, but only three places had been set: one at the head of the table and two more, one to the right and left. Cecilia was already seated in the chair to the left, looking utterly confused and a little nervous. She stared at Isabelle's face with curiosity, especially her bruised cheek. The escort cleared his throat and gestured to the chair on the right.

"You never told me you had an invitation," Isabelle said.

"I received it only an hour ago. They gave me almost no time to dress and prepare. I thought—I assumed the Emperor had changed his mind about dinner with you."

Isabelle looked Cecilia over, her perfect red hair in flowing semi-curls, a touch of cosmetic applied here and there, a dress that looked like it had been sewn for an empress.

"You are beautiful, Cecilia," Isabelle said as she took her seat. She wasn't even certain why those words came out of her mouth.

Cecilia didn't respond.

Each place setting had seven forks, seven spoons, three knives, three plates, three goblets, and two bowls. In Blithmore, this was known as a twenty-five point setting. Seeing it here reminded her of how much tradition the two countries shared. Isabelle gestured to all the tableware in front of them. "Looks like an eight-course meal."

During her education with the Vestin family, Isabelle's parents had insisted that she learn proper etiquette. Mrs. Vestin, to accommodate the Oslan's request, had taken great pains to arrange a table the way it would be set at a royal feast and taught Isabelle, James, Henry, and Maggie how and when to properly use each piece set at the table.

Cecilia cleared her throat. "I've eaten with the Emperor several times, but I still don't know how to use all this correctly."

Isabelle lightly touched each utensil, plate, cup, and bowl, reminding herself and explaining to Cecilia what each piece was for and when it was to be employed. In the five minutes they waited for the Emperor, she was able to recall everything perfectly. Then the footman across the hall turned his head to peer through the doorway behind him, and stood a little straighter as he announced, "His Imperial Majesty, Emperor Ivan Richter Krallick the Third."

Isabelle did not have to think about standing for his entrance. Her legs did it automatically. The Emperor entered impressively, dressed in a glorious ensemble of white, red, and black. Unlike the attire she had seen him wear previously, white was the dominant color of the day. After pausing to examine the injury to Isabelle's face, he smiled at her warmly, something which softened his normally pointed features. He was excited to see her and seemed unsurprised at her injury. She, however, felt nothing but hatred. Knowing she could not show this, she did her best to keep her face a neutral mask and let the Emperor see her as he wanted.

His hands were gloved, but he took Isabelle's own gloved hand in his and brought his lips near her hand and kissed the air above it. Then he repeated this act with Cecilia's hand, only he kissed it fully. The girls waited until he sat. When he did, he turned his attention again to Isabelle. "Let's address the obvious first, shall we? What happened to you?"

Isabelle touched her face as though she had forgotten all about the injury. "Oh this, I—I don't know, Your Majesty." Despite all her time around Ruther, she still hadn't learned how to properly tell a lie. "This morning I woke up and—and there it was!" Her nervous laugh wasn't convincing, either. "The maids believe it might be a bite from . . . um . . . an insect. Or something of that nature."

Emperor Krallick leaned forward, concern filled his face. Isabelle had forgotten how handsome he could be when his features didn't appear so sharp and forbidding. "No, it doesn't appear to be a bite. There are no marks."

"Well, then . . ." Isabelle held up her hands as though she'd given up. "Who knows?"

The Emperor smiled at her, then at Cecilia. "Who indeed?" He clapped his hands once to signal the food bearers to begin. "Of course, I'm reminded of something Cecilia said to me perhaps a month ago as we lunched together. You came up in our conversation, Isabelle. Do you remember, Cecilia, what you said?"

Cecilia cleared her throat and spoke so softly that Isabelle could barely hear her. "No, my Lord, I don't recall."

"You said, 'Any problems Isabelle has in the house would be those caused by others, not her.' Do you remember now?"

"I do, my Lord."

Servants entered the room bearing trays of food. Everything Isabelle and Cecilia did had to be preceded by the Emperor. He had to take the first bite or sip of each course. As the food came, Isabelle observed proper etiquette with great care. She sensed the Emperor watching her movements, looking for any hint of a failure to observe all the decorum of her station.

Halfway through the soup, the Emperor set down his spoon and touched his napkin to his lips. "How are you enjoying life in my palace, Isabelle?"

"It is . . . comfortable, Your Majesty," she said carefully. "I've never experienced such—such a life as this."

"Of course, many find the lifestyle overwhelming at first. If you'd known several months ago how wonderful this life is, we might have avoided all the unpleasantness associated with bringing you here. I take responsibility for that."

His words flabbergasted her. "Erm—well—thank you, Your Majesty."

"But some problems have arisen, haven't they?" he asked, removing a piece of parchment from his pocket and waving it before them. "A nasty streak of jealousy has developed among my concubines. In fact, one of the girls wrote me an anonymous letter detailing an event which occurred last night. It involved the two of you."

Emperor Krallick waved the letter for Isabelle and Cecilia to see. The handwriting was beautiful, with large looping letters. Isabelle was not able to read it as it waved about.

"My Lord," Cecilia stated, "I will explain what happened. The truth." Cecilia glanced at Isabelle, and Isabelle saw that Cecilia knew enough to condemn Isabelle in the eyes of the Emperor. "May I speak?"

Isabelle's palms began to sweat and an itch developed in her throat. Did Cecilia know the truth? What Isabelle was doing with the ruby rose? She prepared herself for what answer—what lie—she'd have to tell if Cecilia did know.

The Emperor took a long drink from his goblet, gazing at both girls. "Yes, Cecilia. Tell me what poor Isabelle Oslan did to make you strike her."

Isabelle's mouth dropped open at this statement and she stared at Cecilia, whose face had gone white.

"*Oslan.*" Cecilia whispered the word like a long forgotten curse. She looked at Isabelle with wide eyes, as though seeing her for the first time. "Richterton."

"Cecilia?" Emperor Krallick said, interrupting Cecilia's thoughts. She blinked several times and seemed to remember that she was in the presence of the Emperor. "Do not make me ask you again. Is it true you struck Isabelle?"

Cecilia recovered quickly. "Strike her, my Lord?" She laughed as though the idea was utterly absurd. "My Lord, she and I have become good friends. I would never strike her. I was asleep during the whole matter. But you know I care about my position, my Lord—my desire to please you. And because of this, I make it my business to know what the other girls know. Last night one of the girls tried to mar Isabelle's face in order to make you displeased with Isabelle. She fears you may develop an attraction to her."

"Who was it?"

"Isabelle knows, my Lord."

"Is this true, Isabelle?" the Emperor asked.

Isabelle did not know how to answer. What did Cecilia know? By implicating someone else, would Isabelle possibly bring her wrath back on herself?

"Isabelle," the Emperor repeated. "Answer me."

Rather than facing the possibility of being caught in a lie, Isabelle nodded.

"Was it Cecilia?"

"I don't . . ." She remembered the scent of lilacs, the harsh voice. "No, my Lord."

His eyes narrowed, sharpening his features again. "Do you know who it was?"

"It was dark, my Lord. I saw no one."

The Emperor straightened himself in his chair. "I did not ask what you saw. I asked what you *know*."

"I do not know anything, my lord." Isabelle would not condemn Kayla, especially without being certain of her culpability.

The Emperor's eyes narrowed and he tapped the letter next to him with his fingers. "Why, then, does this letter name you, Cecilia?"

A long pause preceded Cecilia's answer. "That handwriting appears to have Haxite influence. Jade. She covets the rose, Your Majesty. She may have lied in order to supplant me as the next favorite."

Emperor Krallick's eyes pierced into Cecilia's. The moment lasted long enough that even Isabelle began to feel awkward.

"All the girls wish this," Isabelle added, "It would be easy to let greed or—or jealousy color the way a girl perceives events. Through no fault of her own."

"A fascinating insight into the minds of my concubines, Isabelle. You might be interested to know that Cecilia, however, has been particularly jealous of you since your arrival. Isn't that right, Cecilia?"

Cecilia took a long sip from her goblet. "It's hard for me not to be jealous of any woman to whom you show greater affection than myself, my Lord. Simply because I have developed such strong feelings toward Your Majesty. I hope you will forgive me."

"Cecilia has shown me nothing but kindness, Your Majesty," Isabelle stated. "She has, more than any other girl, been my friend and mentor. While she may feel some jealousy, she has always sought to help me prepare for the day of our union. And I know she does this because she seeks for nothing but Your Majesty's happiness."

The Emperor laughed and clapped his hands and the next course of food was delivered, and the previous one whisked away. "It is a blessing to have someone so educated here, Isabelle," he said. "Not only that, but your beauty . . . not that you're beautiful right now. No, not with the beastly thing on your face, but normally you are exquisite. I do believe you may be my most prized concubine."

He reached forward with his gloved hand and placed it on the back of hers. Isabelle trembled under his touch. When he sensed this, he smiled as though he interpreted her reaction as the skittishness of a girl with a romantic anxiety. His hand traveled up her arm to her shoulder where his fingers slipped under the sleeve of her gown. She glanced at Cecilia, who looked on with pain in her eyes.

Never had anything been so repulsive and yet wonderful at the same time. No one besides the maids had touched Isabelle in weeks. Human contact was something her soul yearned for, but when it came from someone she loathed, her stomach churned. Finally Emperor Krallick withdrew his hand from her shoulder and resumed eating.

"There are two kinds of concubines, Isabelle. The first are those whose company I enjoy at night . . . or any other time of the day. The second are those whom I keep to decorate my palace. Like my statues and portraits. Those in the latter group, I sell or trade like any other possession. But those in the former group are treasured."

"Which am I?" Isabelle asked.

"That remains to be seen. And always continues to remain. Even my favorites can become something I get rid of if I have reason to, even one who wears a token of my affections."

Cecilia frowned at the Emperor's comment and set down her fork.

"I hope you would never rid yourself of Cecilia," Isabelle said. "From what I've seen, she should be the girl who wears the ruby rose, not Kayla. She is your most beautiful concubine. In a class all of her own."

"Of course, beauty is in the eye of the beholder," the Emperor countered.

"Not all beholders are created equally . . . Your Majesty," Isabelle said.

Cecilia gasped at Isabelle's boldness. Emperor Krallick stared at her, then began to laugh, hearty and full. Again he wiped his lips as his body convulsed with amusement. "I'd forgotten how honest you can be, Isabelle! Another reason why I'm so pleased to have you."

Despite all the bitter loathing she harbored for the Emperor, a small part of her also felt guilty for wanting to be rude in the face of his tangible politeness. When he looked upon her, smiled at her, waited patiently for her to speak, she sensed his genuine interest in what she had to say and how she felt. Prior to this evening, she had always thought of him as a terrible and wholly evil man; now she was forced to reassess her opinion, if even slightly. Again, Cecilia was excluded from the conversation. Left to sit, watch, and listen.

"It must be difficult for the other girls," the Emperor said, glancing at Cecilia. He gestured for a servant to take his plate away and bring the next course. "Seeing you every day—you and your great beauty. What a novelty you are. Humble, intelligent, exquisitely formed by the Lord of All Worlds himself. Of course, if I had known all these things when your father first came to me, Isabelle, I would have unleashed every force in Atolas to bring you to my palace. I have never seen greater beauty."

His words made her squirm like the itchy gowns she wore during her cleansing. "I'm not certain that I deserve such praise."

"Your circumstances are nothing like dear Cecilia's. She arrived here broken, desperate, and scared. I had lunch with her, found her to be pretty enough and fairly delightful, and most of all, of course, she didn't cost me a thing! She was a sad sight, but I saw her potential." He reached over and patted Cecilia's hand. She tried to hold his in return, but he withdrew. "Philosophers say that you value things more when they come at a greater cost. Isn't that odd? Yet it's true. And I have few possessions that cost me what you did."

He paused as if he wanted her to say something, but Isabelle was speechless. First because the Emperor thought so highly of her. And second because of the conditions under which Cecilia had arrived at the palace.

"That is why, of course, I must do something about your injury," he informed her through a mouthful of tender veal. "One of the guarantees I make to all the girls who wish to be a concubine is that their lives will be free from worry about safety and health. What has happened to you is contrary to that promise. I will make it up to you. But before I can do that I must have a name. The true name of the one who has harmed you." The tone of his voice changed so abruptly that it frightened Isabelle.

Cecilia's gaze, which was normally focused squarely on the Emperor, turned to Isabelle, who realized he would not let her leave the dining hall without telling him what he wanted.

Isabelle set her fork down. She remembered the scent in the hall, the angry looks, the paranoia. All she had to do was say the name. "Kayla," she whispered. "It was Kayla."

The Emperor's nostrils flared and his eyes burned with fury. Then, in an instant, his rage vanished. "Thank you. Now is there something I can do for you? Something to help heal your wounded spirit?"

Isabelle had to stuff her mouth full of beans to prevent her from retorting back to the Emperor, "Release me from this prison!" Then she thought of a favor for which she could ask, and perhaps have her request granted.

"Yes, Your Majesty, there is something, a wish you could grant. May I be granted time each week to spend in the courtyard?"

Cecilia's eyes narrowed on Isabelle.

The Emperor grinned. It amazed Isabelle how he could still seem dangerous when he wore such a friendly expression. "Again you remind me why you are such a treasure. You ask for something that endears yourself to me: to admire the beauty I've created within the walls of my palace. Of course, I will be happy to grant you this wish. Is there anything else you would ask of me?"

"Please show Kayla mercy."

Her request genuinely moved the Emperor. He took a deep breath and grasped Isabelle's hand, the touch once again more pleasant than she would have admitted. "I cannot wait for the day when your cleansing is complete. I am even considering moving forward the night of your blessing a few days or even a couple of weeks if your maids consider you ready. I admit I am . . . anxious, but perhaps my patience will make the experience all the more special."

There was an air of vulnerability about him, and perhaps a touch of embarrassment that accompanied his confession. "I am certain it will, Your Majesty."

Now the Emperor looked at both Isabelle and Cecilia. "Times are changing. The day may soon come when the thrones of Neverak and Blithmore are united. If that day arrives, a symbolic union will need to take place. I would need to take a wife from among the noblewomen of Blithmore. Such a union would unite the lands. My wife would be crowned as the Empress of Blithmore. It would be a glorious moment in history. A moment never to be forgotten. Think about that . . . both of you."

It was all Isabelle could do not to retch. His words made her ill. His fondness was as welcome as a snake in her private chambers. This was the man who had killed Brandol only weeks earlier, thinking him to be Isabelle's betrothed. She had no tenderness to spare him. What could she do if he decided to marry her? And if his patience for her was running out, how much time did she have?

THIRTY-THREE
Teacher and Student

Maggie clutched her cloak tightly to block out the wind. Sand blasted and bit her hands and face, even blew inside her ears as she made her way from the Sandman inn to the prison, carrying a basket of food and two water skins for James and Henry. The street cutting through Tiller's Thain was empty. Most of the buildings were closed due to the early hour and the unforgiving winds. By the time she reached the prison, her face was raw and sore.

The sleeping prison guard opened a lazy eye and yawned. "Bringing sustenance?" he asked in a gruff voice.

"Yes."

The guard waved her in and inspected the basket for any contraband. Henry and James were both awake, their pale, dirty faces eyeing the basket greedily through the trapdoor. Maggie watched them sadly, dreading what might befall them. Henry reached a shaky hand up and brushed Maggie's fingertips. Maggie's heart broke at the sight of his filthy fingers. The guard cleared his throat, a subtle reminder that she wasn't allowed to touch them. Maggie gave him a pleading glance.

The guard sighed. "Don't be getting me into trouble, miss."

Maggie knelt by the trapdoor and passed the food. The thick bars of metal obscured James's face. His hands wrapped around two of the three bars. Despair filled his eyes. It was exactly what she had seen in her vision outside the Iron Pass.

"Please." He stretched out his arm as though he needed her touch to survive. "Just your hand."

A glance at the guard told Maggie he wouldn't tolerate her breaking the rules. Rather than taking James's hand, she stood, wiped her eyes, and gave him her bravest smile.

The pain and disappointment on James's face broke her heart, but she had no choice. She ran back to the inn, sand and wind stinging her watery eyes. Thirsty was still asleep when Maggie shook her awake. "What? What is it, Maggie?"

"They're not going to live," Maggie said wetly. "Nothing we do will help them."

"If the trial fails," Thirsty answered, "we need to have a plan. Are you willing to try learning how to project?"

Maggie bit her lip. *I am he who will destroy you. Choose not to pursue this—choose not to believe—and none of the things you witnessed will happen.* "I don't know."

"Maggie, the trial is only days away."

"Can't we come up with something else? I can't . . . I don't want to—"

"What other ideas do you have? It won't hurt to at least try, will it?"

"You're right," Maggie said with a reluctant sigh.

Minutes later, she and Thirsty sat on the floor of the main room. A fire roared in the fireplace. Maggie wasn't certain why Thirsty had made the fire so large, but it made the room uncomfortably warm. Thirsty rested her hands on her knees, her back straight and eyes closed. Her breaths came slow and deep.

"The Way of Lyrial is an ancient power," Thirsty began, "older than the Word of Worlds that people now read. Older than mankind, but mostly forgotten. It was passed from the Lord of All Worlds to us as a reminder that this power, the power of Lyrial, governs all. Those blessed with the gift—the Way of Lyrial—must walk the Path.

Each decision made in life is a step toward the Light or toward the Shadow."

"How does it work? How are these gifts possible?"

Thirsty opened her eyes. "The gift is an amalgamation of the power in every man and woman and the power of a greater being."

Thirsty stood and gestured for Maggie to stay seated. She walked around their room and gathered three objects: a wooden bowl, a burning candle, and a cold, baked bread roll. "These will help you develop the gift of projection."

"How will a bread roll help me develop—"

Thirsty picked up the roll and took a large bite. "Not that one," she mumbled through a full mouth. "That's for me. Breakfast." Thirsty laughed at herself and covered her mouth.

"So what do I do?" Maggie asked.

Thirsty hurried to finish her roll. "I will teach you the things that Serenity—the wise woman in our town in Old Avalon—showed me. Using the gift of projection, Serenity could put out a flame. She could levitate anything in her house that wasn't nailed down. See if you can do that."

Maggie concentrated on the flame. It bobbled with each air current, an orange and white dancer held in place only by a thin wick. She watched it for several seconds before looking helplessly at Thirsty. "What do I do?"

"Extend the gift outside yourself. Project it." Thirsty clasped her hands to her chest than pushed them out and spread her arms apart. "Send it out. Reach inward and push outward."

Maggie had no idea what this meant. Closing her eyes, she tried to send whatever was inside of her out, but all she ended up doing was flexing and releasing her stomach muscles so tightly that they began to cramp. When this didn't work, she tried tensing up her arms and imagining the candle blowing out. She peeked one eye open and saw the flame still dancing merrily on the tip of the candle.

"Thirsty, I don't get it. You say these things, but I don't know how to do them. I need more specific instructions."

Thirsty placed her hands on Maggie's. Maggie flinched under the touch. "You're right. Let's try some simple techniques to help you learn to focus. First, clear your mind and think of nothing but your body . . . and how it fits into the space around you."

Maggie sighed. "All right." She closed her eyes again and tried to let go of all her thoughts and worries. With her eyes closed for so long, she became more aware of her other senses. A slight breeze from the fireplace rustled her hair, laughing voices drifted in from another room. Then Henry sprang to mind. His face pale and full of horror. Bubbles floated up from his gaping mouth as he struggled for air, dying.

Choose not to believe, and none of the things you witnessed will happen.

"No, no!" Maggie cried. "I can't do this."

"You have to." Thirsty spoke with a rare note of firmness.

"I can't!"

"You must try harder. Reach inward and—"

"I heard what you said," Maggie snapped at Thirsty. "You're asking the impossible."

Thirsty smiled at Maggie. It wasn't her biggest or brightest smile, and Maggie saw frustration in her face. For some reason, this made her feel better. "Try again, Maggie."

Maggie did as she was asked, but failed.

"Try again, Maggie," Thirsty repeated patiently.

Failure.

"Again."

More failure.

"Again."

No matter how many times she tried, no matter what instructions

Thirsty gave, Maggie couldn't make the flame of the candle waver. The longer she worked at it, the more frustrated she grew. "*I can't do it!*"

"You don't *want* to do it. Why? Because you don't like me?"

Thirsty's honesty made Maggie pause. It was true. She didn't like Thirsty. She had never liked Thirsty. But she had no good reason why. The realization hit her in the gut.

"Do you realize how hard it is to be around you?" Maggie shouted. "I used to be the one who received the compliments for cooking, the one who made James blush ever so slightly with a compliment, but now it's you. How can I compete with you, Thirsty?"

"You aren't comp—"

"I am! You're this ideal, impossibly flawless woman. You have beautiful dark skin, perfect teeth, and you're never, ever, ever sad or annoyed or even angry! Why would James notice me when he's around you?"

"Maggie . . ." Thirsty covered her face and started to cry. "I don't know what to say. No one's ever said such kind things about me, even in an angry way."

Maggie both cried and laughed. "See what I mean? You're so nice! Here I am yelling at you and you just hear me complimenting you!"

The flames from the fireplace and the candle cast a glow over Thirsty's features. Her blue eyes reflected the orange flames as she stroked her own cheek with her fingertips. "I don't know how else to be, Maggie. I haven't had a family since I was a girl. It's always been me. Being happy, positive—it kept me going. Some nights when I first came to Pappalon, I would weep for hours for my mother. I just wanted someone to hold me. All I could do was relive the happy memories I had. You and Henry and James and Ruther, you four saved me. The path I had started to walk was dark and lonely."

Maggie had never thought about how lonely Thirsty must have been in Borderville. Nothing to do but work. No one to come home to. No friends, no one to hug, to lean on, to cry with. "That must have been awful."

Thirsty nodded quickly. She was crying again. "And I'm not perfect, Maggie!" she squeaked through her tears. "I don't read or write well. And I have oddly shaped toes."

Maggie laughed.

"And apparently I can't teach someone how to use the Path."

"It's not you." Emotion welled up inside Maggie like a bursting spring of water. "Weeks ago, I saw four visions: one of me, of Henry, of Ruther, and of James. All of them were . . . terrifying. I didn't want to believe in them. I tried to shut them out because someone told me if I didn't believe, then they wouldn't come to pass. Today James's vision happened exactly as I saw it."

"And he's still alive!" Thirsty said.

"Yes, but if I do start to believe, if I do start to learn, then Henry is going to die."

Lines creased Thirsty's face. But before she answered, Ruther entered. With a sigh, he sat in a chair and rubbed his temples.

"How did it go with Scotty?" Thirsty asked, wiping her eyes.

Ruther's chest heaved. "He's done what he can, but I worry it won't be enough. It's going to take a miracle to win."

Thirsty smiled and took Maggie by the hand. "I think it's time we're due for one."

THIRTY-FOUR
The Trial at Tiller's Thain

Neither James nor Henry slept the night before the trial. It was like being in the Iron Forest again. James dwelt on all the terrible things he'd experienced in his life: his father slapping him until his nose bled because he'd defended his mother, the day he turned seventeen and his father kicked him out, the worst days of guardsman training when he thought he might die of exhaustion, the day Cecilia rejected him, the battle at the Iron Pass. So many dark memories. He hoped to live long enough to replace them with good ones.

Finally morning came, and for the first time in many days, he and Henry left their cell. After dwelling in darkness for so long, the light stabbed his eyes like needles. The jailer provided them with a bucket of water and a towel to scrub themselves clean. It didn't help much with the stench. A posse, swords drawn, escorted them to the town hall, a small building packed with two hundred people. James felt the first trickles of sweat form on his temples and under his arms.

Maggie and Ruther sat in the back of the room and tried to appear optimistic. Thirsty didn't dare attend. Shouts came as James and Henry were led to the center of the hall. More than a few spit at them. When James moved his arm to wipe some of it out of his eye, a guard knocked him hard in the back, sending him to his knees. This brought jeers from the crowd.

The town leader sat behind a tall desk, parchment and quill in front of him. He settled the crowd by clapping loudly and brought the trial to order. He was quite tall and pale. He was bald except for a ring of orange hair running around the sides of his head. "Quiet!" he shouted one last time. "Everyone take your seats, please."

James and Henry were made to stand.

"These two men are charged with the crime of killing my son, Michael." The town leader paused to get control over his emotions. Henry and James exchanged a look of dread. "These two men and their friends came into town accompanied by a dark-skinned woman. They had their fill of drink at our tavern, and once under its influence, they started an altercation with several men. The fight ended only when one man—my son—was brutally killed by having his head shoved into a table. Although I cannot imagine what these men could possibly say to defend their actions, our code states that we must let them speak. But first, we will hear from my other son, Matthew, and those with him that night."

Matthew glowered at James and Henry as he emerged from the throng. He looked older than James remembered. His patches of orange hair had been slicked down, but he'd made no effort otherwise to improve his appearance. He cleared his throat and the audience fell silent. "My brother and I enjoyed frequenting the Thirsty Thief on a weekly basis for the past few years. Everyone there knows us. We don't give people trouble.

"The night my brother died, five travelers came into the tavern. Two of them were these men. Of the other three, one of them was a woman of the devil kind. Knowing that the owner was too good-hearted to ask this woman to leave, Michael and I took it upon ourselves to escort her out. When we did so, the taller of the two strangers," Matthew pointed to James, "pulled out a knife and threatened to gut us if we didn't leave.

"None of us have the skill to fight a man wielding a weapon. Even as we backed off, he taunted us. And his friend, that one," Matthew gestured to Henry, "hit Michael from behind. I was scared so I called over my friends to help us with the troublemakers. But by then, it was too late. The tall fellow with the knife, he stabbed my brother."

The town leader held up James's knife, which was now covered in dried, black blood. "Is this the knife he stabbed him with, son?"

"The same one. Then the other one grabbed Michael, picked him up, and threw him into the table. Busted—busted—" Matthew sniffed and wiped his eyes. "Busted his head right open. He died right that instant."

The town leader blew his nose into his handkerchief, then chased a tear from his cheek. "Thank you, my boy. I've always said you're a brave young man—haven't I always said that?"

At least a dozen murmurs of assent came from the crowd as they rose up and cheered for Matthew. Then one by one, six other people, some who hadn't even been at the tavern, got up and gave the same account as Matthew. Some of them spoke eloquently, some stumbled along, helped out by the town leader whenever they needed it. When they had finished, James saw no way he and Henry could win.

A roar of boos and angry hollers came from the crowd as James began to speak. He and Henry had discussed their best strategy, and decided that they would first share their testimony, then ask if anyone else wanted to speak in their behalf.

However, the second half of the meeting went nothing like the first. As he and Henry told their stories, frequent and loud disruptions drowned out their voices. The town leader did nothing to quell the storm, in fact, he seemed to encourage it with the questions he asked: "How drunk were you when you killed my son?" "What were the last words he said as he died?" With each question, the fury among the spectators swelled like a lake in the midst of a storm.

When Henry and James finished, Ruther came forward. He had combed his hair and donned new, respectable clothes of fine quality.

"Citizens of the good city of Tiller's Thain," he began in perfect blend of Pappalonian and Farmlands accents, "some of you may know who I am. For those who don't, my name is Rumps Liggit. I am a physician, traveling with these gentlemen eastward. Since this tragedy occurred I have been in regular contact with Scotty Brittamon, a man who has provided you with good health and the best remedies. You, in turn, have given Scotty your respect and gold, for which he is grateful.

"Scotty wished to give testimony, but believed himself incapable of doing so in an unbiased manner. Thus he appealed to me to look into the events surrounding the death of your dear son, brother, and friend, Michael Erwick. Such a tragedy. However, let us not, in our anger and pain, allow emotions to cloud our judgment. Remember the Word: the greatest sin is to pass unholy judgments down upon our fellow man.

"He has asked me to convey two pieces of information to you, and nothing more. First, Scotty Brittamon found *no* knife wounds on the deceased Michael, nor bruises upon his body. Indeed, the only injury found was to Michael's head. With the assertions put forth by Matthew and his friends, he was extremely careful in examining every part of dear Michael, particularly his back and abdomen. Again, and I cannot state this clearly enough, there were absolutely no knife wounds in the body.

"Now if you will please indulge me, I would like to have this man step forward for all to see." He pointed his ever-raised left finger at Henry, who did as he was asked. "Now, ladies and gentlemen, will you please raise your hand if you believe that the late Michael Erwick was a man of vigor and strength."

A few hands hesitantly raised, but Matthew and his father's hands shot up.

"Don't be shy," Ruther said, "raise them up if you believe Michael was a strong man."

Almost all the hands in the room reached heavenward. From

somewhere unseen, Rather produced a long, thin reed. He fixed his gaze on Henry. "Sir, please remove your shirt."

Henry did as he was told. Then Ruther shouted at the top of his lungs and ran forward at Henry with the reed raised like a weapon. Henry jumped in place and shielded himself with his one good arm, but Ruther did not strike. "The guards of the prison can confirm that no communication has been made with the prisoners, so you may rest assured that what you just witnessed was unrehearsed. Note how he only raised one arm in defense. This is because he has a lame right arm. If you don't believe me, then watch: Matthew Erwick, please come forward."

Matthew followed orders and Ruther stepped back and handed the reed to Matthew. "Strike this man on his bad arm."

Matthew held the reed awkwardly. "You want me to hit him?"

"That I do."

The swat made a light smacking sound, but left a thin red line on Henry's bicep. Then Ruther ordered Matthew to do it a second time, only harder. Finally, Ruther had Henry place his hand on the back of a chair, and Matthew brought the reed down so hard on Henry's hand that the reed broke in half. Henry showed no reaction at all.

"I brought a second reed," Ruther said, pulling it out of his pocket, "if one of you would like to come up and try. Anyone?"

No one came forward.

"You may sit now, Matthew." Ruther cleared his throat and addressed the hall once more. "The reason I make this demonstration is because, as you all admitted, Michael was a strong man. Matthew, this dear grieving brother, and his friends said that this man threw poor Michael into a table and cracked open his skull, a powerful feat for a man with only one good arm."

"*That's a lie!*" Matthew screamed. "I saw what happened and told the truth! Those men killed my brother!" About twenty voices rose in agreement.

"Rather than dispute the facts, I leave the decision of these men's fate in the hands of the good people of Tiller's Thain, with a friendly reminder that to wrongfully convict a man—let alone two—due to prejudice is to bring down the fiery wrath of the Lord of All Worlds upon your heads. Good day, my dear friends."

The instant Ruther finished speaking, the audience erupted in chatter. James looked around to see that more people regarded them with compassionate eyes than before. The town leader clapped his hands to call everyone to silence. "It is now time to vote on the fate of the accused. All those who believe these men to be guilty, say aye."

A loud cry of ayes rose from all around James. His heart sunk and he clasped Henry's hand to give him strength.

"All those who believe these men to be innocent, say nay."

An equally loud cry of nays erupted. Matthew, red faced and livid, shouted, "The ayes have it. They are guilty!"

The town leader, however, did not seem so convinced. "We will have a vote by hands. All who believe these men are guilty, raise your hands."

James and Henry turned around to count all the hands. Each person raised two hands. James wasn't the best at counting quickly, but he and Henry both came up with two hundred and twelve hands.

"All those who believe these men are innocent, raise your hands."

James's heart beat furiously as he stared around the room. "Ninety," he whispered, "one hundred-twenty, forty, eighty, two hundred." There were very few hands left to count now. His whole body sweated as he finished the count. "Two hundred two . . . four . . . six . . ."

Only two hundred six. There had to be more. There had to be. Two more hands went up. "Two hundred eight." They needed four more hands. He looked around and saw Maggie and Ruther's arms raised high, but he had already counted them. "Four more," he said softly. "Four more, please."

The town leader finished counting. "Has anyone not voted?"

All hands went down, and the room was as silent as death.

"We did nothing wrong!" Henry yelled. Tears were in his eyes as he turned to the audience. "Please! I have killed no one. I started no quarrel. I beg you to release us and let us leave your town in peace."

"I wish to change my vote!" one woman yelled. "I believe these men are innocent."

"Does anyone else wish to change their vote?" the town leader asked.

No one spoke.

The leader's gaze fell upon James and Henry. His eyes were cold, his voice low. "It is a tie, which means my vote is the tiebreaker. By a vote of two hundred eleven to two hundred ten, the town of Tiller's Thain finds you guilty for the crime of murder. You are sentenced to death by beheading. The execution will take place tomorrow morning at dawn. May the Lord of All Worlds reject you and cast your souls to the Endless Abyss where you will serve the Great Demon and suffer for all time."

THIRTY-FIVE
Changes in the House

Three nights after Isabelle and Cecilia's dinner with the Emperor, Isabelle was awakened by the sounds of screaming. "*No!*" a girl screamed. "No, I won't go! I didn't do it! Let me go!"

Isabelle heard the voices of the Emperor's servants speaking in calm but firm tones. "The Emperor has decreed it."

"Let me speak to him! Please! I wear his rose!"

Isabelle crept out of bed and peeked through her curtains. Three guards were carrying Kayla from her chambers through the corridor, but she fought them every step of the way, kicking and scratching and twisting. A few other slaves stood in the hallway, openly staring and whispering.

"I am sorry," one of the servants said, "but you have already been sold to Lord Skorpio."

Kayla's screaming only grew. "Please! I didn't hurt Isabelle! Tell him that!" Her pleas were ignored, and minutes later, the house of concubines fell silent once more.

Kayla's sudden absence had a dramatic effect on the concubines' shifting loyalties. Cecilia began doing all she could to gather others' favor, but two other girls rose in popularity quite rapidly: Jade, the gorgeous Haxite with her cream-colored hair and brilliant green eyes; and Jessika, a tall, willowy girl with jet black hair and extraordinarily proper manners. Raised by a wealthy Neverakan noble, Lord Pok, Jessika was considered by many to be the Emperor's likely choice to be Empress.

Isabelle liked Jade. She was kind, polite, and didn't seem to let the attentions of the Emperor go to her head. Jessika, however, Isabelle didn't care for. Almost certain that she would be the next recipient of the rose, Jessika began to assert her dominance among the concubines the same way Kayla had done. Jade seemed determined to remain her normal, amicable self. Yet each day that Jade was chosen over Jessika, or vice versa, the tension between them grew. Isabelle observed this silent battle for power with a morbid fascination. It saddened Isabelle to see women so bright and beautiful dragged down by something so trivial.

Jade and Jessika received the Emperor's invitation almost nightly, whereas Cecilia hadn't been chosen in days. Whatever was going on inside her head, she did not confess it to Isabelle. In fact, she avoided Isabelle, which meant her friends gave Isabelle the cold shoulder too. More than once Isabelle tried to speak to Cecilia, only to be ignored. Yet Isabelle still couldn't help being concerned for her friend. Something was taking a toll on her. Her face, once happy and bright, was wrinkled with worry. Her tightly pursed lips formed a permanent thin frown that left her looking both forbidding and sickly. And it had all started after their dinner with the Emperor.

One evening the escort arrived to take a woman down to the Emperor, but this time another servant accompanied him. Isabelle recognized him as the Emperor's chamberlain. She had never seen him in the house of concubines before today. In gloved hands he bore the ruby rose.

A few girls hushed the others when they saw him. "The Emperor has delegated to me the assignment," he said in an unnaturally high voice, "of placing the ruby rose into new hands."

Jade leaned forward, eyes hungry, and tall, regal, raven-haired

Jessika glowed triumphantly. The servant cast his gaze about the room, clearly savoring the power he held over this captive crowd. "The girl who wears this will also be blessed by the Emperor tonight." He paused to look at each girl. "And His Majesty gives the rose . . . to Jade."

Jessika shrieked. Jade blushed from ear to ear. Cecilia, pale and trembling but not crying, left the room, leaving the gently swaying curtains in her wake. A few of the girls were so excited for Jade that it might as well have been they and not the Haxite who received the rose. But it dawned on Isabelle that they were simply playing the power game. Their words of congratulations sounded sincere, but Isabelle saw their disappointment in the way their eyes did not match their smiles, and how they so quickly turned away from Jade.

Sitting by herself on a sofa, eating a handful of grapes, Jessika watched the chamberlain pin the rose into Jade's hair and then, with a final condescending glance around the room, exited to her chambers. The escort left with Jade while the chamberlain stayed behind and cleared his throat. "I have a message for Isabelle."

Isabelle stepped out of the corner she'd been lurking in and raised her hand. Several concubines turned their heads, eyeing her with suspicion. The chamberlain reached into his pocket and delivered her a note in a small envelope sealed shut with the Emperor of Neverak's insignia. After he left, Isabelle took the letter to her chamber and opened it.

Miss Isabelle,

During our recent dinner engagement, you mentioned your desire to spend time in the enclosed gardens of my palace. I consider them to be one of the great marvels inside these walls. Please send word with my servants when you would like to go, and I shall make your desires a reality. My thoughts are with you as your cleansing draws to a close.

With great affection,
Emperor Ivan Richter Krallick III

She wrote an equally short response thanking the Emperor and stating her desire to visit the gardens every other day. Then she returned the note to the envelope and set it on her bedside table.

A cool breeze blew lazily in from the window above her bed. Isabelle stood on her headboard and looked out the window, holding onto the two iron rods for support. She rubbed the bar on the right, feeling the deep gouges she had cut with the ruby. It would only take a short amount of work to cut through the remainder of the bar.

Her gaze went to the stars, remembering nights when she and Henry would lay on his roof and watch them, making up their own names for constellations and forgetting where they were minutes later. Below the horizon, the city surrounding the palace was still alive. She could see horses and carriages trundling along roads like insects. Beyond the town were the cliffs of the Towering Mountains. And then the rest of Atolas.

She wondered where Henry was at that moment. The world was so big, and the palace—as massive as it was—was such a small thing when viewed in the proper perspective. The Emperor was only one man; it was the power he wielded that was formidable, not the man himself. He controlled all within his reach: from vast armies and navies to the actions and daily routine of his personal slaves. Isabelle's thoughts went to the ruby, which now belonged to Jade. She was sorry to see Cecilia not receive it. Isabelle missed her friend. She'd thought earning the rose might restore Cecilia's cheery nature.

Later that night, Isabelle snuck into the Haxite's room and familiarized herself with the belongings in the drawers and wardrobe. She slid her hands under a small pile of laundered robes and felt something hard in the back corner. Isabelle pulled it out and found it was a glass vial filled with a clear liquid. She pried off the cork gently but

recapped it immediately, coughing. The smell of lilacs was overpowering. Isabelle put everything back as she'd found it and hurried out.

Every night after, if Jade was not chosen to entertain the Emperor,
Isabelle snuck into her room and searched for the ruby rose. She did
not find it. The problem was Isabelle had to be far more cautious in
her explorations of the Haxite's room than she had been with Kayla's.
If Jade was the one who attacked Isabelle, she'd be less forgiving if
she caught Isabelle again now that she had the rose.

Isabelle's solution was to place herself near Jade as often as possible in hope that she might get some information on where Jade hid
the rose at night. Jessika always seemed to be around Jade, too, but
for different reasons. Not an hour passed without a comment directed
at Jade regarding the jewel. "Jade, did you pick up any bewitching
charms in your native land? Could you teach us some? We'd all love
a chance at hoodwinking the Emperor into thinking we're his favorites." "Will you polish my crown when I'm the Empress? I'm certain to
choose you as my personal slave."

But the one in particular caught Isabelle's ear. Jessika said, "Does
the ruby feel heavy when you wear it, Jade? That's not the weight of
the gem, but your own guilty conscience."

Did Jessika know about the vial of perfume? Had Jade pretended
to be Kayla to trick Isabelle? The thought that she may have accused
Kayla mistakenly did not sit well with Isabelle, no matter how hard
the Emperor had pressed her for information.

More than a week after Isabelle had written her request to the
Emperor, he answered by sending an escort to take her to the gardens.

"Why does she get to go?" Jessika asked.

"Because the Emperor invited her," Jade answered with a tone
that told Jessika to mind her own business. Jade smiled at Isabelle.
"Enjoy yourself."

Cecilia, who sat in a corner by herself painting, watched the exchange without comment. Her gaze met Isabelle's just as Isabelle left the room, and she gave Isabelle a small parting nod.

Since Isabelle wasn't allowed any dresses unless dining with the Emperor, Isabelle went wearing only her light house robe and slippers. She felt uncomfortable and exposed, but when they arrived at the courtyard, the escort took his leave of her and said, "His Majesty says you are welcome to stay here until nightfall."

Though this was her second time in the courtyard, Isabelle found the experience to be even more breathtaking now that she could appreciate it. She set her slippers aside to let her feet touch the manicured grass and feel it between her toes, a sensation she hadn't experienced in months. Two orange-red flamebirds flew over her head, quarreling over a small worm one had plucked from the dirt. A snowsquirrel with fur as white as wool leapt from one branch of a fir tree to another with a nut in its mouth. In the streams, small pale fish swam about, flitting through the water like aquatic ghosts. Three months before she might have found the garden's wildlife bland and domestic, but after being within the palace walls for such a long time, it was an oasis in the middle of a desert.

As she watched the animals, she wondered if they had any sense of imprisonment, living in this domed garden instead of the wild, where they were meant to be. Did the flamebirds ever yearn for open skies and rainfall? Did the fish want something more than small streams and ponds? The Emperor had built an impressive, luxurious garden, but did the animals appreciate that or did they have the same sense of confinement that she felt? Were they like her, so fervent and impatient for freedom that they thought they might burst?

Sunlight streamed down from glass windows built into the domed ceiling, but her attention turned to finding a way to escape. The glass windows built into the dome were over twenty feet high, and none of the trees were tall enough to reach them. Isabelle couldn't see any way to climb that high, so she checked the doors.

Four sets of doors led into the large courtyard. She tried them all, but they were locked. Isabelle wandered the courtyard, methodically searching for something that might help her. Finding nothing, she sat by the pond and watched the fish. The water traveled gently from the small pool at the base of the waterfall to the other end of the court-yard. A slight slope must have been built into the floor to encourage the water to flow in that direction.

The small stream went under the wall, but where did it go from there? It was hard to tell what was going on beneath the surface. She knelt down by the side of the water near the draining conduit. Then she rolled up her sleeve and felt around, putting her arm in the water all the way up to her shoulder. She still couldn't reach the streambed, so she stuck her leg in, holding her robe as high as she could, praying no one would come in and catch her in an indecent state.

By stretching her leg, she was able to scrape her toes against the streambed made of highly polished stone. Where the stream met the wall, stone gave way to a metal screen. She pushed on it with her foot, but it held strong.

But the question remained: Where did the water go beyond the screen?

She crossed the courtyard, following the stream to the pond, where the waterfall began at a heap of large rocks. To get to the rocks, she'd have to swim across the pond. Did she dare? Her clothes and hair would be soaked. Suspicions would be raised. The escort would certainly inform the Emperor. She could lie and say she had only wanted a swim, but she was a terrible liar. If the Emperor saw through it, he would punish her for attempting escape.

She shrank away. There had to be another option. She examined rocks in the depths of the streams and ponds, collecting several dif-ferent kinds and testing them on a boulder to see which ones might be hard enough to cut through the iron bars. In the end, she selected the two hardest rocks with sharp edges and hid them in her armpits.

That night, Isabelle began her work again in earnest. The longer she worked, the more uncertain she became of the rocks. They didn't cut nearly as well as the ruby. After two hours of hard labor, she had accomplished little. She hid the rocks under her bed and went to sleep.

Two days later, the escort arrived and took her back to the gardens, where she chose two different rocks and smuggled them to her room in the same manner as before. One of these cut only marginally better than the first two, so she dropped the other three out the window. Six days had passed, and her progress on the second window bar was nearly nonexistent. She needed the ruby but still couldn't find it.

On the seventh night after her first visit to the gardens, as she was working on the bars, she slipped and cut her hand. Isabelle dropped the rock on her bed, cradled her hand, and started to cry. Her tears weren't from the pain in her hand, though the cut did hurt; they came from loneliness, heartache, fear, her cleansing, the Emperor, the squabbling concubines, the ruby. All these things and more each contributed a tear, and she shed them all.

"So," a voice said from behind the silk curtain in the doorway, "you're trying to escape."

THIRTY-SIX
The Execution

When the trial ended, James and Henry were too stunned to speak. Henry had believed something would happen, some miracle. Fate. Ruther had made Henry and James's innocence plain to see. But it hadn't been enough. Armed men surrounded them before they had a chance to move. Henry looked through the crowd to find Ruther holding a sobbing Maggie in his arms.

A voice cut through the din. "Those men are innocent. Recount the vote!"

Henry could not see the source of the cry, but a few more people shouted their agreement. As Henry and James were led out of the room, dozens of people chanted, "Recount! Recount! Recount!" Dozens more booed and shouted at them, while those closest to the condemned pelted them with spittle and angry screams. The last thing Henry heard as the doors closed was the town leader yelling to dismiss the crowd.

Back to the prison they went. It was the last place Henry wanted to be. When the barred trapdoor slammed over them, he fell to his knees and rested his face in the dirt and wooden planks that made up the floor.

"I'm sorry," he told James, himself, Isabelle, and everyone else. "I'm sorry for whatever I've done to deserve this punishment. I'm sorry

I built that carriage for the smuggler. For not heeding the warnings in my soul to take Isabelle and flee Richterton. For not going straight to Neverak from Borderville. For threatening Fossy Barnic for information. For every lie I've let escape my tongue. Every ill thought I've harbored about someone. Every lustful desire. All of it. Everything. If there must be punishment for these sins, let them be on me. Not James. Not Isabelle. I've tried to live a life of goodness and dignity. If any of my efforts have merited me anything, then I beg for help!"

Henry pounded his fist on the floor, then covered his head with his good arm and continued to pray. He stayed on his knees for a long time, his eyes closed, lips moving without sound. He had never prayed like this. He begged for someone to take pity on them. He begged that if this were not possible, they could find a way to escape. And he begged that if those two things failed, Ruther, Maggie, and Thirsty would think of something. When he finished, he saw James ripping planks of wood from the wall.

"You want to help or just pray?" James asked.

"How far do we have to dig?"

James wiped his brow and stopped for moment. "The shack above us is about twenty feet by twenty feet. The trapdoor is in the middle of it. This . . . cell is about twelve feet by twelve feet. If we tunnel ten feet out and then straight up, we should clear the building. We'll be free."

Henry jammed his stick into the dirt behind the plank James had been working on. "Let's give it our best."

Together they pried three planks out of the wall and eased them to the floor. This gave them enough space to start tunneling. The dirt was compact and difficult to remove. Using the sticks the guards had given them to practice swordplay, they scraped and worked until nightfall. In the darkness of night, they measured the tunnel at just more than three feet long. A commotion above told them that Ruther had arrived with their final meal. Normally the process took less than a minute. Tonight, however, they heard Ruther conversing with the guards in a low voice for a long time.

"Fine," one of the guards finally said, "but get any ideas and you'll be marching to see the executioner right along with them in the morning."

Ruther laughed, a subdued, pitiful sound not at all like his normal jovial self.

The trapdoor opened, and down came Ruther, Maggie, and Thirsty. Maggie didn't look much better than she had when Henry had been taken from the trial. Thirsty, at least, put on a brave front. Maggie threw herself into Henry, the first time they'd touched in a month.

"Henry!" she said thickly. "We've done everything we could. It was our best effort. I'm sorry. I'm sorry! I tried to develop my gift so I could help, but I can't do it. I'm so sorry."

"It's not your fault." Henry patted her gently, savoring the feel of her hair between his fingers. He wouldn't let himself cry. To cry would be to accept his death, and he still had a chance to escape. He had to be a rock. "It's my fault. I made too many poor choices. Now they've caught up to me." Then he whispered in her ear. "We're tunneling through the wall."

Maggie nodded.

"I love you," he told her. Then he kissed her head.

Ruther came forward next while Maggie moved to say her good-byes to James. "No matter what," Henry said to his best friend, "promise me you'll go after Isabelle."

"Of course I will, friend. Of course."

"I appreciate everything you've done to help us. Your arguments in the trial . . . they almost worked."

"I thought it would. I just wish I had done more—" Ruther's voice caught in his throat and he pulled Henry to him tightly. Henry whispered his and James's plan in his friend's ear.

"Is there anything else I can do for you?" Ruther asked.

"Convince the whole town that we're innocent tonight," Henry answered.

Ruther laughed, but again it was mirthless. The sound almost broke Henry. Slowly Ruther pulled away. Then he hugged Henry again. "It should be me locked in here, not you."

"You made the right call to walk away from the tavern," Henry said. "It might have been the first time in your life, but it came at the right moment."

Ruther wiped his eyes.

"Take care of Maggie."

Thirsty stepped forward and embraced Henry warmly. Henry returned the embrace, finding comfort in her arms that he hadn't expected. She hummed something, a tune Henry had never heard before, but he found strength in it.

"You're a good friend, Thirsty."

"As are you, Henry." She kissed his cheek.

"Take care of Ruther. He needs a strong woman in his life."

He couldn't see her face very well, but he could feel her smile, a heated glow from a miniscule sun. As Thirsty pulled away, Maggie finished her goodbye to James, sobbing into her hands. Ruther held her arms and asked the guards to let her out. Then he bid his goodbye to James and left with her. Thirsty wrapped her arms around James and whispered to him. Then Henry heard her kiss him.

"Thank you, James. And don't worry. Everything—everything will be fine."

As Thirsty left the prison hole, Henry heard Maggie ask the guards. "How will you feel tomorrow knowing that you helped two innocent men die? How will you sleep?"

One of the guards mumbled a response.

"No," Maggie said, "their blood will be on this entire town."

Henry and James wasted no time getting back to work. Night

passed like the fleeting memory of a good dream. Henry and James took advantage of every moment. Fatigue came early, trying to cripple them after days of sickness, hunger, and many nights of no sleep. But the men brushed it aside. Their task was set before them. They reached four feet, then five. It was an endless cycle of scraping away the dirt by clods and crumbs, then pushing the mess out to make room for more. At some point in the night, the guards changed. Henry and James stopped then and only then. Afterward, they attacked the wall of dirt like it was their mortal enemy. By the middle of the night, their sticks were broken and useless, leaving them nothing to use but their fingers, which were already tired and raw. The pile of dirt on the floor slowly grew, but it was never big enough. The work kept their minds off the impending doom that awaited them should they fail.

In the twilight hours, they reached nine feet. The tunnel was suffocating and tight, but nothing deterred them. Weariness plagued them like a relentless warrior, but they fought it, finally reaching ten feet. With no time to celebrate, they started the upward climb. Freedom wasn't more than four feet overhead, but they had to be careful not to let the ground cave in on top of them. Dirt and sweat combined to make mud that caked Henry's body. It filled his mouth, ears, and nose. He tasted it in his teeth and spat it out as James returned from pushing out another load of dirt.

"I think we're close to sunrise," James said. "The cell seems to be growing lighter."

Henry attacked the dirt like a man possessed. Perhaps it was his imagination, but it seemed that he could see light coming through the dirt overhead. It had to be close. He thought he even heard a sound like chirping.

"You hear that?" he asked James with a nervous chuckle. "Sounded like a bird."

"What bird lives in the desert?"

Henry heard the sound again, a high-pitched squeak like a mouse. "There it is again."

"That's no animal. They've opened the trapdoor."

From a distance, Henry heard the voices of the guards. "Let's go, men. Big day today."

"Try not to lose your heads as you climb out of there," another said. This drew wild laughter from the others.

"Move faster," James told Henry. "Keep digging. We have to get out now!"

Henry launched a flurry of fist and claw at the dirt above. Not far away, the guards yelled louder. "Come on out!" the men teased. "No need to be shy."

Henry's hand broke through as a cascade of dry soil covered his head, blinding him and filling his lungs with the dirt and sand. Henry coughed, he couldn't help it, but the hole was there. "There's no one out here," he told James. "No one will see us. Lift me!"

James heaved Henry, but the passageway was too tight for it to do much good. Henry scrabbled and pulled with his good arm, but couldn't raise himself.

"Come on, Henry! You can do it!"

Gritting his teeth and holding his breath, Henry poured every ounce of his energy into lifting himself upward. This was the moment they had worked all night for, their last chance. But what good could a crippled man do? Henry hated himself for not having two good hands. He was useless; he wasn't strong enough.

"I . . . can't . . . do it."

James tried to push, shove, anything, but the dirt gave way under Henry's poor grip, and he slipped back down, cursing.

"I don't see them down here!" cried one of the guards. "And where did this pile of dirt come from?"

"One more try!" James urged. "Give it all you have!"

"A hole!" another voice said. "A hole in the wall!"

Henry heaved for the final time. James groaned in his efforts and Henry began to make some headway. Then a sword poked into his back, causing him to cry out in pain and fright.

"Almost." The voice of the town leader came from above. Then he called the guards. Rope was brought to lift them out, then to bind their hands behind their backs. Henry's eyes burned, both from the dirt and the rising sun. "I couldn't sleep all night, boys. My soul ached with agony. I will have justice for my boy."

"And it will still ache with agony for the rest of your life," Henry said, "after you realize you have executed two innocent men."

The town leader stared at Henry, his eyes full of hate and disbelief. Twelve men surrounded the two prisoners and escorted them to the center of town where hundreds had gathered to witness the execution. A raised platform awaited them where a tall executioner with massive arms and a chest as solid as a mountain stood, clad in a black, hooded robe and wielding a mighty sword in his large hands.

Henry's muscles seized up and he fell to the ground. Several hands grabbed him and carried him toward the platform, but Henry would not be dragged like a coward. He shrugged them off and willed his feet to work—to bear the weight they'd always born. Each step took tremendous effort. As he started up the stairs, he looked in the faces of the crowd. Some of them were angry and vile. Others were sorrowful. None of them were friends—Maggie, Thirsty, and Ruther were nowhere to be seen.

It couldn't be real. Everything was happening too fast. How could he have come all this way to die so ignominiously? Where was the just hand of the Lord of All Worlds? Henry's chest heaved like a great bellows, but he could not seem to inhale enough air. Desperately he searched again for Maggie. For Ruther. For Thirsty. James glanced at him. He'd noticed the same thing.

They were alone.

All but two of the guards left the platform. The executioner stepped forward, his hand rubbing the hilt of the bright new sword eagerly. The town leader joined them above the throng.

"Do the condemned have any last words?" he shouted, not to James or Henry, but to the masses gathered to watch.

Henry tried to stand as straight as possible. "For the last time . . ." he said, not in a loud voice, but not softly, either. The crowds grew quiet as he spoke. "With the Lord of All Worlds as my witness, we have done no wrong in your town! We have injured no one. You condemn innocent men to die. I beg you to undo this injustice before it cannot be undone!"

The guards pushed Henry forward first. A tree stump had been brought onto the platform, its surface stained dark red, notched deeply from the deaths of others. At that moment, the finality of it all sunk in.

"Please . . . please . . . please . . ." He said the words many times in those few steps—to the town, to its leader, to Matthew, to the executioner. His vision blurred from tears and sweat. The guard forced him to his knees and placed his tied hands around the stump so he hugged that which would soon bear his severed head. He shut his eyes tightly.

"I'm sorry, Isabelle," he whispered. "I will not see you again in this life, but the next."

The executioner stepped forward. Each fall of his boot sent shockwaves through the stump into Henry's skull. He smelled like a dying animal, like rot. Henry held his breath so he wouldn't gag on the scent. No sound came from the crowd. In the quiet, Henry heard the executioner's breaths, too, as he prepared for the killing blow. Then came the longest breath of them all, the one where he raised the sword. A sudden calm came over Henry as he waited for the stroke. He heard the blade whistle through the air.

Screams rang through the crowd as the blade struck with a *thunk*. Henry opened his eyes to see his guard falling from the platform, kicked in the back by the robed giant. Behind him, Henry heard

James slam the back of his head into the skull of another guard, sending him off the platform, too. The executioner charged forward, dagger pointed, and grabbed the town leader. In one swift movement, his blade was at the leader's throat. It took Henry a moment to realize that his hands were no longer tied. The rope had been cut. He got up and untied James's hands.

"Matthew!" The executioner's voice was a brutal scream, which reminded Henry of when James, disguised as a guard, had shouted at him in Bookerton. "Unless you want your father's head to roll at your feet, get up here."

Matthew scrambled through the crowd and climbed the stairs, tripping twice along the way.

"Please, Hector—please!" Matthew shrieked. Henry could only guess that Hector was the name of the executioner. "Don't hurt my father!"

"Tell the truth!"

Matthew's face had already turned red from hurrying up the stairs and making a fool of himself along the way, but now he turned positively scarlet from his neck to his hairline. "I gave my testimony at the—"

"The *truth!*"

Matthew whimpered, then cried. His shoulders slumped as he faced his fellow citizens. His knees shook as though his legs weren't up to the task of supporting them. Then his whole body rocked with sobs as he confessed the truth in broken, staccato bursts in between his babylike bawling. Bit by bit, the story came out, until the truth was made bare for all to see. When Matthew finished, he crumpled to the floor of the platform and held himself. It was almost as though he had begun to believe his own lies, and he had shocked himself by telling the truth.

"And now what are we to do with these men?" the executioner

asked in his loud, harsh voice. "Shall we kill innocents and stain our town?"

The town leader watched his son with tears in his eyes. Shame filled his face. Henry saw that even though the evidence had shown otherwise, Marcus Erwick had believed his son to the very end. "Let them go."

The executioner pointed with his sword to a post not far from the platform. There, three horses waited: Sissy, Quicken, and Ghost. But where was Ruther? And Maggie and Thirsty? The crowd around the platform parted for the three men, and the executioner walked them to the horses. After Henry and James had mounted their steeds, the executioner planted his sword in the ground and pulled off his robe. A great deal of straw fell out of the cloth, but some of it stuck to his clothes, Ruther's clothes. He shook his mane of red hair and brushed off his clothes as more straw fell away. Then he pulled the sword from the ground and threw it onto the platform where it landed with a loud clatter.

"Give that beautiful blade to Hector with my thanks." Ruther jumped on Ghost and patted his mane. "I hope you all rot.'"

The three men galloped away, leaving a stunned crowd behind.

THIRTY-SEVEN
The Bounty Hunters

With the aid of the Emperor's network of stables and strong horses, the four bounty hunters flew through Neverak and Blithmore with the speed of the Great Demon himself. In less than five weeks, they arrived at the Iron Pass. Skuller had never set foot in the pass, but he knew the stories. He knew the rules. And after explaining them to his three traveling companions, he warned them that if anyone dared to break one of them they should expect a knife in the back or the throat from him if the haunts didn't kill them first.

He didn't trust bounty hunters, and being a smuggler, guessed that they didn't trust him either. It kept him on his guard. Skuller fully expected one or more of them to try to kill him or each other if an opportunity availed itself. Fewer hunters meant fewer people with whom to share the bounty. But the question was who would make the first move? Bonesy? Kelric?

Ivory, the albino, seemed the least dangerous to Skuller, but perhaps that was exactly what Ivory wanted the others to think. Maybe he wanted them to let their guard down around him. Ivory talked for hours on end. He always had a hearty chortle, like all of life was one big laugh but only he was in on the jape. His appearance unnerved Skuller. Besides being dapper and obsessed with his own cleanliness, Ivory's pale skin and pink eyes made Skuller's neck hair stand up straighter than the lavender pine trees of Neverak. And Skuller had never met a man who liked the color white so much—white clothes, white hair, pure white skin, a white bone handle on his dagger, and a white ivory hilt on his sword. But it all made sense somehow, too, as though Ivory any other way wouldn't be quite right.

Kelric didn't like Ivory much. Well, Kelric didn't seem to like *anyone* much, but Ivory the least. Kelric had a nasty streak in him. Skuller saw that plain and clear. He'd seen similar streaks in other smugglers, those who liked getting into trouble with the authorities just to spill a little blood. Not Skuller. Everything he did had a reason. And that reason was usually golden and shiny and could be spent on nice things.

Then there was Bonesy, who gave Skuller the willies even more than Ivory. If Ivory made Skuller's hair stand up, Bonesy made it jump right out of his skin. She never said a word, though he suspected she couldn't if she wanted. He hadn't heard her so much as grunt since they'd met. Cold, calculating, and pretty filthy, too. Always chewing and spitting and watching. Yes, if there was one person he wanted to see bleed out in the middle of the night, it was her. But he wouldn't make the first move. Not against her. He wasn't certain he'd win that fight. Instead, he slept with one hand clutched around the handle of his dagger.

The last place the bounty hunters changed horses was in Reddings, a small town south of the pass. After replenishing their resources, they plunged into the Iron Forest without hesitation. Skuller didn't like it. Perhaps it was all the tales he'd heard over the years, but something about the woods deeply troubled him. Even Ivory, normally as happy as a child eating a zapperbee honey pie, lost his sense of humor. It was difficult to tell with Kelric and Bonesy. Kelric must have been born with a scowl. He would die with a scowl. He even laughed scowling. So whenever he glanced into the woods with the same angry, displeased face, Skuller assumed he was business as usual.

A few days into the woods, the voices began. Judging by Ivory's and Kelric's faces, they heard them, too. Only Bonesy showed no sign that she'd heard them. Day after day, hour after hour, minute after minute, the voices grew worse. The voices dredged up every horrible thing Skuller had done, the names of every girl he'd smuggled and sold, the faces of men he'd killed in skirmishes, all of it played before his mind in whispers and taunts, the girls' screams and pleas, until his ears began to bleed.

Nothing had ever scared him so much as that moment when he felt blood trickling down his neck. When Ivory and Kelric saw it, they checked their own ears. No blood had fallen yet, but it would. Their pace through the Iron Pass doubled that day. They pushed the horses to their limits, but they were strong beasts. At one point the voices became too much for Skuller's mind. They convinced him he could make it all stop by joining them in the trees. He dismounted and started toward the darkness, but was stopped by Bonesy, who grabbed him by the neck and squeezed until he nearly blacked out. When she finally let go, he was so grateful to be able to breathe, he forgot about the voices long enough to regain his sanity.

They crossed the pass in ten days. By then, Ivory's eyes were bleeding, Kelric was as pale as the albino, Skuller could hardly remember his own name—but Bonesy was still seemingly unaffected. All three men knew that if not for her they wouldn't have survived. She intervened for each of them more than once when the madness nearly took them.

When they left the darkness and emerged into the light, tears ran down Ivory's face. Kelric, pale and jittery, vomited repeatedly. Skuller wiped the blood from his eyes and ears. But Bonesy . . . Bonesy didn't even blink. She spat something black out of her mouth and sucked up whatever drool caught on her chin. Skuller looked down where she had spit and saw that she'd been chewing on the strange black bark of the Iron Forest's trees.

At the gate into Pappalon, they checked with the Emperor's spy, a man named Asaron who sat on some self-important Pappalonian committee. He didn't look pleased to see them, but welcomed them into his home anyway once they showed him their letter from the Emperor of Neverak. Skuller was content to let Kelric and Ivory do the talking. It seemed Bonesy felt the same way. It was a simple matter with Asaron. Either he could confirm the information he'd sent to the Emperor or he couldn't.

"Four of them, yes," Asaron said, his eyes flickering to Kelric's scowl. "Uh . . . hmm . . . two men—no, three men and a woman. One of them was injured. His arm. I can't remember if it was right or left. Another one had a nasty cut on his back, I believe. The fat redheaded one. He may not have survived that wound. Hmm . . . The other two, the third man and the woman, were perfectly fine, as I can recall. My spy informed me they stayed at the Sheep's Entrails."

"Descriptions." Kelric gave it as an order, and Asaron obeyed. When the spy had given them all the information he could, the bounty hunters took the road east to Borderville. "Split up here," Skuller said when they reached the town square. "Four inns on the west side of the town. Four on the east. Bonesy and Ivory go east. Kelric and I will go west and check out the Sheep's Entrails."

"Why do I have to go with Bonesy?" Ivory asked. "No one's voted you as leader."

Bonesy spat a large wad of something dark green. It landed on the toe of Ivory's white boot. With a sigh, he knelt down and cleaned up the mess with a handkerchief.

"See my point?"

Skuller looked at Kelric, asking with his eyes if Kelric would go with Bonesy. Kelric fixed Skuller with an extra nasty scowl.

"Bonesy," Skuller finally said, "I'd be honored if you'd come along with me."

Bonesy turned her dead eyes onto Skuller and continued to chew whatever was in her mouth.

"Talk to everyone," Skuller continued. "Show them the portraits. Offer a reward if they can give a name. Meet back at this square by sundown or get left behind."

Using portraits of James, Ruther, Maggie, and Brandol drawn up by the Emperor's best artists, Skuller and Bonesy went to the inns on the western side of Borderville. As the agent at the western gate had said, the Sheep's Entrails was where they found their next informant.

Jessop recognized the travelers' portraits at once. "Oh yes," he said, "they stayed here nearly a month. Always thought there was something odd about them, especially given their arrival."

"What do you mean?"

"They had no money," Jessop explained. "At least, not at first. I kept a close eye on them in case they resorted to stealing. My customers do that sometimes. But nothing went missing except my maid."

"Your maid went missing?"

Jessop laughed, but it sounded nervous. "Thirsty left with them. She was quite taken by the tall one." He pointed at James's picture. "Glad to be rid of her, too. Lazy, sullen, and never satisfied with her station."

Bonesy's head slowly turned at the mention of the name.

"Thirsty?" Skuller repeated. "A name like that can only be from Old Avalon. Black-skinned, is she?"

Bonesy fixed her cold black eyes on Jessop until the small man started to shrink away. "Er, yes," the owner said. "But like I mentioned, I was glad to see her go."

Bonesy reached into her side pack and withdrew parchment and a quill. After spitting a greenish-black wad into a small bowl, she began to draw a picture of a girl perhaps ten years of age. With a disgusted look, Jessop peered around Skuller's side to watch her. When Bonesy finished, she flourished the parchment, displaying an incredibly detailed portrait of a girl. Using the hand holding the quill, she gestured to the picture and then to Jessop.

"Is that her?" Skuller asked. "Thirsty?"

Jessop examined it for only a moment before nodding his head. "That's a near-perfect drawing of what she looked like when I took her in ten years ago."

Although Skuller hadn't thought it possible, Bonesy's eyes turned blacker and colder. She folded the piece of parchment until it fit in her palm, then stuck it in her mouth, chewed it up, and swallowed it. Jessop turned to Skuller for an explanation.

"Safest place for it, I suppose," was all Skuller had to say. He pondered on the strange coincidence that Bonesy knew this Thirsty woman. Skuller's thoughts went back to the Seer's letter, which had promised a chance to be paid handsomely to exact revenge upon the man who had caused Skuller's downfall many months ago. How had the Seer known so much?

"Perhaps you should go," Jessop finally said. "Thirsty isn't here, and I don't want my customers to think there's any trouble."

Skuller produced a coin from his purse and placed it into Jessop's hand. "It's not her we're after. It's the leader. He's a wanted man in Neverak *and* Blithmore. Do you know which direction he was headed? What sort of activities he was involved in during those four weeks?"

"They did what everyone else did," Jessop said. "Rolled the dice."

Jessop's information led Bonesy and Skuller to the dice hall in the center of town where they met another small man, but this one much more irate. His name was Rudolfos. "Those two," the man even tinier than Jessop said, pointing at the portraits of Ruther and James. "Scum. Cheats. Liars. Nearly had that one's hand on my wall. If you catch him, take his hand. I'll pay you handsomely for it."

Skuller smiled and made a note of that. "What else can you tell us? We're trying to find out where they went from here."

"Only one person I know might have knowledge of that. A man who lives in a nearby city, Poppinghock. Plays dice here two, three months out of the year. Richer than a king. Name is Fossy Barnic."

"Can you help us find him?"

Rudolfos nodded his little head. "Of course I will. This business of getting that hand on my wall . . . It's become quite personal."

That same day, the four hunters departed Borderville and headed for Poppinghock. Finding Barnic's grand home wasn't difficult. When his butler saw Skuller, Ivory, Bonesy, and Kelric at the door, he called to his master rather than inviting them in. Mr. Barnic was finishing supper and came to the door with a napkin in his hand. He eyed his four visitors with suspicion, and his hand went to the large dagger hanging at his belt. "Gentlemen and . . . err . . . madam, I presume, how may I be of service?"

Skuller showed Fossy Barnic the portraits. "I know these men. Not the woman. This one," he tapped on the picture of Henry Vestin, "is a scoundrel of the lowest order. Worse than a bounty hun— Err, excuse me. Worse than a smuggler he is. Broke into my room at an inn several weeks ago. Forced me to give him directions to a cartographer's house."

"Why would any man do such a thing as that?" Ivory asked.

"Desperate for maps into Neverak."

"But we have information stating that when the group left Borderville," Skuller said, "they were headed east. Any idea why?"

Mr. Barnic pondered on this for a moment before shaking his head. "I clearly recall the man wanting advice and maps on visiting Neverak."

"Can you remember anything else?" Kelric pressed, getting uncomfortably close to Fossy Barnic's face. "Anything of consequence?"

"Well, you do already know that the man who accosted me has a lame arm, do you not? Hask Vornbit!" Mr. Barnic snapped his fingers. "It just came to me. That was his name."

"We know about the lame arm," Kelric said, now so close to Mr. Barnic that Barnic had to step back, "but how's that s'posed to help us know where he's going? Are you wasting our time?"

"There's—there's a healer. A well-known healer in the Far Eastern Irons. A valley in Greenhaven, to be exact. If that scoundrel is looking to get his arm healed, perhaps he's headed that direction. I'm only saying it's worth your consideration."

"Can you give us directions?"

A gleam of triumph appeared in Fossy's eyes. "I most certainly can."

Once convinced that Fossy Barnic was of no further use, they excused themselves and left the house. They spent that night camping in a grove of trees a stone's throw from the road. Stew bubbled in a pot over the campfire. Ivory preferred to do the cooking if any was to be done, which was fine with Skuller. The stew didn't smell half-bad.

Kelric sat on a log, his shoulders slumped and his face scowling at the sword he was sharpening. "I expected 'em to be headed north, not east."

"I thought the same," Skuller said. "Old Avalon was my guess, then into New Avalon and back through the forest or perhaps by boat to Neverak."

"Not me," Ivory said. "I thought Oslan would lead them south to the ports and into foreign lands."

Bonesy stared dully into the flames, the orange light casting a glow in her black eyes.

"What's so important about the healer?" Skuller asked. "That question's been bugging me all day."

"When I met 'em in Blithmore, seemed they followed orders from Henry," Kelric said as he helped himself to a second bowl. "I think that magician was right. I think Henry ain't dead."

Bonesy drew another piece of parchment and a quill from her bag, using it in the same revolting manner as before. She scribbled some words down and showed them to the men.

Hask Vornbit
Henry Vestin

"Not likely a coincidence, is it?" Ivory said.

"So he ain't one head shy of a full body like the Emperor thought," Kelric concluded. "I bet they're still following his orders. If the man says he wants to get his arm fixed, the rest will fall in line to find this healer."

"I agree," Ivory said. He picked his pearly white teeth clean using a small looking glass, occasionally stopping to smile at himself. "Oslan is a well-trained soldier, but often the best soldiers are poor leaders."

"Let's not forget," Kelric said, "that the storyteller helped orchestrate the original attack on the Emperor. And as much as I hate that cocky slob, he is smart."

"If the soldier were in charge," Skuller wondered aloud, "he'd go straight for his sister, don't you think?"

Kelric scowled. "I s'pose."

"We need to send word to the Emperor," Skuller said. "Inform him that Henry is alive but injured. And that he's likely headed to Greenhaven to find a healer."

Bonesy spat more black bark juice into the fire. It sizzled and stank. No one complained.

"I shoulda killed them when I had a chance," Kelric said. "Since I'm splitting the money with you three, that leaves me only a thousand when we get all four heads. If I'da bagged the whole group in Blithmore, I'da made more'n that."

Skuller laughed at the irony. Kelric scowled at him. "Sorry to burst your bubble, but I can beat that. I met Henry Vestin long before he put a sword to the Emperor's throat in the name of love. That bastard cost me my entire smuggling operation. If it weren't for him, I would be as wealthy as a king."

"How did a carpenter manage to do that?" Ivory asked.

"Ratted me out." The memory of it still made Skuller's stomach boil. "I misjudged him, and he helped the King's Guard hunt me down. Forced me out of business. In exchange for my freedom, I helped them round up other smugglers." Skuller chortled at his own story. "Now there's a bunch of men—my own men—who hope to put a blade of steel deep into my heart. I tried to get even with Henry Vestin. Went to his home to put a dagger in him, but he was gone. The house was deserted."

"And how'd you get sucked into this affair, albino?" Kelric asked. "Have you met Henry Vestin as well?"

Ivory smiled, showing off his pearly whites. "No, never met Henry Vestin or his sister. But I'm just as connected as you are."

"And you, Bonesy?" Ivory asked. "Have you ever met these bandits?"

Bonesy stared at Ivory blankly, nodded her head, and went back to her food.

"But you were a soldier," Kelric muttered at Ivory. "King's Guard. How'd you change from that . . . to this?"

Ivory chuckled and stroked his white chin. "I thought you already knew about me. Up until a few months ago, I was in the King's Guard. But certain events made it apparent to me that I was no longer wanted. I had no chance for promotion despite my stellar career. A couple of my colleagues in the Guard decided to become bounty hunters, and no sooner had I enlisted with them than I received a summons from the Seer. He found me with little trouble."

"Did you know Oslan in the King's Guard?" was Skuller's question.

Ivory looked at Skuller and laughed. It wasn't his normal, good-natured humor, but something deeper and more primal. "No," he said, still laughing, "He's never met me. But I can't wait to introduce myself."

Days later, the four crossed into Desolation. They rode east to Tiller's Thain with all haste. Finding information there wasn't difficult. Only a week earlier, three men and two women had caused a stir such as the town had not seen in years. A tavern brawl, a death, imprisonment, a trial, executions, and a dramatic escape.

"Show me their heads on your journey back to Neverak," the town leader told Skuller and the others, "and I will reward you handsomely."

The four hunters hurried onward, eager to catch their prey. According to Skuller's maps, they would easily overtake their targets in the valley of the healer. Now was not the time to rest. He could smell the scent of blood in the air—blood which coursed through the veins of Henry Vestin and his sister, Maggie. Skuller would see that blood spilled.

THIRTY-EIGHT

The Valley of the Healer

T wo weeks after Tiller's Thain, Henry's small band reached the valley of the healer. The deserts of Desolation were behind them, lush green rivers and lakes all around. Ruther couldn't believe it. He had started to wonder if their quest had been cursed, but this valley teemed with life. Birdsong and the calls of other animals, sparse in Desolation, were abundant here.

Ruther rode Ghost next to Maggie and her horse, Fury. He watched Maggie's eyes light up as they left the Dusty Mountains behind. It had been Maggie's idea to bribe the executioner. It had been Maggie who helped Ruther prepare his arguments for the trial. Those hours spent with her had been especially wonderful. Making Maggie laugh despite their troubles made Ruther feel like a king. He had savored her smile, her eyes dancing with delight. The compliments she had paid him, encouraging his efforts, were a feast for his famished soul.

James and Henry had been both grateful and furious about their rescue. Grateful because Ruther, Maggie, and Thirsty had saved their lives, and furious because they hadn't been told about the plan to have Ruther in the executioner's place. Maggie patiently explained that if Henry and James had known about the plan, they might have behaved suspiciously.

The first town they came to after leaving the mountain passes was called Juniper. While they were purchasing supplies, a fisherman took great interest in Thirsty, and followed her around from booth to booth. He didn't bother to hide his curiosity, which made her visibly uncomfortable. Finally Ruther approached the man. "Do you have a problem, sir?" he asked.

The man pointed at Thirsty. He had a long beard that matched his long gray hair. His clothes stank of fish. "She with you?"

Ruther couldn't bite back the anger in his voice. "What business is it of yours?"

The bearded man laughed in such a way that it diffused the tension in the conversation. "Didn't mean no harm, sir. It's just we don't get many of her folk around. Thought she might be looking for the others."

"What others?"

"Others like her. Came through town two weeks ago. Making their way toward the healer. Looking for the rest of their group."

"How big was the group?" Thirsty asked.

The man scratched his beard so fiercely that Ruther wondered if he had fleas. "About a dozen. Rest of the group is much bigger. Been coming through here for weeks now—a few here, a few there. Maybe as many as a hundred of 'em."

"Where can I find them? Do you remember any of their names?" Thirsty asked. "Did any go by Stinker?"

"I don't—"

"Or Smile? Furious? Do you remember anything?"

"No names, I'm sorry to say. All I can recall is they've come through here. Never got a chance to get to know any."

The next morning they pushed deeper into the forest, following the guidance that Markus Finkley had given Henry more than two months prior. Late in the afternoon, they came to a wrought iron and silver archway. Just beyond it was a large sign of gilded wood that read:

SECRETS OF NEVERAK

WELCOME TO THE VALLEY OF THE GREENHAVEN HEALER

PLEASE FOLLOW THE RULES

The healer will see all in the healer's time.
Only the afflicted may see the healer.
The healer does not accept compensation.
The healer will not heal everyone.
Some may not survive the healing process.

The forest was quieter here, but no less beautiful or green. For a time, the only sounds they heard were rich breezes ruffling the leaves and the clopping of hooves. The change in scenery cheered everyone but Thirsty, who scanned the far-off woods somberly. A mile down the trail from the archway and sign, they started passing groups camped in clearings off the trail. Some had tents, others none. Some had wagons or carts covered in blankets. Thirsty broke off and visited all of them, asking if anyone had seen a group of dark-skinned travelers or knew their whereabouts. Many confirmed that a group had passed through days ago but had not been seen since.

At last they came to an empty clearing not far from the shore of a small lake. There they built camp. While they were clearing the area of fallen branches and rocks, a woman approached them. She wore a simple blue gown with gold embellishments. Her long brown hair was braided behind her, flowers and leaves intertwined in the braid. Ruther thought her elegant. She was tall, probably a little taller than Isabelle. Her eyes fell on each of the travelers, but rested the longest on Maggie.

When she looked at Henry, she said, "It's you."

"Me?" Henry responded

"Yes, your party has come here for you. Your arm."

"Are you the healer?" Maggie asked.

"No. My name is Gretchen. I work for the healer. There are many

358

of us who find joy and purpose in aiding those who come seeking rejuvenation. You can identify us by our attire."

Ruther jerked his thumb at Henry. "Think he can be fixed?"

"I'm not a broken axle, Ruther," Henry said. Then he faced Gretchen, "I want to see the healer as soon as possible."

"Remember the rules." Gretchen smiled patiently, her eyes fixed on Henry. "The healer will see all in the healer's time."

"I know, but we will pay whatever—"

"The healer does not accept—"

"I've read the rules."

Ruther put a hand on Henry's shoulder. "Then act like it. We're on the healer's land; we play by the healer's rules."

"Any idea on how long we may have to wait?" James asked.

"The healer will see all in the healer's time."

"But can you offer us any insight?" Thirsty asked.

"It could be an hour. It could be a month. Today, however, I wish to inform the healer of this man's condition. The more knowledge I gather, the more helpful the healer may be."

Ruther spoke up. "Now would be a good time for the rest of us to take a little walk while Henry and Gretchen get to know one another better."

"Good idea," James said. "We'll be back later."

Maggie volunteered to stay with her brother, which made Ruther reconsider going off with James and Thirsty. However, he guessed Henry didn't want a crowd around while dealing with this Gretchen woman, so he hopped back on Ghost.

"Miss Gretchen," Thirsty said, "we've heard talk that a group who look like me are in the area. Can you tell me where I might find them?"

Gretchen smiled sadly. "The healer asks that we respect the privacy of those who come to see her. If you are meant to find your friends, you'll find them."

Ruther sighed pointedly and rode down one of the trails with

James and Thirsty. For the remaining daylight hours, they searched for someone who might know the location of Thirsty's people. When night began to fall, they decided to return before getting lost. Thirsty didn't say a word, but Ruther could not mistake her disappointment.

At camp, over dinner, Henry and Maggie filled them in on what had taken place with Gretchen. "She asked him questions for hours," Maggie said. "I helped answer them when Henry wasn't being entirely truthful."

"Did Gretchen say when the healer will see Henry?" James asked.

"No," Henry answered.

"She walks the Path," Maggie told the others in an abnormally quiet voice. "Gretchen, I mean. She walks it. I'm certain of it."

"How are you certain?" Ruther asked.

"Her eyes. The color."

"They were green," Henry said.

"They weren't," Maggie said. "They were lyrial. I wonder if she sees mine as that color, too. She stared at me with such curiosity. Perhaps she wondered why I don't heal Henry myself."

"Remind me what lyrial is?" James asked.

"Lyrial is the central star," Thirsty said, "from it comes the color which marks those who walk its Path. Maggie, if you say you saw the color lyrial in her eyes, then you are correct. She does walk the Path."

"They were *green*," Henry insisted. "I saw them."

"Lyrial can only be seen by those who walk the Path," Thirsty said. "Only Maggie can see it. To everyone else, lyrial is missing. Another color takes its place."

"Perhaps she can find someone to teach you, Mags," Ruther suggested.

Maggie stared at the ground, frowning. "Yes, perhaps."

Thus began their days of living in the valley. They had nowhere to go, nothing to do but wait. The four months of Isabelle's cleansing were almost up, and Ruther knew Henry was dreading the day when time ran out. In the meantime, the five friends explored the area, looked for Thirsty's people, and tried to enjoy themselves. Food was purchased at the markets in the nearby town. Drinking water came from the plentiful brooklets and streams.

On their third day in the valley, Maggie discovered a waterfall. Ruther had never seen anything like it. Pure, beautiful, magnificent, and only a ten-minute ride from their camp. It came down from the cliffs at a height of more than a hundred feet and splashed into a small lake surrounded by trees, wildflowers, and the southern wall of the Dusty Mountains. Ruther suggested they should teach Thirsty how to swim. They returned to the area almost daily, and it was during one of their swims that they met several men emerging from the woods, bare-chested, shirts slung over their dark-skinned shoulders, their black feet bare. When they saw Thirsty, they stopped and watched her.

She called out to them and paddled to shore. James and Ruther followed. The men (Ruther counted seven) waited for her, even politely turned around while she slipped her dress over her soaked underclothes. Once decent, Thirsty introduced herself. All of them had strange names, the oddest of which was Bookness, who seemed to be the one in charge.

"Do any of you know men named Smiles, Stinker, or Furious? They're my brothers. I haven't seen them in years."

"We all know a man named Smiles," Bookness responded. "He's at our camp among the wounded. I don't know anyone named Stinker or Furious."

"Is Smiles a common name?" James asked.

Thirsty looked at James with a hopeful expression. "Maybe. I'm not certain. Could you take me to Smiles? If he's my brother, he'll remember me."

Bookness looked Thirsty over, then James, Ruther, Henry, and Maggie. Ruther saw suspicion in the man's eyes. "No offense, Miss, er . . . Thirsty, is it? Well, Miss Thirsty, I don't want to give you the wrong idea, but we've run into some evil folk on our travels. And we have plenty of reason to be concerned about the Baron's spies trying to find us. Before I agree to take you to Smiles, I need to speak with him first. Give me directions to your camp, and if he consents to your visit, I'll find you."

Thirsty eagerly agreed to the proposal, and Bookness and his men bid her farewell. On their way back to camp, Thirsty rambled on about how exciting it would be if her brother was nearby. James tried to temper her enthusiasm by suggesting it might be days before Bookness came to find her, or that the man named Smiles might not be her brother.

Thirsty laughed James's warnings away. "Don't be such a pessimist. If it is my brother, I bet my horse that Bookness will be at our camp by nightfall. You watch and see."

No one thought much of Thirsty's wager, yet it was a bet Ruther was glad he didn't take. Just as dinner had finished cooking, several men entered their camp, led by Bookness. His dark face glowed in the firelight. Four of his men flanked him, two of whom Ruther recognized from earlier. Bookness greeted everyone in Henry's group by name, which impressed Ruther since he couldn't remember the names of Bookness's companions.

"I spoke to Smiles, Miss Thirsty," Bookness said. "He's quite ill, but he's never grinned so big as when I mentioned your name. He asked that I bring you at once."

Thirsty jumped and clapped, her eyes wide with delight, and her teeth shining in the firelight. "James, you must come with me. Please! I want you to meet him."

"We're about to eat supper," Maggie said.

"Oh please?" Thirsty repeated. "I need someone to come with me."

"I can come," Ruther said, grabbing his stomach in his hands. "Heaven knows I could miss a meal or two."

Thirsty looked at James with her big blue eyes.

"No, Ruther," James said. "I can go."

Maggie frowned and averted her gaze to the flames. Bookness gestured for two of his companions to step forward. Both held a cloth bag. "I hope you'll forgive these," Bookness said, "but we value our privacy and our secrets. Right now, our location is our biggest secret. Until Smiles authenticates your identity, Miss Thirsty, you'll need to wear it. You, too, Mr. James."

"Is your location that great a secret?" James asked as he allowed them to place the bag over his head.

"It is. After all, we aren't just any rebels. We lead the rebellion. And Thirsty's brother is our leader."

THIRTY-NINE

The Rebels of Old Avalon

J ames rode Sissy at a leisurely pace, Bookness holding the horse's reins. The bag over James's head smelled like moldy potatoes. The cloth of the bag was slightly porous, and allowed him to see bits of the forest through the material. He could not see well in the darkness, but the rebels' torches gave enough light that he could figure out who and what was around him. Thirsty touched his hand and gripped it tightly. James held it, and his heart beat a little faster. Her palm was sweaty. Or perhaps it was his palm. Maybe both.

Branches clawed at him as he rode through the forest for what he guessed was about an hour, holding Thirsty's hand most of the way. Occasionally Bookness and the other rebels conversed in low tones. James caught random words, but not enough to put together an idea of what they were saying.

Despite the rapidly diminishing sunlight, James spotted a tiny shack on stilts built against the sheer wall of the mountains. With no other destination in sight, he had to assume that this was where they were headed, but it was impossible that so many men could live in such small quarters. When they stopped outside the tiny dwelling, the rebels helped James and Thirsty off their horses, but did not remove the bags from their heads. As Bookness marched James and Thirsty up the stairs—the only part of the shanty that seemed sturdily built— the rest of the men led the horses up behind them. This confused

James even more, but he said nothing, not wanting to reveal that he could see through the cloth over his head.

"Almost there." Bookness knocked three times in rapid succession, then three more times with a short pause between each knock. The door opened for them, and all James saw beyond it was darkness. Then he understood what was going on. The shack was not a dwelling at all, but had been built to cover the entrance to a cave. A humongous cave.

The bags came off, and James noted several things immediately. First, Bookness had let him keep his sword. Second, the cavern was well-lit by dozens of torches along the cave walls. Third, he had severely underestimated the number of rebels hiding with Bookness. And fourth, Thirsty had finally let go of his hand, and he wished she hadn't.

"Welcome to our home," Bookness announced. "Smiles is this way." He walked in front of them carrying a large torch. They passed many men who sat against the walls and looked up as James and Thirsty walked by. Some were reading, others playing cards. A few practiced swordplay with scraps of wood. "We still haven't explored all the caves, but we didn't discover this place, either."

"Who did?" James asked.

Bookness shrugged. "When we arrived, Gretchen brought us here knowing that we needed to keep a low profile. She said we are free to stay here until it is time."

"Time for what?" Thirsty asked.

"To return." He ducked through a low passage but the ceiling quickly raised again. They came to a large room with a bad smell, where the wounded were being kept and treated. "This way. Not far now."

James tried not to stare at the injured men. It reminded him too much of men he'd seen suffer and die after skirmishes while serving in the King's Guard. Most of those memories were bitter and cold. How many of these rebels were going to die and didn't know it?

"Smiles?" Bookness whispered.

"Here," a faint voice said behind them.

James turned with Thirsty and Bookness and saw a man lying on two thin blankets. His resemblance to Thirsty couldn't be mistaken. He wore no shirt and a bandage covered his chest. His right hand was two fingers short of a full set of five, but he wore the largest smile that James had ever seen, showing off all of his teeth.

"Smiles!" Thirsty cried, hugging him. "My brother!"

"Oh! Oh! Oh!" he muttered, laughing weakly. "Careful. These bandages aren't pretend."

Thirsty gently pulled away from him. "Smiles, I—I really can't believe it. You look exactly the same as I remember. Exactly. It is so good—so good to—to—" She wiped her eyes and took his hand, placing it over her heart. Then she did the same with her hand to his. "It really is you, isn't it?"

Smiles nodded with tears in his own eyes. "My sister!" he shouted to those around him. "Can you believe after more than ten years, I finally get to see my sister?"

Thirsty laughed and kissed his cheeks. As she pulled away, James caught a whiff of something foul. He leaned in a little closer and realized it was coming from his bandages. He wondered if Thirsty could smell it, too.

"So tell me—tell me whatever you can," Smiles said. "Gretchen said she's coming tonight to take me to the healer. We don't have much time."

Thirsty covered her mouth with one hand and brushed back Smiles's white hair with the other. "I don't know what to say. I have years too much to tell."

Smiles took her hand and patted it. "Start with this man. What are you doing with him?"

"This is James." Thirsty patted James's leg, winking at him. "He's the most handsome man I've ever met. Along with Maggie, Henry, and Ruther, he's my best friend. It feels like we've traveled halfway across the world together, the five of us. And now that I'm here with you, I can't imagine being any happier."

Smiles coughed, a wet, nasty hack that went deep into his lungs. "Did you—" Again he coughed, this one not as bad. "Did you see Furious?"

"Furious is here?" Thirsty stood up and looked around. "He's actually here? No one told me. This is amazing! What about Stinker?"

"Furious was sitting here only ten minutes ago. We were talking about you, then he said he needed to meet with his men. Stinker is still in Old Avalon doing important work."

"Furious has men?" Thirsty repeated. "You make it sound like he's important!"

"Don't you know? Furious, Stinker, and I are the heads of the rebellion. The most wanted men in all of Old Avalon."

Thirsty giggled. "Listen to you go on. Furious is too young to be doing something so big and important."

Smiles gave his sister a big grin. "You'll see for yourself. It will amaze you to see the man he's become. He's like a general."

Thirsty didn't seem to know what to do except look at her brother and grin. James remembered what it was like to see his sister and parents after several months of training, but after ten years? He couldn't imagine such a thing. Did Thirsty even know her brothers anymore?

"Smiles?" Bookness said, reentering the room. "Gretchen's here."

Smiles nodded happily to Bookness. "Been waiting days to see the healer. Hoping I can get fixed up. My cough gets worse every day. All the men you see here injured—happened to us in Desolation. Tiller's Thain, Grotto Dunes, the Town Beyond . . . people chased us. Attacked us. We lost two men in Grotto. I got hurt on the road.

People followed us. Someone shot a bow." Smiles tapped his ribs where the arrow had struck him.

Gretchen wore the same dress and braids that James had seen several days ago. As she drew close, she finally noticed James and Thirsty. James stared at her eyes to see if he could detect a hint of the magical color, lyrial.

"Ah, you are friends of Henry Vestin, aren't you?" She nodded, answering for them. "Tell him the healer is anxious to see him. In fact, he's next after Smiles."

"Oh," James responded. "We'll be certain to tell him. He'll be thrilled at the news."

Gretchen turned back to Bookness. "I require some assistance to take Smiles to the home of the healer."

Bookness called in four men, who put Smiles on a crude stretcher and picked him up. Smiles reached down and took his sister's hand, then kissed it. "I can't wait to see you again, Thirsty. You're such a beautiful woman. When I come back healed, I'll hug you properly."

Thirsty kissed his hand with the same tenderness he had shown her. Then the other rebels took him away, leaving James and Thirsty standing there with Bookness looking on. "I suppose you are ready for me to take you to Furious?"

"Yes!" Thirsty exclaimed. "Why did you tell me you had never heard such a name?"

"It's my duty to protect him. Furious is the most hunted man in Old Avalon. You might have been a spy or bounty hunter pretending to be his sister so you could get close to him. We've heard reports of bounty hunters around, though who they're hunting is anyone's guess. I assume the worst because it's my job." Bookness started to walk away. "Follow me. I'll take you to Furious."

Again Bookness led them through the caverns. James continued to marvel at the size of the caves and the sheer number of people they held. He guessed that well over a hundred men were holed up inside the stone walls. They traveled deep into the mountain before reaching Furious's quarters. A half-dozen armed men guarded the halls here. At the sight of James, they all unsheathed their swords, but they stood down when Bookness gave them a signal.

"At ease, men. He's with me."

They entered a small chamber. It was better furnished than the other rooms, a small cot instead of blankets for a bed, candlesticks instead of torches, and a table that held several maps.

Once James got past the obvious resemblances that the siblings shared, he noted how different in temperament Furious was from Smiles. It was as though their names had proven prophetic. Whereas Smiles always appeared jovial, Furious seemed cross and uninviting.

"Thirsty," he said, "I still recognize you." He held her at arm's length, his large hands on her shoulders while his eyes traveled from her face to her toes. "So long ago and yet you've hardly changed!" A small tight grin crossed his face as he pulled her into a tight hug. "We always wondered what happened to you . . . whether or not you made it."

"I missed you, Furious. I missed all of you." She wiped her eyes as he let her go. "I have so many questions. Smiles didn't have much time to talk."

"Did the healer finally summon him?"

"Yes, so I need you to fill me in on our family. How did you get involved with the rebellion? Are you really the leader?"

Furious asked Thirsty and James to sit on his cot while he produced two three-legged stools from a corner, one for himself and one for Bookness. "First, tell me about you. Have you had a good life? What have you been doing?"

James listened while Thirsty spoke about growing up in Pappalon, working at inns, becoming a maid, and then joining Henry's group in search of adventure. Furious nodded, chuckling here and there, but never allowing himself a good laugh. "You're just like the rest of us. The need for adventure is strong in our blood."

"Is that why you started a rebellion?" Thirsty asked.

A somber expression fell over Furious, more so than usual. "Do you remember Father well, Thirsty?"

"Yes, I think so."

"They say I got my temperament from him. He was an angry man. He was driven. He couldn't bear to see his children grow up as slaves knowing that the rest of Atolas rejected such practices. That's why he sent you to Pappalon first."

"Sent me?" Thirsty asked. "We drew straws."

"He rigged it. You were his only daughter, and he could only afford to send one child. I remember those events as though they happened yesterday. After you left, he grew anxious. Your freedom weighed heavily on his mind. One day, he'd had enough. He left his master's house, rounded up any slave who would follow him, and started a march for freedom to the Baron's castle. He hoped that if enough slaves marched, the Baron would see their numbers and bow to the pressure. Instead, they were met by an army. All of them were cut down. Because Father led the march, they hanged Mother, too."

"I didn't know." Thirsty covered her nose and mouth with her hands, crying silently. James put an arm around her.

"They would have hanged me, Smiles, and Stinker, but friends hid us."

Thirsty's sobs shook her body.

"I've never forgotten that day," Furious said. Flames roared in his eyes as though he were witnessing their deaths afresh. "Seeing Mother hang changed me. It changed all three of us. Everything we did was devoted to finishing Father's work. We studied, we learned, we talked to people, but we also kept our heads down and acted like everyone else, waiting for the right time. Mother always said that I had a gift for rage, so I spread it like a wildfire. I made other people angry. I made them dissatisfied with their lives. I helped them see a chance for something better."

"You started the rebellion?" James asked.

"Yes. More than a year ago. We tried to coordinate it with our spies in the Baron's castle to give us the best chance at success."

James's interest climbed. "What spies? What information?"

"Slaves who serve in the castle risked their lives to help us time our rebellion to perfection. The Baron has been in communication with the Emperor of Neverak for several months. They plan to invade Blithmore soon. It was supposed to take place several weeks ago, but our informants misinterpreted a key conversation between the Baron and his generals. We acted too soon and were punished."

"Invading Blithmore?" James laughed. "You must be kidding. Blithmore and Neverak were working together to find us! Elite Guards were all over . . ." Suddenly he saw the brilliance of the Emperor's plan. He understood why the Emperor had not wanted his Elite to slaughter Henry's group. It was all a ruse. "I can't believe—" Though he felt no real loyalty to Blithmore anymore, he still cared about his friends in the Guard, men that would be slaughtered in a surprise invasion. "Is that why you lost, Furious? Bad information?"

Furious's eyes burned as he nodded. "It was glorious for a few days, our uprising. We had over a thousand men ready to fight. The plan we had—we thought it was brilliant. But none of us have military training. What did we know? When the Baron's armies came down upon us, our rebels scattered like chickens. Only a few hundred of us remain—some here, others hiding in Old Avalon. We fought with passion, with fury, but martyrs was all we were . . . not soldiers. Some suffered horrible deaths at the hands of the Baron. Other men were lucky and died on the field of battle."

"And now what?" Thirsty asked. "What about Stinker? What about you and Smiles? Do you plan to return, or hide in this cave forever?

Or will you be wise and seek your freedom in lands where people will treat you as equals?"

Furious looked deep into his sister's eyes. James felt a kinship to this man because of his bravery and valor. "Have you ever known me to be wise? I'm over thirty years old. I have no wife or children. My life is dedicated to the cause of freedom."

"So what is your plan?" James said.

"Stinker is laying the groundwork for a second rebellion. I am gathering men and women, former slaves, overseeing efforts to get our leaders healed and prepared for a second strike. The Baron's armies will leave soon—if not already—to march to Neverak and, from there, invade King Germaine's lands. During that time, the Baron will be vulnerable. If we ever have a chance to succeed, it will be very soon."

"What will happen once the armies return in force?" James asked. "How will you fight with untrained slaves?"

"We will not be alone," Furious answered. "I have a plan. The Emperor and the Baron plan to strike the Blithmore army encamped around the Emperor's palace. They reside there as part of an agreement the Emperor made to search for a band of criminals who attacked him during his visit to Richterton. The Emperor will wipe them out and then swiftly march south before alarms can be raised. We will send a letter to the King of Blithmore informing him of this treachery beforehand. Our request in exchange for our help will be to stand with us and fight for our freedom."

"That's a lofty goal, Furious," James said. "Very lofty."

"When we achieve it, we will negotiate a treaty with Old Avalon. In exchange for peace, we will take land and form our own country, our own government, and rule ourselves."

James gripped the edge of the cot and scooted himself forward so Furious could see his face better. "Furious, you have heart, and I think well on you for that. But sometimes heart can cloud the brain. If you do this, you will lose. Your Baron would be a fool to commit anything more than half his armies to Neverak. Frankly, an untrained army will lose to a well-trained one even if they outnumber them five to one."

"You may be right. We do need help. We need someone who can train us."

"It's more than training, Furious. It's leadership. Who will make the difficult decisions and send men to their deaths? Who will rally them in the face of defeat? Your men need someone who is experienced in war and battle. Someone they look to for courage. I don't know where you can find such a man, but that's what you need."

"You speak like a soldier. Do you have experience leading men in battle?"

"Well, yes, but—"

"If so, your abilities with the sword and the knife must be exceedingly skilled."

James put up a hand to stop Furious. "That's not all—there's more—"

Furious got down on one knee, clasped his hands together tightly, and bowed his head. "James, you are the man we need. Will you train us and lead us in battle?"

"No . . . no . . . stop! I am trying to steal my sister from the Emperor of Neverak! I can't get involved in your rebellion. I am one of the bandits who was hunted by Emperor Krallick because he stole her."

Furious looked up at James, surprised. "Don't you see? It was fate that we should meet. With your aid in our rebellion, we will enable the armies of Blithmore to retaliate effectively against the initial attack on their troops. The Baron's armies will have to abandon the Emperor and return to Old Avalon. When Blithmore learns of the Emperor's treachery, they will thirst for blood. They will remove Ivan from his throne, and his slaves will be freed! Your sister will be freed!"

"I'm sorry, but I can't abandon my friends. We have come so far. To desert them would be something they would never forgive."

Tears of frustration sprang from Furious's eyes. "I understand, but I know you will change your mind. Our cause is just, and the Lord of All Worlds has sent you to lead us. So I accept your decision for now, knowing that this setback is only temporary."

James didn't know what to say, so he clasped Furious's hand and muttered, "We will see. I don't pretend to know the future. For now, Thirsty and I should return to our camp."

"Not tonight," Furious said. "It is unsafe to travel in the dark. We will make beds for you here. Thirsty and I still have much to discuss." He hugged his sister again. "Will you stay with us or return to your friends in the morning?"

Thirsty looked at James, then at her brother. "I don't know. I will have to consider it. It's been so good to see you and Smiles, and I long to see Stinker. But James and his friends have become my family as well. No matter what I decide, I won't leave this valley without leaving people I love."

Furious kissed her forehead. "Mother always knew you would do great things."

Furious's men helped set up beds for James and Thirsty, who accepted the hospitality gratefully. As James lay in bed listening to whispered conversation between Thirsty and Furious, and later Furious, Bookness, and other leaders, he couldn't help but think about Furious's offer. When he fell asleep, he dreamed of leading an army of Old Avalon's slaves into battle.

At some point during the night crying woke him. James rolled off his mat of blankets to find Thirsty, but she was not in her bed. Only two faint candles gave illumination to the cavern, but it was enough to see several people standing over Furious's cot where someone else lay. James walked over to the group. Thirsty grabbed him and sobbed into his chest.

"Screaming?" Furious asked one of his men. "You're certain you heard him scream?"

"It curdled my blood," the rebel answered. "But they wouldn't let me see what was happening. I told them the screaming wasn't natural, but it didn't make a difference. They wouldn't let me in no matter what I said. Finally it stopped—it stopped very suddenly, and then the healer's people bore him out of the house with their apologies. Said he couldn't be healed."

James looked down at Smiles's body. His face was not one of pain, but serenity, smiling even in death. Thirsty continued to cry. "It's not fair," she moaned. "It just isn't fair."

James stroked her hair. Furious knelt to the ground and put his arms around his brother. "This is the third man we've lost to the healer. It's time we leave before we lose any more."

"Has anyone been healed yet?" James asked.

"Yes," Furious said, "some have, but their injuries were minor. I should not have let Smiles go, but his wounds were beyond our ability, and he insisted on trying."

"Henry!" Thirsty said, looking at James with wide, fearful eyes. "Gretchen said he's next. He needs to be warned!"

James agreed. "We have to return to our camp now. Perhaps we can finish our conversation before you leave for Old Avalon."

"No, we're leaving now. If you change your mind, look for us on the Old Desert Road. It's the safest way to travel through Desolation. Take the road to the Cave of Bones."

Furious gave orders to his men to take James and Thirsty back to their camp. They took horses, holding torches to light the way, riding as quickly as the trails would allow. When they reached camp, they found Maggie and Ruther awake and sitting by the fire. Maggie regarded James coldly, while Ruther gave a friendly welcome.

"Where's Henry?" James asked.

"You just missed him," Ruther answered lazily. "Left not long ago with that Gretchen woman. I don't think he could wait another second. Where have you two been?"

FORTY
Cecilia's Mistake

"So, you're trying to escape." Cecilia entered Isabelle's room, a crazed look in her eyes that moved from the iron bars to Isabelle's wounded hand and then to the rock Isabelle had dropped on the bed. Isabelle scrambled to grab it, but Cecilia was quicker. Once she had it, she sat on the bed and tossed it from hand to hand.

Hot guilt drove every thought from Isabelle's mind. "You can't just come in my . . . why are you still . . . it's late! This is my private chamber!"

"I heard a strange sound. I wanted to see if you were all right."

Isabelle hid her bleeding palm between her calf and her thigh. "As you can see, I'm perfectly fine." Her tone made it clear that she was inviting Cecilia to leave.

Rather than going, Cecilia, with ungloved hands, pulled Isabelle's hand out from its hiding place and examined the wound. "It's not that bad, but you should clean it. If you don't, the maids will have a fit."

"You shouldn't be touching me." Isabelle pulled her hand away. "You'll have to be cleansed again. I don't want to mess up your chances with the Emperor."

Cecilia grinned at Isabelle. It was the first bit of fire and life Isabelle had seen in her in days. "Who's going to tell His Majesty? Not you. And certainly not me."

Isabelle sniffled through a polite laugh. Yet it was true. Isabelle would never report Cecilia to the Emperor.

"I don't understand you," Cecilia said, searching deep into Isabelle's eyes for an answer that eluded her. "What are you doing here?"

Uncertain what Cecilia meant, Isabelle said, "I'm the Emperor's slave, just like you."

Cecilia took a cloth, wetted it with Isabelle's water pitcher, and dabbed her wound with it. "Exactly. You're *his* now. You know he desires you. He'll follow in his father's footsteps and marry a concubine. Why give up your chance at the throne?"

"I don't have a chance at it."

"One of us," Cecilia continued. "You heard him. He will choose one of us. And all the girls know you have the upper hand right now. Despite all my effort . . . all my attentions . . . he leans toward you. Play the game right and you could be the Empress of Neverak . . . and Blithmore."

Isabelle shook her head. "You don't know what you're talking about."

"Why, Isabelle? Why would you try to escape? Why not ask the Emperor to let you go?"

A rush of laughter escaped from Isabelle. She hadn't expected such a naive statement from Cecilia, of all people. "You think . . . let me go? No. You have no idea what he went through to bring me here. The man I love rescued me *from* Emperor Krallick. He and I tried to flee Blithmore to escape. He sent his armies and the armies of the King of Blithmore to capture me. Why do you think he was so doting at dinner?"

"Why would he capture you?" The questioning tone in her voice, the wary look in her eyes, Isabelle could tell Cecilia did not believe her.

"Because he's an evil man!" Isabelle cried. How could Cecilia not see this? "My father sold me to him."

"Why would your father do that?"

"Because he's an evil man, too! I will do everything I can to escape before I give myself up to the Emperor and become his whore."

Cecilia reacted as though Isabelle had spit on her. "That is not what I am."

"Then what are you, Cecilia? You want the ruby rose as much as the rest of them. But it isn't real! The Emperor cares no more for you than any of his prized horses. You are beautiful, healthy, intelligent, and skilled. A man would be lucky to marry you. He would wake up every morning and praise the Lord of All Worlds that you're sleeping next to him."

"Stop it," Cecilia said coldly.

"No! You could have something genuine, passionate, and lasting, like what I had—what I hope to have—with Henry. But you're chasing a mirage instead of a wellspring of joy."

"Shut up!" Cecilia said. She raised her hand to hit Isabelle but stopped herself. "The Emperor cares about us, but he doesn't know how to show it. You should see him when he is alone with me. He is kind, gentle, loving . . ."

"I know how much you adore the Emperor, Cecilia, but he is a vile monster."

"He's not."

"He poisoned me."

"He wouldn't."

"It took me weeks to recover, and then when we tried to flee the country for safety from him, he caught us and ripped me from the man I love!"

"I don't believe you!" Cecilia shouted.

"Why not?" Isabelle cried.

"Because you're an *Oslan!*"

Though she'd never heard her family name spoken with much respect back in Blithmore, Isabelle had never heard it spoken with such
a venomous tone. She stared at Cecilia. "Why—what does that mean?
What does my family have to do with this?"

A flash of sudden emotion blazed in Cecilia's eyes, but Isabelle
couldn't tell what it was. Fury? Hate? Grief? Something more?

"The—the Oslan name . . . is not well-spoken of throughout
Blithmore," Cecilia finally stated in a quieter voice. "They are not
known for being honorable or . . . trustworthy."

"Cecilia . . . You could accomplish things that have meaning. You
can leave something better than yourself behind, but not here serving
the whims of the Emperor."

Cecilia got up again and rinsed the blood from the cloth. The cut
wasn't deep, but it stung. "Like what?" Cecilia asked.

"Love."

Cecilia shook her head and wiped her eyes. Isabelle hadn't even
noticed that she'd been crying. "What is *love*?" Cecilia's laugh was
even more sarcastic than Isabelle's had been. "I used to believe in
such things, you know. I used to dream about a life with a man I
loved. Isabelle, you fool, you should be grateful to live in a place
where all your wants and needs are met. We all grow old, we all become ugly, and we die. There is no such thing as love."

"You're wrong. And what I'm telling you about the Emperor is
true. He hunted me down—and the man I truly love. And I would still
give all this up to be with that man. I would not hesitate."

"You make it sound as though he's still alive." Isabelle still heard a
quiet, dangerous undertone in Cecilia's voice.

"I—I—I still love him." The faltering in Isabelle's voice betrayed
her. She cursed herself for being such a terrible liar. "He lives in me."

"Foolishness." Cecilia's tears fell more steadily now. Her cheeks
were the color of a setting sun, and her eyes were puffy and downcast.
"I thought I knew love. I thought it was when you tell someone that

you're devoted to him. Or when you offer your life to him because you trust him with it."

"It is!" Isabelle cried.

"But then, despite standing by him during a time when everyone else is against him, he rips your life apart with a few words and—and—strikes you down like an unwanted dog . . ." Cecilia gingerly touched the corner of her lips as though lost in a memory. "The only way you can be happy again is by forgetting he exists. And when it finally sinks in that he's gone, you have nothing left but a shattered dream."

Isabelle had been holding her breath while Cecilia spoke, and finally let the air from her lungs. "That's horrible. If you felt the same way for him that I do about the man I love, you must have been devastated."

"I was!" Cecilia snarled and glowered at Isabelle as though it was she, not some man, who had wounded Cecilia's heart. Then the look was gone, and Cecilia wiped her face with her sleeve. When she withdrew her arm, her face was an expressionless mask. "Excuse my blubbering. I don't enjoy dwelling on the past."

"I don't mind you sharing your personal life with me. In fact, I welcome it. Sometimes I feel like I don't have a friend in the world."

"I'm not your friend, Isabelle," Cecilia said. "I never could be."

The words hurt Isabelle more than she wanted to believe. Cecilia was the person Isabelle had connected with, the one she'd looked up to and trusted. She needed Cecilia to be a friend. "What have I done to you? Why can't we be—"

Cecilia got up and walked to the drapes covering Isabelle's chamber doorway. She trailed her fingers along the cloth, half-looking over her shoulder. "It will never happen. Your name brings me nothing but pain." Her eyes briefly met Isabelle's, but there was hate there, not love. "What you're searching for is under Jade's pillow. She's a heavier sleeper than I am. But Isabelle . . . if you're caught and mention my name at all, a bruise on your cheek will be the least of your worries."

FORTY-ONE

The Healer

While Gretchen rode her pony to the house of the healer, Henry tried to keep up on foot. The walk was long, and the strange woman made no attempt at conversation. She forced Henry to move at a strenuous pace, and by the time they came to a rest, he was clutching at his aching ribs and gulping down air. Gretchen didn't seem to notice, or perhaps she didn't care.

"This way," she called to him over her shoulder as she rode into a dense grove of trees.

If Gretchen was following a trail, Henry could not see it in the darkness. The night air was warm in the grove, and stinging sweat dripped into his eyes. Between the rocky terrain and the abundant foliage, he found it difficult to maintain his balance with only one arm. When Henry contemplated sitting down and falling asleep, Gretchen announced, "Nearly there."

The foliage grew denser until every step Henry took was a fight through a wall of branches and leaves, scratching at his arms, legs, and face. "Are we going to the healer's house?" he asked, puffing for air with each step. "We are far from any road or trail."

"The healer has many homes in the valley."

"Does the healer walk the Path?"

"It is not my place to reveal such things," Gretchen answered politely.

"And you? Do you walk the Path?"

Gretchen glanced down at Henry. "Why would you ask such a question?"

"Lyrial. It is the color of your eyes."

This time Gretchen looked hard at Henry, examining him. "You speak of things you do not understand. Your sister told you that."

"She has the gift, but knows little of the power or how to use it."

Gretchen smiled as she turned away. "Do not call it a gift. We call it the Path for a reason. If no journey or effort was required to use it, then *gift* would be a fine word. Your sister fears it. That is her weakness."

"Where can she go to be taught? Could the healer teach her?"

"No."

"Well . . . wait . . ." Henry struggled to talk and walk at the same time. "Let me . . . explain more. My sister has no one to teach—help her—"

"Not here, no," Gretchen repeated. "The valley is not an academy for those who walk the Path. It is a place of healing. Nothing more."

"Could you teach her?"

"No."

Henry snorted and kicked at a twig in his path. "Do you know anyone who *could* help?"

Gretchen's laugh was airy and bright and made her braid dance. "Now you're asking the right questions. There is someone. Perhaps the healer will give the name to you."

By the time Henry reached the home of the healer, he was nearly faint from exhaustion. The lack of sleep and the hard hike through the night had worn him down mentally and physically. The sun had begun to rise over the peaks of the Dusty Mountains when Gretchen stopped and pointed. "If you follow that path, you'll find a small cottage that doesn't belong where it sits. That's where the healer will see you." Then she and her pony disappeared into the woods.

Henry stopped to catch his breath. Even his bones were exhausted. Knowing what a mess he must look, he used his good hand to brush the twigs out of his hair and off his clothes, then dragged his feet forward.

The cabin was the strangest sight he had seen in a while, a log homestead covered in ivy of a bright, almost poisonous orange. A haphazard garden grew around all four sides, tomatoes, beans, fruit trees, and corn stalks scattered throughout the whole of it. Stones had been placed every few feet as if someone had simply tossed them up into the air and then planted around them. Henry stepped on the stones until he reached the large brown door.

He knocked, but heard no sounds of movement. After waiting a few moments, he knocked again. This time the door opened. A girl of about eight or nine answered the door. She was barefoot and wore a simple white dress that made her dark brown hair shine vibrantly and gave her milky skin the appearance of an unblemished daisy. Henry returned her pleasant smile as best he could in his fatigued state.

"Hello," he told her, "I'm here to see the healer."

"Come in, Henry," the girl said. "I've been expecting you." She left the door and retreated inside. "Close the door behind you, please?"

Henry's smile faded as he hurried to follow her orders. The inside of the home was different than he'd expected from his experiences with the Winmore brothers who had treated Isabelle, or the physician in Borderville who worked on Ruther. He saw no jars or bottles of herbs or medicines, no towering bookcases. It was a one-room homestead and quite small. A tiny bed occupied one corner. A large pot hung in the fireplace, and nearby were two chairs made of thin tree branches bent into shape and held together with metal bands. The healer already sat in one of them, her legs crossed and her arms folded. She wore only one embellishment, a silver bracelet with a large blue pearl set into it which she caressed with her fingers.

"Please sit," she said. "Tell me why you are here."

Henry gestured with his good arm to his bad. "I've—I've lost the ability to move my arm—and—and my hand."

The girl smiled again. Henry noticed that she had large teeth like an adult, not a child's. Her eyes had the beginnings of wrinkles around them, making her appear far more wise and calculating than a girl of eight or ten. "No, Henry. I mean, why are you *here?*"

It took a moment before Henry understood her meaning. "Er—I've come expecting to see the healer. Is that you?"

The girl nodded. "I am the healer, but I can't heal you."

"How do you know? Won't you examine my arm before you make a decision?"

"Very well, let me see it." Henry didn't like her tone. It was flippant and cold.

He had to take off his shirt to show the arm. He hated dressing and undressing because it was nearly impossible to do with one hand, which meant Ruther or James often had to help him. Once he managed to get his arm out of his sleeve, he felt silly standing half-naked in front of such a young girl. He showed her the scar where the blade of the Elite Guard had done the worst damage. When she finished her examination, he put the shirt back on.

"Weren't you hit anywhere else during the attack?"

"Yes, I was hit in the head. The wound was just as bad, if not worse."

"Your head moves perfectly well. How very interesting. Yet I stand by my decision. I can't heal you."

Henry tried to argue again. "Can't you at least try—?"

The healer raised two fingers and placed them over her lips. When Henry fell silent, she spoke again. "You misunderstand me. *I* cannot heal you. Only *you* can heal yourself. Tell me how your arm came to be this way."

Before Henry launched into a story of his adventures, he wanted to ask her questions of his own. He wanted to know how old she was, how she came to be a healer, and why she operated as she did. However, he did things her way, and if this turned out to be a sham, he would make her deeply regret wasting his time.

The girl listened intently as he spoke, never interrupting. When he finished, she did not move or speak for a long time. The only sound was the crackling of the fire and the soft rustling of the ivy leaves as the morning wind blew past the house. Her head was cocked slightly to one side, her bracelet pressed over her heart, giving Henry the impression she was listening to something he could not hear. When this had gone on long enough that Henry felt uncomfortable, he said, "What's your name?"

"I don't remember. You may call me the healer."

"How old are you?"

The girl's faraway gaze ended when he spoke and her smile returned at his question. "How old do you think I am?"

Henry shrugged. "You look like a child, but I doubt that I'm the first person to say that."

"Some people are so astonished when they see me that they turn around and leave."

Henry could see why. He, too, was skeptical. "So . . . how old do you think you are?"

The healer's smile remained as enigmatic as ever. "Older than you, but as for my exact age, I no longer remember that either. I have no memory of my parents. Perhaps I have been healing people in this valley since the beginning of time, though I very much doubt it."

She crossed the room and pulled a trunk out from under her bed. From within, she removed a long piece of rope. "I have no memory of any family," she said as she walked to the fire. "It is the cost of prescience, one of the powers of the Path I walk. Which your sister walks. To glimpse events which have not yet occurred, one must sacrifice a memory. Do it enough, and you become like me, a lost soul with no memory of the past. Eventually I will grow so lost that I will go mad. And then my days as a healer will end. How does that strike you, Henry?"

"The cost is too great. Memories are things to treasure."

"Not my memories." The healer toyed with the rope in her hands like it was a snake. "Or so I assume. I can't remember now why I wanted to rid myself of them, but I believe they must have been terrible."

The healer burned the ragged ends of the rope and then dipped them in a pot of glue until each end smoked and fused. The fumes reached Henry's nose. They smelled sweet and tangy. "Or perhaps I was born of Atolas itself and, through the power of the Lord of All Worlds, placed in the womb of the healer before me. And one day, I'll begin to age and a child will be placed in my womb. I'll raise her and teach her and then die. It's a nice fantasy, isn't it?"

"You sound as if you've already gone mad. Or are you putting on a performance to create a mystique around yourself?"

She blew on both ends of the rope. "For those who do not understand or believe in the Path, it makes a better story. Many who visit me want something supernatural, not the truth."

"Is it a difficult life? Healing?"

The healer smiled. "I have a wonderful life. I heal people from all over Atolas." She touched his bad arm with her small, delicate fingers. Her eyes were filled with sympathy for him, but her tone was strong. "We all have struggles. To complain about them is a waste of time and air."

"I agree," he finally said.

"I have peered into the future for you, Henry," she said carefully, clutching the pearl on her bracelet. "I have seen a course of action that will give you the greatest chance to be healed. But it is dangerous. It may kill you. I want to be certain that you are willing to endure it to the bitter end if that's what it takes."

"What do you mean?" Henry asked.

"I don't think I can be clearer. For the last few days, I have contemplated your injury based on your answers to Gretchen's extensive questions. I used that information to put together a treatment which I believe has the best chance of healing you. However, if it does not work, you will die."

"Well—wait—do people often die during these treatments?"

"This morning I saw a man who received a chest wound from an arrow. I did everything I could to save him, but the injuries were too great and he passed on. I see much death, Henry."

Despite having rested the last few minutes, Henry felt more tired than ever. "What are my chances of surviving this?"

The healer's ethereal smile returned and she seemed to be looking into his soul. "It depends on your strength."

"I don't feel strong at all. I haven't slept much tonight, and I walked for miles to come here. Perhaps if I rest first . . ."

The healer showed her teeth as she giggled girlishly. "Not your physical strength." She touched his chest, and her fingers lingered as though feeling for his heartbeat. Then she moved them up his body until they rested on his forehead. Her skin was cool and soft, her touch something Henry found pleasant and inviting.

"I'm sorry, but I don't understand. Why are you being so mysterious? You said you looked into the future. What did you see? Did I survive or not?"

"The Path does not allow me to see forthcoming events as simply as putting my head under a blanket to learn what is hidden underneath. It only shows me probability and chance. My question to you remains the same."

"What question?"

"Are you willing to put your life in danger to be healed?"

"I don't know." Henry looked inside himself, trying to find the answer. "I wasn't prepared for this."

"Would it have mattered if you knew I was going to ask?"

"Yes."

"How?"

"I might not have wasted so much time traveling here!"

The healer pointed to the door. "You are free to leave if you wish."

He looked at the door and pondered over his options. But the truth was he had no faith in his ability to make the right decision.

"What do you wish to do, Henry?"

"Tell me about the treatment. What is the process?"

"I can't tell you what it is until the moment we begin."

"Why?"

"Because part of the treatment is the unknown. And because I enjoy being mysterious." Henry caught the hints of a smile on her face, but was in no mood to share in her mirth.

"I can't decide," he said.

"Why?"

"I can't. What if I make the wrong choice?"

"Why do you think your arm has become lame?"

"It was injured in battle. You saw the scars."

In a quick movement, the healer tore Henry's shirt from his body. Then she tossed the garment into the fire. Again she examined Henry's body. "Yes, I see a scar, but it's not in a place suggesting a complete loss of the use of your limb."

"I don't know! I am not a man of science nor am I a physician."

"What are you?"

"I'm a carpenter. I'm just a carpenter."

"How will you work with wood if you have only one arm?"

Despite having asked himself this very question a thousand times in the last few months, Henry still had no answer.

"How will you support yourself? A woman? What good will you be to anyone with only one arm?"

"I don't know," Henry whispered.

"Will you beg for money? Find another trade? Raise pigs or sheep?"

Tears threatened to gather in Henry's eyes, but he fought them. "Yes, I'm worthless. My entire journey from Richterton to here was littered with poor choices. You couldn't imagine someone more inept than me leading a band of travelers."

The healer went to the door at the back of her house, left, and returned moments later with two goblets. One she handed to him. He took a sip. While the water was refreshingly cold and tasted wonderful, Henry noticed these things distantly, as if someone else was drinking it through him.

"What is your decision?" she asked again, a touch of impatience in her voice now.

"Part of me thinks what you offer may simply be my last terrible mistake among many."

"I guess it comes down to one question, Henry. If you walk away today without the treatment, will you always wonder? Will you look back on that choice with regret? Will you bumble through life with a bad arm and wish you had tried?"

Henry thought this over and realized that every time he had imagined himself embracing Isabelle, it had always been with two arms, not one. He had seen himself picking her up, twirling her, holding her tightly. James had been right.

He needed to be whole.

FORTY-TWO
At the Waterfall

I
t wasn't easy waiting around for Henry to return, especially for
Maggie. Ruther watched her closely. She couldn't seem to sit still.
One minute she sat by the fire, then she got up and paced around
the camp, then dug through the packs, then paced some more. After
several minutes of this, she'd sit down only to get up moments later.
Finally Ruther decided he'd had enough.

"Maggie, would you like something to take your mind off waiting?"

She looked back at him with an eyebrow raised and her jaw set.
"Like what?"

Ruther put up his hands as he tried to think of something. "We
could go to the waterfall. Or ride to town for supplies."

Maggie appeared to have every intention of declining, but then,
for some reason, she said, "Good idea. James, will you accompany me
to the waterfall?"

James lay on the ground, wrapped in blankets, trying to catch up
on missed sleep. He looked at Thirsty and Ruther for help, but neither
offered to go along. It was clear from Maggie's tone that she wanted to
be alone with him. "Er . . . now, Maggie?"

"Yes, if you don't mind."

Reluctantly, James agreed. Ruther watched with disappointment
as his friends rode off to the waterfall on Sissy and Fury. He wanted
to be the one to comfort Maggie, not James. Thirsty sat on the ground

near the fire, her focus also on the departing riders. She and Ruther exchanged a look.

"We should let them have some time alone," he said.

Thirsty nodded. Her eyes were on James but also filled with tears.

"Thirsty, what's wrong?"

She put a hand over her eyes and let out a heart-wrenching sob. "My brother died, Ruther! I hadn't seen him in over ten years. And I don't know if I should be thankful that I got those few minutes, or angry at having him ripped away from me so suddenly."

Ruther wished for James to come back and console Thirsty. He did not know what to say, so he held her as she cried on his shoulder and he rubbed her back. Gradually her sobbing subsided, her body relaxed, and her breathing softened until he noticed that she was no longer crying, but sleeping. Not wanting to wake her, he gently lowered her to the ground, then retrieved a blanket to put under her head and another to cover her.

"Thank you, James," she mumbled. "I love you."

"Uh . . ." Ruther hesitated. Then in his best impression of James, he responded, "I love you, too."

Satisfied that Thirsty would be all right, Ruther mounted Ghost and headed to the waterfall. As he drew near, he slowed his horse to a lazy trot. Then Ruther tied him up a short way off the trail. He half expected to find James and Maggie swimming, but they were not in the water. It took a while to find them while staying hidden, but he eventually spotted them sitting on the shore near the falls.

He heard Maggie first, the agitation in her voice apparent. "You've already discussed this with Thirsty?"

"She was right there when he asked me."

"I can't believe you're considering it. Isabelle needs you. Henry needs you! What are Henry and Ruther supposed to do without you?"

"They'll have you."

"*Me?*" Maggie laughed, but it was a hollow, pitiful thing. "Ruther's the one who gets people out of binds. You're the one who is good with a sword. Thirsty can cook, clean, and make everyone smile. What am I?"

"You're—you're—"

"I'm nobody! I'm worthless! I add nothing to this group."

"You walk the Path!"

"A Path I know nothing about. A gift that has benefitted us nothing. We have to stay together. You can't do this, James."

"I haven't made a choice. I don't know what I'm going to do." Ruther noted the exasperation in James's tone. "We could all come, Maggie. You, Henry, and Ruther. We don't need to split up."

"You sound like you've made up your mind." Maggie folded her arms and pursed her lips. Ruther couldn't count how many times he'd seen her make that same face, only directed toward him, not James. "So why are we discussing it?"

James took her hand. "Because your opinion is important to me. Furious made a point, and it stuck in my brain. His rebellion could change everything. If his information is correct, and Old Avalon plans to join Neverak in their invasion, then the whole crux of the war may hinge on their actions. It could very well be the key to saving Isabelle."

"It doesn't make any sense!"

James slapped his palm against the wet ground, making a sharp *splat!* The effect made both Ruther and Maggie jump. "It does! I've explained it, but you don't want to see it."

"Markus Finkley gave us directions on how to sneak into the palace to get Isabelle. Those same directions led us safely to this valley. Why shouldn't we keep trusting him? Why get involved in wars?"

"I never said we couldn't trust him. I only said that his plan is risky."

Maggie looked around wildly, as though not certain what to say or how to react. "Would—would you be so willing to do this if that man—their leader, Angry or—"

"Furious."

"If he wasn't Thirsty's brother, would you still go?"

"Why does that matter?"

"It matters to me! Will you be honest with me for once and tell me what is going on inside your cursed head?"

James's face was ashen, his eyes wide. His left hand played with his boot while the other fidgeted with his belt. "You're right," he admitted in a hushed voice. "I don't know why I make things so torturous for everyone around me, but that's how I am. I apologize." His breaths came deep and fast, and his grip on the belt tightened. If Ruther hadn't known better, he'd have guessed James was terrified of something.

"I do care for you, Maggie, but not in the way you would like. Or maybe not the amount you would like. I—I was in love . . . once. I thought I could feel that way again with you. But I realized it wasn't the same as what I had experienced before. Your affections made me want to believe something that—that wasn't real because—because I enjoyed the attention, the warmth. I wanted to hope I felt something in return. When you asked me several weeks ago if I felt anything toward Thirsty, I told you the truth. I do feel something, but I don't know what. I don't know her very well."

"Have you expressed your feelings toward her?" Maggie asked, but she sounded fearful of his answer. "In any way?"

"No!" James said, "That wasn't me who—she kissed *me*, Maggie!"

"*What?*" Maggie shrieked.

James looked like he wanted to punch himself. "The night before the execution . . . she kissed me. I don't know why. I didn't ask—I didn't know what—"

Maggie's body trembled. "Did you kiss her back?" Her tone was low and menacing.

"Maggie, things were so intense. My emotions—and she—I don't know what I did."

"Did you or didn't you?"

Ruther had never seen James so uncomfortable. It would have

been hilarious in any other situation. For whatever reason, James couldn't bring himself to answer Maggie's question.

Maggie leaned over and kissed James. It lasted less than a second before James leaned away from her. "What are you doing?"

Maggie bit her lip. "You have never kissed me. No one has ever kissed me. I wanted to experience it once."

James reached out to touch her shoulder, but Maggie pushed his hand away.

"Go away, James." She clutched her stomach. Her eyes grew red and puffy, but Ruther could see her determination to not cry in front of James.

"I'm sorry for hurting you," James said helplessly.

"Just go! Take your impenetrable heart and your buried secrets and your past loves. I don't care anymore."

Maggie hid her face in her hands. Ruther wanted to go to her and hold her. He wanted to tell her that he cared for her deeply. He wondered if James would do those things instead. But James didn't. He stood up, watching Maggie with a face of stone. Then he climbed on Sissy and rode away without a backward glance. And only then did Maggie let herself cry.

Ruther stepped forward to help her, stepping on and cracking a stick as he did so. Maggie's head jerked up in alarm, and she wiped her face and eyes quickly. "Who's there?"

Her voice was still heavy and thick. Ruther stopped, wondering if he should continue forward or leave her alone. The longer he watched her from his hiding place, the more he knew that he couldn't walk away from her.

"Is someone there?" she called. "Please don't—" she began to say, but before she was able to finish, Ruther stepped out of the woods.

"What's wrong, Mags?" He tried to sound as ignorant as possible. The last thing he wanted was her knowing that he'd overheard her argument with James.

"Nothing, Ruther, please, I'm just—"

"Did James hurt you?" he pressed, taking her hands in his.

She seemed surprised at the concern in his voice and on his face. "No!"

He pulled her head against his chest and a second later, her tears flowed again.

"Please don't cry, Maggie," he whispered. He combed his long fingers through her hair more gently than anything he had ever done. "Don't cry. Is this because of James?"

She didn't answer, but her crying increased.

"You deserve better."

Saying this didn't help Maggie's tears, so he held her tighter and tried to think of something profound to say or something amorous from one of the stories he'd memorized. He remembered Pippynn's story. He needed to confess his love. This was the moment he needed to act, to say exactly the right thing and win her heart, but nothing came to mind. So rather than waste the moment, he took a deep breath and pulled Maggie's face up until her lips met his. Her lips were dry and tight, not at all as he'd expected they'd be. Almost immediately, Maggie jumped and pulled away from his grasp.

The blood drained from Ruther's face, and he stared at her with wide eyes. "I love you, Maggie," he said in one breathless gasp. "I don't know when it started or why, because we've always struggled to get along. But somewhere I developed feelings for you and now I can't make them go away."

Maggie still looked shocked from the kiss. "I—Ruther—I—James and I just had an argument, that's all. This is just a bump in the road for us."

"It wasn't just an argument, Mags. You know that. He doesn't care about you the way you want him to. I've known that for a long time. He told me that when we went hunting. Remember? When I killed that buck?"

Maggie slid away from him, still with that frightened expression that he couldn't stomach. "Ruther . . . no. I can't. I'm in no position to be dealing with your troubled or—or—or warped sense of love."

Ruther started to sneer, but covered it with a cough. "A warped sense of love? Do you even know what I feel?"

"Sometimes I wonder if you feel at all!" Maggie cried.

The realization slowly dawned on Ruther that he'd made a terrible mistake, but this didn't make the words she hurled at him any less damaging. "Of course I feel! Remember that time I stubbed my toe and yelled *Ow*?" His attempt at a jest fell flat.

Maggie looked away. "Is this some lame attempt to make me feel worse?"

"No. I'm sorry, Maggie. I'm not good at this, but I do care about you. That's what I've been trying to tell you. I care deeply for you."

"Stop, Ruther. Stop telling me how you feel."

"No. You're beautiful, and when you want to be, you're charming as well. Sometimes I've found myself wanting to step out of my own skin so I can be someone else for you. But I can't do that. I'm only me. I'm Ruther, the boy you've known for more than eleven years. Who teased you and made you laugh and who took you and Henry and Isabelle on all those crazy adventures. Don't tell me you feel nothing for me. Don't tell me you're that callous."

Maggie flinched at the word *callous,* and Ruther instantly wished he could take it back. "I find you revolting, Ruther. The only time I can't remember feeling that way was when you first moved into my family's house, but once I realized what you were, I have never looked at you the same again. My mother—"

Ruther put up a hand to silence her. "Please stop."

"Put your hand down. I am not callous. I once had a little girl's fancy for you, yes. But then my mother set me straight. Do you know what one of the last things she ever said to me was? 'Don't marry a man like Ruther. Don't marry *anyone* like him.' And it wasn't the first time. She must have told me that a hundred times. Maybe more."

"Your mother? Why—what does she have to do with us now?"

"Because she was right. It took me a long time to see it. At first all I saw was your charming personality, but eventually I realized you amounted to nothing more than a lazy boy who stole from and lied to my parents after they took you in. I hated you for years. And it wasn't until you saved my life during that battle at the pass that I finally moved past those feelings. But still, when I look at you, I see a fat, lazy, and crude man—"

"I don't need to hear this!" Ruther turned to leave, but Maggie continued on.

"A crude man who received an enormous gift of talent just so he could throw it to the wind and let it blow into the Beyond. I see the man who teased me endlessly despite knowing how much I hated it. I see the boy who lured Henry into trouble time and again to my parents' great frustration. Don't you ever look at yourself, Ruther—truly gaze into your own soul?"

"Of course . . . What does that—?"

"You're lazy. You're wasteful! You convinced James and Henry to cheat and steal. Is that someone I should love?"

"That was for Isabelle . . ."

"How can you say you love me, Ruther? You don't know what that is. How could you? You've loved you and only you all your life. You're not the kind of man I could ever want as a husband."

When she had finished, Ruther could hardly remember what she'd said. Stricken, he stared past her as though she was nothing more than air. All his emotions were spent. With nothing more to say, Maggie wiped her face one last time, and hugged herself. Ruther ran in the opposite direction, not stopping until he reached Ghost. He rode as fast as he dared, and when he was far enough away, he let out a primal scream until his exhausted lungs burned as hot and painfully as his soul.

FORTY-THREE

The Healing Basin

The healer led Henry to the back of her house. More orange ivy climbed up the back side of the house and onto the roof. Patches of flowers speckled the grounds like a quilt, and a well-worn trail ran through them. The slopes of the Dusty Mountains rose up sharply no more than a few hundred yards away. Somewhere in the distance Henry heard the sound of rushing water.

"I have over a dozen homes in the valley. I don't use this one often, but it's quite lovely. Simple. I had this basin dug out and built just for you. It took six of my helpers five days to do the work." She pointed to a shallow pit in the ground, perhaps five feet deep and wide enough that Henry could stretch out in it and not touch the sides. The walls were lined with flat stones embedded into the dirt. At the bottom were smooth rocks, a stone chair, and a coil of rope. A small trough approached the basin at the back side, but it was bone dry. The healer surveyed everything with the same detached smile on her face that Henry had now grown accustomed to. "Take off your boots, Henry."

"What do I have to do?" Henry asked, pointing into the basin as he struggled to remove his boots with one hand. "Use the rope to pull the stone chair up?"

"No, I will tie you to the chair, and you will free yourself. Can you climb down by yourself or would you like my assistance?"

Her question struck Henry's pride. "I can do it myself."

The basin appeared deeper from the bottom than from the top. The healer asked Henry to sit in the chair while she muttered to herself. Henry tried to catch what she was saying, but she spoke too softly. Finally she stood up straight and walked around to face him.

"This is your last chance to—"

"I said I was going to do it, and I'm here. Stop trying to talk me out of it."

"Very well," the healer glowed triumphantly. "Remember . . . I will not aid you." Her words had an eerie tone of finality to them.

From behind her, she produced a strip of black cloth. "This blindfold is to help you focus," she told him as she tied it around his head, robbing him of his sight. "Sit."

The stone chair was uncomfortably cold against Henry's bare back, but he gradually grew accustomed to it. Meanwhile, the healer tied the ropes tightly around his calves, thighs, waist, chest, and his good arm. The only thing Henry could move was his head. He noticed his lame arm remained untied.

"Focus on yourself, Henry," the healer said. "You have a tremendous amount of guilt." As the healer spoke, Henry could tell that she was walking around him. "Why do you carry that with you? Does it help?"

Before Henry could answer, he heard a small stream splashing nearby. He remembered the narrow trough that fed into the basin. "I don't know any other way to live. My guilt helps me prevent future mistakes."

"Does it?"

"I believe so."

"How?"

As Henry tried to think about this, the first drops of water touched his bare feet, distracting him. What was the point of the water? "I—I don't—"

"Forget about the water, Henry. How has your guilt helped you?"

"My father once taught me that life is like carving wood. You can cover up a small scratch or chip, but big mistakes can't be fixed. They can't be smoothed over. You have to live with those forever."

"What did you learn from the battle? Have you learned from your mistakes?"

"I learned swordplay!" He didn't know why he was shouting, but something about the water made him uneasy. "James and I have spent almost every spare moment of the last four months training."

"What else do you feel guilty about?"

Henry closed his eyes even though he couldn't see anything through the blindfold. Ignoring the water was not easy, but it was more difficult to put the answers to the healer's questions into words.

"They looked to me as the leader of the group," he admitted. "It wasn't something I asked for, but it made sense because my friends had gathered around my cause . . . except Brandol. He wasn't meant to come along. He was supposed to be gone the night we left. Brandol is imprisoned because of me—or dead. Also because of me."

"How is it your fault?"

"I asked for his help getting the last of our belongings to the carriage. In my selfishness, in my panic, I abused my status as his master. He was seen as the King's men rode up the street and so we were forced to take him with us. It's my fault."

"Continue."

"I could have done more for him as we rode south. Brandol was always so afraid, and his fear forced him to do things he would never have done otherwise. If I'd chosen another route . . . We shouldn't have stopped in Bookerton." He knew stopping in Bookerton had been a necessity, but he regretted it nonetheless. "I made so many poor decisions—all things I could have done better if I had just taken the time to think."

"Why didn't you take the time to think?"

"What else could I do?" he exclaimed. "We were always moving, constantly afraid, we rarely even had time to rest! But as the leader, I consistently made poor choices. Now I'm too scared to think about what Isabelle must be . . ." Henry felt his anger extinguish like a small flame doused in a great deluge. "It terrifies me to think what she's gone through and what she must still endure because of me. I told her once that I wouldn't let us be separated. Now I look back and think what a foolish thing that was to promise."

"You can't be together now?"

"Any day her cleansing will end. The Emperor will take her for himself, and if she fights him—when she fights him—she'll die. Everything is my fault."

"Is it?"

"Yes!" he shouted. The fire inside his belly he'd thought was gone was now a roaring blaze. "If I had never built that carriage for the smuggler, I wouldn't have become cursed. If I'd shown courage back in Richterton to get Isabelle far away as soon as I could, this entire catastrophe would never have happened."

The water in the basin now covered Henry's feet. It was cold as ice. A shiver ran up his legs to his spine, but didn't quench his anger.

"James . . . Maggie . . . Ruther . . . Brandol . . . Thirsty . . . Isabelle. All have suffered. All my fault." He hung his head and waited for the healer to say something, but he heard only the sounds of water as it continued to splash into the basin.

"Your sin is as old as man. As old as Atolas and her moons. As old as time."

"*What is my sin?*" Henry yelled.

"Pride, Henry. Your guilt comes from your pride in thinking you have to be perfect. Guilt in knowing that you are not."

"I don't think—"

"You do. Because you are a carpenter to the core, you think you must be perfect, not only with wood but with life. You cannot accept your flaws. Because of your pride, you carry guilt. It poisons you.

It prevents you from the cleansing power of forgiving yourself. Your mind cannot cope with so much guilt, so your feelings turn into powerlessness, which has manifested itself in a different way—by paralyzing your arm. When you decide to move past it—to let it go—your arm will reawaken."

He heard the healer move forward, sloshing the water about her. Then came a thick wet *smack* to his right, which splashed freezing drops of water onto his bare skin.

"I have wedged a dagger into the ground next to you. With minimal effort, you can reach it with your afflicted arm. Then you can use it to cut through the ropes that bind you to the chair. This basin will take hours to fill. I'm not certain exactly how long, but probably not until the sun begins to set." Her tone told Henry she knew exactly how long it would take the basin to fill. "When it does fill completely, if you are still in it, you will drown."

Henry sputtered. "You can't be serious!"

"Good luck, Henry. Should you fail, your body will be returned to your friends."

Henry pulled at his restraints, but the effort was futile. The healer had tied the knots well. "You're supposed to be a healer! Healers don't kill."

"You were warned this was a possibility multiple times."

"I thought it only applied to those who were gravely injured!"

"Then you were gravely mistaken."

He tried to break free of the ropes again, straining every muscle in his body to create some wiggle room, but all he received from his efforts were rope burns.

"This can't be the way! Let me go!" When she didn't respond, he called out to her again. "Healer? Healer! Don't leave me!"

Whether or not she had stayed to watch, Henry couldn't tell. But he'd heard the tone in her voice, the utter solemnity with which she had spoken. He had to save himself.

He tried to clear his mind. It was impossible, though—his limbs were quaking from both the rising frigid water and the terror coursing through him. Instead, he thought about the lessons he'd given Brandol back in his woodshop in Richterton. Brandol often made mistakes and then got so worked up about them that his face became red, his chest heaved, and he couldn't focus. Henry would tell him to breathe first, and deal with the mistake later.

"Breathe," he whispered to himself. "You have until sunset."

He tried to sort his thoughts. What did the healer want of him? She apparently believed that his paralysis was of his own doing. Could she be correct? He wanted her to be, and perhaps that was enough for now. Why would he want her to be wrong? If she was, it meant he'd never use both arms again. Even his friends had believed in this healer enough to cross Pappalon, the United Farmlands, and Desolation to see her. The evidence was there. All Henry had to do was to choose to believe.

Closing his eyes, he stated his belief aloud. "I believe in the healer." Saying the words felt silly but good at the same time, validating the months of toil and sweat it had taken to journey to this place when he could have gone after Isabelle instead. That feeling of goodness was all he had at the moment, but he embraced it as the water crept up his ankles.

Admitting his belief was the easy part. Henry withdrew into his mind, trying to figure out some way to follow the healer's advice. He listened to her words again, talking about his pride, powerlessness, and guilt. She had said he needed to release those feelings. How? How could he not blame himself for what had happened to Isabelle, to Brandol? A thought struck him.

What would Isabelle say if they could speak now? His first reaction was that she would be furious with him for letting her be captured and subjected to such treatment from the Emperor. But he knew this was wrong.

Isabelle was not the kind of person to be furious with anyone—even her own father. Despite years of unkindness and mistreatment, she had given him one last chance to make amends and do the right thing. Some might have called her gullible or hopelessly naive, but there was more to her than that. She was full of charity, kindness, and goodness. Perhaps it was wiser, in the end, to always give someone another chance. Perhaps forgiveness was better. Could Isabelle help him forgive himself?

He imagined them having a conversation on the grass near the hedge that separated her father's manor from his own homestead. It was late at night, and they both wore cloaks to fight off the cold evening wind. Isabelle had snuck out of her house to see him, and Henry had barely finished putting the last touches on a project for an important customer. Wood dust still covered his hair and skin. Isabelle laughed at it when she saw him, and brushed it out of his hair, making her sneeze.

"Why did you bring me here?" she asked. "You could've brought me anywhere to talk."

A bitterly cold wind blew across Henry's legs, chilling them. "I know this place best. It's where we had some of our most important conversations."

She reached up and wiped more dust from his face. Then she kissed him. Her lips were cold and stiff. "What do you want to talk about?"

"I need you to help me let go of my pride. Help me forgive myself. If not—if I can't—I'm going to die."

FORTY-FOUR

In Dangerous Waters

One week remained until Isabelle's night of blessing. With only a few hours of work remaining to cut through the second bar of her window, and Jade gone nearly every night, Isabelle's need to escape now bordered on panic. Meanwhile, tension between Jade and Jessika continued to mount, which set Jade on edge and made Isabelle more wary about attempting to borrow the ruby.

Bad dreams about Henry filled her sleep. Most of them had something to do with him falling fatally ill, getting caught in a trap, or traveling toward a terrible, looming danger. The sadness she felt upon waking was enormously oppressive and sometimes lasted for hours. Whether these dreams were portents of bad things to come or merely the effect of being a prisoner for too long, she didn't know, but she wished they would end. She found herself spending as much time as possible in the courtyard, the one place she found peace.

Normally the luscious gardens gave her an opportunity to reflect in quiet meditation, something she needed to focus her thoughts. But today, as she sat on a boulder by the pond, tossing pebbles into the water, only one thought occupied her mind: escape.

By her calculation, she needed two more nights with the ruby rose to cut through the bars. She also needed to make a rope to climb down from the window. To make it, she'd have to shred several blankets and tie the pieces together end to end. She would have to wait until the last two nights because if several blankets suddenly went missing, suspicions might arise with dire consequences.

"I have so little time!" she cried in frustration, tossing several pebbles into the water at once. The fish in the vicinity scattered like leaves in the wind. Escaping before her night of blessing was looking more and more impossible. The thought of the Emperor's hands on her body, his lips on her neck and face, his body pressing . . . "There has to be another way," she muttered, again and again.

The stream in the courtyard flowed in from the Drewberry River and back out again. If Isabelle could go with the water, she would be free. She already knew that the courtyard's outflow point was blocked by a screen because she'd tested it with her foot. But what about where the water entered, at the top of the rock pile? To get there, she'd have to cross the pond. There was no other alternative.

Isabelle decided it was worth the risk. Kicking off her slippers, she eased into the frigid water and crossed the pond to the base of the waterfall. Large boulders were artfully cemented together to appear like a natural rockfall, and at its peak, a flat slab jutted out farther than the rest, the waterfall spilling over its edges.

Isabelle had difficulty scaling the boulders with her wet hands and feet; her soaked robe clung to her body. When she reached the top, she waded through an upper pool to the courtyard's back wall, where the water flowed in. Here she found a screen built into the wall, similar to the one she'd felt at the stream's outflow. The only difference was that this one had a corner that was no longer flush with the stone wall.

The opening was wide and tall enough that she could crawl into the space if the screen were removed. Using her robe to protect her hands, she wrenched on the screen until it tore away. Sound bounced off the walls, and Isabelle's heart began to pound, but no one came to investigate. She dropped the screen into the water and crawled into the space.

Water gushed around her hands, knees, and feet as she scrambled along the cramped stone water chute. The passageway sloped upward at a sharp angle, making the going slick and slow. From somewhere unseen ahead, she heard the sound of something mechanical dumping water into the chute. When she reached the end of the chute, she discovered a massive wood and metal waterwheel enclosed on all sides. She grabbed onto one of the wheel's water troughs and rode it down into the moat.

The moat was deep and clean, fed by the Drewberry River. Swimming was extremely difficult in the robe, but Isabelle managed to dive under the surface to investigate how the water entered the enclosure. To her dismay, she found strong metal bars running down from the walls embedded deep into the river floor, the space between them too narrow for her to squeeze through.

There was no escape here.

Distraught, Isabelle swam back to the water wheel and climbed into one of the troughs. She rode it up until she came back to the dumping well that fed the courtyard's pond, and then reentered the tight passageway. The incline felt much steeper on the way down. She tried to slow her descent with her hands, but the slick stone and rushing water caused her to lose her grip. Unable to slow down, she slid headfirst into the pool and tumbled over the waterfall. As she fell into the lower pool, she smacked her head on a rock. Stars flashed before her eyes, and she blacked out face down in the water.

• • •

Emperor Krallick had just entered the courtyard when he heard a splash from the pond. "Isabelle?" he called out.

There was no response.

"Isabelle?" he shouted, running to the pond's edge. There, in the pool, was Isabelle, floating face down in the water. The Emperor pulled her to him, flipped her over, and examined her.

Blood oozed from a wound in her head and covered her face. The Emperor was glad he had requested gloves on his way to visit her, knowing that the temptation to touch her would be too great. Her flesh was cold, even through his gloves, and her robe was filthy. The Emperor shook her. "Isabelle, wake up. *Wake up.*"

When she didn't respond, he tipped her onto her side and smacked her back as hard as he could. He repeated this three times until finally she coughed and retched a great deal of water. As she continued to cough and gag, the Emperor brushed her hair back behind her ear, amazed at how beautiful she was, even when half-drowned and bleeding. And when she gazed at him, realizing it was he who had saved her, something powerful stirred in his chest.

"You're going to scare all my fish away," he said with a smile. "Of course, I couldn't have that happen. Could I?"

Isabelle sat up quickly. The Emperor moved back in case she tried to touch him. "Your Majesty, I was—you—I can explain!"

Emperor Krallick noted again her filthy state. "Please do."

"I was—I fancied a swim—" She put a hand to her head, obviously in pain. The Emperor helped her to her feet. "Did I hit my head?" She swayed as though she were about to fall again, but Emperor Krallick held her steady.

"These pools are not meant for swimming, Isabelle. To endanger yourself in such a way is foolish beyond measure." He took her by the arm and felt her body shudder. "Let me help you. You need examination by the Imperial Physician."

"It's nothing, my Lord," she tried to say, "I merely—"

"Any injury of yours is an injury of mine, Isabelle," he replied as they crossed the courtyard, hand in gloved hand. "I want you to be happy and healthy in my palace."

"Please—please, don't trouble yourself with my problems. You have much more important—"

"Not another word," the Emperor said. "One thing I pride myself on is the lifestyle my concubines enjoy. I don't want you to experience even a second of unhappiness if I can prevent it. Are you being mistreated by anyone in the house?"

"No, Your Majesty," she answered quickly.

The Emperor gazed at her intently to discern if she was being truthful. "Are you missing your . . . home?"

"A little, I suppose."

Isabelle looked uncomfortable in her soaked robe, but also exhausted. At that moment, he thought back to the Seer—the accusation that the man he'd killed in front of Isabelle was not the carpenter. Perhaps it was time to ask her and see if she answered truthfully.

"When you say you miss home, Isabelle, do you mean you miss the man who stole you from me at the inn in Richterton?"

Isabelle swallowed. "I do miss him."

He looked straight into her eyes. "Do you hate me for what I have done?"

"I don't know, Your Majesty," she whispered.

Emperor Krallick watched her closely. "There are rumors that the man I killed was not Henry Vestin, but another . . . What do you say to this?"

Isabelle began to cry, again stirring feelings inside the Emperor that he had no recollection of ever experiencing. He tightened his grip on her hands. "The only way I know how to comfort you is to promise that I will do all I can for you. You have an effect on me that I have never felt before. Why is that?"

Isabelle shook her head, her other hand over her face.

"There's something about you, Isabelle. My servants say you are more polite to them than the other concubines. Is that true?"

"I only behave the way my mother raised me."

"Your parents taught you to treat people beneath you as equals?"

"It had nothing to do with my parents. Growing up the daughter of a poor nobleman and—and . . . being educated by the wife of a laborer taught me that the only difference between kings and stable boys is the way we treat them."

The Emperor of Neverak chuckled as he watched two fish chase each other in the pond. "You don't really believe that, do you?"

"I do."

"Isabelle . . . consider this for a moment. Do you believe that the Lord of All Worlds is a kind and good being?"

"Yes."

"If you were a kind and loving entity with all power, why would you place one man in the position of Emperor, a few as noblemen and women, and almost everyone else as stable boys or maids or common laborers?"

"I don't know. I've never thought on it."

"The reason is because the stable boy and the Emperor may talk alike. They may somehow dress alike. The may even look alike, but they are not alike in *being*. I was placed here by the Lord of All Worlds to be the Emperor of Neverak. It is my divine calling. The same as my father and his father and so on. It is because I am a greater being than a stable boy. I am, of course, a shepherd of stable boys and noblemen, and farmers, and so forth. My responsibilities are greater because my abilities are greater because I am a greater kind of being. Were I not a greater being, it would make the Lord Almighty unfair and unkind to put me in a high station and others so low."

"I . . . never thought of it that way." She pointed at the fish. "Are some fish better than other fish? Or are all fish just . . . fish?"

He cleared his throat. "I don't know. Beautiful creatures, aren't they? I used to have them brought in from the local lakes, but now they've survived in captivity for three generations."

"These gardens are a wonder, Your Majesty."

The compliment made his lungs burn. He wanted to touch her face, caress it, kiss it . . . He closed his eyes and remembered the day he first learned what uncleanliness could do to a man. He would wait a few more days.

"I think about you often," he said. "It's amazing how a few weeks can feel like an eternity. Of course, time passes more slowly when we have something to look forward to. And yet I—I can't remember looking forward to something with such fervor. Do you understand?"

He looked at her again, waiting for her to say something. She finally stammered, "Yes. I—I think I understand what you mean."

"How—how is the cleansing?" he asked in a heavy voice. "Are the maids doing all they are supposed to each day?"

"Yes, I believe so."

Their gaze connected for an instant until the Emperor broke away, his entire body quaking. "Restraint is a difficult thing sometimes, especially for a man powerful enough to have anything he wants," he said and leaned in closer to her. His eyes were half-closed and his lips parted slightly. "My mother used to say that wanting a thing is better than having it. What do you think of that?"

"I don't know."

"Of course, under the present circumstances, I can't imagine that sentiment being true."

The Emperor opened his eyes. Her nearness worried him. What would he do if she kissed him? If their lips touched, he would need to hold her. And if he held her now, nothing would stop him from having her brought to his chamber that very night.

His voice came out lower than normal. "Do you know how my grandfather chose my grandmother to wed?"

"I am not familiar with the history of Neverak royalty, Your Majesty. However, I will learn it if you want."

"She was his concubine. A noblewoman from the southwest corner of Neverak. He told my father that the moment he laid eyes on her, he sensed something special. I used to think that was silly. But when I first saw you at the Glittering Fountain—"

"You mean the Glimmering Fountain?"

The Emperor grinned guiltily. "Yes. When I saw you, something touched me—touched my soul deeply. That is why I pursued you to the ends of Atolas, why I had to have you. Isabelle, if you only knew how I yearn for you . . ." He closed his eyes and leaned toward her. Perhaps this was the right thing. Her cleansing was nearly complete. What did a few days matter?

A knock sounded on the courtyard door. The Emperor's eyes opened and regained their focus. He saw Isabelle properly for the first time in minutes. She was a mess, bleeding, fatigued, and cold. He pulled his gloves tighter and observed them with disgust. After clearing his throat, he called out, "Come in!"

A footman entered through the nearest door. If he found the Emperor and Isabelle's wet state and humble position—sitting in the grass—at all strange, he made no sign. "Your Majesty, correspondence just arrived from General Derkop. You asked to be informed."

"I will read it right away." He turned back to Isabelle. "It was a pleasure spending time with you. I pray these last few days will fly by as quickly as possible." He stood up and offered her his hand in assistance. "Goodbye, Isabelle. I hope you think of me often." As he passed his footman, he ordered him, "Escort her back to the house of concubines when she is ready. And summon Cecilia to dine with me tonight."

• • •

The Emperor was gone. Isabelle exhaled slowly, gathered her wits, and told the footman to take her back to the house. Despite her throbbing head, her thoughts were clear and her mind was set. Only one way existed out of the palace—through the window. And the only way through the window was with the aid of the ruby. If Jade caught her, so be it. Even if Isabelle had to stay up all night wearing her fingers down to nubs, she would do so.

Fortunately, Cecilia entertained the Emperor that night. Isabelle waited patiently until the sounds of slumber came from Jade's bedroom. Isabelle said a silent word of gratitude to both the Lord Almighty and Cecilia, then snatched the jewel from under her pillow before Jade awoke.

Just as unnoticed as she had come, Isabelle stole back to her room and worked feverishly. She accomplished a great deal before she knew she must go to bed or risk raising suspicion. She needed just one more day to cut through the last bar. That would give her enough time to make a rope to descend from the window to the moat. Sleep came easily that night, and as she rested, a smile stayed on her rosy lips—a smile she believed the Emperor would never have the pleasure to kiss.

• • •

The Emperor kept a close eye on Cecilia during dinner. Regal, poised, witty, and charming, she could make a wonderful and formidable Empress. While he was not as infatuated with her as Isabelle, he knew that such feelings were not to be the sole determiner of whom he should marry. After all, the Emperor, though married, would still be entitled to his concubines.

She chose roast goose for the meal, an excellent selection by the Emperor's standards. They chatted amicably through the first three courses. Cecilia even told a highly amusing story about a boy trying to ride a neighboring farmer's dragonox. Hearing her voice and seeing the excitement in her eyes made him look forward to their night together.

"Where did you hear such a tale?"

Cecilia glanced away. "Oh, somewhere . . . the specifics escape me."

When the main course was served, the Emperor paused before eating to ask, "Have you noticed anything strange regarding Isabelle?"

Cecilia pursed her lips and regarded the Emperor with a look of suspicion. "Why—how—what do you mean, my Lord? What should

I see as strange? She has always been different from the rest of the girls."

"Different how?"

"More melancholy. Withdrawn. She speaks often of a man who she loved."

"Have you ever noticed her . . . doing anything that might indicate she wants to leave the palace? I know that may surprise you, but take your time and think. Anything at all that might raise your suspicions?"

Cecilia did as commanded and thought before answering. "My Lord, I can think of nothing she has done that might indicate she wants to leave. However, the person you may wish to speak to regarding this matter is Jade."

"Jade?" he repeated. Emperor Krallick liked Jade well enough, but he saw her more as a tool to be used to spark jealousy between Cecilia and Jessika. He had heard no reports from any concubines that Jade and Isabelle were especially close.

"Yes, my Lord. They are very good friends. Closer than she and I. It is a rare occasion when they are not spending time together during the day. Playing games, painting, reading the same books, telling stories. Jade has many fascinating tales about her days in the land of Hax. Has she never told you them?"

The Emperor stroked his goblet with his thumb. "No. I have never asked. Distant lands and their customs do not interest me."

"My Lord, if you wish, I shall keep an especially close watch on them—Isabelle in particular. But I do not think she wishes to leave. You are so good to us, so doting and lavish, who could possibly wish to leave your care?"

Emperor Krallick looked on her with great pleasure. "Who indeed? But yes, keep a close watch. If you notice anything, do not hesitate to alert me."

"Serving you is my greatest pleasure, my Lord."

FORTY-FIVE

The Water Rises

When James returned from the waterfall, Thirsty was asleep and Ruther gone. He hadn't wanted to leave Maggie alone at the lake, but knew nothing he could say or do would make her happy. Exhausted from getting so little sleep, he lay on his blanket and closed his eyes. He didn't wake until Maggie shook him. She kneeled over him, her eyes swollen and red, her cheeks pale and drawn.

"Whassamatter?" he mumbled.

"Ruther's gone . . . We need to look for him."

It was past noon and a hot day already. The air in the forest had a heavy feel to it, like rain was coming, though James didn't see any clouds. "Why do we need to look for Ruther?"

"He took off into the forest. On Ghost."

"What do you mean he took off?" James asked. "Why would he do that?"

Maggie's face contorted into an expression of horrible pain. "He kissed me!" she squeaked, wiping tears from her eyes. "And I didn't know what to do. I was crying, and he kissed me. I got angry and said things I didn't mean. They were hurtful things. It . . . I—I didn't mean to, but I did! I wanted to hurt him! I wanted to hurt anyone I could. Now he's gone."

"Which direction did he go?"

Maggie let out a small sob. "I want to go home, James. I want to go back to Richterton before all this started. Before you came back, before Ruther and I talked Henry into letting Isabelle have dinner with the Emperor. I want to do it all over again!" The longer she spoke the more panicked and shrill her voice became.

"Stay calm, Maggie!" James said. "Think about Ruther. Which way did he go?"

"West."

"If I know Ruther, he's headed to a tavern."

The nearest town was almost a half-day's journey, so they woke Thirsty and set out immediately. James made certain that he had money to pay for an inn. The trails were easy to follow. As they rode, they saw other groups riding in or setting up their camps. The farther they rode, the harder the wind blew. It was a sweltering wind, offering no cooling respite from the stifling heat. In the gaps of the leaves and branches above, he caught glimpses of massive black clouds moving in from the south.

Thirsty was silent as they rode. James knew she grieved for Smiles. "Are you all right?"

"No." Thirsty rubbed the sleep from her face and eyes. "But I will be. Smiles was always so kind. I wish I'd—I wish I'd had more time with him."

"I understand." James thought of his mother.

"It's strange how you can be apart from family for so long, and even after the shortest of reunions, sense such terrible loss. Love can be both cruel and kind."

"Yes." James saw Cecilia in his mind's eye, her beautiful face twisted in hate, her sweet voice uttering cruel words. Fresh pain stabbed his gut.

A drop of rain splashed James's hand. Another hit his face. "Great," he muttered. He turned to Maggie and Thirsty. "We need to ride faster."

They pushed on, but the wind grew worse, slamming into them from the southwest, slowing them down. Soon droplets of rain and pebbles of hail pelted them. James cursed the weather and pushed on, bowing his head so the water and ice slammed into his cloak, not his skin. Leaves fell around them like a green shower as the hail tore through the trees. Above, the sky darkened as deep black clouds rolled in, occasionally lighting the forest in bright flashes and sudden booms.

Despite being drenched and uncomfortably warm from the blanket of humidity, James had the feeling that someone was watching them. He glanced all around, straining to see through the rain and trees. Then he heard something behind him, a slick, wet sound like someone slipping in the mud. A moment later, a dark object whizzed thought the air, barely missing his head. James didn't have a good look at it, but having thrown a knife thousands of times, he recognized it for what it was.

"We're under attack!" he yelled to Thirsty and Maggie. "Ride!"

. . .

"Die?" Isabelle asked Henry, her face frozen in shock. "Why are you going to die?"

Henry explained the situation to her. The longer he spoke, the less conscious he became of what was reality and what was a dream. By the time he finished, his conversation with Isabelle was more real than the freezing water inside the basin halfway up to his knees. Isabelle caressed his face, her lips near his, and her breath blowing gently on his skin.

"Why do you carry this guilt, Henry?"

"I don't know." He shivered and rubbed his legs. His hands came away wet, and he shook off the water. "It's not something I mean to do."

"Do you remember our first day of school?"

"When I dumped dirt in your hair?"

Isabelle nodded, grinning at the memory they shared.

"What about it?"

"Don't you remember how you reacted after that? You were so guilty about it that you could hardly talk to me. When your mother brought you over to the manor to apologize, you cried for almost an hour. You've always had a heightened sense of guilt. You've always demanded perfection from yourself. That's what makes you such a brilliant carpenter."

"That's how my father raised me."

"So many of our talks revolved around you fretting over your decisions because they affected other people. However noble your intentions, you spend too much time looking backward instead of forward."

Henry threw his hands up in frustration. "Can I help the way I am?"

Isabelle stared off into the distance of Richterton's skies. "That depends on you."

"How do I change?"

Isabelle grabbed Henry's shoulders and faced him. "Use that intelligent brain and figure it out. In the meantime, I need to go."

"Go? Go where? What do you mean?"

"You're asleep, Henry. You need to wake up. Today is an important day. It's a fork-in-the-road kind of day."

"What? Why?"

Isabelle kissed his forehead and stood up. "We'll talk more later."

Henry opened his eyes and everything was dark and loud and wet. The blindfold still covered him. The cloth itched, and he was sick of not being able to see. He rubbed his head up and down against the stone chair on which he sat, shoving the fabric upward and getting his own hair caught in it painfully. Finally the cloth came loose and he was able to shake it off the top of his head. The healer was nowhere in sight.

The sky was dark, not because the sun had set, but from storm clouds. Rain and hail hammered the water in the basin and bit his skin like angry ants. He had to figure something out quickly. The water would rise faster because of the rainfall. It was already nearing his waist, about halfway to his death.

With no better idea of what to do, Henry screamed at the top of his lungs, *"I forgive myself!"* He felt completely foolish, but it was the best thing he could come up with. He tried moving his arm, but it was as limp as ever. And the water continued to rise.

• • •

Bounty hunters. Who had sent them? Rudolfos? The town leader from Tiller's Thain? The Emperor of Neverak himself? It didn't matter. Whoever it was, they were out for blood. Four hunters rode strong mounts, which would overtake James's group shortly.

"We have to get off the horses," he told Maggie and Thirsty. "We'll be safer in the trees. If the wood is dense enough, they'll have to dismount."

"Why are they after us?" Maggie shouted.

Thirsty said nothing. Her wide eyes stayed fixed ahead, unmoving and unblinking. James wondered if she had gone into shock. He glanced back over his shoulder and knew they didn't have much time to act. A particularly thick patch of trees was coming up . . . "In there!" he told the girls, but Thirsty still didn't respond. "Thirsty, did you hear me? Jump off your horse and then run for your life!"

She turned her blue eyes to James. Tears were there, but also strength. How much strength, he wasn't certain, hopefully enough to get her through this.

"Three . . ." he said, "two . . . one . . . *now!*"

Maggie threw herself off Fury, who continued to gallop down the path. James jumped a moment later. Thirsty thought twice about the decision to jump, but finally followed suit. All three of them hit soft, muddy ground covered in wet leaves, grass, and other forest detritus, but the landing still hurt. With no time to spare, they pulled themselves out of the muck and ran. James let the girls stay in front of him so he wouldn't lose them.

Not far back, the bounty hunters dismounted in a less hasty fashion. James urged the girls on, though he couldn't imagine them moving any faster. The wetness slowed everyone down. Looming far ahead was a large rock formation jutting out of the ground like a miniature mountain ridge. All James saw was the high ground they needed to mount a defense.

As they drew closer, James realized that the ridge was actually a long tendril of the southwestern wall of the Dusty Mountains. He hurried Thirsty and Maggie onto the rocks. The slope wasn't steep, but slick. Twice Thirsty lost her footing and nearly tumbled down. Maggie and James each slipped once. Once they reached the summit, James considered mounting a defense using his throwing knives, but from afar he saw that two of the hunters had bows and quivers. Instead, he led the girls over the ridge. One of hunters nocked an arrow and loosed it, but the gale blew the arrow to the right, and the hunter put his bow away.

The top of the ridge was long, bumpy, and narrow. The three friends stepped carefully across. It led directly to an enormous concavity in the side of the cliffs where a small city of tall but ancient dwellings of stone and mortar had been built. The dilapidated dwellings stretched for at least a mile east to west and nearly a hundred yards deep into the mountainside.

They reached the end of the ridge and were forced to shimmy over a dangerously thin path along the face of the cliff in the pouring rain. A sheer drop of a hundred feet greeted anyone unfortunate enough to slip and fall. Rain fell in their eyes and ran down their faces in steady streams. James took the middle position between Thirsty and Maggie, ready to grab either woman if she needed aid. It was James, however, who required the help. When glancing back to see the hunters,

James's foot slipped and he gave a cry. Thirsty's hand reached him first, steadying him before his weight tipped him backward. Maggie quickly lent a hand to support. By the time all three made it safely into the concavity, the bounty hunters were already halfway across the ridge. James took the girls deep into the dwellings.

The cave provided shelter from the rain, but the wind was loud and low, reverberating off the walls and filling James's ears. "Remove your boots," he told them as he slipped off his own. After hiding their sopping wet boots and cloaks, James pulled his sword from its sheath and went further into the settlement.

James had never seen such elaborate cave dwellings. In the Towering Mountains of Western Blithmore, he had explored some crude dwellings, but nothing like these. Here, the tallest stood almost fifty feet high, nearly reaching the top of the cavern. Elevated walkways of stone and wood carved with pictorial writings connected many of the buildings together; low walls offered protection for people traveling from building to building. Inside the dwellings were windows cut into the walls, stone staircases and ladders in various states of disrepair, and dozens of fire pits, some that had seen use recently.

It was dark, and James had no idea where he was leading Maggie and Thirsty, but he had to find somewhere safe to hide until they figured out what to do.

"Mr. Oslan . . . Miss Vestin . . . there's only one way out of this place!" a low, harsh voice called out. James knew he'd heard the voice before, but wasn't certain where. "If you think we're gonna budge from it, you're mad! One way or another, the two of you ain't leaving this place alive. Your dark-skinned friend can go. We have no quarrel with her. But if she chooses to stay, maybe we'll get a bonus for her head."

• • •

Henry looked at his right arm. "Move," he whispered to it. He squeezed his eyes shut, clenched his jaw, and mentally ordered his fingers to bend. In his mind, he tried to picture them moving, wiggling, anything. But nothing happened.

Mouthing the order again, he concentrated so hard that his head and neck trembled under the strain. He tried to feel for the connection between the muscles and ligaments in his shoulder, arm, hand, and fingers, tried to piece it all together so that his brain could give commands and have them obeyed, but still nothing happened.

"*Move!*" he bellowed.

It was well into the afternoon. He had tried calling for the healer, begged her to return so he could talk sense into her, but she ignored his pleas. For all he knew, she might be across the valley healing someone else. Between his yelling, trembling, concentrating, and the icy water now climbing three inches above his navel, exhaustion was becoming a very real factor in his attempt to survive this "healing."

He wasn't ready to face death but somewhere in the back of his mind he knew it was drawing closer to reality. Despite facing death multiple times in the last several months and walking away, meeting his demise was still terrifying. He looked down at the dagger jammed into the floor of the basin between two stones. His hand hung limply by his side, soaking in the water only inches above the dagger's hilt. With only a slight bend of his torso, he could reach the knife, bring it up, and cut through the ropes . . .

"*Move!*" he ordered his fingers again, imagining them working nimbly as they always had. For years his father had taught and developed Henry's woodworking skill, carefully crafting his son like a piece of wood; only instead of creating a fine piece of furniture, he'd turned his son into a master artist. But what good did that do him now?

• • •

James, Thirsty, and Maggie hid on the top floor of one of the tallest cliff dwellings. From their vantage point they could see the four bounty hunters conversing while scouting for their targets.

Unfortunately, they couldn't overhear them, but it seemed as though they were arguing. Their conversation ended abruptly when the group broke in half. Two hunters entered into the dwellings while the others stayed back to guard the ridge that provided the only passage to and from the cliff.

"Can we try to get behind them?" Thirsty asked. "Sneak up on them?"

"We can try," James said. He removed two throwing knives from their sheaths on his belt. "Here, one for each of you. Don't throw them; use them to stab, and only if you have to." James demonstrated a proper knife thrust before handing over the blades.

Maggie and Thirsty took the weapons. James ignored their skeptical expressions and led them back through the dwellings. They took extra caution to move in silence. James held his sword at the ready, even when he knew the hunters weren't close. Maggie and Thirsty had their daggers at the ready, too. They paused frequently to peek out of windows and doorways, looking and listening for the hunters, but the hunters moved with equal stealth.

As they crept from dwelling to dwelling, the wind and heavy rainfall masked their sounds. It was hard for James to keep his emotions in check. He had raided caves filled with robbers, battled bands of rebels, and been involved in a dozen other skirmishes, but he'd never felt so anxious. He glanced over his shoulder repeatedly to check on Thirsty and Maggie.

They came to another tall dwelling and crept up floor by floor, spying through each window for signs of the hunters. Out the topmost window, James saw them emerging from an adjacent dwelling. Of the two men, he instantly recognized one as Kelric, the bounty hunter from the Friendly Fenley.

"This can't be a coincidence," James muttered.

Kelric wore a sour expression as he looked up and down the walled walkway. It was Kelric's voice James had recognized earlier. The second hunter wore white clothes, grimy from many days of travel. His back was turned, and all James could see was the man's shockingly white hair and ghostly pale skin. The bounty hunters turned toward the back wall of the cliffs.

"Let's head down, Ivory," Kelric said. "See if we can get behind them."

James, followed by Thirsty and Maggie, swiftly descended the stairs, taking care to avoid places that appeared hazardous. They crossed through two dwellings and reached the walkway where James had seen the two bounty hunters. Moving in the hunters' direction, James, Maggie, and Thirsty turned into a third dwelling with only one upper floor. Thirsty found a small window through which they could watch the street below. Only a minute later the two hunters sauntered down the lane, swords drawn. Kelric faced forward, the man in white watching the opposite direction. Something about the man triggered an eruption of hatred inside James. But why? He had never met an albino before.

"There's something about that albino," James hissed to Thirsty. "He reminds me of . . . But it can't—it looks nothing like him."

Yet that wasn't true. The man in white was the right height and build. He held his sword with the same practiced balance and training as the man James had sworn revenge upon. Even his gait was eerily similar. But the hair, the eyes, the skin . . . it was all wrong.

Maggie stirred behind James and her foot crunched on loose stone. The two hunters stopped and looked around. "Did you hear something?" the man in white asked Kelric.

"His voice is identical . . ." James whispered.

The bounty hunters passed below. James's eyes were fixed on the man in white, his mouth dry as sand. His chest thumped as if one of Henry's hammers had been loosed inside his ribs. As the man in white's face came into better view, the urge to vomit built up until James thought a steel glove was squeezing his insides.

"It's him," James whispered. "It's him."

"Who?" Thirsty asked.

"Him."

Yet he wasn't certain of it. James knew what a terrible mistake it would be to give away his position, but he *had* to know. He had dreamed a hundred times of putting his sword into his sworn enemy. Was his mind playing tricks on him? He had to know. Gripping the edge of the window, he leaned out as far as its small frame would allow and roared the name.

"Vreagan!"

FORTY-SIX
A Blade in the Dark

Whence James yelled the name, the albino bounty hunter's face whipped around. James knew the face. He didn't know how the eyes and hair had changed, but he knew those features. The man in white was Logan Vreagan.

The hunters moved quickly, tracing back their steps until they came to the dwelling where James, Maggie, and Thirsty had been.

"What are you doing?" Maggie hissed. "You gave us away!"

"I want them to find me."

"Why?"

"This way," James said. "We have to find the right ground."

He took the girls into the adjacent dwelling, hiding just inside the doorway.

"Come on," James said so quietly that even Thirsty standing right next to him wouldn't hear. "We're waiting for you."

"Don't be surprised that Oslan is hiding," Vreagan announced from a distance. "That man is a coward through and through. Even in battle, he hid behind other men, let them die for him. I witnessed it with my own eyes."

James quaked with rage. He tensed his muscles, ready to spring. It didn't matter that he was outnumbered with two women to protect. It didn't matter that he was ignoring years of training. All that mattered was Vreagan dying by his sword. Just as he decided to attack, a hand rested on his arm. It was nothing more than a simple touch, but it was enough. He looked up in the darkness and saw Thirsty watching him. He saw her eyes, the care she had for him and the hope she placed in him. It was enough to clear his mind and make him rethink his revenge.

"That pot," Maggie whispered, pointing to a broken clay pot against the wall. "Throw it into the dwelling across from us. Then we can hurry up these stairs and hide. If they follow the sound, then we come back downstairs—"

"And hit them from behind," James added. "Good thinking."

He picked up the cracked pot and heaved it across the walkway into the adjacent home. Moments later, he, Thirsty, and Maggie scrambled up the shabby staircase as quietly as possible and huddled around a window to watch. It didn't take long for Vreagan and Kelric to locate the source of the crash. As soon as they entered the opposite dwelling, James, Maggie, and Thirsty went back downstairs and crossed into the dwelling behind the bounty hunters.

James entered first. Kelric and Vreagan were just exiting through the door on the other side. If James hurried, he could eliminate Kelric unawares, and then have a fair fight to the death with Vreagan. Stepping lightly on his toes, he dashed across the room, ready to strike. In his haste, he failed to see a piece of the smashed pottery on the floor. The moment he put his weight on it, the pottery crunched.

Vreagan acted as any experienced soldier of the King's Guard would have. He spun fluidly, his hand raised to the level of his ear, his fingers clenched around the hilt of a throwing knife similar to the set that James owned, but with handles made of pure white bone. James threw himself aside, reaching for a knife of his own. Vreagan's blade missed James, but whistled onward, hitting Thirsty.

• • •

With the water up to his neck, Henry closed his eyes and returned back into his own mind. How he did it, he still wasn't certain, but it was easier the second time, and he knew Isabelle would be waiting for him on the lawn, right where he'd left her. His premonition proved to be precise. She sat on the grass, a light wind blowing through her long, light brown hair and a smile on her lips as she watched him approach through the hedge. Her legs were outstretched, covered to the ankles by her gown, her upper body supported by her arms. Henry had never seen anything so perfect, and it broke his heart.

He fell to his knees and clutched at the grass. Isabelle reached to him and pulled him down beside her. "Henry, it's all right." Her tone was that of a mother soothing her sick child. Her touch sent a shudder through his body. He hadn't realized how cold he was until her warm hands provided a contrast. He felt wrapped in a sheet of ice.

"I can't move my arm, Isabelle. I'm going to die. Help me."

"I can't do anything except remind you that I love you and that the only way we can be together is for you to survive."

"It broke me, Isabelle," Henry said. "Losing you broke me in ways I didn't think were possible. If I survive this—if I somehow do what the healer is asking me to do—and I lose you again . . . How can I survive that? What if it's all for nothing?"

"That's the chance we all take every day of our lives, the chance that it might all be for nothing. But what's the point of living without hope? Where does true joy come from if everything we have means nothing? Every person at some point has to ask *why*."

"Does the why even matter if I've already damaged things beyond repair?"

"That's foolishness."

Henry opened his mouth to speak again but water came out. It ran down his chin and neck, soaking his shirt. He coughed up more, trying to ask her questions, specific questions about what she meant, but the water poured out of his mouth. Nothing he did could make the water stop. Frigid water drenched his clothes. He could hardly breathe through his nose.

"You have little time, Henry!" Isabelle said. "Listen to me. Listen closely. You do not need my forgiveness. You never needed it. I know how hard you tried; I know you've made mistakes. The key to healing yourself is not here." She pointed to herself. "It's here." Isabelle placed a hand on Henry's chest. "Your father was *wrong*. You must believe that."

Henry wanted to speak.

"Go, Henry! And remember—"

Henry opened his eyes and saw the basin. The water had reached his chin. His mouth was filling with water. He spat it out and raised his chin. "Healer?" he called out. "Healer, are you near?"

She did not answer. It finally sank in that she truly wasn't going to save him. He was on his own and had mere minutes left to live.

• • •

"Pull her back!" James told Maggie. "Help her! I'll hold them off!"

Thirsty staggered back into Maggie, who caught her in her arms. A knife protruded from her abdomen. Maggie dragged Thirsty by the shoulders, away from James, away from the hunters, and back into the stone dwelling where they'd been hidden. Thirsty groaned with each step but Maggie didn't stop until they were safely hidden.

There wasn't much light to see the wound, but when Maggie touched the skin near the knife, she felt the hot, thick wetness of blood. Maggie gasped.

"I need to see . . . the healer." Pain laced every word Thirsty uttered. "What are we . . . going to do? I can't walk. Oh, Maggie . . . it hurts."

"Just hold still, Thirsty. I need to think."

Thirsty grunted. "I can't . . . Maggie, this pain . . . Am I going to die?"

Maggie got up and looked around for help, but there was nothing. No one. "I can't carry you out of here. I can't do anything!"

Thirsty took Maggie's hand. "You—you have to do it. Please. *Please.*"

"But Henry . . . the vision. He'll die."

Thirsty placed a weak hand on Maggie's shoulder. "Let Henry decide his own fate, Maggie." They looked into each other's eyes and an understanding passed between them.

"Squeeze my hand." With one hand entwined with Thirsty's, Maggie took the knife by the hilt and pulled it out. Thirsty screamed in pain and arched her back, but Maggie clamped a hand over her mouth.

"Let me concentrate," Maggie told Thirsty as she placed her hand to cover the wound.

Thirsty fell silent, but her breathing was heavy and wet.

"I want to heal you, Thirsty. I want you to surv—" Maggie stopped speaking when she felt her hand bond to Thirsty's stomach accompanied by a rush of heat. Her own breath grew ragged as she dreaded what was to come.

It started slow, a slight discomfort, but blossomed into a twisted, stabbing pain in her gut. Maggie doubled over, her hand still connected by an unbreakable bond. The pain became agony, and Maggie stuffed her fist into her mouth to stifle her screams. But something was coming up, and she had twist onto her side to let it out. Vomit, all of it blood, poured onto her dress and down to the floor. It tasted filthy and salty. The bond broke between her fingers and Thirsty's abdomen.

Somewhere in the distance, James bellowed, a primal shout of fury and rage. Thirsty sat up quickly. "You did it." She wrapped her arms around Maggie, which only made the pain worse. "Thank you, Maggie!" She kissed Maggie's cheek.

Maggie couldn't respond, the pain all-consuming. But she had to. "G—g—go . . ." she finally managed to say. "Go to James . . . Save him."

"What about you?"

"Go now."

Maggie watched Thirsty leave. As she did, Maggie felt something else besides debilitating pain.

Happiness.

• • •

As Maggie dragged Thirsty back, James pointed his sword at Vreagan. "Enjoy the sunset. It will be your last."

Vreagan hooted in derision. "Always full of empty promises, Oslan."

James backed away while Vreagan and Kelric advanced. He knew that Vreagan could not defeat him one-on-one with the sword. Kelric couldn't either. But a fight against both Vreagan and Kelric would almost certainly end in James's death.

As soon as Kelric and Vreagan reached the walkway, Kelric gave a loud, shrill whistle. James knew what it meant. It was a call for reinforcements. James's hand flew to his belt and unleashed a knife at Kelric with a speed that would have impressed even Ruther. Kelric whipped his body to the side and let it fly past.

"Told you to watch for the knives, didn't I?" Vreagan said to his partner.

Behind him, James heard Maggie dragging Thirsty into the neighboring dwelling. He couldn't go that way. He needed to lead the hunters in the opposite direction. As soon as he cleared the door, James turned and ran down the walkway. Kelric and Vreagan were only seconds behind. The next dwelling he came to was on his right. He dashed in and climbed the stone steps. As soon as he put his weight on the bottom stair, the rock groaned and cracked, but did not crumble.

On the stairs, he made his stand, daring Vreagan and Kelric to challenge him while he held higher ground. Kelric and Vreagan entered together, both obviously wary of James's throwing knives.

"Oslan," Vreagan said, "I must admit, this is a fine day."

"The day you die is a fine day, indeed."

Vreagan laughed again and threw a knife. James ducked, and the knife sailed over his head, clanged off the wall, and bounced away. The rock and cement forming the stairs shifted and groaned again, but held. Vreagan heard the sound and cackled. "You're on dangerous ground." He moved toward James's front while Kelric flanked James's right.

"Prove you're not a coward," James said. "Fight me man to man."

Vreagan slashed at James's legs, but James parried and countered, barely missing Vreagan's left ear. Then he drew one of his larger daggers to defend against Kelric's attack, which he only just deflected. "A coward?" Vreagan repeated. "I know such a man. A man who steals another man's woman, lies in order to secure another's honors, and then leaves him deformed. That man is a coward!"

Kelric thrust at James, but it was a clumsy effort which James knocked aside. James watched Vreagan's eyes for the next attack. "You don't blame me," James responded. "You know what happened. You're a vile, low, spineless excuse for a man."

Vreagan rushed James, hacking and slashing; Kelric took advantage of the moment to aim a thrust at James's heart. James parried and backed up the stairs, putting enough distance between himself and Vreagan that Vreagan had to climb the stairs as well to reach James.

"Run, Oslan," Vreagan taunted. "Run like the coward you are. You deserve worse than death by the sword."

"Shut up!" As James yelled, he flung another knife at Vreagan. Vreagan moved, but a fraction of a second too slow. The knife grazed his cheek and left a trail of red from just below his eye to his ear. Vreagan touched the cut and stared at the blood on his fingers. His hand trembled and he roared.

Pushing Kelric aside, Vreagan dashed up the stairs and met James's sword with his own. "First you deform me, now you cut my face!"

"You framed me!" James punctuated his accusations with thrusts of his sword, but Vreagan matched him blow for blow. "Imprisoned me! Took everything from me!"

"Look!" Vreagan said. "My hair, my eyes, my skin. You did this."

James pushed his attack on Vreagan, determined to end it quickly. "Lies."

"Remember that arrowhead? That cursed arrowhead? You transformed me with it . . . transformed me into a beast. I was handsome." Vreagan's sword flew with such fury that he knocked James's own blade from his grip. It whirled through the air and landed several feet away. "I told you it had been cursed! You knew."

"Are you mad?" James asked. "I did *nothing* to you! I was your friend!"

"The arrowhead, Oslan!" Spit flew from Vreagan's mouth as he screamed the words. "I told you it had been cursed. Remember the sorcerer? Gaddano? It turned my hair and skin white! My eyes pink! It cursed me." Vreagan raised his shirt and exposed his chest, covered in scars, mutilated beyond revulsion.

"Then I would do it again," James replied grimly.

Vreagan laughed, high and loud, unnatural and crazed. As he howled, he struck at James with mighty blows that James could only dodge and redirect with his dagger. His fury equaled Vreagan's madness, but each time Vreagan's sword clashed with James's dagger his laughter grew more frenzied.

Kelric let out another long whistle, and this time Vreagan dived away from James. An arrow from Kelric's bow flew at James, who jumped aside without an instant to spare. Vreagan wasted no time resuming his attack. He brought his sword at James's head at the same time that James raised his knife. They locked in a match of strength, each pushing back and forth until Vreagan brought his elbow up and smashed it into James's face. James fell back toward the edge of the roof, stumbling and then rolling until he stopped, his head hanging off the edge. Vreagan pressed his advantage, but James snatched up his sword from the ground just in time to block the fatal blow.

Kelric fired another arrow, but it struck the ground near James's leg and bounced away. Vreagan roared at him. "Go kill the girls. This is my vendetta."

The lack of sleep took its toll in James's limbs. His arms were logs and his feet bricks. But this was Vreagan. James had planned to hunt the man down in Blithmore, yet fate had brought him here. This was his chance. James darted forward with a speed that surprised even himself. Vreagan brought his sword around to parry, but James slipped under the blade and thrust his dagger forward.

Vreagan spun to the side, but not fast enough. The blade cut deeply into the soft flesh of Vreagan's left side, leaving behind a nasty, but not fatal wound. Vreagan looked at it and laughed again. "You can't kill me, Oslan."

"I can."

"You can't! You know why?" Vreagan's face began to soften, like butter melting in the sun. His hair darkened and grew. Even his clothes transformed. James didn't know what he was seeing. He didn't even believe it at first. "Do you see yet, Oslan? Do you *hear*?"

The voice wasn't Vreagan's. It was a woman's. A voice James hadn't heard in months. The hair turned from brown to auburn, a deep, rich red. The eyes blurred from pink to blue to green like emeralds. The face thinned, the cheekbones pronounced themselves more prominently on his face. In the end, Vreagan became Cecilia. He even wore one of her gowns. The only things that hadn't changed were the wounds, still fresh and bleeding on Vreagan's face and torso, the blue gown already stained red with blood.

James stepped back and screamed every curse he knew. And then Vreagan, a mirror copy of the woman James once loved, attacked again, laughing like Cecilia might during a walk on a cool summer's eve.

• • •

Henry had to crane his chin upward to breathe. The water numbed his blanched limbs and turned his lips a deep, dark blue. His thoughts weren't on the water, though—they were on Isabelle's words.

"Your father was wrong. You must believe that."

What had his father been wrong about? What had Isabelle wanted him to remember?

No answer came. Something was just beyond the light of his understanding, dancing in the shadows. "What was it?" he shouted and spat out the water that had splashed into his mouth while it was open. "What am I supposed to remember?"

The wind whipped wildly through the yard, rustling the trees and the overgrown ivy that clung to the walls of the healer's small cottage. It rippled the water in the basin, making a small wave that covered Henry's face. His shivering grew worse as he felt every drop of water on his nose and ears. The rustling of the branches and leaves made a loud hissing noise that sounded to Henry like a word:

Us.

A revelation opened in Henry's mind. In a single instant, he beheld every mistake he believed he had made since his time in Richterton to now, placing him in his current, wretched state. What woman could forgive a man after so many missteps?

Isabelle. She still loved him.

Isabelle had always been quick to forgive and slow to anger. It was one of the reasons he loved her. Why had he forgotten something he'd come to know as second nature? Why had he let himself believe otherwise? His mind, clouded in darkness for so long, was now illuminated with bright light. Believing was easy again. Isabelle had seen Henry's faults, his darkest moments and brightest days since they were children. She knew him as well as he knew himself. She accepted the bad with the good, the imperfections.

Even as this realization came, the water level continued to climb over his mouth. Only by straining his neck could he keep his nose above the brim. By his reckoning he had a few precious minutes left to breathe. All of his attention and energy went to the arm. The arm had plagued him for months. The healer said it could be fixed. He chose to believe that, too.

A shock traveled from the fingertips of his right hand to his shoulder. It was the first sensation he'd felt in months. Despite nights of pinching, scratching, and bruising himself, he hadn't felt anything. Now he felt a shock. It was something.

But his fingers . . . Henry reached out to them with his mind, wiggling the fingers in his good hand and trying to mirror it with the other. He strained and groaned in his effort, but all that resulted was a second, more painful shock up the arm, this time followed by the agony of a thousand red-hot needles pressing into his skin.

Water cascaded into his nose. Henry pulled himself up against the ropes and breathed out forcefully. This cleared out the water and allowed him to take a deep breath. He savored it, knowing there was a good chance it could be his last. The fire in his arm grew worse until Henry thought he might pass out from the pain before he ran out of air. He stuck his head under the water. In the dimness, he could still see the dagger, inches away from his grasp. All he had to do was close his fist and get it.

He willed himself to do it, pouring every ounce of himself into the effort. Still his fingers did not obey. He raised his head, expelled the air from his lungs, and took one last breath, nearly inhaling water as he did so. The beginnings of panic were already setting in. Henry dipped his head into the water to see the dagger. His eyes fixed on it, yearning for it. His arms and legs strained against their bonds, testing the knots to the extreme, but he still found them unyielding. At that moment he knew he was going to die.

FORTY-SEVEN

A Red Dawn

The Emperor of Neverak greeted Attikus in the throne room, a more formal setting than their previous encounters. Ivan always had a reason for what he did, because Attikus had taught those principles to the prince years ago. Watching his lessons being thrown back at him so obviously was both fascinating and humiliating.

"Greetings, General," the Emperor said. "I congratulate you on your work in Blithmore. King Germaine believes we have removed almost all of the Elite Guard from his borders."

"Yet hundreds remain, hidden and waiting, led by my best lieutenants. It is a risky game you play, Emperor."

"We are well poised to strike, thanks to your efforts. The red dawn will rise tomorrow. Are you prepared for it?"

"I am at your command."

A smile grew on the Emperor's lips. "I have chosen the battalions that will be employed for our strike against King Germaine's soldiers. The 19th, the 30th, and the 42nd. I believe they will perform their tasks with great efficiency."

Attikus paused before answering. Despite his formidable intellect, he had not anticipated the Emperor doing something like this—something so bold and provoking. "I am in danger," he told himself silently. "Perhaps more grave than I realized."

The Emperor observed him for a reaction. Attikus gave him none.

Instead he asked, "My Lord, why do you leave me at the head of your armies if you do not trust me?"

"If I did not trust you, you would already be removed from your position."

This was a lie. And a test. Attikus's eldest son, possessing a bright mind and strong will, had risen in the military after Attikus's first tenure as general. Consequently, two years ago, he had been promoted to the rank of colonel and placed in charge of his own battalion. That battalion was the 42nd.

Attikus's second son had joined the Elite Guard more than four years previously. He, too, showed a strong military aptitude. A year prior, he'd been promoted to second major and given command over a company, which equaled a third of a battalion. That battalion was the 30th.

The general's youngest was new to the Emperor's service and too green to be anything but a field officer on the front lines. His battalion was the 19th.

"Please, Emperor, do not insult me. The battalions you've chosen are no coincidence."

"Of course not! This is an opportunity for your entire family to shine, to prove to the rest of the empire that your family is made of stronger stuff than a dozen families combined. I thought you would thank me for this blessing."

"I am grateful, Emperor." Attikus's tone conveyed anything but gratitude. "But I believe my performance in your service would improve knowing that my sons' lives are not dependent upon my decisions."

The Emperor nodded thoughtfully. "Of course, every soldier in my service has a father, mother, wife, or child whose lives will be affected by what you do."

Attikus could not argue with the Emperor on that point, nor did he wish to. "Will you permit me to speak my feelings on the matters at hand?"

Ivan's expression turned sour. "No. The die is long cast. We are at war."

"We are not at war."

"Tomorrow Blithmorian soldiers who should be marching back south to their families will be dead. In their place the Elite Guard will arrive in Blithmore alongside the best soldiers the Baron of Old Avalon has to offer. Under your leadership, we will bring swift and unrelenting death to Blithmore's forces until they surrender their lands and their King. We could not be more at war."

Attikus fell to one knee. "Please hear me . . . should you reach old age as your father was so blessed to do, how would you be remembered? Emperor Peter was loved by his people, and well regarded by those in neighboring lands. His name was spoken with gladness by thousands of tongues. It will not be so with you. You will be cursed. They will call you a tyrant. Is this what you wish for your legacy?"

Emperor Krallick's lip curled. "Get up, old man. If you were anyone else, I would have you thrown out of my hall with your head removed. I don't care what they think of me. They are subjects. I rule them. It is my right as an agent of the Lord of All Worlds to take the land of Blithmore if I am able. And I am able! Where are your loyalties, Attikus?"

"They lay where they have always lain! To the throne of Neverak!" Attikus stood and saluted not the Emperor, but the throne on which he sat. "If you strike with the sword, it stains the blade. The consequences of this war will be a needless weight around your neck."

"I will choose different battalions for the morning battle," the Emperor said, "if you can tell me the location of my father's journals."

"Your father's journals?" Attikus repeated. This was the second time the Emperor had raised the subject. "How should I know their location?"

"I have spent weeks searching for them in the archives. No one can locate them."

"Why the sudden interest in them, Your Majesty?"

"Because I wish to put my mind at ease regarding . . . rumors."

"What rumors? Of my ability to conquer Blithmore in under a month? Or perhaps something more troubling to the east . . . in the Iron Forest?"

The Emperor bristled at both of Attikus's suggestions, leading him to believe he had guessed correctly. "I have my own reasons. If anyone knows where my father's journals are, it is the man who was his most trusted advisor. Where are they?" The Emperor stared into the general's deep brown eyes, waiting for the answer.

"My home is yours to search. I do not have them. Emperor Peter, though a friend he was, never showed me his books. Nor did he confide in me where he hid them. Perhaps you should ask that mapmaker where they are—the one whose house and family you burned to ash. He was privy to all the palace's secrets."

Attikus had pushed the Emperor too far. Ivan seethed as he sat on his throne, and for a brief moment, Attikus believed he was going to die.

"Attikus . . . You are not invincible. Remember that I have seen you bleed. If I discover you have kept this information from me, I will destroy you from root to branch."

The discussion was closed. Attikus had already received his orders from the Emperor regarding the battle. Once out of the palace, he visited the barracks and spoke to his lieutenants, ensuring that all preparations for battle had been carried out to his specifications. Then, before returning home, he made two special preparations of his own.

By the time he finished, his hands were covered in rope burns and he had two bite marks: one on his wrist, the other on his hand. He was tired, not having slept in twenty-four hours. At home, his wife sat in her rocking chair, waiting for him despite the late hour. He confessed to her what he had done, and she comforted him with words of wisdom. Then, before the sun rose, Attikus left the house again, this time ready for war.

He had not overseen a battle of this magnitude since the trade skirmish between Neverak and Drapoli three years after he was first made general. That battle had lasted thirty-two hours before the Drapolian ships were repelled from Neverak's northern shores. Attikus had emerged from that battle as a proven leader, and he'd won the respect of the Neverakan armies. In the aftermath, Drapoli had speedily organized a convoy to negotiate a compromise, their ships laden with gifts and gold.

In the darkest hours of morning, long before the sun would rise, Attikus held a brief meeting with his lieutenants to settle their final strategy. It would be a four-pronged attack with double the men on the south flank and most of the cavalry riding in from the north. The northern push would wedge the Blithmorians southeast and southwest, then pinch off the army into two segments surrounded by Neverak's Elite Guard. No one questioned him when he put his youngest son's company in the south flank where it would be safer with larger numbers.

Five hundred soldiers of Blithmore slept, prepared to march home in a few hours after months of scouting Neverak lands and maintaining a presence just outside the palace. Two dozen of the five hundred men stood guard around their camp: twelve kept watch on towers, another twelve patrolled the grounds.

By the time the general reached his position, Neverak soldiers had already lined up into formations, concealed from the eyes of the Blithmore guards. The mixture of excitement and fear was palpable among them. Most of the Emperor's men were untested in real battle; some of them would not live to see the noon sun. Voices peppered the misty air, orders quietly relayed from several directions. A light fog rested on the eastern city and stretched all the way to the Drewberry River. The fog would have served them better on the western side, but Attikus's reports said conditions on the battlefield were clear.

One of his lieutenants saw Attikus and rode out to meet him. "General," he said with a salute that Attikus returned, "all preparations of the western battalion are complete."

The general looked over everything once more. The Emperor was correct. They were already at war. Nothing he did could prevent that. "My orders stand. Move your men into position as soon as you can."

Over the next ten minutes, more riders arrived and reported that the southern, eastern, and northern battalions were ready at their positions. "Remind them to move as soon as the signal is given," Attikus said, then sent them on their way.

"Are you ready, General?" his newest lieutenant asked with hints of anxiety in his voice.

Attikus did not have to work hard to mask his own fear regarding his or his sons' safety. He was well practiced at it. Besides, emotions were left to the men on the front line. They earned them. "Get into position."

Attikus was followed to his battle station—the bell tower of a monastery overlooking the battlefield—by one lieutenant and one boy with a signal horn. Each man had a job: Attikus would decide on any adjustments to be made, the boy would communicate them to the field, and the lieutenant would learn from Attikus.

Four watchtowers bordered the Blithmore camp, three guards on each. Two Elite Guard assassins were sent to each of the four watchtowers. It wasn't uncommon for Neverakan soldiers to pay a visit to these guards. In fact, it was a testament to the unbreakable bond of friendship between the old Emperor and the King, the general noted sadly. The assassins would be welcomed to the tower; they might even enjoy a minute or two of conversation. Then they would strike quietly and cleanly. At that moment, when twelve bodies hit the floor of the watchtowers, war would be inevitable.

Five minutes later the signals came that the assassins had done their work.

Attikus gave the order for forty marksmen to move in. They would target the remaining twelve Blithmore guards with their crossbows. Attikus faintly heard the sounds of forty bows firing in near-perfect harmony. Bodies fell to the ground. Cries were swiftly silenced.

Next came the third order. Bales of hay were placed at the openings of the barracks tents that held dozens of men in bunks. When Attikus gave the signal, the bales of hay were set on fire. As he watched them blaze then spread to the tents, he prayed that he would be forgiven for his part in this. It wasn't much longer before alarms sounded from within the camp, but by then it was too late.

The battle unfolded exactly as Attikus had envisioned it. As the troops of Blithmore awoke to the crackle of flame and the smell of smoke, pandemonium broke out. Some of the Blithmorian officers tried to marshal their men to order, but they were woefully outnumbered and unprepared. The general's men cut them down like farmers reaping with sharpened sickles.

The general's western flank attacked too fast and allowed a small group of about twenty men to get behind them, outside of the ring of death. Horns signaled the breach and the matter was speedily fixed. The eastern attack, on the other hand, was executed with astounding precision. Attikus noted with satisfaction that his eldest son commanded this battalion.

The southern line held strong. As companies from the north, west, and east fell upon the Blithmorians, who now realized that they were penned in with no hope of survival, Attikus turned away from the scene. The screams of death were curses of damnation. This was war in its most hellish state.

The last fifty men of Blithmore made a valiant defense and nearly broke through the western flank for a second time. If they had succeeded, it might have been impossible to hunt them all down, but the southern battalion hurried to reinforce the line. A few men of Neverak were cut down in the process, but the Blithmore armies were finally overwhelmed. Then came the worst part. White flags were waved in surrender—but the Neverakan army was under orders to fight until every last man had perished.

"No surrender!" one of the colonels yelled to the Blithmorian soldiers. "Pick up your weapons and fight! There will be no surrender!"

When word came that the last enemy had fallen, the mercy killing began. Attikus left his post on the bell tower and met his lieutenants on the ground. As a whole, the battle had gone perfectly . . . if such a term could be applied to such horrific acts.

"I will meet with the Emperor," he informed a lieutenant. "If he wishes you to be there, I will send word. Otherwise, you are dismissed. See to the wounded and bring me word when all five hundred men of Blithmore are accounted for."

"Yes, General," the lieutenant replied, followed by a sharp salute.

Attikus left the battle and mounted his horse. Rather than returning home or riding to the palace to report to the Emperor, he rode to a location known only to himself and four others. Five miles to the east of the palace, fir trees grew in abundance but little else in the hilly, rocky terrain. The ground was rough, and patches of weeds sprung up in the few sunny places. Anyone riding through would find the area unpleasant, uninteresting, and uninhabited.

Attikus noted the familiar though subtle landmarks and followed them to a large rocky outcropping jutting up from a tall hill. At the base of the hill, he tied up his horse and hiked upward. Even at the hill's peak, the spot he was looking for could not be seen. Then, in the midst of several tall stones protruding skyward at sharp angles, he found the small entrance to a hidden cave formed by the unusual layering of the rock.

After lighting a torch, Attikus removed a large dagger from its sheath and approached the opening. Between footsteps, he could hear the sounds of two men breathing raggedly in the darkness. Cautiously, Attikus descended into the cave. In the farthest corner from the entrance were two men. Both were nude, gagged, and tied like hogs with the same rope that had given Attikus burns on his hands. Attikus hurried to remove their gags and put them at ease.

"I will release you of your bonds now," he said, "but if either of you try to harm me again, I will not be forgiving. Do you agree to be compliant?"

The men glanced down at Attikus's dagger. In hoarse voices they stated their agreement.

"Very well. I will release you."

As Attikus did so, he saw in the men's eyes a desire to strike out again. "Every last soldier from Blithmore encamped around Neverak Palace is dead . . . except the two of you. You are not safe unless you put on these clothes." From his pack, the general removed two bundles which he dumped onto their laps. Then he pointed to the man on the right, who seemed the dimmer of the two. "Your name is Freddick Hektor, field officer of the 40th battalion, heading to Richterton to deliver a message to King Germaine. Here is the letter you will deliver."

Tapping the man's cheek with his open palm, Attikus got the man to look him in the eye. "Did you understand all that? Repeat it."

"Freddick Hektor. Fortieth battalion."

Attikus pulled out the letter and showed "Freddick" the seal of the General of Neverak on it. "Deliver this to the King personally—no one else. If you are caught with this letter, we will both lose our lives."

The soldier of Blithmore nodded gravely.

"When I let you out of here, head southwest twenty miles until you get to a town called Kerkland. Can you find your way southwest?"

"Sun rises in the east," Freddick answered.

"Can you walk twenty miles by sundown?"

Freddick nodded.

"Good. A stable is at the northern end of that town. Tell the man who manages it that you are *too tired to stand.* Use those words exactly. He'll give you a horse. Take the horse back to Blithmore using the Old King's Road south and cross the Bloody River at Fangleton. The old road fades in places to the point that you think it will stop, but it won't. If you don't deliver that letter to King Germaine, you will be making the gravest mistake of your life. Even your children's children's children will curse your name. Do you understand? What were the words?"

"Too tired to stand," the man hurried to repeat.

Attikus was satisfied and tossed another item out of his pack. "Get dressed, take this water skin, and leave."

Attikus watched the confused soldier dress and then climb out of the hole. Then he turned his attention to the second man. This man seemed to be the brighter of the two. He was tall, strong, and even-tempered. He had resisted strongly when Attikus had snuck into camp the previous night and kidnapped the soldiers one at a time. He even bit Attikus.

The general removed a second letter and another water skin from his pack. Then he looked the man in the eye. "Are you loyal to the King of Blithmore?"

The man stared back at Attikus. The general liked the fire he saw there. If this man had been born in Neverak, he would have promoted him through the ranks quickly. "I am."

"Do you know who I am?"

"You're General Attikus, leader of the armies of the Emperor."

"Your name?"

"Matheu Mullins."

"Your rank?"

"Captain."

Attikus handed Matheu the water skin and the letter. "I cannot overstate the importance of the items I am entrusting to you. If you are truly loyal to your King, and wish to end a war, then you must listen to me. But first I must ask you a question."

"What?" Matheu asked.

Attikus rested a hand on Captain Mullins' shoulder. "Are you brave enough to enter the Iron Forest for your King?"

Matheu paled, though the fire never left his eyes. "I am."

"Then that is what I must ask you to do. But you must listen carefully."

Attikus spoke to him at length, then released him with the same confidence he had in the man now named Freddick. After Matheu left, Attikus remained in the small cave. He knelt down on the floor in the corner near where the men had lain. He packed up the ropes and removed all traces of their presence. Then, unable to help himself, he brushed at the dirt until he revealed a small crack in the floor. Getting his fingers under the lip of a rock, he pulled it up with all his might. It was a large slab of stone which he'd buried and concealed. Beneath it was a box made of brick and cement. A large man could almost fit inside this box, which Attikus and his sons had constructed a decade ago under the old Emperor's orders. But there was no man inside.

Only books and papers. Dozens of them. Each of them authored by the same man: Emperor Peter Richter Krallick IV, the father of Emperor Ivan Richter Krallick III.

FORTY-EIGHT

The Death of the Carpenter

As Thirsty ran after James, she felt for the wound in her stomach. It had healed, the blood dried over her skin and in her clothes. She even felt more rested than she had in days. The dagger that had once been embedded inside her was now clenched in her fist. She thought she would be more afraid, but she didn't have time for that. James needed her.

She dashed out of the dwelling, following his voice, but the moment her bare foot hit the ground, a sword sliced at her neck. Thirsty threw her weight back and watched as the blade passed a hair's width above her nose. The sword smashed into the doorframe, scattering bits of rock and cement. A woman's grunt came from Thirsty's right, so she ran left, away from the attackers, and down the walkway.

On a rooftop high overhead, she saw James near the edge fighting a woman, a beautiful woman in a gown stained with blood. Two pairs of boots followed her, their heavy footsteps echoing down the walkway like drums. Thirsty sprinted inside the dwelling where she had seen James and jumped onto the stairs. A loud *crack* reverberated off the walls as the stairs gave way beneath her. She scrambled up them just as they collapsed, leaving her pursuers with no way to reach her. But another bounty hunter waited for her at the top of the stairs, a man with a scowling, evil face.

"James!" Thirsty cried.

James swung his head around in surprise.

"Kill her, Kelric!" the woman in the blood-stained gown shouted.

Kelric, the evil-faced hunter, brought his sword down on Thirsty, but she threw her body into the wall and slashed his hand with her dagger. Kelric dropped his sword and grabbed his gashed hand. Thirsty picked his weapon up, pointed it at him, and crossed the remaining stairs to the rooftop. Kelric backed up and shouted to the woman in the gown.

"We got company, Ivory!"

Thirsty wasn't certain if James was grateful or disappointed to see her. Her real problem, though, was that she had no idea what to do with the sword or dagger in her hands besides keeping them pointed at the man who wanted to kill her.

"You let her take your sword?" the woman named Ivory said. "You're as worthless as you are ugly." The beautiful red-haired woman transformed into an albino man wearing all-white clothes. It was a ghastly process to witness. He tossed a knife from his belt to Kelric.

Then the albino man changed again. Only this time he wasn't a woman, he was an exact copy of James.

Kelric didn't seem accustomed to the sight of his fellow bounty hunter transforming himself. His scowl deepened as he brandished the knife at Thirsty. Thirsty held the sword aloft, but Kelric saw in her eyes that she did not know what to do with it.

"Get away from him!" James told her. "Jump to the next rooftop."

"I'm not leaving," she answered.

"I'll follow. Go now!"

Before clashing swords again with his duplicate, James pointed to a neighboring rooftop about ten feet away from and six feet below the roof she stood on. Could she make the jump? If James believed she could, then so did she.

Steeling herself, she took a deep breath and ran. Kelric watched her with a look of astonishment. As she soared through the air, she felt like a swan. A moment later, she hit the roof and rolled to a stop. Immediately she picked up the sword and pointed it at Kelric, daring him to follow her.

"You ain't got no guts, girl," he cackled. "Run or I'm gonna get you."

Then he jumped. Thirsty knew what she had to do, but couldn't bear to watch. She closed her eyes and held the sword out where she knew he would land.

"No! No! No!" Kelric screamed. Then a tremendous weight hit Thirsty, shoving her onto her back and ripping the sword from her grip. A terrible, gurgling groan came from the hunter on top of her, impaled on his own weapon. He looked at her, scowling, and shook his head.

"You got guts after all." His smile was red and fluid. Then he closed his eyes.

Shouts came from the other rooftop mixed with the clashes of steel as James fought the albino, still disguised as James. From her position, Thirsty could not see well. But the albino seemed to enjoy taunting James, trying to goad him into making a mistake. Finally she saw James run to the edge of the rooftop and leap across. He had two cuts, both small. When he landed he winced.

"Good work," he said, nodding at Kelric, "but we need that sword."

Thirsty tugged at the sword lodged in her enemy. "There's more of them. The other two hunters attacked me downstairs, but the stairs collapsed. I think they're nearby."

The albino called for his fellow hunters to cut off James and Thirsty's escape as James led Thirsty downstairs. "Where's Maggie?"

"She's hurt from healing me. She told me to help you."

"I hope she had the sense to hide. We have to find her."

"But the hunters—" Thirsty said.

"You'll have to fight one of them. I'll handle the other two."

"I can't fight with a sword!"

James glanced at the weapon in her hand, still dripping red. "Tell that to Kelric."

• • •

Your father was wrong.

The level of the water passed Henry's nose, cutting off his air supply. He had only a minute or two left to live. He focused on the dagger, ordering his hand to grab it. The pain in his arm began to subside as the burning in his chest grew, passing off one torture for a new one. All his body knew was cold and pain. Pain and cold.

Pride in thinking you have to be perfect.

Still his fingers refused to move. The light faded inside the basin, and Henry knew it wasn't from a setting sun or the blackening clouds; it was his brain turning off without the precious air it needed.

Guilt in knowing that you are not.

A grim acceptance came over him as his lungs and ribs began to spasm, ready to force him to open his mouth and breathe in a watery death. It was no longer just his arm on fire, but his body as it screamed for one more gulp of air to survive. He closed his eyes as his thoughts turned to Isabelle, and he spoke to her.

"It wasn't enough. I'm sorry, but my best wasn't enough."

A man is like a block of wood. Everything we do stays with us. Carves us pleasantly or scars us hideously.

Henry tried to reach the dagger again. "I don't believe you, Father," he said as he strained his body, willing his arm to move. "I am a carpenter, yes. You gave me the capability to make beautiful works with wood, but flaws and mistakes are not permanent fixtures in wood. They are erasable, changeable, reparable, organic. Life allows us the chance to fix our errors."

Henry embraced this idea. If only the realization had come to him months ago . . . Perhaps he might have been able to do more. But if he had to die, he would die like a man, owning his mistakes.

He had given it all he could and had no regrets. Even in his moments of failure, he had acted in the best interest of his friends and Isabelle. He could die knowing that.

As though some part of him deep inside had been waiting for this moment—not for weeks, not even months, but years—a piercing heat invaded his body, including his right arm and hand. Henry clasped the hilt of the dagger, yanked it from the ground, and sliced through the ropes binding him in three swift strokes as if the fibers of the rope were nothing more than wisps of clouds. Free from the stone chair, Henry's feet touched the bottom of the basin, and he pushed himself upward.

His lungs burst open for air the moment he breached the surface. He was a man reborn. Cold, clean, and clear-minded. The healer stood at the edge of the basin, watching him with grim satisfaction. When he saw her, she offered him a hand and pulled him out with a strength that surprised him. The rain still came down with force. Thunder boomed overhead. Henry stood and flexed his right arm. It was weak and ached badly.

"Did you always know?" he asked her.

"I suspected. Gretchen said she saw great strength in you. I admit I began to doubt."

This statement brought a smile to Henry's lips. "So did I. You wouldn't have pulled me out, would you?"

"No. Were you not strong enough to survive the basin, you would have died somewhere else, in some other way, and quite soon. You still have dangers left to face, but now I believe you're strong enough to conquer them. Like I said, I had my doubts."

"It wasn't me. It was her. No . . . it was both of us together."

"When you slept, you kept saying her name. Isabelle."

"Was she really there?" Henry asked. "Did I actually see her?"

The healer smiled. "She was never here, but if you saw her, then she was real. Now you need to listen. My servants have informed me that your friends are in danger. They need you right away. I have your horse and your gear ready. Follow me and I'll give you directions." She pressed a slip of paper into Henry's hand. "If Maggie survives, that is for her."

• • •

They found Maggie where Thirsty had left her. James reached her first. She was bone white, listless, and her limbs were cold to the touch. Blood soaked her dress. James lifted her to her feet. Her eyes fluttered, unfocused and heavy. "Are we . . . safe?" she asked.

"Not yet," James grunted. "How are you?"

"Awful."

"And it's only going to get worse," a new voice said in the dark.

Two of the bounty hunters blocked their way. One man, one woman. Thirsty recognized the woman at once. Her breath caught in her chest and her eyes watered as terrible memories flooded her. Horror rose inside her like vomit. The woman, skeletal and soulless . . . it had to be her. It had been more than ten years, but she looked exactly the same.

Thirsty tightened her grip on her sword, but wondered what good it would do. She had seen this woman in action, watched as slaves were brutally subdued on the trail to Pappalon. This woman was an animal. When she locked eyes with Thirsty, her face changed from one of calm observation to cold fury. She yelled unintelligibly, revealing a tongue-less mouth. Thirsty as a girl had witnessed the removal of that tongue.

James and Thirsty couldn't retreat, not with Maggie in such poor condition. James sat Maggie back down and moved in front of her; Thirsty joined him, facing the three remaining bounty hunters.

"If you value your lives—" James began.

"Always the coward," Vreagan, the copy of James, said. "Knows he's outnumbered . . . as good as dead, but tries to convince us to run."

"I will kill you first." James swung at Vreagan, but immediately pulled back as the other two bounty hunters moved in with swords.

Thirsty knew James could not match swords with three opponents. Vreagan and the woman were particularly skilled. The third hunter went after Maggie, but Thirsty blocked his path. He pointed his sword at her heart. "You're willing to die for this girl?" he asked Thirsty.

Thirsty thrust at him, but he slapped her blade away with his.

"You can't win," he said. Then he swiped at her with a slash, which she leaned to avoid.

Wanting his focus on her, not Maggie, Thirsty attacked again, following it with a quick swipe with her dagger. She never came close to cutting flesh, but it angered him, and that was what she needed. He cursed at her, aiming blows at her head and arms, but rather than trying to parry and counter his maneuvers, Thirsty backed away from James and Maggie, giving James a better chance at winning his battle.

"What's the matter, girl?" the bounty hunter mocked. "Too afraid to fight? Never used a sword before?"

Thirsty voiced no response. He lunged again, but she jumped back, stepped on a rock, and hit the ground. Not willing to give her assailant time to attack again, Thirsty picked up the rock, roughly the size of her fist, and threw it at his head. Her aim was true. The hunter seethed in pain, clutching a cut above his eye. Thirsty hopped up and ran out the rear door.

"You filthy wretch!" he shouted as he chased after her. "I will cut the devil out of you!"

Thirsty didn't think. She darted in and out of dwellings, trying to lose her pursuer. But he was faster. Her luck ran out when she entered a dwelling without a second entrance. With nowhere else to go, she climbed the stairs two at a time, the bounty hunter only a breath behind. She hoped to find a nearby rooftop to jump to as she had done before, but they were all too far away.

The hunter had her cornered, his face smug, victory in his eyes. "I don't have much taste for killing . . . It's Thirsty, right? So you pick: the sword or the fall? Either way, Bonesy down there is going to be very happy to acquire your head."

• • •

James could not gain the upper hand on the bounty hunters. An injured Vreagan he could beat, but this other one—*Bonesy*, Vreagan called her—she was deadly. He had fought with the sword more times than he could ever count. Some opponents had been better than him, not many, but some. But he could not recall anyone who fought with the fury and intensity of this woman. She was a savage beast, cutting, slicing, and overwhelming James with her speed and ferocity. Each time he parried and deflected, she moved in closer with her shorter sword, making it hard to maneuver his longer blade in such proximity. It forced him to give up ground toward Maggie as Bonesy continued to punish him with her superior skill.

His sword clashed with Bonesy and Vreagan's in a wild waltz of metal and sparks. Bonesy retained the upper hand, keeping James on the defensive. He summoned all his strength and skill to prevent himself from losing any more ground, but his body was already worn from fighting Vreagan, whose injury prevented him from getting too involved. Bonesy ground her teeth, eyes blazing death. She stepped forward to jab at him, but her foot slipped. James took advantage of her stumble and thrust forward, but even still he was too slow. She caught his sword with her own, bringing both blades up high. Then her foot swept his leg, and he tumbled.

Vreagan sliced at James's head at the same time that Bonesy sent a thrust at James's midsection. James twisted his body and ducked under the slice, using his blade to send away Bonesy's blow. But Vreagan was quick, and with the butt of his hilt, gave James a hard knock to the head. His vision blurred, James rolled on the ground while

Vreagan struck again, slicing James on the arm. On his back, James raised his sword, but it was knocked away by Bonesy.

Laughter came from Vreagan as he regarded James with a look of supremacy. "Never good enough. Not to keep your position in the Guard. Not to beat me. And certainly not to keep your girl. Isn't it time to just die, Oslan?"

As Vreagan and Bonesy moved to strike, two knives flew in through the door. One flew past harmlessly, the other hit Bonesy in the thigh. She clutched at it, grunting incoherently. James blocked Vreagan's thrust with his last remaining dagger and slammed his foot into Vreagan's knee. With a loud crunch, Vreagan crumpled, clutching his inverted leg, and groaning, "Bonesy! Help!"

But Bonesy wasn't helping anyone anytime soon. Still nursing her thigh, she hobbled away, out of sight. James watch her go as he got to his feet. His focus stayed on Vreagan as he readied his sword.

"Sorry, James," Henry said, entering the dwelling. "You make throwing knives look easier than it is."

"Get to Thirsty!" James told Henry, pointing in the direction Thirsty had gone. "I'll help Maggie and get her out."

Henry took off. James waited he'd left to pick up his blade and press it to Vreagan's pale neck. Vreagan put a hand up.

"Oslan, stop! You can't do this."

"It was you I met in front of Cecilia's house, wasn't it? You posed as her after my release from prison. You robbed me of the life I was meant to have!"

Vreagan, still transformed as James, tried to scoot away across the rocky floor, his skin shimmering and melting as he did so. His pale pink eyes were as wide as gyri, until he took on the form of Cecilia. He kept his hand raised as though it could ward off James's sword.

"I know I did wrong! I'll make it up to you. I was a different person then, so angry after you stabbed me . . . the albino skin, the hair . . .

I was enraged. I went to her, changed to look like you. I did horrible things to her."

"What!" James screamed. "What did you do?"

"I hit her, insulted her . . . and I—I—"

"Say it!"

"I can't!" Vreagan wailed.

James pressed his sword into Vreagan's arm.

"I dishonored her! Then I waited for you outside her house. It was wrong, Oslan, I know. And I am sorry!"

"Where is she now?"

"I don't know—I searched—but nothing—No one knew anything."

James redirected his sword to Vreagan's ribs. "More lies!"

"By the Lord of All Worlds, I know *nothing!* She vanished like a ghost. Her parents, friends, none of them knew where she went. Believe me, I tried to find her. I wanted her, too."

James screamed in rage and frustration. He had waited so long for this moment, but Vreagan knew nothing. "Curse you! Curse you for everything!"

James looked down at Vreagan, the man these hunters apparently called *Ivory*. Looking into Cecilia's eyes, he recalled the day he had been betrayed, the twisted scar left on his scalp, the conversation with Cecilia, the days spent in prison, and the oaths he'd uttered to avenge himself. It rose up in him like a bitter well of water.

Vreagan saw the look in James's eyes. "Forgive me!"

"I can't." Without another thought, James thrust his sword forward between Vreagan's ribs, piercing his heart. Instead of watching Vreagan—disguised as the woman he loved—bleed to death, he hurried away to help Maggie.

• • •

The bounty hunter facing Thirsty was a handsome man with light brown hair, lighter than Henry's. But he was not handsome in the same manner as James. This man's gray eyes had a malevolent shine to them. And when he grinned at the way she held the sword, it made her feel helpless. Yet he moved forward with caution.

"I've already killed one hunter," she warned. It took considerable effort to keep her voice steady. "That ugly man . . . I—I stabbed him. Leave now and—and you won't get hurt."

"Thirsty, don't fool yourself. I used to smuggle girls destined to become slaves. Took them to Neverak, Old Avalon, the Farmlands . . . all over. I went wherever the money sent me. And you know what I saw?"

Thirsty did not answer because she didn't want to hear what he had to say. But the man pointed a damning finger at her face.

"That look. Not scared . . . not even terrified. *Petrified*."

"Then you've misjudged me." Thirsty stepped forward and swung the sword. The hunter took a step back and deflected it. Before Thirsty could bring the heavy weapon around for another strike, the hunter kicked her in the chest. She absorbed the blow and swung back. He parried and kicked again. This time, Thirsty hit the ground on her backside but rolled into a kneeling position and raised her sword just in time to save her own life.

The hunter kicked her yet again, this time in the face. Pain exploded in her nose and mouth. But she held strong and swung the sword blindly, catching him on the leg. He grunted as the sword's edge sliced his skin. Thirsty smiled and spat the blood from her mouth at him.

"Do you think you're winning, Thirsty?" he asked as he raised his sword.

Thirsty lifted her weapon as she tried to get up, but the hunter knocked the sword out of her hand and with a backhanded fist, sent her sprawling to the stone. The sword was too far for her to reach. Her face was puffy and bleeding, her mouth full of hot, wet metal. The hunter was too strong and fast. And Thirsty simply couldn't beat him.

He was going to kill her. She would see her brother, Smiles, and her parents sooner than she'd expected. Only a brief amount of pain, and then it would end.

"Can't say I didn't try," she said grimly, but still with a smile.

The hunter shook his head. "No, I can't."

"Put the sword down, Theodore," came a new voice from behind the hunter.

• • •

Skuller recognized the voice. "Henry Vestin," he said, turning, his arms wide in welcome. "My favorite carpenter. Alive and well. The Emperor thinks you're dead. I guess he killed the wrong man."

"My face must be more common than I realized," Vestin said.

James Oslan was with him, helping along a feeble Margaret. Both Oslan and Vestin had swords. Vestin held the sword in his left hand, though Skuller was almost certain the man was right-handed from watching him work on the carriage many months ago.

Skuller had to move quickly to preserve his life, so he stepped behind Thirsty and grabbed her hair. Before she even had time to scream, his blade was at her throat. "I will leave here alive, or she will die with me."

"Who sent you after us?" Vestin asked. "How did you find us?"

"I'm not going to answer your questions. We're going to strike a deal."

Vestin lowered his sword. "We didn't come here to kill you, Theodore. We have no quarrel. Let her go and leave in peace. Hurt her and you'll die."

Skuller tightened his grip. Vestin took two steps forward. "Easy, carpenter," the hunter warned. His gaze darted from Vestin's sword to Oslan's sword to Vestin's feet. This was a dangerous moment. They would try to trick him. Everyone played tricks. No one could ever be trusted. "These hands of mine aren't as steady as yours. Slips can happen."

"There won't be any slips," Vestin said. "No more blood will be shed tonight."

"So you've killed the other hunters?"

"No. The woman is alive. We let her go."

Skuller laughed. "Liar. I know Bonesy. She wouldn't just walk away."

"She didn't walk," Oslan said. "She limped. Put the sword away and you'll be able to walk after her."

Skuller felt Thirsty tremble in his clutches. It gave him a sense of power, which, in turn, fed his defiance. These men thought him a fool. "Put the swords and daggers down." He looked pointedly at Vestin, knowing the soldier had several throwing knives. "She and I will go down together. Once I leave this place, I'll—"

"I've heard enough," Vestin said. His sword was now pointed at Skuller's throat and he advanced again.

"Don't take another step!" Skuller barked.

"Do you want to die?" Vestin asked. "Because that's where this leads. You take my offer or you die."

Skuller stared at Vestin for a long time. This was not the same man he'd met in Richterton many months ago. That man had been naive, uncertain of himself, and soft. The Henry Vestin in front of him now was someone to be wary of, someone who knew what he wanted and took it. Skuller decided to change tactics. Slowly he put his sword away. After he did so, Vestin lowered his own weapon and stepped aside for Skuller to pass.

Oslan, however, did not seem so keen to let him go. It wasn't until Vestin nodded to the soldier that Oslan's sword found its sheath. When Skuller finally passed them without injury, he let out a sigh of relief and ran. By the time he reached the heart of the forest where he'd tied his horse, it was past sunset. The pale light of two moons shone down on him. The third was nowhere to be seen. Bonesy was there, tending to a wound in her thigh. Her hair had turned to a shocking white. Her skin, normally pale, was now as white as the moon. Her eyes shone pink by the light of her torch. When she saw him approaching, she spat.

"And I'm glad to see you as well," Skuller remarked. "How bad is the wound?" He didn't need to ask the question. He could already tell. It was deep and risked getting worse.

Bonesy turned toward him and spat a thick, black wad on the dirt between them.

"I'll find you herbs and bandages in Ivory's bag." Skuller glanced again at the shock of white hair and skin. He thought about asking what had happened, but decided against it. He fumbled through Ivory's belongings until he found healing supplies. After lighting a torch he moved to assist her with the leg.

"Don't touch me," a gravelly voice said, scaring Skuller so badly that he fell back onto his backside.

"You—you—you can speak?" He held up the torch to her and saw that she had transformed. "How did you change into Margaret Vestin? The albino?"

Bonesy nodded. "Just before he died, I told him to give it to me—give me the power and I would avenge his death." She shifted back into her own form, a process Skuller found both fascinating and disgusting.

"Why did your hair and skin become white like his?"

Bonesy tried to speak but couldn't because in her natural, hideous state she still had no tongue. She transformed again, but it seemed to take her longer, as though doing it took great effort. When she finished, her hair was still the color of snow, but her skin was black as the night, and her eyes sparkled blue. "I don't know why I've become an albino. But I intend to learn the answer."

"And you can transform into Thirsty. How convenient for us."

"Both women bled, and I imbibed their essences. Once my leg is healed, we will pick up their trail and kill them all." Then she spat a black, tar-like wad onto the fire, where it crackled and stank.

FORTY-NINE
One Last Roll

Ruther peered through the rain, trying to figure out where he was. All the trees looked the same. All the trails looked the same, too.

"Everything she said was a lie," he told himself. "Just—just laugh it off. It's not true."

But if Maggie had been lying, why did he feel like she'd ripped off his mask and exposed him? Why had he screamed the way he did?

The answers weren't important. Only pushing Ghost onward mattered—deeper into the woods was where he needed to go. An abyss chased after him, an abyss of dark truth, and to keep himself from falling into it, he had to move forward. His face felt fat and clammy as cold sweat and rain dripped from his temples and forehead. His breaths came in sharp, irregular gasps and he began to feel dizzy.

He hated this place. They called it the valley of the healer, but he had yet to see anyone healed. "Fat," he muttered with great distaste. "More like big boned."

The words stung his ears and punched him in the gut. Absentmindedly, he rubbed his stomach. "I'm not lazy, either. I do . . . plenty. I've done lots for our group. Saved Henry three times. Saved James twice. Saved Maggie. I'm not lazy. I'm the saving guy."

A voice in his head told him that it would be wise to go back to his friends, to help them now. Thirsty was in emotional pain. Maggie was upset. James, too. Henry hadn't returned. Ruther knew he was needed.

"No," he said aloud. "I have to clear my head. Have to think."

And Ruther knew of only one place where proper thinking was done: taverns. Money jingled in his pocket. It yearned to be spent. But whenever the urge to drink hit him, he remembered the oath he had sworn to James. He had sworn off ale forever.

"I didn't touch the stuff in Tiller's Thain! I can have one mug to help get these memories out of my head. I want to forget . . . I *need* to."

He closed his eyes and let the rain hit his face. Ale would be bought tonight. He would find Henry and the others tomorrow. Heading west, he made poor time in the rain. By evening, cold and soaked through and through, he arrived at a tavern in the village outside the healer's valley. He didn't care what it was called. He was thirsty, hungry, and tired.

Walking into a tavern for the first time was the same no matter where he went. People always turned to see who entered. Some conversations paused, others didn't. Most could tell he wasn't trouble at a glance and went on with their business. The nosier ones stared longer. More often than not, at some point during a tavern visit, someone ventured over to chat, drain him of information, then leave. Normally he was fine with that, but tonight he didn't want to talk.

He found an empty table in a corner and fell into a chair. It wasn't long before a woman came by asking him how he would best be served. Ruther looked her over with heavy eyes. She was short and plump, tan with brown hair made lighter by the last sun of the evening, but she had a definite glow about her that came from being a girl near the age of twenty.

"I want ale and food," Ruther groaned into his hands. "Whatever dish is your cook's best. I have plenty of money, so plenty is how much I want."

Soon his table was decorated with a loaf of bread that smelled as though a baker in the King's castle had made it. A roasted goose neighbored it. He sniffed the ale and sighed; it was fresh and sweet. Ruther lifted the mug to his lips and held it there. He savored the scent, but couldn't bring himself to drink it.

Maggie's words rang in his ears. Ruther set down the mug and called the serving girl back to his table. "I can't drink this," he said.

"Is it not to your liking?" she asked.

"No, I'm certain it tastes heavenly, but do you have anything else?"

"Wine?"

"Unfermented?" he asked.

"Goat's milk. Water?" the serving girl eyed him as though he were the first person to ask for something of such a nature.

"Goat's milk," Ruther finally decided. "I'll try that."

After a large dinner washed down with goat's milk, Ruther felt better. Life was almost good again. The girl bringing him more food looked prettier, and the scene around him seemed terribly welcoming. What the good people of Greenhaven needed more than anything now . . . was entertainment.

Ruther stood dramatically. "Gentlemen! Ladies! Count yourselves among the most blessed children in all of Atolas this evening, for you have in your midst a man from Blithmore of renowned ability in the noble and ancient art of storytelling!"

Every set of eyes in the tavern turned toward him. The last ounce of self-pity vanished from Ruther's heart. He was alive. "I do not come here today for employ but as a traveler who seeks to put a smile on the face of his brothers and sisters and invite joy into their souls. Let me tell you a story—with no charge to the owner of this good establishment—of a man and his three daughters named Rosemary, Rebecca, and Ratface."

It was one of Ruther's best stories. He had invented it a couple of years ago, and it had taken him far, earning him hundreds, if not thousands, of coins. The crowd loved it. Ruther had just enough energy left to deliver it well, and enough wit to improvise beautifully. No matter that it had been months since his last performance, he delivered it spot on.

The owner, a tall thin man with a bad twitch in his shoulders, shook Ruther's hand and offered him pay. When Ruther refused, he offered him even more if he would come back for the rest of the week. The second offer was very tempting, but Ruther again refused with an explanation that he had to be getting back to his friends the next day, but he did ask the owner if he would let him a room for the night.

Stranger after stranger came to his table, now located in the center of the tavern. All of them offered Ruther a drink or proposed a toast. Ruther raised his mug of milk and declined them all politely. The fatigue from his long ride vanished as he enjoyed the high spirits that always came post-performance. When dice games began, Ruther was invited to join. He knew he shouldn't but the men who had pronounced themselves his friends insisted on it.

"How about if I watch?" he finally suggested.

The men at the table were friendly indeed and didn't mind when Ruther declined to place a bet. He was content to sit back and let the men at his table laugh at his stories. They seemed to truly enjoy his company, asking question after question about Blithmore while the serving girl stopped by to watch and pour more drinks. As the night wore on, she and Ruther spoke for longer lengths of time. Her name was Lucinda, and Ruther adored her nervous giggle. He couldn't help but stare at her as she went from table to table.

Late in the evening, a large group of men came in and started a high stakes rolling game on the far side of the room. Lucinda spent more time with the new group, seeing to their needs. When she finally returned to Ruther's table, she said, "I'm supposed to give those men most of my attention. They spend a lot of money, and the owner wants them happy. If you join their group, we can keep talking. They won't mind."

Ruther caught her hint and smiled. "That, my dear lady, is a sound idea."

He excused himself from his newfound friends, though they were sorry to see him leave. One man caught Ruther by the sleeve and said, "Mr. Ruther, you don't want to spend your time with that crowd. Ain't going to lead to naught but trouble."

"Trouble? I can handle myself," he said as he left with a friendly wave.

Lucinda introduced him, and all the men greeted him cordially. Ruther noticed that one in particular, a monster of a man named Leland, had his eye on Lucinda too. He had no doubt that if these men were regulars, they must know the staff and ownership of the establishment well. They played unusually high stakes for a small tavern. It was not uncommon for forty or fifty gyri to be bet on a roll. And as Ruther's head grew fuzzier from the late hour and his full stomach, the value of the bets climbed higher.

Leland had a good sense of humor. He laughed off big losses, and never bragged when he won. Twice he invited Ruther to make a roll, but both times Ruther declined. Ever present in the back of his mind, even in his semi-dazed state, was the bitter quarrel that ended with him nearly losing his most prized possession: Henry's friendship.

Lucinda split her time chatting amicably with both Leland and Ruther. The more Ruther saw her giving Leland that same beautiful giggle, the more his jealousy flared. He also saw that her interest in Leland waxed as he won and waned as he lost. He had seen her type before: a girl who shares the highs of winning with the men she flirts with. When she brought Ruther his next mug of milk, she gave him a wink and pointed at the dice table.

"You really should give it a shot. I have a feeling you'll have good luck tonight."

When she giggled, some of Ruther's resistance melted away. "Do you think I'm fat?" he asked.

Lucinda was astounded at his question. Then she giggled as if he'd said something terribly funny. "You don't need me to tell you how handsome you are."

As she turned to help the other patrons, her hair flipped behind her and as the brown strands caught the light it mesmerized Ruther. Handsome. *Handsome.* He couldn't remember a girl ever calling him that. He smiled stupidly as she left, but she glanced over at him twice while speaking to others, grinning and winking.

Leland noticed that Ruther was showing much more interest in the dice game. "Certain you won't have a roll?" he asked, holding out the dice.

Ruther stared at the dice in Leland's palm. They looked almost exactly like his. Lucinda . . . Leland . . . similar eyes and nose structure. Almost identical hair color. Siblings.

This was a ruse.

Leland was cheating and Lucinda was trying to sucker Ruther into losing big to her brother. "Maybe later," Ruther told Leland, "for now I'm just an observer."

Ruther started to notice how Leland almost always handled the dice, and the others were comfortable letting him. How many other rollers were in on the scheme? The longer Ruther studied them, the more certain he became that Leland was working with one other man, a short, fat fellow named Chester who was nearly bald on top with thin graying hair on the sides.

Some of the men gambling with them seemed despondent. One of them said to another in a whisper. "I can't remember the last time I had such bad luck."

"I'm in over my head," the other man answered. "Down two hundred gyri!"

"You don't want to be down to this man," the first warned. "He's bad news."

"You tell me this *now?*"

Something about the situation struck Ruther's soul. Perhaps there was a way here to repay the debt for what he'd done in Borderville. He didn't like Leland, or the way his sister had tried to manipulate him. He made up his mind and cleared his throat. "You know, gentlemen, I think I will join the game. May I have the cubes?"

With smart play and deft handling of his own lucky dice, Ruther started on a hot streak. The better he rolled, the more time Lucinda spent pressed against his arm; her arm once even moved around his waist for a split second. Ruther laughed and talked with the rest of the men as though they were kin. Occasionally he looked back at the table he'd come from and saw men watching him. Most of them had wary expressions on their faces. Ruther wondered if they'd lost money to Leland, too, and still had bitter feelings.

Leland seemed to bet against Ruther the most, and consequently he lost big. Ruther was astonished at the man's ability to laugh away such large sums. By the time the game was winding down, Ruther's tired and blurry eyes counted at least seven hundred gyri that had moved from Leland's bag to the hands of the men he'd cheated, and a smile stuck on his face.

"We have a tradition among friends that we call 'one last roll,'" Leland said. "The honor always goes to the person who's been the luckiest. Would you like the honor tonight? Just you and I betting on your roll."

All the men around the table banged their knuckles to show Ruther their support. Lucinda rubbed Ruther's shoulder excitedly and slipped her arm around his waist a second time. Ruther basked in the praise these men gave him and asked, "What will the wager be?"

Leland clapped Ruther on the back and patted the money bag that Ruther had slowly emptied during the night. "Everything I've got."

Leland dropped the dice into Ruther's hand. Ruther had no doubt that these were ordinary dice, and that Leland planned to switch them after he rolled.

He pretended to consider the offer while fingering the dice in his pocket, and then slipping them into his hand for the switch. When he won, he could give his winnings to the men whom Leland had cheated. Justice would be served, and Ruther would—perhaps in a twisted way—have made up for his actions in Borderville. "All right," he said, "I'll take the bet."

As Ruther prepared to throw, all the men but Leland chanted his name. Lucinda stood beside him and watched excitedly. Her fingers tickled the back of his neck, teasing the edges of his hair. Ruther rubbed his hands together and felt the special, winning dice click happily between his palms.

Then he let them fly.

Ruther should have sensed something was wrong the moment he let them go because Lucinda walked away from the table without waiting for the dice to stop. The first one bounced off the back of the trough and landed showing a one. The second die twirled majestically in the air. It would be a six. Between his two weighted pairs, one always rolled a one and a six. The other rolled a three and a four. But it wasn't a six.

It was another one. And two ones always meant . . .

"Dead man's stare," Leland announced. "You lose, friend."

The men around Ruther groaned, but Ruther merely shrugged, masking his confusion about what had gone wrong. "Luck comes and goes," he said, repeating the words of his uncle, "but a winner is anyone who quits ahead." Somehow Leland had made certain he got some of his money back, and Ruther was fine with that. He had cheated enough in his life that perhaps this was true justice. He chose to say nothing.

"How much is in your bag?" he asked Leland as he scooped coins from his purse.

The faces of every man at the table turned grave. Ruther had never seen laughter die so quickly. "You owe me three thousand gyri," Leland said quietly, opening his bag. "I'll let you count it if you want."

Ruther peered inside the bag and saw a large sum of coins deep inside. Leland hefted the bag as though it was nothing. No laughter came from Ruther's lips now. He saw the expectation of payment in the eyes of Leland and the other men. "You—you aren't serious," he pleaded. "Le—Leland, you know I haven't got such a sum. I'll give you everything I've got."

The murmurs at the table put panic in Ruther's heart. "If everything you have is three thousand gyri," Leland countered, "then I accept."

"You know I haven't got that much money!" Ruther cried. This had to be a game. At any moment, these men would smile and laugh and tell him that all was well. "Three thousand . . . I have never seen someone carry such a sum! Much less wager it! I have given you all I have. Do you want the clothes off my back? Then I will walk naked to my people and they will be all the more impressed with me."

"Pay the money or pay the penalty."

"Those dice were fakes," Ruther said, pointing at them where they lay in the trough. "Let me see them!"

Lucinda swooped in, picked them up, and handed them to Ruther. Ruther rolled them down the trough again. A five and a three. The two other men at the table regarded Ruther with an expression of pity, shook their heads, and walked away.

"Don't go," Ruther said as they passed him. "Please! You know he was cheating."

One of them put his hands up. "I can't get involved. Sorry, chum."

"Can you pay me or not?" Leland demanded.

"Of course I can't!" Ruther yelled, "What do you want me to do?"

From the back of the tavern, Lucinda led the owner out. "What's the trouble here, Leland?" the owner asked. "Lucinda tells me you're having problems again."

Leland resumed his easygoing manner and pointed at Ruther. "We made bets, and this man says he either can't or won't pay."

When the owner looked to Ruther for an explanation, Ruther told him everything from the fake dice to the outrageous bet. As he finished, the owner's attention was on Leland again. Chester, Leland's balding, fat friend, refuted it all and called Ruther's story hogwash.

"This is what . . . the third time something like this has happened in the last year, isn't it?" the owner asked Leland and Chester.

"We play high-stakes dice games, you know that," Leland answered. "If you don't like it, we'll stop bringing you our business. But in high stakes, sometimes people get caught up and they don't play by the rules."

"You weren't playing by the rules!" Ruther shouted. "You used fake dice. You should have told me you were betting such a sum! Three thousand!"

"What did you see happen, Lucinda?" the owner asked.

Lucinda didn't seem to want to answer, but she had little choice in the matter. "I didn't see any fake dice," she answered, eyes on Leland, not Ruther. "They looked normal. I handed them to Ruther, and he rolled them."

"Did Ruther make the bet of three thousand?" the owner asked next.

It was the longest seven seconds of Ruther's life while he waited for Lucinda to answer. Finally she nodded her head. "He made the bet." When she said *he,* she pointed at Ruther. He stared at her hand. Then he remembered her hand around his waist, right before he pulled the dice from his pocket. Her hand had been next to his pocket. She had handed the dice from the trough to Ruther. It was *her.* He had been played, beaten at his own game.

Ruther's jaw dropped. "How dare you? You stood right next to me! You saw him point to his bag. You were right there! You lying—"

"The law is clear on this," Leland said. "This man belongs in prison until his debts are paid . . . unless he and I can make other arrangements."

The owner looked terribly sorry, but he agreed with Leland. "I don't want your business anymore, Leland. It's fishy and it stinks. Now get out of here and settle this yourselves."

Leland and Chester went to put their hands on Ruther, but he bolted from them. He shoved through the tavern door and sprinted for Ghost. Leland and Chester shouted after him as they gave chase. Ruther reached his horse without a moment to spare, undid the lashings and jumped on the saddle. "Go Ghost!" he cried. "*Go!*"

Leland tried to grab Ruther's leg but slipped. Ghost jerked around to trot off, but Ruther lost his balance. He slipped to the side, which put him within reach for Leland the second time. Before Ruther knew it, he was ripped from the saddle as Ghost galloped away.

Almost all the patrons had come outside to watch, including the owner. Ruther cried for help to anyone who would listen. "They're cheating me! I never agreed to that bet!"

Chester stood Ruther up, pinning his arms behind his back. Leland slugged Ruther so hard in the gut that he lost his dinner. When he was able to speak again, he continued yelling for help.

"Shut up!" Leland struck Ruther across the face. "Now I'm going to give you a generous offer because that's the kind of man I am. I own a mine up north in the Quarry Lands. I could use an extra hand for a while. You come work for me for, say, six months. Five hundred gyri a month, and I'll call our debt even. Your alternative is rotting in a prison hole, a year for every thousand you owe me or until someone can pay your debts."

"I—I have people who'll be looking for me," Ruther complained, but his mind wasn't working very quickly. What should he do? Henry had nowhere close to that kind of money. Nor did Henry know where Ruther was. Even if he did, would Henry be willing to wait six months while Isabelle stayed locked in the Emperor's palace? Ruther made his decision.

He yanked himself from Chester's grasp and sprinted down the road. He had made it about twenty steps when Leland's larger and fitter body caught up and pulled him into the mud. Leland shoved Ruther's face into the mud until Ruther thought he was going to suffocate. When Leland finally let him up, he gasped for air. Leland shoved Ruther's arm up behind him, threatening to break it. The pain was unbearable.

"That was foolish. Now the deal is a full year of work to repay me. Make your choice now or rot in prison!"

"Fine!" Ruther cried out just to make the pain stop. "All right! I'll work the mine!"

Leland jerked Ruther up and dragged him to his wagon. Ruther was tossed roughly into the back, and Chester got in with him, shackling him. The patrons who had been watching started to head back into the tavern, many of them shaking their heads. Lucinda stayed behind watching everything. Leland came back around and spoke to her. Ruther noted the way the large man grabbed Lucinda's hair roughly and shoved her back toward the tavern. Then just before leaving, he placed a handful of gyri in her hand and bid her farewell.

"Make yourself comfortable," one of the men in the back said to Ruther. "We have a long ride ahead of us."

FIFTY

The Fork in the Road

Despite the darkness, despite their exhaustion, Henry's company left the valley of the healer. They traveled by moonlight and torchlight. The rain had stopped, replaced by a vast stillness following the storm. Henry's thoughts were on Ruther. James had informed him what Maggie said to Ruther, and how Ruther had reacted. Everyone knew the foolish mistakes Ruther was prone to when left to his own devices. And in a distraught state, he would certainly turn to ale. They had to check the taverns.

They trudged on for as long as they could on the main road to the nearest western town. Henry rode one of the pack horses with Maggie in front, sleeping in the saddle. When James almost fell off his horse due to lack of sleep, Henry suggested they camp on the side of the road.

The sun was well on its way to its zenith when they awoke the next morning. By noon they had reached the nearest town. A riderless horse greeted them as they approached the first tavern. Henry recognized Ghost right away. James and Henry exchanged a dark look. Ruther prized Ghost above almost anything.

Knowing they would likely find answers in the tavern, they entered the small but respectable establishment called the Fork in the Road. The owner—a tall, thin, twitchy man—welcomed them in for breakfast. He gave them a second lookover when he heard their Blithmorian accents.

When he brought them food, the owner paused and joined them at their table. "You looking for your friend?" He didn't even wait for an answer before springing into a story of how Ruther had come for a meal, been tricked into making an enormous bet, and dragged off in chains by a large man named Leland.

"He was drunk, wasn't he?" Maggie asked.

"No," the owner insisted, "in fact, he bought ale, and then thought better of it. Drank goat's milk, of all things. Can't remember the last time someone drank goat's milk here."

Maggie's cheeks blossomed red and she fell silent.

"How long ago did they leave?" James asked. "Can we catch them?"

The owner's shoulders twitched. "Might. But I'm certain they rode through the night. Leland travels fast. You won't likely catch them before they reach the quarries."

"The man told Ruther he had to work for six months?" Henry asked.

"A year after he tried to run away. Who could pay three thousand gyri?"

"Three *thousand*?" Henry repeated.

"Where is the quarry?" James asked.

The owner jerked his thumb to the north. "Lots of different men have business operations in the Quarry Lands. No idea where any specific one is. That place is as dangerous as Desolation. Lawless and brutal."

"Thank you for the time and information," Henry said, placing a few copper coins in the man's hand as they shook.

The owner looked down at the money and shook his head. "Can't take that. Wouldn't be right after what those men did in my establishment." He stood, the left side of his face twitching as he walked away.

No one spoke at first. The silence made Henry uneasy. He knew what everyone was thinking, or he thought he did.

"You want to go after him, don't you?" James asked.

Henry put his hands in his hair and sighed. "Yes. But who knows where he is, what that will entail . . ."

"It's my fault," Maggie said in a quiet voice. Henry saw the shame in her eyes. "I have to go for him. I have to make it right."

Henry's gaze went to Thirsty. She had been quiet for hours. If there was one person whose thoughts he didn't know, it was her.

Rather than answering him, she spoke to James. "I've been traveling for the last three months or so. When I said I wanted adventure, I had no idea what I was getting into." She forced a laugh at her own words, but no one joined her. "Now I've met my brothers again. They've left the valley to return to Old Avalon. They may be only a day's ride ahead. They're trying to do something great, something important. It's bigger than me, bigger than anything I know. I have to help them. No matter what you all decide, I have to go back. James, the invitation is still there for you, too. All of you, really. But I know some of you can't come." She looked at Henry and Maggie.

"You're certain you want to go?" James asked.

Thirsty nodded without hesitating.

There was a strange look in James's eyes. Henry didn't like it. "James?" he asked. "What are you planning to do?"

"You don't want to know what I'm thinking, Henry," James stated.

"Yes, I do."

Maggie's eyes stayed on her mug. Thirsty's eyes, however, were locked on James, hopeful. When James finally spoke, his voice was firm, the voice of a soldier. "I used to despise Ruther, but as I've gotten to know him, gambled with him, I've come to love him as a friend. Perhaps not the same way I love you as a brother, Henry, but close. If you weren't going after him, Henry, then I would. But I know he'll be in safe hands. I know the two of you will find a way."

"What about Isabelle?" Henry asked.

"I've thought about this for hours on end. Thirsty's brother made a point. If the Emperor is truly on the verge of invading Blithmore, then their rebellion can make a difference. Think of it: the Emperor and the Baron of Old Avalon go to war with Blithmore, but suddenly the slave rebellion ignites again, and the Baron finds himself fighting on two fronts, one at home in his own capital, the other across the Iron Forest. What will he do? He'll be forced to withdraw his troops to save his own throne. Emperor Krallick will be left to fend for himself against the might of Blithmore and her allies. Not even the Lord of All Worlds could save him."

"That's much bigger than us, James," Henry said. "You have no idea how to start a war, how to—"

"I do have a pretty good idea, actually. And I know I can help Isabelle by aiding the rebellion in Old Avalon. If we can rekindle the slaves' rebellion, a real one with teeth, then we can turn back the armies of the Baron and hurt the Emperor in ways we couldn't possibly dream of otherwise. It's possible that Thirsty's brothers may be the key to saving Isabelle. I don't think it's a mere coincidence that we met them . . . or Thirsty. This is something more. I feel a powerful hand guiding us."

Henry couldn't believe it. James was willing to stall his journey to Neverak for an indeterminable amount of time. "The Quarry Lands lie to the north. It's hardly a diversion from Neverak. It's practically on the way!"

"I know what I know, Henry. I know a band of fifty is stronger than five. I know that men deserve to be free. I can help Furious. Perhaps my path is not on the direct road to Neverak. But when you find Ruther . . . or *if* you find him, look for us in Old Avalon. If you choose not to look for us, I hope you have success where the road leads you."

Henry put up his hands. "I don't think splitting up is wise."

"Ruther is your brother. You must help him. And Thirsty must help her brothers. I will give you the bulk of the money we have left. Thirsty and I can manage with less. I've taken two of the maps; the rest I know well enough to do without them. Once we join the slaves, we'll know our path."

Henry said nothing more. James had set his mind. It was the end of their journey together. Furious's instinct about James had been right. Maggie didn't say anything for or against James's decision. The group left the tavern. The sun continued to shine brightly, but the prospect of a warm, beautiful day held no interest for Henry. James had been with the group every step of the way. They'd spent days together locked in a prison cell. He could not imagine the journey without him.

James and Thirsty went to work getting their belongings from the horses. Maggie and Henry looked on awkwardly, not knowing what to say or do. They glanced at each other every few minutes, but remained silent. When James and Thirsty finished, the four friends faced each other—friends who had been through the worst of times together, now parting. Henry's heart ached to see them leave.

James and Maggie shook hands and mumbled empty words. James and Henry embraced as brothers, each offering well-wishes to the other. When they let go, James wiped the corner of his eye and smiled in embarrassment. Thirsty and Maggie shook hands, too, but said nothing.

The four friends mounted their horses and rode together a little ways down the road, no one speaking. Not far ahead, just as the tavern said on its sign, was a fork. Quarry Road turned almost perfectly north. The second veered to the northwest—Old Desert Road. The third road continued west, the same route they'd taken on their way into the valley. At the junction, James abruptly stopped.

"Goodbye," he said to both Henry and Maggie. "I truly do wish you blessings, and hope we meet again soon."

"I know we'll see each other again," Thirsty said. "I feel it."

Henry couldn't help but agree. Maggie stayed silent, her gaze to the sky.

"Maggie . . ." James said with great tenderness, but she didn't answer. "Maggie, I don't want to leave you like this."

Maggie finally turned her head and surveyed both James and Thirsty. "Good luck, James. And you, too, Thirsty."

James waved one last time and rode with Thirsty down the Old Desert Road. Henry wondered if they would turn back and give a final wave, but they didn't.

"Are you ready?" he asked Maggie.

She was reading the note from the healer that Henry had given her.

The worst is yet to come.
Seek the secret teacher.
Find him, and your future has hope.
Fail, and darkness will reign.

They started on the road to the north—Quarry Road. Henry was much less certain of himself now than he had been only hours before, but he trusted in instinct, in his fate, and in his love for Isabelle—now more than ever.

FIFTY-ONE

The Night of Blessing

After four months of cleansing, the dawn of the dreaded day arrived. Isabelle had done everything in her power to prepare for her escape. The bars were all but cut through. Only a few hairs' width of iron remained to sever them from the window. She had stowed away blankets, staying up late the past two nights to rip them into long pieces and tie them together. She estimated the drop into the moat at two hundred feet. Any injury sustained during the drop would greatly reduce her chances of escape. To be safe, she wanted a length of one hundred and fifty feet. Last night, after working on it for three hours, she estimated the rope's reach at only a hundred.

She woke in the morning to the sounds of other concubines and even the maids fussing at the windows. Large plumes of smoke filled the sky on the western side of the palace, leaving a burnt scent in the air.

"Must have been a battle—" Jade said. "How awful!"

"What if the Emperor was injured?" Cecilia whispered with dread.

Isabelle hoped he'd been stuck like a pig. The maids were distracted during her baths, fussing about Isabelle's big day and gossiping about the cause of the smoke outside.

The servants who brought breakfast also delivered a letter to Isabelle with detailed instructions of what time to expect the tailor and the escort for her special night. After reading it, the food turned to ash in her mouth; she ate only to keep up her strength. Cecilia was never far away, as though she was keeping watch over Isabelle but wanted no contact. The dark circles around Isabelle's eyes and her sallow face gave her a sickly, fatigued appearance. Only Jade offered Isabelle comfort and reassurance.

"I dreaded it, too," she kept saying. "I assumed the worst. But it wasn't at all what I expected. You'll be fine. I promise."

"Well, look who it is," Jessika said when her cold and calculating gaze fell on Isabelle on her way out of the common room. "The last virgin."

Several of the girls around Jessika sniggered.

"Good morning, Jessika," Isabelle said politely. "You look lovely."

"Don't try to act cheerful. We all know you've been terrified of this day since the moment you arrived. But now you're clean and pure, just as the Emperor wants you. Normally I get a little jealous when the Emperor has other girls in his chambers, but not tonight. No . . . I'm going to sleep with a smile on my face knowing that you're right where you don't want to be." Jessika set her plate down on Jade's lap and patted Isabelle's cheek roughly. "You've always thought yourself so much better than us. Now you see that we're all the same. All competing for the prize."

Isabelle could not suppress her laugh. "And what would that prize be?"

Jessika took a step back as though Isabelle had caught on fire. "Empress, of course."

"And what then? What if he *does* make you his wife? What will that mean?"

No one else shared Isabelle's amusement. Jessika looked at Isabelle as if she was the dumbest woman in all of Atolas. "It will make me above everything but him. It will mean I am better than you. And you will be no better than a commoner."

Isabelle stood. "To the Emperor, everyone is a commoner. Do you know what's uncommon, Jessika?"

Jessika sneered at Isabelle. "What?"

"Being cherished by someone."

Though she hesitated for a moment, Jessika clucked her tongue, stuck her nose in the air, and walked away.

It was a horse-riding day. Servants escorted any concubine who wanted to ride out to the stables and grounds. Today was the first day Isabelle was allowed to go, but she was the only girl to decline. No one questioned her when she did so. They all assumed she was saving her strength for the Emperor. As soon as they left, Isabelle finished cutting through the bars with one of her rocks. Each took about fifteen minutes of work. A great thrill went through her as they came down. She set the bars underneath her bed, and felt around for her rope made of torn sheets. Not feeling it, she got down on her hands and knees and looked for it.

The rope wasn't there. Isabelle hadn't moved it. She'd put it in the same place each night. Someone must have taken it. She searched each room for her rope, careful not to disturb anyone's belongings, but the longer she hunted, the more desperate she became. After going through every room, she started to sob. Who would do this? Why? She had no choice but to try to make a new one with the little time remaining.

Hurrying to the linen cabinets, Isabelle threw the doors open to find them all bare.

"No!" she cried.

She touched the empty shelves just to make certain that what she saw was real. It didn't make sense. The house always had extra blankets. Was it possible someone had figured out what she was doing and had taken them to stop her? It could only be Cecilia. But if she was trying to stop Isabelle, why not inform a servant?

Her plan was ruined. Isabelle had no other options except to jump to her death or let herself be taken to the Emperor's chambers. Suicide wasn't a choice she would entertain. For now, she had to cover up what she'd done to her window. Thinking quickly, she went to the main room and retrieved a small jar of honey sitting on the lunch table. Using honey and strips of black cloth from napkins, she attached the bars back to the window. She would have to fashion another rope, but not today.

Not long later, the other concubines returned, exhilarated from horseback riding. Derrick the tailor arrived about the same time to have Isabelle try on her evening gown. He had used the measurements from her previous dinner, but he had to be certain that everything was still perfect. As he looked her over, he noted her glum face, but said nothing. Isabelle couldn't find it in herself to feign excitement.

"Well, dear," he said as he finished, ignoring her behavior, "there's really nothing more I can do. Isabelle is as lovely as a ripened apricot. Isabelle will enjoy her evening. The Emperor asked me to tell Isabelle that dinner will be served later than usual. As Isabelle may have guessed, what with the battle and all, he's had a rather busy day."

When afternoon turned into early evening, two of the maids came for Isabelle for a second bathing. "You must be absolutely clean," they told her. "And your hair must be perfect, your skin flawless. Everything will be wonderful!"

"Yes, wonderful," Isabelle muttered.

"You don't seem excited!" the same maid chastised.

"She's nervous!" another answered. "I was so frightened that I couldn't sleep for a week before the night. The matrons—as we called people like myself back then—made me sleep the whole day before. This was wise counsel because I didn't get much rest that night!"

Both of the maids giggled like silly children. Isabelle wanted to scream, but knew she couldn't.

"Listen to her go on," the first maid exclaimed merrily. Instead, Isabelle ducked her head under the hot water and tuned them out.

As they dried her off at the end of her bath, Isabelle casually brought up the blankets. "Last night I was so cold," she began. "When I went to the cabinet to get a second blanket, all of them were gone. Where did they go?"

The maids looked at each other, puzzled. "Do you suppose they were taken for washing?" one asked the other.

"I know nothing about it," the other replied. "But I'll look into it. You can always borrow one from another girl. Some of them keep two or three blankets in their chamber so they don't have to wander out of their room at night."

Isabelle thanked them with a weak smile. "I'll think about that. Will you please find out where they've gone and bring them back soon?"

After the maids assured her they would, they started washing and then arranging her hair. "You still have some time before the escorts arrive. We should wait to put your cosmetics on until then."

"Otherwise we'll have to touch you up again."

"Best you go rest in your room, dear."

But her room was the last place Isabelle wanted to be. The thought of the missing rope sent a sharp pang to her midsection strong enough to double her over.

"Oh my! Stomach pains, dear?"

"Yes," Isabelle replied weakly.

Both of them smiled at her. "That's good," came the answer as they guided her out of the baths and back to her private chamber. "That means you're excited. I can't imagine feeling any other way."

"No!" Isabelle protested.

"Trust us," they insisted, stopping outside her chamber. "Every girl experiences it. We'd be more alarmed if you didn't have them. Now, it's time to rest. We'll be back later to apply your cosmetics. If you need anything, ask one of the girls to inform us." They both patted her shoulders and drew the curtain closed after her.

Isabelle burst into tears again and fell onto her bed. When she hit her pillow, she struck something hard. Sitting up, she moved the sheets aside and saw a large bundle of knotted cloth wrapped into an enormous coil. She examined the rope and found that it was much longer now than it had been when she tied it. Furthermore, one end of the coil extended from under her sheets to where it had been tied tightly to the leg of the bed. Giving a hard tug at the knot, she found it—and the bed—would not budge. Suddenly aware of what this meant, she glanced back to see if anyone was watching her from the doorway, but all she saw was that the girls were in the common room playing games.

In the middle of the coil of rope was a small piece of parchment. Isabelle picked up and turned it over. Printed on it, she saw only one word:

Go.

She needed no further invitation. If they caught her, so be it, but right this second, she had a chance. Within a minute's time she'd removed the bars from the windows, threw them into the moat, and then fed the rope out the window. After waiting a moment to make certain no alarms were raised, she squirmed out the opening wearing a plain black dress. With the sun nearly gone in the west sky, the timing could not be more perfect.

Down, down, down she climbed, relying on her arm strength and her feet to keep her steady from the buffeting winds on the west side of the palace. The more she descended, the more she realized that she had underestimated the drop from her window to the water. When she reached the end of the rope, she gazed down, guessing that at least seventy feet remained to the moat. She looked around to see if any guards were nearby, but saw none. No one seemed to be aware of the strangeness of her presence outside the palace walls.

She hung in place for more than a minute, staring down and

wondering what madness had made her think her idea could work. It wasn't only the height that frightened her, but also the possibility of being spotted. How would she proceed once she reached the water? Where would she go with no money or food?

The muscles in her arms ached for her to let go of the rope, but she clung to it, terrified. She closed her eyes and in her mind summoned up a picture of Henry. This steeled her nerves.

"I'm coming, Henry," she said as she took a deep breath, pushed off the wall with her feet, and let go of the rope.

The wind whipped her gown around her, forcing blinding tears from her eyes. Then her feet hit the frigid water of the moat. Bolts of pain shot up her feet into her legs and hips. She gasped in shock and inhaled water. Nearly losing consciousness, she struggled to swim to the shore, her dress threatening to drag her down to the depths. Finally she reached land and pulled herself out, dripping, muddy, and coughing up fluid. The pain in her arms and legs told her to rest, but in her mind she saw again the note that had been left for her. That one word burned into her mind and consumed every mental obstacle like fire.

"Go!" she told herself. "*Go!*"

• • •

Almost three hours after Isabelle reached the moat, Attikus appeared before an infuriated Emperor. He did not know why he'd been summoned again. He had already delivered his report to Emperor Ivan, and received full commendations for eliminating all five hundred Blithmore soldiers while limiting casualties to just thirty-nine of the Emperor's Elite Guard.

"Your Majesty," he said, bowing. "Your message was unexpected. How may I be of service?"

Rage showed in every facet of the Emperor's face. Attikus pitied whatever foolish person had dared cross him in such fashion. "A girl has escaped," he spat. Then he drove his fist into the armrest of his throne and screamed, "ISABELLE OSLAN *ESCAPED FROM MY PALACE!*"

Attikus took a step back. "I know nothing of this, my Lord. Nor do I see what I can do—"

"Find her!" he yelled. He pulled a black envelope from his jacket. Orders. He threw it at Attikus, who watched it flutter down and land near his feet.

"My Lord, I am willing to obey your commands always, but we have begun a war with our powerful neighbor. How many Elite Guard are you willing to commit to this endeavor?"

"It's all in the letter." The Emperor's violent rage had calmed to a coolly restrained fury. While the general would rather listen to a calm Emperor than he would a screaming one, he also knew that this was Emperor Krallick at his most dangerous.

"I shall read it immediately and follow your orders with exactness. But Your Majesty, if word of this gets out, it will prove to be an embarrassment."

The Emperor slowly turned his head from the statue of his father against the wall to fix his eyes on Attikus. He enunciated each word deliberately. "Then see that it doesn't."

The chamberlain entered the room from a side door. "Your Majesty," he said in a quieter tone than he typically used in the Emperor's presence, "you asked to see the concubine as soon as possible."

"Bring her now."

The general did not dare ask permission to leave. If the Emperor wanted him gone, he would have dismissed him already. A moment later, a cowering girl stood before Emperor Krallick, wearing a pale robe that highlighted her long, dark auburn hair. She was a magnificent creature, far more beautiful than the other concubines the Emperor kept in his dollhouse.

"Speak, Cecilia," the Emperor commanded. "What do you know? The other slaves say that you were closest to Isabelle."

"My Lord," Cecilia said, "I—I have told you, remember? Jade was closest to her. Perhaps she knows more. I can only tell you what little I heard from her. Isabelle was unhappy here. She was secretive. I spoke to you once already of my suspicions."

"Why was she unhappy?" the Emperor demanded. "I gave her everything she wanted!"

Cecilia jumped at the Emperor's bark. Attikus watched her closely. She was lying, or at least knew more than she let on. What reason would she have to lie? He didn't know much about the habits of the Emperor's concubines, but one thing was certain: they all plotted and schemed, hoping to become Empress someday.

"My Lord, she told me you hunted her down and forced her to come here."

"Yes, but why would she risk such a danger? She has nothing to run to. NOTHING! She has only *me!*"

Three more servants entered the throne room. Between the three of them, they carried a large rope made of ripped cloth. The Emperor watched them with the same cold stare he gave to everyone at the moment. "What did you find?" Emperor Krallick asked.

One of the servants stepped forward, holding out an open hand. Attikus saw nothing there. The Emperor leaned forward, narrowing his gaze on the hand. "Your Majesty, we found hairs."

Attikus noted that Cecilia did not react to this news. Emperor Krallick signaled for his gloves. Once he had them on, he accepted the hairs from the servant and studied them. Finally he turned to Cecilia.

"They're white."

And then Cecilia's face took on an expression of surprise. But it wasn't real. Attikus might have laughed—if he did such things.

"Your suspicions are proved correct, Cecilia. I should have

listened more closely to your counsel. You shall be well rewarded for your loyalty."

Cecilia bowed. "My Lord, I serve you with pride and . . . and love. Isabelle . . . she also . . . she let something slip. Something that perhaps I should have thought to mention sooner. Whenever she spoke of the man—the carpenter—she spoke of him as though he still lives."

The Emperor sat up straight at these words. Even Attikus turned toward the girl. It dawned on him just how astute she was: her cowering a clever deception, her fear a farce. She knew exactly how to play the Emperor for a fool.

Emperor Krallick's eyes flared with rage, but also something else. Attikus saw doubt there, perhaps fear. The Emperor had to wonder now about what Attikus had warned. This Henry Vestin fellow was proving harder to kill than a giant scorpion. He was a threat.

Cecilia knelt before the Emperor and kissed his feet. "My Lord, if only I had known that this information was new to you, nothing could have stopped me from alerting you. I offer my most humble apologies. I am your most devoted, your most *loyal* companion. I beg you to forgive my foolishness."

The Emperor surveyed Cecilia, then Attikus. "You may leave us, General."

Epilogue

Attikus saluted the Emperor, knowing that he would not receive a returning gesture. Then he nodded to the concubine at the Emperor's feet and left the throne room. The moment the doors closed behind him, a strange expression appeared on Attikus's face. Not quite a smile—for Attikus never smiled—but something closer to one than had graced his face in years. It stayed there until he returned home, miles away. He found his wife still awake, writing a letter by firelight.

"'What did the Emperor want with you?' she asked without looking up. 'Has he figured out your secret yet?'

"Attikus said nothing at first, but walked over to the flames to stare into their depths. He thought of the various events currently at play. It fascinated him to see all the connections. It made him wonder at the great many more things that might be in play that he did not know about.

"'Not yet,' Attikus finally answered his wife, 'but he will eventually . . . when he begins asking the right questions. And then it will only be a matter of time. I must do all I can to prevent this war, my dear.'

"He pulled the Emperor's letter out of his travel bag and rubbed his thumb along the seal. Then he dropped the letter into the flames. 'Go, Isabelle. Go and find your man. Perhaps somehow you and he will make this world better . . . simply by being together.'"

EPILOGUE

• • •

I sat stiffly, sweating as I finished writing my notes. The room had grown much warmer with the great body of people gathered inside the tavern, pressing around the tables. Many more stood against the walls, blocking the windows and allowing little fresh air to reach us where we sat. When I finished, I flexed and rubbed my cramping hand.

The old woman who had sat with me nodded lightly as though she had fallen asleep. The silence that had fallen over the crowd was even more special tonight, perhaps because more people had come to witness this extraordinary man. He indicated he had finished for the day by taking one last drink of water and then using his cane to stand. He was greeted with thunderous applause mixed with groans from those who wanted more. No one put those desires to words, however, knowing they would fall on unyielding ears.

Determined to talk to the old man this time, I excused myself from my host and made my way to where the crowd had parted for the old storyteller to leave. Behind him, the break in the crowd collapsed as others followed him out. I asked the pardon of those I pushed past, but his unimpeded exit was much faster than I could work my way through the throng.

Just as I reached the doorway, the owner found me and put his hand on my shoulder. "I'm glad you got a good seat," he said. "Wasn't that a marvelous night?"

I sighed in frustration as the old man disappeared from my view. However, remembering the great service Benjamin had done for me, I gave him a warm smile and thanked him again for his hospitality. As I returned to my table to collect my notes, he spoke up once more.

"Who is paying you to write down this old man's story?"

I gave Benjamin a mysterious smile—because the whole situation was still a mystery to me. "If I had to guess, which is the best I can do, I'd have to say it's the storyteller himself."

"No, that can't be. What mad fool would pay you to write his own story?"

"I haven't the faintest idea," I answered. "That's why I keep trying to speak with him after he finishes, but I haven't managed to track him down."

The owner lit up with an idea. "Tomorrow night, don't worry about a thing! I'll save you a seat close to the door. It'll be so quiet, you'll be able to hear from anywhere, so don't worry about that. As soon as he's done, slip out and wait for him. We'll get to the bottom of this yet, good man!"

I shook Benjamin's hand gratefully and told him he was too kind. Then I bid him goodnight. Knowing I had no chance now to catch the old man, I turned to my table, where my ink and papers waited. The old woman was still there. She turned when she heard me packing my things. Tears ran down her face.

"Are you well, Madam?" I asked. I set down my things again so I could help her.

"Oh, yes," she chuckled. "Don't mind an old fool like me! These kinds of stories touch me so deeply. You'll understand better." She wiped her eyes with both hands, and something seemed odd, though I couldn't place what it was. Her wrinkled, bony face gave me one last smile so warm I felt the glow of it on my own face. She placed her hand on my shoulder and patted me, then left. I watched her go, hoping I would be able to speak with her again. It wasn't until she was long gone and I in my room reviewing my notes that I realized what had struck me as odd when she had wiped her face. Her left hand had only three fingers and a thumb. The smallest of the four was missing.

No doubt she had an interesting story of her own.

Acknowledgments

My special thanks go to all those who helped me make this book a reality and get it into your, the reader's, hands. My beta readers: John Wilson, Natasha Watson, Britta Peterson, Dan Hill, Benjamin Van Tassell, and Jana Jensen. Also: Chris Schoebinger and Heidi Taylor at Shadow Mountain for their excellent suggestions to improve the manuscript. Derk Koldewyn for his editing work, and all those in the art department who made the book look as great as it does. Most of all: my wife, Kat, and my kids, who allow me the time to write and get my books out there into the world.

READ THE PREQUEL!

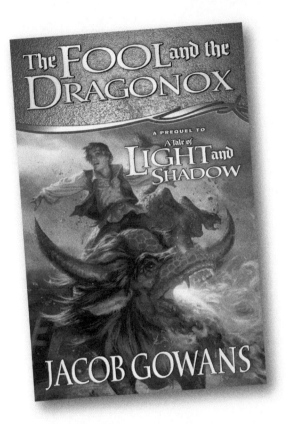

FREE download at
ShadowMountain.com
Amazon.com

1.18